Praise for Harlan Coben

'Bolitar is a glorious character, full of the right kind of quips and wise-ass backchat. Coben's thrillers always have a dramatic twist at the end, sometimes even two or three, and this does not disappoint on that score'
Guardian

'One of the most gripping and clever mysteries we've read in ages. An instant classic' *Heat*

'Tense and tightly plotted . . . a master of thrillers'
Shortlist

'Coben's dialogue is as punchy and readable as ever . . . another novel that will manage both to raise the heart rate and serve as a relaxing treat' *Independent on Sunday*

'Cunningly plotted and dependably entertaining'
Evening Standard

'Coben's characters are believable archetypes, his dialogue honest and pleasingly familiar . . . as always with Coben, it's the fun of the switchback ride that counts'
Financial Times

'If you haven't been caught by Coben's intelligent, gripping thrillers yet, this will hook you' *Daily Mirror*

'His trademark is twists that you don't see coming and his writing is not just exciting but also thought-provoking'
Daily Mail

'Rejoice. After a temporary absence, Myron Bolitar is back. Coben proves yet again that mean, twisted minds inhabit the deceptively squeaky-clean suburbs of New Jersey' *Time Out*

Promise Me

HARLAN COBEN

An Orion paperback

First published in Great Britain in 2006
by Orion Books
This new paperback edition published in 2014
by Orion Books,
an imprint of The Orion Publishing Group, Carmelite House
50 Victoria Embankment,
London EC4Y 0DZ

An Hachette UK company

25

A CIP catalogue record for this book
is available from the British Library.

ISBN 978-1-4091-5050-3

Printed and bound by Clays Ltd, Elcograf S.p.A.

The Orion Publishing Group's policy is to use papers that
are natural, renewable and recyclable products and
made from wood grown in sustainable forests. The logging
and manufacturing processes are expected to conform to
the environmental regulations of the country of origin.

www.orionbooks.co.uk

For Charlotte, Ben, Will and Eve.
You're a handful, but you will always be my world.

Promise Me

Chapter 1

The missing girl—there had been unceasing news reports, always flashing to that achingly ordinary school portrait of the vanished teen, you know the one, with the rainbow-swirl background, the girl's hair too straight, her smile too self-conscious, then a quick cut to the worried parents on the front lawn, microphones surrounding them, Mom silently tearful, Dad reading a statement with quivering lip—that girl, that missing girl, had just walked past Edna Skylar.

Edna froze.

Stanley, her husband, took two more steps before realizing that his wife was no longer at his side. He turned around. "Edna?"

They stood near the corner of Twenty-first Street and Eighth Avenue in New York City. Street traffic was light this Saturday morning. Foot traffic was heavy. The missing girl had been headed uptown.

Stanley gave a world-weary sigh. "What now?"

"Shh."

She needed to think. That high school portrait of the

girl, the one with the rainbow-swirl background . . . Edna closed her eyes. She needed to conjure up the image in her head. Compare and contrast.

In the photograph, the missing girl had long, mousy-brown hair. The woman who'd just walked by— woman, not girl, because the one who'd just walked by seemed older, but maybe the picture was old too—was a redhead with a shorter, wavy cut. The girl in the photograph did not wear glasses. The one who was heading north up Eighth Avenue had on a fashionable pair with dark, rectangular frames. Her clothes and makeup were both more—for a lack of a better word—adult.

Studying faces was more than a hobby with Edna. She was sixty-three years old, one of the few female physicians in her age group who specialized in the field of genetics. Faces were her life. Part of her brain was always working, even when far away from her office. She couldn't help it—Dr. Edna Skylar studied faces. Her friends and family were used to the probing stare, but strangers and new acquaintances found it disconcerting.

So that was what Edna had been doing. Strolling down the street. Ignoring, as she often did, the sights and sounds. Lost in her own personal bliss of studying the faces of passersby. Noting cheek structure and mandibular depth, inter-eye distance and ear height, jaw contours and orbital spacing. And that was why, despite the new hair color and style, despite the fashionable glasses and adult makeup and clothing, Edna had recognized the missing girl.

"She was walking with a man."

"What?"

Edna hadn't realized that she'd spoken out loud.

"The girl."

Stanley frowned. "What are you talking about, Edna?"

That picture. That achingly ordinary school portrait. You've seen it a million times. You see it in a yearbook and the emotions start to churn. In one fell swoop, you see her past, you see her future. You feel the joy of youth, you feel the pain of growing up. You can see her potential there. You feel the pang of nostalgia. You see her years rush by, college maybe, marriage, kids, all that.

But when that same photograph is flashed on your evening news, it skewers your heart with terror. You look at that face, at that tentative smile, at the droopy hair and slumped shoulders, and your mind goes to dark places it shouldn't.

How long had Katie—that was the name, Katie— how long had she been missing?

Edna tried to remember. A month probably. Maybe six weeks. The story had only played locally and not for all that long. There were those who believed that she was a runaway. Katie Rochester had turned eighteen a few days before the disappearance—that made her an adult and thus lowered the priority a great deal. There was supposed trouble at home, especially with her strict albeit quivering-lipped father.

Maybe Edna had been mistaken. Maybe it wasn't her.

One way to find out.

"Hurry," Edna said to Stanley.

"What? Where are we going?"

There was no time to reply. The girl was probably a block ahead by now. Stanley would follow. Stanley Rickenback, an ob-gyn, was Edna's second husband. Her first had been a whirlwind, a larger-than-life figure too handsome and too passionate and, oh yeah, an absolute ass. That probably wasn't fair, but so what? The idea of marrying a doctor—this was forty years ago—had been a fun novelty for Husband One. The reality, however, had not sat as well with him. He had figured that Edna would outgrow the doc phase once they had children. Edna didn't—just the opposite, in fact. The truth was—a truth that had not escaped her children—Edna loved doctoring more than mother-hood.

She rushed ahead. The sidewalks were crowded. She moved into the street, staying close to the curb, and sped up. Stanley tried to follow. "Edna?"

"Just stay with me."

He caught up. "What are we doing?"

Edna's eyes searched for the red hair.

There. Up ahead on the left.

She needed to get a closer look. Edna broke into a full-fledged sprint now, a strange sight in most places, a nicely dressed woman in her mid-sixties sprinting down the street, but this was Manhattan. It barely registered a second glance.

She circled in front of the woman, trying not to be too obvious, ducking behind taller people, and when she was in the right place, Edna spun around. The possible-Katie was walking toward her. Their eyes met for the briefest of moments, and Edna knew.

It was her.

Katie Rochester was with a dark-haired man, prob-ably in his early thirties. They were holding hands. She did not seem too distressed. She seemed, in fact, up until the point where their eyes met anyway, pretty content. Of course that might not mean anything. Elizabeth Smart, that young girl who'd been kidnapped out in Utah, had been out in the open with her kidnapper and never tried to signal for help. Maybe something similar was playing here.

Edna wasn't buying it.

6

The redheaded possible-Katie whispered something to the dark-haired man. They picked up their pace. Edna saw them veer right and down the subway stairs. The sign read c and e trains. Stanley caught up to Edna. He was about to say something, but he saw the look on her face and kept still.

"Come on," she said.

They hurried around the front and started down the stairs. The missing woman and the dark-haired man were already through the turnstile. Edna started toward it.

"Damn it."

"What?"

"I don't have a MetroCard."

"I do," Stanley said.

"Let me have it. Hurry."

Stanley plucked the card from his wallet and handed it to her. She scanned it, moved through the turnstile, handed it back to him. She didn't wait. They'd gone down the stairs to the right. She started that way. She heard the roar of an incoming train and hurried her steps.

The brakes were squeaking to a halt. The subway doors slid open. Edna's heart beat wildly in her chest. She looked left and right, searching for the red hair.

Nothing.

Where was that girl?

"Edna?" It was Stanley. He had caught up to her.

Edna said nothing. She stood on the platform, but there was no sign of Katie Rochester. And even if there was, what then? What should Edna do here? Does she hop on the train and follow them? To where? And then what? Find the apartment or house and then call the police. . . .

Someone tapped her shoulder.

Edna turned. It was the missing girl.

For a long time after this, Edna would wonder what she saw in the girl's expression. Was there a pleading look? A desperation? A calmness? Joy, even? Resolution? All of them.

They just stood and stared at each other for a moment. The bustling crowd, the indecipherable static on the speaker, the swoosh of the train—it all disappeared, leaving just the two of them.

"Please," the missing girl said, her voice a whisper. "You can't tell anybody you saw me."

The girl stepped onto the train then. Edna felt a chill. The doors slid closed. Edna wanted to do something, do anything, but she couldn't move. Her gaze remained locked on the girl's.

"Please," the girl mouthed through the glass.

And then the train disappeared into the dark.

Chapter 2

There were two teenage girls in Myron's basement.
That was how it began. Later, when Myron
looked back on all the loss and heartbreak, this
first series of what-ifs would rise up and haunt him
anew. What if he hadn't needed ice. What if he'd opened
his basement door a minute earlier or a minute later.
What if the two teenage girls—what were they doing
alone in his basement in the first place?—had spoken in
whispers so that he hadn't overheard them.

What if he had just minded his own business.

From the top of the stairs, Myron heard the girls giggling. He stopped. For a moment he considered closing
the door and leaving them alone. His small soiree was
low on ice, not out of it. He could come back.

But before he could turn away, one of the girls' voices
wafted smoke-like up the stairwell. "So you went with
Randy?"

The other: "Oh my God, we were like so wasted."

"From beer?"

"Beer and shots, yeah."

"How did you get home?"

"Randy drove."

At the top of the stairs, Myron stiffened.

"But you said—"

"Shh." Then: "Hello? Is someone there?"

Caught.

Myron took the stairs in a trot, whistling as he went. Mr. Casual. The two girls were sitting in what used to be Myron's bedroom. The basement had been "finished" in 1975 and looked it. Myron's father, who was currently lollygagging with Mom in some condo near Boca Raton, had been big on two-sided tape. The adhesive wood paneling, a look that aged about as well as the Betamax, had started to give. In some spots the concrete walls were now visible and noticeably flaking. The floor tiles, fastened down with something akin to Elmer's Glue, were buckling. They crunched beetle-like when you stepped on them.

The two girls—one Myron had known her whole life, the other he had just met today—looked up at him with wide eyes. For a moment no one spoke. He gave them a little wave.

"Hey, girls."

Myron Bolitar prided himself on big opening lines.

The girls were both high school seniors, both pretty in that coltish way. The one sitting on the corner of his old bed—the one he had met for the first time an hour ago—was named Erin. Myron had started dating Erin's mother, a widow and freelance magazine writer named Ali Wilder, two months ago. This party, here at the house Myron had grown up in and now owned, was something of a "coming out" party for Myron and Ali as a couple.

The other girl, Aimee Biel, mimicked his wave and tone. "Hey, Myron."

More silence.

He first saw Aimee Biel the day after she was born at St. Barnabas Hospital. Aimee and her parents, Claire and Erik, lived two blocks away. Myron had known Claire since their years together at Heritage Middle School, less than half a mile from where they now gathered. Myron turned toward Aimee. For a moment he fell back more than twenty-five years. Aimee looked so much like her mother, had the same crooked, devil-may-care grin, it was like looking through a time portal.

"I was just getting some ice," Myron said. He pointed toward the freezer with his thumb to illustrate the point.

"Cool," Aimee said.

"Very cool," Myron said. "Ice cold, in fact."

Myron chuckled. Alone.

With the stupid grin still on his face, Myron looked over at Erin. She turned away. That had been her basic reaction today. Polite and aloof.

"Can I ask you something?" Aimee said.

"Shoot."

She spread her hands. "Was this really your room growing up?"

"Indeed it was."

The two girls exchanged a glance. Aimee giggled. Erin did likewise.

"What?" Myron said.

"This room . . . I mean, could it possibly be lamer?"

Erin finally spoke. "It's like too retro to be retro."

"What do you call this thing?" Aimee asked, pointing below her.

"A beanbag chair," Myron said.

The two girls giggled some more.

"And how come this lamp has a black lightbulb?"

"It makes the posters glow."

More laughs.

"Hey, I was in high school," Myron said, as if that explained everything.

"Did you ever bring a girl down here?" Aimee asked.

Myron put his hand to his heart. "A true gentleman never kisses and tells." Then: "Yes."

"How many?"

"How many what?"

"How many girls did you bring down here?"

"Oh. Approximately"—Myron looked up, drew in the air with his index finger—"carry the three . . . I'd say somewhere between eight and nine hundred thousand."

That caused rip-roaring laughter.

"Actually," Aimee said, "Mom says you used to be real cute."

Myron arched an eyebrow. "Used to be?"

Both girls high-fived and fell about the place. Myron shook his head and grumbled something about respecting their elders. When they quieted down, Aimee said, "Can I ask you something else?"

"Shoot."

"I mean, seriously."

"Go ahead."

"Those pictures of you upstairs. On the stairwell."

Myron nodded. He had a pretty good idea where this was going.

"You were on the cover of *Sports Illustrated*."

"That I was."

"Mom and Dad say you were like the greatest basketball player in the country."

"Mom and Dad," Myron said, "exaggerate."

Both girls stared at him. Five seconds passed. Then another five.

"Do I have something stuck in my teeth?" Myron asked.

"Weren't you, like, drafted by the Lakers?"

"The Celtics," he corrected.

"Sorry, the Celtics." Aimee kept him pinned with her eyes. "And you hurt your knee, right?"

"Right."

"Your career was over. Just like that."

"Pretty much, yes."

"So like"—Aimee shrugged—"how did that feel?"

"Hurting my knee?"

"Being a superstar like that. And then, *bam*, never being able to play again."

Both girls waited for his answer. Myron tried to come up with something profound.

"It sucked big-time," he said.

They both liked that.

Aimee shook her head. "It must have been the worst."

Myron looked toward Erin. Erin had her eyes down. The room went quiet. He waited. She eventually looked up. She looked scared and small and young. He wanted to take her in his arms, but man, would that ever be the wrong move.

"No," Myron said softly, still holding Erin's gaze. "Not even close to the worst."

A voice at the top of the stairs shouted down, "Myron?"

"I'm coming."

He almost left then. The next big what-if. But the words he'd overheard at the top of the stairs—*Randy drove*—kept rattling in his head. Beer and shots. He couldn't let that go, could he?

"I want to tell you a story," Myron began. And then he stopped. What he wanted to do was tell them about

13

an incident from his high school days. There had been a party at Barry Brenner's house. That was what he wanted to tell them. He'd been a senior in high school—like them. There had been a lot of drinking. His team, the Livingston Lancers, had just won the state basketball tournament, led by All-American Myron Bolitar's forty-three points. Everyone was drunk. He remembered Debbie Frankel, a brilliant girl, a live wire, that spark-plug who was always animated, always raising her hand to contradict the teacher, always arguing and taking the other side and you loved her for it. At midnight Debbie came over and said good-bye to him. Her glasses were low on her nose. That was what he remembered most—the way her glasses had slipped down. Myron could see that Debbie was wasted. So were the other two girls who would pile into that car.

You can guess how the story ends. They took the hill on South Orange Avenue too fast. Debbie died in the crash. The smashed-up car was put on display in front of the high school for six years. Myron wondered where it was now, what they'd eventually done to that wreck.

"What?" Aimee said.

But Myron didn't tell them about Debbie Frankel. Erin and Aimee had undoubtedly heard other versions of the same story. It wouldn't work. He knew that. So he tried something else.

"I need you to promise me something," Myron said.

Erin and Aimee looked at him.

He pulled his wallet from his pocket and plucked out two business cards. He opened the top drawer and found a pen that still worked. "Here are all my numbers—home, business, mobile, my place in New York City."

Myron scribbled on the cards and passed one to each of them. They took the cards without saying a word.

"Please listen to me, okay? If you're ever in a bind. If you're ever out drinking or your friends are drinking or you're high or stoned or I don't care what. Promise me. Promise me you'll call me. I'll come get you wherever you are. I won't ask any questions. I won't tell your parents. That's my promise to you. I'll take you wherever you want to go. I don't care how late. I don't care how far away you are. I don't care how wasted. Twenty-four-seven. Call me and I'll pick you up."

The girls said nothing.

Myron took a step closer. He tried to keep the pleading out of his voice. "Just please . . . please don't ever drive with someone who's been drinking."

They just stared at him.

"Promise me," he said.

And a moment later—the final what-if?—they did.

Chapter 3

Two hours later, Aimee's family—the Biels—were the first to leave.

Myron walked them to the door. Claire leaned close to his ear. "I heard the girls were down in your old room."

"Yep."

She gave him a wicked grin. "Did you tell them—?"

"God, no."

Claire shook her head. "You're such a prude."

He and Claire had been good friends in high school. He'd loved her free spirit. She acted like—for lack of a more appropriate term—a guy. When they'd go to parties, she'd try to pick someone up, usually with more success because, hey, she was an attractive girl. She'd liked muscle-heads. She'd go with them once, maybe twice, and then move on.

Claire was a lawyer now. She and Myron had messed around once, down in that very basement, on a holiday break senior year. Myron had been much more uptight about it. The next day, there had been no awkwardness for Claire. No discomfort, no silent treatment, no "maybe we should discuss what happened."

No encore either.

In law school Claire had met her husband, "Erik with a *K*." That was how he always introduced himself. Erik was thin and tightly wound. He rarely smiled. He almost never laughed. His tie was always wonderfully Windsored. Erik with a K was not the man Myron had figured Claire would end up with, but they seemed to work. Something about opposites attract, he guessed.

Erik gave him a firm handshake, made sure that there was eye contact. "Will I see you on Sunday?"

They used to play in a pickup basketball game on Sunday mornings, but Myron had stopped going months ago. "I won't be there this week, no."

Erik nodded as though Myron had said something profound and started out the door. Aimee smothered a laugh and waved. "Nice talking to you, Myron."

"Same here, Aimee."

Myron tried to give her a look that said, "Remember the promise." He didn't know if it worked, but Aimee did give him a small nod before heading down the path.

Claire kissed his cheek and whispered in his ear again. "You look happy."

"I am," he said.

Claire beamed. "Ali's great, isn't she?"

"She is."

"Am I the greatest matchmaker ever?"

"Like something out of a bad road production of *Fiddler*," he said.

"I'm not rushing things. But I am the greatest, aren't I? It's okay, I can take it. I'm the best ever."

"We're still talking about matchmaking, right?"

"Fresh. I know I'm the best at the other."

17

Myron said, "Eh."

She punched his arm and left. He watched her walk away, shook his head, smiled. In a sense, you are always seventeen years old and waiting for your life to begin.

Ten minutes later, Ali Wilder, Myron's new lady love, called for her children. Myron walked them all to the car. Jack, the nine-year-old boy, proudly wore a Celtics uniform with Myron's old number on it. It was the next step in hip-hop fashion. First there had been the retro uniforms of your favorite greats. Now, at a Web site called Big-Time-Losahs.com or something like that, they sold uniforms for players who became has-beens or never-weres, players who went bust.

Like Myron.

Jack, being only nine years old, didn't get the irony.

When they reached the car, Jack gave Myron a big hug. Unsure how to play this, Myron hugged back but kept it brief. Erin stayed back. She gave him a half-nod and slipped into the backseat. Jack followed his big sister. Ali and Myron stood and smiled at each other like a pair of newly dating doofs.

"This was fun," Ali said.

Myron was still smiling. Ali looked up at him with these wonderful green-brown eyes. She had red-blond hair and there were still remnants of childhood freckles. Her face was wide and her smile just held him.

"What?" she said.

"You look beautiful."

"Man, you are smooth."

"I don't want to brag, but yes. Yes, I am."

Ali looked back at the house. Win—real name: Windsor Horne Lockwood III—stood with arms folded, leaning against the doorframe. "Your friend Win," she said. "He seems nice."

"He's not."

"I know. I just figured him being your best friend and all, I'd say that."

"Win is complicated."

"He's good-looking."

"He knows."

"Not my type though. Too pretty. Too rich-preppy-boy."

"And you prefer macho he-men," Myron said. "I understand."

She snickered. "Why does he keep looking at me like that?"

"My guess? He's probably checking out your ass."

"Good to know somebody is."

Myron cleared his throat, glanced away. "So you want to have dinner together tomorrow?"

"That would be nice."

"I'll pick you up at seven."

Ali put her hand on his chest. Myron felt something electric in the touch. She stood on tiptoes—Myron was six-four—and kissed his cheek. "I'll cook for you."

"Really?"

"We'll stay in."

"Great. So it'll be, what, like a family-type thing? Get to know the kids more?"

"The kids will be spending the night at my sister's."

"Oh," Myron said.

Ali gave him a hard look and slipped into the driver's seat.

"Oh," Myron said again.

She arched an eyebrow. "And you didn't want to brag about being smooth."

Then she drove off. Myron watched the car disappear, the dorky smile still on his face. He turned and walked back to the house. Win had not moved. There had been many changes in Myron's life—his parents' moving down south, Esperanza's new baby, the fate of his business, even Big Cyndi—but Win remained a constant. Some of the ash-blond hair around the temples had grayed a bit, but Win was still the über-WASP. The patrician lockjaw, the perfect nose, the hair parted by the gods—he stank, deservedly so, of privilege and white shoes and golfer's tan.

"Six-point-eight," Win said. "Round it up to a seven."

"Excuse me?"

Win raised his hand, palm down, tilted it back and forth. "Your Ms. Wilder. If I'm being generous, I give her a seven."

"Gee, that means a lot. Coming from you and all."

They moved back into the house and sat in the den. Win crossed his legs in that perfect-crease way of his. His expression was permanently set on haughty. He looked pampered and spoiled and soft—in the face anyway. But the body told another story. He was all knotted, coiled muscle, not so much wiry as, if you will, barbed-wiry.

Win steepled his fingers. Steepling looked right on Win. "May I ask a question?"

"No."

"Why are you with her?"

"You're kidding, right?"

"No. I want to know what precisely you see in Ms. Ali Wilder."

Myron shook his head. "I knew I shouldn't have invited you."

"Ah, but you did. So let me elaborate."

"Please don't."

"During our years at Duke, well, there was the delectable Emily Downing. Then, of course, your soul mate for the next ten-plus years, the luscious Jessica

Culver. There was the brief fling with Brenda Slaughter and alas, most recently, the passion of Terese Collins."

"Is there a point?"

"There is." Win opened the steeple, closed it again. "What do all these women, your past loves, have in common?"

"You tell me," Myron said.

"In a word: bodaciousness."

"That's a word?"

"Smoking-hot honeys," Win continued with the snooty accent. "Each and every one of them. On a scale of one to ten, I would rate Emily a nine. That would be the lowest. Jessica would be a so-hot-she-singes-your-eyeballs eleven. Terese Collins and Brenda Slaughter, both near-tens."

"And in your expert opinion . . ."

"A seven is being generous," Win finished for him.

Myron just shook his head.

"So pray tell," Win said, "what is the big attraction?"

"Are you for real?"

"I am indeed."

"Well, here's a news flash, Win. First off, while it's not really important, I disagree with your awarded score."

"Oh? So how would you rate Ms. Wilder?"

"I'm not getting into that with you. But for one thing, Ali has the kind of looks that grow on you. At first you think she's attractive enough, and then, as you get to know her—"

"Bah."

"Bah?"

"Self-rationalization."

"Well, here's another news flash for you. It's not all about looks."

"Bah."

"Again with the *bah*?"

Win re-steepled his fingers. "Let's play a game. I'm going to say a word. You tell me the first thing that pops in your head."

Myron closed his eyes. "I don't know why I discuss matters of the heart with you. It's like talking about Mozart with a deaf man."

"Yes, that's very funny. Here comes the first word. Actually it's two words. Just tell me what pops in your head: Ali Wilder."

"Warmth," Myron said.

"Liar."

"Okay, I think we've discussed this enough."

"Myron?"

"What?"

"When was the last time you tried to save someone?"

The usual faces flashed strobelike through Myron's head. He tried to block them out.

"Myron?"

"Don't start," Myron said softly. "I've learned my lesson."

"Have you?"

He thought now about Ali, about that wonderful smile and the openness of her face. He thought about Aimee and Erin in his old bedroom down in the basement, about the promise he had forced them to make.

"Ali doesn't need rescuing, Myron."

"You think that's what this is about?"

"When I say her name, what's the first thing that comes to mind?"

"Warmth," Myron said again.

But this time, even he knew he was lying.

*

Six years.

That was how long it had been since Myron had played superhero. In six years he hadn't thrown a punch. He hadn't held, much less fired, a gun. He hadn't threatened or been threatened. He hadn't cracked wise with steroid-inflated pituitary glands. He hadn't called Win, still the scariest man he knew, to back him up or get him out of trouble. In the past six years, none of his clients had been murdered—a real positive in his business. None had been shot or arrested—well, except for that prostitution beef out in Las Vegas, but Myron still claimed that was entrapment. None of his clients or friends or loved ones had gone missing.

He had learned his lesson.

Don't stick your nose in where it doesn't belong. You're not Batman, and Win is not a psychotic version of Robin. Yes, Myron had saved some innocents during his quasi-heroic days, including the life of his own son. Jeremy, his boy, was nineteen now—Myron couldn't believe that either—and was serving in the military in some undisclosed spot in the Middle East.

But Myron had caused damage too. Look what had happened to Duane and Christian and Greg and Linda and Jack. . . . But mostly, Myron could not stop thinking about Brenda. He still visited her grave too frequently. Maybe she would have died anyway, he didn't know. Maybe it wasn't his fault.

The victories have a tendency to wash off you. The destruction—the dead—stay by your side, tap you on the shoulder, slow your step, haunt your sleep.

Either way, Myron had buried his hero complex. For the past six years, his life had been quiet, normal, average—boring, even.

Myron rinsed off the dishes. He semi-lived in

Livingston, New Jersey, in the same town—nay, the same house—where he was raised. His parents, the beloved Ellen and Alan Bolitar, performed aliya, returning to their people's homeland (south Florida) five years ago. Myron bought the house as both an investment, a good one, in fact, and so that his folks would have a place to return to when they migrated back during the warmer months. Myron spent about a third of his time living in this house in the burbs and two-thirds rooming with Win at the famed Dakota apartment building on Central Park West in New York City.

He thought about tomorrow night and his date with Ali. Win was an idiot, no question about that, but as usual his questions had scored a hit, if not a bull's-eye. Forget that looks stuff. That was utter nonsense. And forget the hero complex stuff too. That wasn't what this was about. But something was holding him back and yes, it had to do with Ali's tragedy. Try as he might, he couldn't shake it.

As for the hero stuff, making Aimee and Erin promise to call him—that was different. It doesn't matter who you are—the teenage years are hard. High school is a war zone. Myron had been a popular kid. He was a Parade All-American basketball player, one of the top recruits in the country, and, to trot out a favorite cliché, a true scholar-athlete. If anyone should have had it easy in high school, it would be someone like Myron Bolitar. But he hadn't. In the end, no one gets out of those years unscathed.

You just need to survive adolescence. That's all. Just get through it.

Maybe that was what he should have said to the girls.

Chapter 4

The next morning Myron headed into work.

His office was on the twelfth floor of the Lock-Horne Building—as in Win's name—on Park Avenue and Fifty-second Street in midtown Manhattan. When the elevator opened, Myron was greeted with a big sign—a new addition to the place—that read

MB REPS

in some funky font. Esperanza had come up with the new logo. The *M* stood for Myron. The *B* for Bolitar. The *Reps* came from the fact that they were in the business of *rep*resentation. Myron had come up with the name by himself. He would often pause after telling people that and wait for the applause to die down.

Originally, when they just worked in the sports field, the firm was called MB SportsReps instead of MB Reps. Over the past five years the company had diversified, representing actors, authors, and celebrities of various stripes. Ergo the clever shortening of the name. Getting rid of the excess, cutting away the fat. Yep, that was MB Reps right down to the name.

Myron heard the baby cry. Esperanza must be in already. He poked his head into her office.

Esperanza was breast-feeding. He immediately looked down.

"Uh, I'll come back later."

"Stop being an ass," Esperanza said. "You'd think you've never seen a breast before."

"Well, it's been a while."

"And certainly not one this spectacular," she added. "Sit."

At first, MB SportsReps had just been just Myron the super-agent and Esperanza the receptionist/secretary/Girl Friday. You may remember Esperanza during her years as the sexy, lithe professional wrestler named Little Pocahontas. Every Sunday morning on Channel 11 here in the New York area, Esperanza would take to the ring, donning a feathered headband and drool-inducing bikini of pseudosuede. Along with her partner, Big Chief Mama, known in real life as Big Cyndi, they held the intercontinental tag-team championship belt for FLOW, the Fabulous Ladies Of Wrestling. The wrestling organization had originally wanted to call itself the Beautiful Ladies Of Wrestling, but the network had trouble with the ensuing acronym.

Esperanza's current title at MB Reps was senior vice president, but she pretty much ran the sports division now.

"Sorry I missed your coming-out party," Esperanza said.

"It wasn't a coming-out party."

"Whatever. Hector here had a cold."

"Is he better now?"

"He's fine."

"So what's going on here?"

"Michael Discepolo. We need to get his contract done."

"The Giants still dragging their feet?"

"Yes."

"Then he'll be a free agent," Myron said. "I think that's probably a good move, what with the way he's been playing."

"Except Discepolo is a loyal guy. He'd rather sign."

Esperanza pulled Hector away from her nipple and put him on the other breast. Myron tried not to look away too suddenly. He never quite knew how to play it when a woman breast-fed in front of him. He wanted to be mature about it, but what exactly did that mean? You don't stare, but you don't divert your eyes either. How do you mine the area between those two?

"I have some news," Esperanza said.

"Oh?"

"Tom and I are getting married."

Myron said nothing. He felt a funny twinge.

"Well?"

"Congrats."

"That's it?"

"I'm surprised, that's all. But really, I think that's great. When's the big day?"

"Three weeks from Saturday. But let me ask you something. Now that I'm marrying the father of my baby, am I still a fallen woman?"

"I don't think so."

"Damn, I like being a fallen woman."

"Well, you still had the baby out of wedlock."

"Good point. I could run with that."

Myron looked at her.

"What's wrong?"

"You, married." He shook his head.

"I was never big on commitment, was I?"

"You change partners like a cineplex changes movies."

Esperanza smiled. "True."

"I don't even remember you staying with the same gender for more than, what, a month?"

"The wonders of bisexuality," Esperanza said. "But it's different with Tom."

"How so?"

"I love him."

He said nothing.

"You don't think I can do it," she said. "Stay true to one person."

"I never said that."

"Do you know what bisexual means?"

"Of course," Myron said. "I dated a lot of bisexual women—I'd mention sex, the girl would say, 'Bye.'"

Esperanza just looked at him.

"Okay, old joke," he said. "It just . . ." Myron sort of shrugged.

"I like women and I like men. But if I make a commitment, it's to a person, not a gender. Make sense?"

"Sure."

"Good. Now tell me what's wrong with you and this Ali Wilder."

"Nothing's wrong."

"Win said you two haven't done the deed yet."

"Win said that?"

"Yes."

"When?"

"This morning."

"Win just came in here and said that?"

"First he made a comment about my increased cup size since giving birth, then yes, he told me that you've been dating this woman for almost two months and haven't done the nasty yet."

"What makes him think that?"

"Body language."

28

"He said that?"

"Win is good when it comes to body language."

Myron shook his head.

"So is he right?"

"I'm having dinner at Ali's house tonight. The kids are staying with her sister."

"She made this plan?"

"Yes."

"And you haven't . . . ?" With Hector still feeding, Esperanza still managed to gesture the point.

"We haven't."

"Man."

"I'm waiting for a signal."

"Like what, a burning bush? She invited you to her house and told you the kids would be away for the night."

"I know."

"That's the international signal for Jump My Bones."

He said nothing.

"Myron?"

"Yes."

"She's a widow—not a cripple. She's probably terrified."

"That's why I'm taking it slow."

"That's sweet and noble, but stupid. And it's not helping."

"So you're suggesting . . . ?"

"A major bone jump, yes."

Chapter 5

M yron arrived at Ali's at seven P.M.

The Wilders lived in Kasselton, a town about fifteen minutes north of Livingston. Myron had gone through a strange ritual before leaving his house. Cologne or no cologne? That one was easy: no cologne. Tighty-whiteys or boxers? He chose something between the two, that hybrid that was either tight boxers or long tighties. Boxer briefs, the package said. And he chose them in gray. He wore a Banana Republic tan pullover with a black T-shirt underneath. The jeans were from the Gap. Slip-on loafers from the Tod's outlet store adorned his size-fourteen feet. He couldn't be more American Casual if he tried.

Ali opened the door. The lights behind her were low. She wore a black dress with a scooped front. Her hair was pinned back. Myron liked that. Most men, they liked it when the hair came down. Myron had always been a fan of keeping it off the face.

He stared at her for another moment and then said, "Whoa."

"I thought you said you were smooth."

"I'm holding back."

"But why?"

"If I go all out in the smooth department," Myron said, "women all over the tri-state area begin to disrobe. I need to harness the power."

"Lucky for me then. Come on in."

He had never made it past her foyer before. Ali walked to the kitchen. His stomach knotted. There were family photographs on the wall. Myron did a quick scan. He spotted Kevin's face. He was in at least four different photographs. Myron didn't want to stare, but his gaze got caught on an image of Erin. She was fishing with her dad. Her smile was heartbreaking. Myron tried to picture the girl in his basement smiling like that, but it wouldn't hold.

He looked back at Ali. Something crossed her face.

Myron sniffed the air. "What are you cooking?"

"I'm making Chicken Kiev."

"Smells great."

"You mind if we talk first?"

"Sure."

They headed into the den. Myron tried to keep his head about him. He looked around for more pictures. There was a framed wedding photo. Ali's hair was too big, he thought, but maybe that was the look then. He thought that she was prettier now. That happens with some women. There was also a photograph of five men in matching black tuxedos with bow ties. The grooms-men, Myron figured. Ali followed his gaze. She walked over and picked up the group shot.

"This one is Kevin's brother," she said, pointing to the man second on the right.

Myron nodded.

"The other men worked at Carson Wilkie with

Kevin. They were his best friends."

Myron said, "Were they—"

"All dead," she said. "All married, all had children."

The elephant in the room—it was as if all hands and fingers were suddenly pointing at it.

"You don't have to do this," Myron said.

"Yeah, Myron, I do."

They sat down.

"When Claire first set us up," she began, "I told her that you'd have to raise the subject of 9/11. Did she tell you that?"

"Yes."

"But you didn't."

He opened his mouth, closed it, tried again. "How was I supposed to do that exactly? Hi, how are you, I hear you're a 9/11 widow, do you want Italian or maybe Chinese?"

Ali nodded. "Fair enough."

There was a grandfather clock in the corner, a huge ornate thing. It chose then to start chiming. Myron wondered where Ali had gotten it, where she had gotten everything in this house, how much of Kevin was watching them now, in this house, in *his* house.

"Kevin and I started dating when we were juniors in high school. We decided to take time off during our freshman year of college. I was going to NYU. He would be off at Wharton. It would be the mature thing to do. But when we came home for Thanksgiving, and we saw each other . . ." She shrugged. "I've never been with another man. Ever. There, I said it. I don't know if we did it right or wrong. Isn't that weird? I think we sorta learned together."

Myron sat there. She was no more than a foot away from him. He wasn't sure of the right move here—the story of his life. He put his hand close to hers. She

32

picked it up and held it.

"I don't know when I first realized I was ready to start dating. It took me longer than most of the widows. We talk about it, of course—the widows, I mean. We talk a lot. But one day I just said to myself, okay, now maybe it's time. I told Claire. And when she suggested you, do you know what I thought?"

Myron shook his head.

"He's out of my league, but maybe this will be fun. I thought—this is going to sound stupid and please remember I really didn't know you at all—that you'd be a good transition."

"Transition?"

"You know what I mean. You were a pro athlete. You probably had a lot of women. I thought maybe, well, it would be a fun fling. A physical thing. And then, afterwards, maybe I'd find someone nice. Does that make sense?"

"I think so," Myron said. "You just wanted me for my body."

"Pretty much, yeah."

"I feel so cheap," he said. "Or is it thrilled? Let's go with thrilled."

That made her smile. "Please don't take offense."

"No offense taken." Then: "Hussy."

She laughed. The sound was melodic.

"So what happened to your plan?" he asked.

"You weren't what I expected."

"That a good thing or bad?"

"I don't know. You used to date Jessica Culver. I read that in a *People* magazine."

"I did."

"Was it serious?"

"Yes."

"She's a great writer."

33

Myron nodded.

"She's also stunning."

"You're stunning."

"Not like that."

He was going to argue, but he knew that it would sound too patronizing.

"When you asked me out, I figured that you were looking for something, I don't know, different."

"Different how?" he asked.

"Being a 9/11 widow," she said. "The truth is, and I hate to admit this, but it gives me something of a warped celebrity."

He did know. He thought about what Win had said, about that first thing that pops in your head when you hear her name.

"So I figured—again not knowing you, just knowing that you were this good-looking pro athlete who dates women who look like supermodels—I figured that I might be an interesting notch on the belt."

"Because you were a 9/11 widow?"

"Yes."

"That's pretty sick."

"Not really."

"How's that?"

"It's like I said. There's a weird sort of celebrity attached. People who wouldn't give me the time of day suddenly wanted to meet me. It still happens. About a month ago, I started playing in this new tennis league at the Racket Club. One of the women—this rich snob who wouldn't let me cut through her yard when we first moved to town—comes up to me and she's making the poo-poo face."

"The poo-poo face?"

"That's what I call it. The poo-poo face. It looks like this."

34

Ali demonstrated. She pursed her lips, frowned, and batted her eyes.

"You look like Donald Trump being sprayed with mace."

"That's the poo-poo face. I get it all the time since Kevin died. I don't blame anyone. It's natural. But this woman with the poo-poo face comes up to me and she takes both of my hands in hers and looks me in the eyes and has this whole earnest thing going on so that I want to scream, and she says, 'Are you Ali Wilder? Oh, I so wanted to contact you. How are you doing?' You get the point."

"I do."

She looked at him.

"What?"

"You've turned into the dating version of the poo-poo face."

"I'm not sure I follow."

"You keep telling me I'm beautiful."

"You are."

"You met me three times when I was married."

Myron said nothing.

"Did you think I was beautiful then?"

"I try not to think that way about married women."

"Do you even remember meeting me?"

"Not really, no."

"And if I looked like Jessica Culver, even if I were married, you'd have remembered."

She waited.

"What do you want me to say here, Ali?"

"Nothing. But it's time to stop treating me like the poo-poo face. It doesn't matter why you first started dating me. It matters why you're here now."

"Can I do that?"

"Do what?"

"Can I tell you why I'm here now?"

Ali swallowed and for the first time she looked unsure of herself. She made a go-ahead gesture with her hand.

He dove in. "I'm here because I really like you— because I may be confused about a lot of things and maybe you're making a good point about the poo-poo face, but the fact is, I'm here right now because I can't stop thinking about you. I think about you all the time and when I do, I have this goofy smile on my face. It looks like this." Now it was his turn to demonstrate. "So that's why I'm here, okay?"

"That," Ali said, trying to hold back a smile, "is a really good answer."

He was about to crack wise, but he held back. With maturity comes restraint.

"Myron?"

"Yes?"

"I want you to kiss me. I want you to hold me. I want you to take me upstairs and make love to me. I want you to do it with no expectations because I don't have any. I could dump you tomorrow and you could dump me. It doesn't matter. But I'm not fragile. I'm not going to describe the hell of the past five years, but I'm stronger than you'll ever know. If this relationship continues after tonight, you're the one who'll have to be strong, not me. This is a no-obligation offer. I know how valiant and noble you want to be. But I don't want that. All I want tonight is you."

Ali leaned toward him and kissed him on the lips. First gently then with more hunger. Myron felt a surge go through him.

She kissed him again. And Myron felt lost.

An hour later—or maybe it was only twenty minutes—
Myron collapsed and rolled onto his back.

"Well?" Ali said.

"Wow."

"Tell me more."

"Let me catch my breath."

Ali laughed, snuggled closer.

"My limbs," he said. "I can't feel my limbs."

"Not a thing?"

"A little tingle maybe."

"Not so little. And you were pretty good yourself."

"As Woody Allen once said, I practice a lot when
I'm alone."

She put her head on his chest. His racing heart
started to slow. He stared at the ceiling.

"Myron?"

"Yes."

"He'll never leave my life. He'll never leave Erin and
Jack either."

"I know."

"Most men can't handle that."

"I don't know if I can either."

She looked at him and smiled.

"What?"

"You're being honest," she said. "I like that."

"No more poo-poo face?"

"Oh, I wiped that off twenty minutes ago."

He pursed his lips, frowned, and batted his eyes.
"But wait, it's back."

She put her head back on his chest.

"Myron?"

"Yes?"

"He'll never leave my life," she said. "But he's not
here now. Right now I think it's just the two of us."

Chapter 6

On the third floor of St. Barnabas Medical Center, Essex County investigator Loren Muse rapped on a door that read EDNA SKYLAR, MD, GENETICIST.

A woman's voice said, "Come in."

Loren turned the knob and entered. Skylar stood. She was taller than Loren, but most people were. Skylar crossed the room, hand extended. They both offered up firm handshakes and plenty of eye contact. Edna Skylar nodded in a sisterhood way to her. Loren had seen it before. They were both in professions still dominated by men. That gave them a bond.

"Won't you please have a seat?"

They both sat. Edna Skylar's desk was immaculate. There were manila folders, but they were stacked without any papers peeking out. The office was standard issue, dominated by a picture window that offered up a wonderful view of a parking lot.

Dr. Skylar stared intently at Loren Muse. Loren didn't like it. She waited a moment. Skylar kept staring.

Loren said, "Problem?"

Edna Skylar smiled. "Sorry, bad habit."

"What's that?"

"I look at faces."

"Uh-huh."

"It's not important. Well, maybe it is. That's how I got into this predicament."

Loren wanted to get to it. "You told my boss that you have information on Katie Rochester?"

"How is Ed?"

"He's good."

She smiled warmly. "He's a nice man."

"Yeah," Loren said, "a prince."

"I've known him a long time."

"He told me."

"That's why I called Ed. We had a long talk about the case."

"Right," Loren said. "And that's why he sent me here."

Edna Skylar looked off, out the window. Loren tried to guess her age. Mid-sixties probably, but she wore it well. Dr. Skylar was a handsome woman, short gray hair, high cheekbones, knew how to sport a beige suit without coming across as too butch or overly feminine.

"Dr. Skylar?"

"Could you tell me something about the case?"

"Excuse me?"

"Katie Rochester. Is she officially listed as missing?"

"I'm not sure how that's relevant."

Edna Skylar's eyes moved slowly back to Loren Muse. "Do you think she met up with foul play—"

"I can't really discuss that."

"—or do you think she ran away? When I talked to Ed, he seemed pretty sure she was a runaway. She took money out of an ATM in midtown, he said. Her father is rather unsavory."

"Prosecutor Steinberg told you all that?"

"He did."

"So why are you asking me?"

"I know his take," she said. "I want yours."

Loren was about to protest some more, but Edna Skylar was again staring with too much intensity. She scanned Skylar's desk for family photographs. There were none. She wondered what to make of that and decided nothing. Skylar was waiting.

"She's eighteen years old," Loren tried, treading carefully.

"I know that."

"That makes her an adult."

"I know that too. And what about the father? Do you think he abused her?"

Loren wondered how to play this. The truth was, she didn't like the father, hadn't from the get-go. RICO said that Dominick Rochester was mobbed up and maybe that was part of it. But there was something to reading a person's grief. On the one hand, everyone reacts differently. It was true that you really couldn't tell guilt based on someone's reaction. Some killers cried tears that'd put Pacino to shame. Others were beyond robotic. Same with the innocent. It was like this: You're with a group of people, a grenade is thrown in the middle of the crowd, you never know who is going to dive on it and who is going to dive for cover.

That said, Katie Rochester's father . . . there was something off about his grief. It was too fluid. It was like he was trying on different personas, seeing which one would look best for the public. And the mother. She had the whole shattered-eye thing going on, but had that come from devastation or resignation? It was hard to tell.

"We have no evidence of that," Loren said in the most noncommittal tone she could muster.

Edna Skylar did not react.

"These questions," Loren went on. "They're a bit bizarre."

"That's because I'm still not sure what to do."

"About?"

"If a crime has been committed, I want to help. But . . ."

"But?"

"I saw her."

Loren Muse waited a beat, hoping she'd say more. She didn't. "You saw Katie Rochester?"

"Yes."

"When?"

"It'll be three weeks on Saturday."

"And you're just telling us now?"

Edna Skylar was looking out at the parking lot again. The sun was setting, the rays slicing in through the venetian blinds. She looked older in that light.

"Dr. Skylar?"

"She asked me not to say anything." Her gaze was still on the lot.

"Katie did?"

Still looking off, Edna Skylar nodded.

"You talked to her?"

"For a second maybe."

"What did she say?"

"That I couldn't tell anybody that I saw her."

"And?"

"And that was it. A moment later she was gone."

"Gone?"

"On a subway."

The words came easier now. Edna Skylar told Loren the whole story, how she'd been studying faces while

41

walking in New York, how she spotted the girl despite the appearance change, how she followed her down into the subway, how she'd vanished into the dark.

Loren wrote it all down, but fact was, this figured into what she'd believed from the beginning. The kid was a runaway. As Ed Steinberg had already told Skylar, there had been an ATM withdrawal at a Citibank in midtown near the time she vanished. Loren had seen the bank video. The face had been covered by a hood, but it was probably the Rochester girl. The father had clearly been on the over-strict side. That was how it always was with the runaways. The too-liberal parents, their kids often got hooked on drugs. The too-conservative, their kids were the runaways with the sex issues. Might be a stereotype to break it down like that, but Loren had seen very few cases that broke those rules.

She asked a few more follow-up questions. There was nothing that they could really do now. The girl was eighteen. There was no reason, from this description, to suspect foul play. On TV, the feds get involved and put a team on it. That doesn't happen in real life.

But Loren felt a niggling at the base of her brain. Some would call it intuition. She hated that. Hunches . . . that didn't really work either. She wondered what Ed Steinberg, her boss, would want to do. Nothing, probably. Their office was busy working with the U.S. Attorney on two cases, one involving a possible terrorist and the other a Newark politician on the take.

With their resources so limited, should they pursue what appeared to be an obvious runaway? It was a tough call.

"Why now?" Loren asked.

"What?"

"Three weeks, you didn't say anything. What made you change your mind?"

"Do you have children, Investigator Muse?"

"No."

"I do."

Loren again looked at the desk, at the credenza, at the wall. No family pictures. No sign of children or grandchildren. Skylar smiled, as if she understood what Muse was doing.

"I was a lousy mother."

"I'm not sure I understand."

"I was, shall we say, laissez-faire. When in doubt, I'd let it go."

Loren waited.

"That," Edna Skylar said, "was a huge mistake."

"I'm still not sure I understand."

"Neither do I. But this time . . ." Her voice faded away. She swallowed, looked down at her hands before turning her gaze to Loren. "Just because everything looks okay, maybe it's not. Maybe Katie Rochester needs help. Maybe this time I should do more than just let it go."

The promise in the basement came back to haunt Myron at exactly 2:17 a.m.

Three weeks had passed. Myron was still dating Ali. It was the day of Esperanza's wedding. Ali came as his date. Myron gave away the bride. Tom—real name Thomas James Bidwell III—was Win's cousin. The wedding was small. Strangely enough, the groom's family, charter members of the Daughters of the American Revolution, was not thrilled with Tom's marriage to a Bronx-born Latina named Esperanza Diaz. Go figure.

"Funny," Esperanza said.

"What's that?"

"I always thought I'd marry for money, not love." She checked herself in the mirror. "But here I am, marrying for love and getting money."

"Irony is not dead."

"Good thing. You're going to Miami to see Rex?"

Rex Storton was an aging movie star they were repping. "I'm flying down tomorrow afternoon."

Esperanza turned away from the mirror, spread her arms, and gave him a dazzling smile. "Well?"

She was a vision. Myron said, "Wow."

"You think?"

"I think."

"Come on then. Let's get me hitched."

"Let's."

"One thing first." Esperanza pulled him aside. "I want you to be happy for me."

"I am."

"I'm not leaving you."

"I know."

Esperanza looked into his face. "We're still best friends," she said. "You understand that? You, me, Win, Big Cyndi. Nothing has changed."

"Sure it has," Myron said. "Everything has changed."

"I love you, you know."

"And I love you."

She smiled again. Esperanza was always so damned beautiful. She had that whole peasant-blouse fantasy thing going on. But today, in that dress, the word *luminous* was simply too weak. She had been so wild, such a free spirit, had insisted that she would never settle down with one person like this. But here she was, with a baby, getting married. Even Esperanza had grown up.

"You're right," she said. "But things change, Myron. And you've always hated change."

"Don't start with that."

"Look at you. You lived with your parents into your mid-thirties. You own your childhood home. You still spend most of your time with your college roommate, who, let's face it, can't change."

He put up his hand. "I get the point."

"Funny though."

"What?"

"I always thought you'd be the first to get married," she said.

"Me too."

"Win, well, like I said, let's not even go there. But you always fell in love so easily, especially with that bitch, Jessica."

"Don't call her that."

"Whatever. Anyway, you were the one who bought the American dream—get married, have two-point-six kids, invite friends to barbecues in the backyard, the whole thing."

"And you never did."

Esperanza smiled. "Weren't you the one who taught me, *Men tracht und Gott lacht*?"

"Man, I love it when you shiksas speak Yiddish."

Esperanza put her hand through the crook of his arm. "That can be a good thing, you know."

"I know."

She took a deep breath. "Shall we?"

"You nervous?"

Esperanza looked at him. "Not even a little."

"Then onward."

Myron walked her down the aisle. He thought it would be a flattering formality, standing in for her late father, but when Myron gave Esperanza's hand to Tom, when Tom smiled and shook his hand, Myron started to well up. He stepped back and sat down in the front row.

The wedding was not so much an eclectic mix as a wonderful collision. Win was Tom's best man while Big Cyndi was Esperanza's maid of honor. Big Cyndi, her former tag-team wrestling partner, was six-six and comfortably north of three hundred pounds. Her fists looked like canned hams. She had not been sure what to wear—a classic peach maid of honor dress or a black leather corset. Her compromise: peach leather with a fringed hem, sleeveless so as to display arms with the relative dimensions and consistency of marble columns on a Georgian mansion. Big Cyndi's hair was done up in a mauve Mohawk and pinned on the top was a little bride-and-groom cake decoration.

When trying on the, uh, dress, Big Cyndi had spread her arms and twirled for Myron. Ocean tides altered course, and solar systems shifted. "What do you think?" she asked.

"Mauve with peach?"

"It's very hip, Mr. Bolitar."

She always called him Mister; Big Cyndi liked formality.

Tom and Esperanza exchanged vows in a quaint church. White poppies lined the pews. Tom's side of the aisle was dressed in black and white—a sea of penguins. Esperanza's side had so many colors, Crayola sent a scout. It looked like the Halloween parade in Greenwich Village. The organ played beautiful hymns. The choir sang like angels. The setting could not have been more serene.

For the reception, however, Esperanza and Tom wanted a change of pace. They rented out an S&M nightclub near Eleventh Avenue called Leather and Lust. Big Cyndi worked there as a bouncer and sometimes, very late at night, she took to the stage for an act that boggled the imagination.

Myron and Ali parked in a lot off the West Side Highway. They passed a twenty-four-hour porn shop called King David's Slut Palace. The windows were soaped up. There was a big sign on the door that read NOW UNDER NEW MANAGEMENT.

"Whew." Myron pointed to the sign. "It's about time, don't you think?"

Ali nodded. "The place had been so mismanaged before."

When they ducked inside Leather and Lust, Ali walked around as though she were at the Louvre, squinting at the photos on the wall, checking out the devices, the costumes, the bondage material. She shook her head. "I am hopelessly naïve."

"Not hopelessly," Myron said.

Ali pointed at something black and long that resembled human intestines.

"What's that?" she asked.

"Dang if I know."

"Are you, uh, into . . . ?"

"Oh no."

"Too bad," Ali said. Then: "Kidding. So very much kidding."

Their romance was progressing, but the reality of dating someone with young kids had set in. They hadn't spent another full night together since that first. Myron had only offered up brief hellos to Erin and Jack since that party. They weren't sure how fast or slow they should go in their own relationship, but Ali was pretty adamant that they should go slow where it concerned the kids.

Ali had to leave early. Jack had a school project she'd promised to help him with. Myron walked her out, deciding to stay in the city for the night.

"How long will you be in Miami?" Ali asked.

"Just a night or two."

"Would it make you retch violently if I say I'll miss you?"

"Not violently, no."

She kissed him gently. Myron watched her drive off, his heart soaring, and then he headed back to the party.

Since he planned on sleeping in anyway, Myron started drinking. He was not what one would call a great drinker—he held his liquor about as well as a fourteen-year-old girl—but tonight, at this wonderful albeit bizarre celebration, he felt in the mood to imbibe. So did Win, though it took far more to get him buzzed. Cognac was mother's milk to Win. He rarely showed the effects, at least on the outside.

Tonight it didn't matter. Win's stretch limo was already waiting. It would take them back uptown.

Win's apartment in the Dakota was worth about a billion dollars and had a décor that reminded one of Versailles. When they arrived, Win carefully poured himself an obscenely priced vintage port, Quinta do Noval Nacional 1963. The bottle had been decanted several hours ago because, as Win explained, you must give vintage port time to breathe before consumption. Myron normally drank a chocolate Yoo-hoo, but his stomach was not in the mood. Plus the chocolate wouldn't have time to breathe.

Win snapped on the TV, and they watched *Antiques Roadshow*. A snooty woman with a lazy drawl had brought in a hideous bronze bust. She started telling the appraiser a story about how Dean Martin in 1950 offered her father ten thousand dollars for this wretched hunk of metal, but her daddy, she said with an insistent finger-point and matching smirk, was too wily for that.

He knew that it must be worth a fortune. The appraiser nodded patiently, waited for the woman to finish, and then he lowered the boom:

"It's worth about twenty dollars."

Myron and Win shared a quiet high five.

"Enjoying other people's misery," Win said.

"We are pitiful," Myron said.

"It's not us."

"No?"

"It's this show," Win said. "It illuminates so much that is wrong with our society."

"How so?"

"People aren't satisfied just to have their trinket be worth a fortune. No, it is better, far better, if they bought it on the cheap from some unsuspecting rube. No one considers the feelings of the unsuspecting yard salesman who was cheated, who lost out."

"Good point."

"Ah, but there's more."

Myron smiled, sat back, waited.

"Forget greed for the moment," Win went on. "What really upsets us is that everybody but everybody lies on *Antiques Roadshow*."

Myron nodded. "You mean when the appraiser asks, 'Do you have any idea what it's worth?' "

"Precisely. He asks that same question every time."

"I know."

"And Mr. or Mrs. Gee-Whiz act like the question caught them totally off guard—as if they'd never seen the show before."

"It's annoying," Myron agreed.

"And then they say something like, 'Gasp-oh-gasp, I never thought of that. I have no idea what it might be worth.'" Win frowned. "I mean, please. You dragged your two-ton granite armoire to some impersonal convention center and waited in line for twelve hours—but you never, ever, not in your wildest dreams wondered what it might be worth?"

"A lie," Myron agreed, feeling the buzz. "It's up there with 'Your call is very important to us.' "

"And that," Win said, "is why we love when a woman like that gets slammed. The lies. The greed. The same reason why we love the boob on *Wheel of Fortune* who knows the solution but always goes for the extra spin and hits Bankrupt."

"It's like life," Myron pronounced, feeling the booze.

"Do tell."

But then the door's intercom buzzed.

Myron felt his stomach drop. He checked his watch. It was one-thirty in the morning. Myron just looked over at Win. Win looked back, his face a placid pool. Win was still handsome, too handsome, but the years, the abuse, the late nights of either violence or, as with tonight, sex, were starting to show just a little.

Myron closed his eyes. "Is that a . . . ?"

"Yes."

He sighed, rose. "I wish you'd told me."

"Why?"

They'd been down that road before. There was no answer to that one.

"She's from a new place on the Upper West Side," Win said.

"Yeah, how convenient."

Without another word Myron headed down the corridor toward his bedroom. Win answered the door. As much as it depressed him, Myron took a peek. The girl was young and pretty. She said, "Hi!" with a forced lilt in her voice. Win did not reply. He beckoned her to follow him. She did, teetering on too-high heels. They vanished down the corridor.

As Esperanza had noted, some things refuse to change—no matter how much you'd like them to.

Myron closed the door and collapsed onto the bed. His head swam from drink. The ceiling spun. He let it. He wondered if he was going to get sick. He didn't think so. He pushed thoughts of the girl out of his head. She left him easier than the girls used to, a change in him that was definitely not for the better. He didn't hear any noises—the room Win used (not his bedroom, of course) was soundproof—and eventually Myron closed his eyes.

The call came in on his cell phone.

Myron had it set on vibrate-ring. It rattled against his night table. He woke from his half-sleep and reached for it. He rolled over, and his head screamed. That was when he saw the bedside digital clock.

2:17 a.m.

He did not check the caller ID before he put the phone to his ear.

"Hello?" he croaked.

He heard the sob first.

"Hello?" he said again.

"Myron? It's Aimee."

"Aimee." Myron sat up. "What's wrong? Where are you?"

"You said I could call." There was another sob. "Anytime, right?"

"Right. Where are you, Aimee?"

"I need help."

"Okay, no problem. Just tell me where you are."

"Oh God . . ."

"Aimee?"

"You won't tell, right?"

He hesitated. He flashed to Claire, Aimee's mother. He remembered Claire at this age and felt a funny pang.

51

"You promised. You promised you wouldn't tell my parents."

"I know. Where are you?"

"Promise you won't tell?"

"I promise, Aimee. Just tell me where you are."

Chapter 7

Myron threw on a pair of sweats.

His brain was a little hazy. There was still some of the drink in him. The irony did not escape him—he had told Aimee to call him because he didn't want her to get in a car with somebody who'd drank, and here he was, slightly tipsy. He tried to step back and judge his sobriety. He figured that he was okay to drive, but isn't that what every drinker thinks?

He debated asking Win, but Win was otherwise preoccupied. Win had also drunk even more, despite the sober façade. Still, he shouldn't just rush out, should he?

Good question.

The fine wooden floors in the corridor had recently been redone. Myron decided quickly to test his sobriety. He walked along one plank as though it were a straight line, as though a cop had pulled him over. He passed, but again Myron was, all modesty aside, pretty damned coordinated. He could probably pass that test whilst wasted.

Still, what choice did he have here? Even if he found

someone else to drive at this hour, how would Aimee react to him showing up with a stranger? He, Myron, had been the one to make her promise to call him if such a situation were to arise. He had been the one who jammed his card with all the phone numbers into her hand. He had been the one, as Aimee had just pointed out, who swore complete confidentiality.

He had to go himself.

His car was in a twenty-four-hour lot on Seventieth Street. The gate was closed. Myron rang the bell. The attendant grudgingly pressed the button and the gate ascended.

Myron was not a big-car guy, and thus he still drove a Ford Taurus, which he dubbed the "Chick Magnet." A car got him from point A to point B. Period. More important to him than horsepower and V6 was having radio controls on the steering wheel, so he could constantly flip stations.

He pressed Aimee's number on the cell phone. She answered in a small voice.

"Hello?"

"I'm on my way."

Aimee did not reply.

"Why don't you stay on the line?" he said. "Just so I know you're okay."

"My battery is almost dead. I want to save the power."

"I should be there in ten, fifteen minutes tops," Myron said.

"From Livingston?"

"I was staying in the city."

"Oh, that's good. See you soon."

She disconnected the call. Myron checked the car clock: 2:30 a.m. Aimee's parents must be worried sick. He hoped that she'd already called Claire and Erik.

He was tempted to place the call himself, but no, that wasn't part of how this worked. When she got in the car, he'd encourage her to do it.

Aimee's location, he'd been surprised to hear, was midtown Manhattan. She told him that she'd wait on Fifth Avenue by Fifty-fourth. That was pretty much Rockefeller Center. What was strange about that, about an eighteen-year-old girl in the Big Apple imbibing in that area, was that midtown was dead at night. During the week, this place hustled with enterprise. On weekend days, you had the tourist trade. But on a Saturday night, there were few people on the street. New York might be the city that never sleeps, but as he hit Fifth Avenue in the upper Fifties, midtown was taking a serious nap.

He got caught at a traffic light on Fifth Avenue at Fifty-second Street. The door handle jangled, and then Aimee opened the door and slipped into the back.

"Thank you," she said.

"You okay?"

From behind him a small voice said, "I'm fine."

"I'm not a chauffeur, Aimee. Sit up front."

She hesitated, but she did as he asked. When she closed the passenger door, Myron turned to face her. Aimee stared straight out the front window. Like most teens, she'd splattered on too much makeup. The young don't need makeup, especially that much. Her eyes were red and raccoon-like. She was dressed in something teenage-tight, like a thin wrapping of gauze, the kind of thing that, even if you had the figure, you couldn't carry past the age of maybe twenty-three.

She looked so much like her mother had at that age.

"The light's green," Aimee said.

He started driving. "What happened?"

"Some people were drinking too much. I didn't want to drive with them."

"Where?"

"Where what?"

Again Myron knew that midtown was not a young-people hot spot. Most hung out in bars on the Upper East Side or maybe down in the Village. "Where were you drinking?"

"Is that important?"

"I'd like to know."

Aimee finally turned toward him. Her eyes were wet. "You promised."

He kept driving.

"You promised you wouldn't ask any questions, remember?"

"I just want to make sure you're all right."

"I am."

Myron made a right, cutting across town. "I'll take you home then."

"No."

He waited.

"I'm staying with a friend."

"Where?"

"She lives in Ridgewood."

He glanced at her, brought his eyes back to the road. "In Bergen County?"

"Yes."

"I'd rather take you home."

"My parents know I'm staying at Stacy's."

"Maybe you should call them."

"And say what?"

"That you're okay."

"Myron, they think I'm out with my friends. Calling them would only make them worry."

She had a point, but Myron didn't like it. His gas light went on. He'd need to fill up. He headed up the West Side Highway and over the George Washington

Bridge. He stopped at the first gas station on Route 4. New Jersey was one of only two states that did not allow you to pump your own gas. The attendant, wearing a turban and engrossed in a Nicholas Sparks novel, was not thrilled to see him.

"Ten dollars' worth," Myron told him.

He left them alone. Aimee started sniffling.

"You don't look drunk," Myron began.

"I didn't say I was. It was the guy who was driving."

"But you do look," he continued, "like you've been crying."

She did that teen thing that might have been a shrug.

"Your friend Stacy. Where is she now?"

"At her house."

"She didn't go into the city with you?"

Aimee shook her head and turned away.

"Aimee?"

Her voice was soft. "I thought I could trust you."

"You can."

She shook her head again. Then she reached for the door and pulled the handle. She started to get out. Myron reached for her. He grabbed her left wrist a little harder than he meant to.

"Hey," she said.

"Aimee . . ."

She tried to pull away. Myron kept a grip on the wrist.

"You're going to call my parents."

"I just need to know you're okay."

She pulled at his fingers, trying to get free. Myron felt her nails on his knuckles.

"Let go of me!"

He did. She jumped out of the car. Myron started after her, but he was still wearing his seat belt. The shoulder harness snapped him back. He unbuckled and

57

got out. Aimee was stumbling up the highway with her arms crossed defiantly.

He jogged up to her. "Please get back in the car."

"No."

"I'll drive you, okay?"

"Just leave me alone."

She stormed off. Cars whizzed by. Some honked at her. Myron followed.

"Where are you going?"

"I made a mistake. I should have never called you."

"Aimee, just get back in the car. It's not safe out here."

"You're going to tell my parents."

"I won't. I promise."

She slowed down and then stopped. More cars zoomed by on Route 4. The gas station attendant looked at them and spread his arms in a what-gives gesture. Myron held up a finger indicating that they needed a minute.

"I'm sorry," Myron said. "I'm just concerned for your welfare. But you're right. I made a promise. I'll keep it."

Aimee still had her arms crossed. She squinted at him, again as only a teenager can. "Swear?"

"I swear," he said.

"No more questions?"

"None."

She trudged back to the car.

Myron followed. He gave the attendant his credit card, and they drove off.

Aimee told him to take Route 17 North. There were so many malls, so many shopping centers, that it almost seemed as though it were one continuous strip. Myron remembered how his father, whenever they would drive past the Livingston Mall, would shake his head and point and moan, "Look at all the cars! If the economy is so bad, why are there so many cars? The lot's full! Look at them all."

Myron's mother and father were currently ensconced in a gated community outside of Boca Raton. Dad had finally sold the warehouse in Newark and now spent his days marveling at what most people had been doing for years: "Myron, have you been to a Staples? My God, they have every kind of pen and paper there. And the price clubs. Don't even get me started. I bought eighteen screwdrivers for less than ten dollars. We go, we buy so much stuff, I always tell the man at the check-out counter, I say—oh, he laughs at this, Myron—I always say, 'I just saved so much money, I'm going bankrupt.' "

Myron cast a glance at Aimee. He remembered his own teenage years, the war that is adolescence, and thought about how many times he'd deceived his own parents. He'd been a good kid. He never got in trouble, got good grades, was lofted high because of his basket-ball skills, but he'd hidden stuff from his parents. All kids do. Maybe it was healthy. The kids who are watched all the time, who are under constant parental surveillance—those were the ones who eventually freaked out. You need an outlet. You have to leave kids room to rebel. If not, the pressure just builds until . . .

"Take that exit over there," Aimee said. "Linwood Avenue West."

He did as she asked. Myron did not really know this area. New Jersey is a series of hamlets. You only knew yours well. He was an Essex County boy. This was Bergen. He felt out of his element. When they stopped at a traffic light he sighed and leaned back, and used the move to take a good hard look at Aimee.

She looked young and scared and helpless. Myron

thought about that last one for a moment. Helpless. She turned and met his eyes, and there was a challenge there. Was helpless a fair assessment? Stupid as it might be to think about it, how much of a role was sexism playing here? Play the chauvinism card for a moment. If Aimee was a guy, a big high school football jock, for example, would he be this worried?

The truth was, he was indeed treating her differently because she was a girl.

Was that right—or was he getting mired in some politically correct nonsense?

"Take the next right, then a left at the end of the road."

He did. Soon they were deep in the tangle of houses. Ridgewood was an old albeit large village—tree-lined streets, Victorians, curvy roads, hills and valleys. Jersey geography. The suburbs were puzzle pieces, interconnected, parts jammed into other parts, few smooth boundaries or right angles.

She led him up a steep road, down another, a left, then a right, then another right. Myron obeyed on autopilot, his thoughts elsewhere. His mind tried to conjure up the right words to say. Aimee had been crying earlier tonight—he was sure of that. She looked somewhat traumatized, but at her age, isn't everything a trauma? She probably had a fight with her boyfriend, the basement-mentioned Randy. Maybe ol' Randy dumped her. Guys did that in high school. They got off on breaking hearts. Made them a big man.

He cleared his throat and aimed for casual: "Are you still dating that Randy?"

Her reply: "Next left."

He took it.

"The house is over there, on the right."

"At the end of the cul-de-sac?"

"Yes."

Myron pulled up to it. The house was hunkered down, totally dark. There were no streetlights. Myron blinked a few times. He was still tired, still more foggy-brained than he should be from the earlier festivities. He flashed to Esperanza for a moment, to how lovely she looked, and, selfish as it sounded, he wondered again how this marriage would change things.

"It doesn't look like anybody's home," he said.

"Stacy's probably asleep." Aimee pulled a key out. "Her bedroom is by the back door. I always just let myself in."

Myron shifted into park and turned off the ignition. "I'll walk with you."

"No."

"How will I know you got in okay?"

"I'll wave."

Another car pulled down the street behind them. The headlights hit Myron via the rearview mirror. He shaded his eyes. Odd, he thought, two cars on this road at this time of night.

Aimee snagged his attention. "Myron?"

He looked at her.

"You can't tell my parents about this. They'll freak, okay?"

"I won't tell."

"Things—" She stopped, looked out the window toward the house. "Things aren't so great with them right now."

"With your parents?"

She nodded.

"You know that's normal, right?"

She nodded again.

He knew that he had to tread gently here. "Can you tell me more?"

61

"Just . . . this will only strain things more. If you tell, I mean. Just don't, okay?"

"Okay."

"Keep your promise."

And with that, Aimee was out the door. She jogged toward the gate leading to the back. She disappeared behind the house. Myron waited. She came back out to the gate. She smiled now and waved that everything was just fine. But there was something there, something in the wave, something that didn't quite add up.

Myron was about to get out of the car, but Aimee stopped him with a shake of her head. Then she slipped back into the yard, the night swallowing her whole.

Chapter 8

I n the days that followed, when Myron looked back at that moment, at the way Aimee smiled and waved and vanished into the dark, he would wonder what he'd felt. Had there been a premonition, an uneasy feeling, a twinge at the base of his subconscious, something warning him, something that he just couldn't shake?

He didn't think so. But it was hard to remember.

He waited another ten minutes on that cul-de-sac. Nothing happened.

So Myron came up with a plan.

It took a while to find his way out. Aimee had led him into this suburban thicket, but maybe Myron should have dropped bread crumbs on the way. He worked rat-in-a-maze style for twenty minutes until he stumbled upon Paramus Road, which led eventually to a main artery, the Garden State Parkway.

But now, Myron had no plans to return to the apartment in New York.

It was a Saturday night—well, Sunday morning now—and if he went to the house in Livingston instead,

63

he could play basketball the next morning before heading to the airport for his flight to Miami.

And, Myron knew, Erik, Aimee's father, played every Sunday without fail.

That was Myron's immediate, if not pathetic, plan.

So, early in the morning—too early, frankly—Myron rose and put on his shorts and T-shirt, dusted off the old knee brace, and drove over to the gym at Heritage Middle School. Before he headed inside, Myron tried Aimee's cell phone. It went immediately to her voice mail, her tone so sunny and, again, teenage, complete with a "Like, leave your message."

He was about to put the phone down when it buzzed in his hand. He checked the caller ID. Nothing.

"Hello?"

"You're a bastard." The voice was muffled and low. It sounded like a young man, but it was hard to know. "Do you hear me, Myron? A bastard. And you will pay for what you did."

The call disconnected. Myron hit star sixty-nine and waited to hear the number. A mechanical voice gave it to him. Local area code, yes, but otherwise the number was wholly unfamiliar. He stopped the car and jotted it down. He'd check it out later.

When Myron ducked into his school, it took a second to adjust to the artificial light, but as soon he did, the familiar ghosts popped up. The gym had the stale smell of every other middle school gym. Someone dribbled a ball. A few guys laughed. The sounds were all the same—all tainted by that hollow echo.

Myron hadn't played in months because he didn't like these sort of white-collar pickup games. Basketball, the game itself, still meant so much to him. He loved it. He loved the feel of the ball on his fingertips, the way they would find the grooves on the jump shot, the arch as the ball headed for the rim, the backspin on it, the positioning for the rebound, the perfect bounce pass. He loved the split-second decision making—pass, drive, shoot—the sudden openings that lasted tenths of a second, the way the world slowed down so that you could split the seam.

He loved all that.

What he did not love was the middle-age machismo. The gym was filling up with Masters of the Universe, the wannabe alpha males who, despite the big house and fat wallet and penis-compensating sports car, still needed to beat someone at something. Myron had been competitive in his youth. Too competitive perhaps. He had been a nutjob for winning. This was, he had learned, not always a wonderful quality, though it often separated the very good from the greats, the near-pros from the pros: this desire—no, need—to better another man.

But he had outgrown it. Some of these guys—a minority for certain, but enough—had not.

When they saw Myron, the former NBA player (no matter for how short a time), they saw their chance to prove what real men they were. Even now. Even when most of them were north of forty. And when the skills are slower but the heart still hungers for glory, it can get physical and downright ugly.

Myron scanned the gym and found his reason for being there.

Erik warmed up at the far basket. Myron jogged over and called out to him.

"Erik, hey, how's it going?"

Erik turned and smiled at him. "Good morning, Myron. Nice to see you show up."

"I'm usually not much of a morning guy," Myron said.

Erik tossed him the ball. Myron took a shot. It clanged off the rim.

"Late night?" Erik asked.

"Very."

"You've looked better."

"Gee, thanks," Myron said. Then: "So how are things?"

"Fine, you?"

"Good."

Someone shouted out and the ten guys jogged toward center court. That was how it was. If you wanted to play in the first group, you have to be one of the first ten to arrive. David Rainiv, a brilliant numbers guy and CFO of some Fortune 500 company, always made up teams. He had a knack for balancing the talent and forming competitive matchups. No one questioned his decisions. They were final and binding.

So Rainiv divided up the sides. Myron was matched up against a young guy who stood six-seven. This was a good thing. The theory of men having Napoleon complexes may be debatable in the real world but not in pickup games. Little guys wanted to harm big guys—show them up in an arena usually dominated by size.

But sadly, today the exception proved the rule. The six-seven kid was all elbows and anger. He was athletic and strong but had little basketball talent. Myron did his best to keep his distance. The truth was, despite his knee and age, Myron could score at will. For a while that was what he did. It just came so naturally. It was hard to go easy. But eventually he pulled back. He needed to lose. More men had come in. It was winners-stay-on. He wanted to get off the court so he could talk to Erik.

So after they won the first three games, Myron threw one.

His teammates were not pleased when Myron dribbled off his own foot, thus losing the game. Now they'd have to sit out. They bemoaned the moment but relished the fact that they'd had a great streak going. Like it mattered.

Erik had a water bottle, of course. His shorts matched his shirt. His sneakers were neatly laced. His socks came up to the exact same spot on both ankles, both having the same size roll. Myron used the water fountain and sat next to him.

"So how's Claire?" Myron tried.

"Fine. She does a Pilates-yoga mix now."

"Oh?"

Claire had always been into some exercise craze or another. She'd gone through the Jane Fonda leggings, the Tae Bo kicks, the Soloflex.

"That's where she is now," Erik said.

"Taking a class?"

"Yes. During the week, she takes one at six thirty in the morning."

"Yikes, that's early."

"We're early risers."

"Oh?" Myron saw an opening and took it. "And Aimee?"

"What about Aimee?"

"Does she get up early too?"

Erik frowned. "Hardly."

"So you're here," Myron said, "and Claire is working out. Where's Aimee?"

"She slept at a friend's last night."

"Oh?"

"Teenagers," he said, as if that explained everything. Maybe it did.

"Trouble?"

"You have no idea."

67

"Oh?"

Again with the Oh.

Erik said nothing.

"What kind?" Myron asked.

"Kind?"

Myron wanted to say *Oh* again, but he feared going to the well once too often. "Trouble. What kind of trouble?"

"I'm not sure I understand."

"Is she sullen?" Myron said, again trying to sound nonchalant. "Does she not listen? Does she stay up late, blow off school, spend too much time on the Internet, what?"

"All of the above," Erik said, but now his words came out even slower, even more measured. "Why do you ask?"

Back up, Myron thought. "Just making conversation."

Erik frowned. "Making conversation usually consists of bemoaning the local teams."

"It's nothing," Myron said. "It's just . . ."

"Just what?"

"The party at my house."

"What about it?"

"I don't know, seeing Aimee like that, I just started thinking about how tough those teenage years are."

Erik's eyes narrowed. On the court someone had called a foul and someone was protesting the call. "I didn't touch you!" a guy with a mustache and elbow pads shouted. Then the name-calling began—something else you never outgrow on a basketball court.

Erik's eyes were still on the court. "Did Aimee say anything to you?" he asked.

"Like what?"

"Like anything. I remember you were in the basement with her and Erin Wilder."

"Right."

"What did you guys talk about?"

"Nothing. They were just goofing on me about how dated the room was."

Now he looked at Myron. Myron wanted to look away, but he held on. "Aimee can be," Erik said, "rebellious."

"Like her mother."

"Claire?" He blinked. "Rebellious?"

Oh man, he should learn to shut his mouth.

"In what way?"

Myron went for the politician response: "It depends on what you mean by rebellious, I guess."

But Erik didn't let it slide. "What did you mean by it?"

"Nothing. It's a good thing. Claire had edge."

"Edge?"

Shut up, Myron. "You know what I mean. Edge. Good edge. When you first saw Claire—that very first second—what attracted you to her?"

"Many things," he said. "But edge was not one of them. I had known a lot of girls, Myron. There are those you want to marry and those you just want, well, you know."

Myron nodded.

"Claire was the one you wanted to marry. That was the first thing I thought when I saw her. And yes, I know how it sounds. But you were her friend. You know what I mean."

Myron tried to look noncommittal.

"I loved her so much."

Loved, Myron thought, keeping quiet this time. He'd said loved, not love.

As if reading his mind, Erik added, "I still do. Maybe more than ever."

Myron waited for the "but."

Erik smiled. "You heard the good news, I assume?"

"About?"

"Aimee. In fact, we owe you a great big thank-you."

"Why's that?"

"She got accepted to Duke."

"Hey, that's great."

"We just heard two days ago."

"Congratulations."

"Your recommendation letter," he said. "I think it pushed her over the line."

Myron said, "Nah," though there was probably more truth in Erik's statement than Erik knew. Myron had not only written that letter, but he also had called one of his old teammates, who now worked in admissions.

"No, really," Erik went on. "There's so much competition to get into the top schools. Your recommendation carried a lot of weight, I'm sure. So thank you."

"She's a good kid. It was my pleasure."

The game ended. Erik rose. "Ready?"

"I think I'm done for today," Myron said.

"Hurting, eh?"

"A little."

"We're getting older, Myron."

"I know."

"There are more aches and pains now."

Myron nodded.

"Seems to me you have a choice when things hurt," Erik said. "You can sit out—or you can try to play through the pain."

Erik jogged away, leaving Myron to wonder if he'd still been talking about basketball.

Chapter 9

B ack in the car, Myron's cell phone rang again. He checked the caller ID. Again nothing.

"Hello?"

"You're a bastard, Myron."

"Yeah, I got that the first time. Do you have any new material or are we going to follow up with that original line about me paying for what I've done?"

Click.

Myron shrugged it off. Back in the days when he used to play superhero, he had been a rather well-connected fellow. It was time to see if that still held. He checked his cell phone's directory. The number for Gail Berruti, his old contact from the telephone company, was still there. People think it's unrealistic how private eyes in TV can get phone records with a snap. The truth is, it was beyond easy. Every decent private eye has a source in the phone company. Think about how many people work for Ma Bell. Think how many of them wouldn't mind making an extra buck or two. The going rate had been five hundred dollars per billing statement, but Myron imagined the price had gone up in the past six years.

Berruti wasn't in—she was probably off for the weekend—but he left a message.

"This is a voice from your past," Myron began.

He asked Berruti to get back to him with the trace on the phone number. He tried Aimee's cell phone again. It went to her voice mail. When he got home, he headed to the computer and Googled the number. Nothing came up. He took a quick shower and then checked his e-mail. Jeremy, his sorta-son, had written him an e-mail from overseas:

> Hey, Myron—
> We're only allowed to say that we're in the Persian Gulf area. I'm doing well. Mom sounds crazy. Give her a call if you can. She still doesn't understand. Dad doesn't either, but at least he pretends he does. Thanks for the package. We love getting stuff.
> I got to go. I'll write more later, but I might be out of touch for a while. Call Mom, okay?
> Jeremy

Myron read it again and then again, but the words didn't change. The e-mail, like most of Jeremy's, said nothing. He didn't like that "out of touch" part. He thought about parenting, how he had missed so much of it, all of it really, and how this kid, his son, fit into his life now. It was working, he thought, at least for Jeremy. But it was hard. The kid was the biggest what-could-have-been, the biggest if-only-I'd-known, and most of the time, it just plain hurt.

Still staring at the message, Myron heard his cell phone. He cursed under his breath, but this time the caller ID told him it was the divine Ms. Ali Wilder.

Myron smiled as he answered it. "Stallion Services," he said.

"Sheesh, suppose it was one of my kids on the phone."

"I'd pretend to be a horse seller," he said.

"A horse seller?"

"Whatever they call people who sell horses."

"What time is your flight?"

"Four o'clock."

"You busy?"

"Why?"

"The kids will be out of the house for the next hour."

"Whoa," he said.

"My thoughts exactly."

"Are you suggesting a little righteous nookie?"

"I am." Then: "Righteous?"

"It'll take me some time to get there."

"Uh-huh."

"And it'll have to be a quickie."

"Isn't that your specialty?" she said.

"Now that hurt."

"Only kidding. Stallion."

He brayed. "That's horse-speak for 'I'm on my way.'"

"Righteous," she said.

But when he knocked on her door, Erin answered it. "Hey, Myron."

"Hey," he said, trying not to sound disappointed.

He glanced behind her. Ali shrugged a sorry at him.

Myron stepped inside. Erin ran upstairs. Ali came closer. "She got in late and didn't feel like going to drama club."

"Oh."

"Sorry about that."

"No problem."

"We could stand in a corner and neck," she said.

"Can I cop a feel?"

"You better."

He smiled.

"What?" she said.

"I was just thinking."

"Thinking what?"

"Something Esperanza said to me yesterday," Myron said. "*Men tracht und Gott lacht*."

"Is that German?"

"Yiddish."

"What does it mean?"

"Man plans, God laughs."

She repeated it. "I like that."

"Me too," he said.

He hugged her then. Over her shoulder, he saw Erin at the top of the stairs. She was not smiling. Myron's eyes met hers and again he thought about Aimee, about how the night had swallowed her whole, and about the promise he had sworn to keep.

Chapter 10

Myron had time before his flight.

He grabbed a coffee at the Starbucks in the center of town. The barista who took his order had the trademark sullen attitude. As he handed Myron the drink, lifting it to the counter as though it were the weight of the world, the door behind them opened with a bang. The barista rolled his eyes as they entered.

There were six of them today, trudging in as though through deep snow, heads down, a variety of shakes. They sniffled and touched their faces. The four men were unshaven. The two women smelled like cat piss.

They were mental patients. For real. They spent most nights at Essex Pines, a psychiatric facility in the neighboring town. Their leader—wherever they walked, he stayed in front—was named Larry Kidwell. His group spent most days wandering through town. Livingstonites referred to them as the Town Crazies. Myron uncharitably thought of them as a bizarre rock group: Lithium Larry and the Medicated Five.

Today they seemed less lethargic than usual so it

must be pretty close to medication time back at the Pines. Larry was extra jittery. He approached Myron and waved.

"Hey, Myron," he said too loudly.

"What's happening, Larry?"

"Fourteen hundred eighty-seven planets on creation day, Myron. Fourteen hundred eighty-seven. And I haven't seen a penny. You know what I'm saying?"

Myron nodded. "I hear you."

Larry Kidwell shuffled forward. Long, stringy hair peeked out of his Indiana Jones hat. There were scars on his face. His worn blue jeans hung low, displaying enough plumber-crack to park a bike.

Myron started heading for the door. "Take it easy, Larry."

"You too, Myron." He reached out to shake Myron's hand. The others in the group suddenly froze, all eyes—wide eyes, glistening-from-meds eyes—on Myron. Myron reached out his hand and clasped Larry's. Larry held on hard and pulled Myron closer. His breath, no surprise, stank.

"The next planet," Larry whispered, "it might be yours. Yours alone."

"That's great to know, thanks."

"No!" Still a whisper, but it was harsh now. "The planet. It's slither moon. It's out to get you, you know what I'm saying?"

"I think so."

"Don't ignore this."

He let go of Myron, his eyes wide. Myron took a step back. He could see the man's agitation.

"It's okay, Larry."

"Heed my warning, man. He stroked the moon slither. You understand? He hates you so bad he stroked the moon slither."

The others in the group were total strangers, but Myron knew Larry's tragic backstory. Larry Kidwell had been two years ahead of Myron in school. He'd been immensely popular. He was an incredible guitarist, good with the girls, even dated Beth Finkelstein, the hometown hottie, during his senior year. Larry ended up being salutatorian of his class at Livingston High. He went to Yale University, his father's alma mater, and from all accounts, had a great first semester.

Then it all came apart.

What was surprising, what made it all the more horrific, was how it happened. There had been no terrifying event in Larry's life. There had been no family tragedy. There had been no drugs or alcohol or girl gone wrong.

The doctor's diagnosis: a chemical imbalance.

Who knows how you get cancer? It was the same thing with Larry. He simply had a mental disease. It started as mild OCD, then became more severe, and then, try as they might, no one could stop his slide. By his sophomore year Larry was setting up rat traps so he could eat them. He became delusional. He dropped out of Yale. Then there were suicide attempts and major hallucinations and problems of all sorts. Larry broke into someone's house because the "Clyzets from planet three hundred twenty-six" were trying to lay a nest there. The family was home at the time.

Larry Kidwell has been in and out of psych institutes ever since. Supposedly, there are moments when Larry is entirely lucid, and it is so painful for him, realizing what he has become, that he rips at his own face—ergo the scars—and cries out in such agony that they immediately sedate him.

"Okay," Myron said. "Thanks for the warning."

Myron headed out the door, shook it off. He hit

Chang's Dry Cleaning next door. Maxine Chang was behind the counter. She looked, as always, exhausted and overworked. There were two women about Myron's age at the counter. They were talking about their kids and colleges. That was all anybody talked about right now. Every April, Livingston became a snow globe of college acceptances. The stakes, if you were to listen to the parents, could not have been higher. These weeks—those thick-or-thin envelopes that arrived in their mailboxes—decided how happy and successful their offspring would be for the rest of their lives.

"Ted is wait-listed at Penn but he made Lehigh," one said.

"Do you believe Chip Thompson got into Penn?"

"His father."

"What? Oh wait, he's an alum, right?"

"He gave them a quarter million dollars."

"I should have known. Chip had terrible boards."

"I heard they hired a pro to write his essays."

"I should have done that for Cole."

Like that. On and on.

Myron nodded at Maxine. Maxine Chang usually had a big smile for him. Not today. She shouted, "Roger!"

Roger Chang came out of the back. "Hey, Myron."

"What's up, Roger?"

"You wanted the shirts boxed this time, right?"

"Right."

"I'll be right back."

"Maxine," one of the women said, "did Roger hear from schools yet?"

Maxine barely looked up. "He made Rutgers," she said. "Wait-listed at others."

"Wow, congratulations."

"Thank you." But she didn't seem thrilled.

78

"Maxine, won't he be the first in your family to go to college?" the other woman said. Her tone could only have sounded more patronizing if she'd been petting a dog. "How wonderful for you."

Maxine wrote up the ticket.

"Where is he wait-listed?"

"Princeton and Duke."

Hearing his alma mater made Myron think again about Aimee. He flashed back to Larry and his spooky planet talk. Myron wasn't one for bad omens or any of that, but he didn't feel like poking the fates in the eye either. He debated trying Aimee's phone again, but what would be the point? He thought back over last night, replayed it in his head, wondered how he could have done it differently.

Roger—Myron had forgotten that the kid was already a high school senior—came back and handed him the box of shirts. Myron took them, told Roger to put them on his account, headed out the door. He still had time before his flight.

So he drove to Brenda's grave.

The cemetery still overlooked a schoolyard. That was what he could still not get over. The sun shone hard as it always seemed to when he visited, mocking his gloom. He stood alone. There were no other visitors. A nearby backhoe dug a hole. Myron remained still. He lifted his head and let the sun shine on his face. He could still feel that—the sun on his face. Brenda, of course, could not. Would never again.

A simple thought, but there you go.

Brenda Slaughter had only been twenty-six when she died. Had she survived, she'd have turned thirty-four in two weeks. He wondered where she'd be if Myron had kept his promise. He wondered if she'd be with him.

When she died, Brenda was in the middle of her residency in pediatric medicine. She was six-foot-four, stunning, African-American, a model. She was about to play pro basketball, the face and image that would launch the new women's league. There had been threats made. So Myron had been hired by the league owner to protect her.

Nice job, All-Star.

He stood and stared down and clenched his fists. He never talked to her when he came here. He didn't sit and try to meditate or any of that. He didn't conjure up the good or her laugh or her beauty or her extraordinary presence. Cars whizzed by. The schoolyard was silent. No kids were out playing. Myron did not move.

He did not come here because he still mourned her death. He came because he didn't.

He barely remembered Brenda's face anymore. The one kiss they shared . . . when he conjured it up he knew it was more imagination than memory. That was the problem. Brenda Slaughter was slipping away from him. Soon it would be as though she never existed. So Myron didn't come here for comfort or to pay his respects. He came because he still needed to hurt, needed the wounds to stay fresh. He still wanted to be outraged because moving on—feeling at peace with what happened to her—was too obscene.

Life goes on. That was a good thing, right? The out-rage flickers and slowly leaks away. The scars heal. But when you let that happen, your soul goes dead a little too.

So Myron stood there and clenched his fists until they shook. He thought about the sunny day they buried her—and the horrible way he had avenged her. He summoned up the outrage. It came at him like a force. His knees buckled. He tottered, but he stayed upright.

He had messed up with Brenda. He had wanted to

protect her. He had pushed too hard—and in doing so he had gotten her killed.

Myron looked down at the grave. The sun was still warm on him, but he felt the shiver travel down his back. He wondered why he chose today of all days to visit, and then he thought about Aimee, about pushing too hard, about wanting to protect, and with one more shiver, he thought—no, he feared—that maybe, somehow, he had let it all happen again.

Chapter 11

Claire Biel stood by the kitchen sink and stared at the stranger she called a husband. Erik was eating a sandwich carefully, his tie tucked into his shirt. There was a newspaper perfectly folded into one quarter. He chewed slowly. He wore cuff links. His shirt was starched. He liked starch. He liked everything ironed. In his closet his suits were hung four inches apart from one another. He didn't measure to achieve this. It just happened. His shoes, always freshly polished, were lined up like something in a military procession.

Who was this man?

Their two youngest daughters, Jane and Lizzie, were both wolfing down PB&J on white bread. They chatted through their sticky mouths. They made noise. Their milk sloshed into small spills. Erik kept reading. Jane asked if they could be excused. Claire said yes. They both darted toward the door.

"Stop," Claire said.

They did.

"Plates in the sink."

They sighed and did the eye-roll—though they were only nine and ten, they had learned from the best, their older sister. They trudged back as though through the deep snow of the Adirondacks, lifted plates that must have seemed like boulders, and somehow scaled the mountain toward the sink.

"Thank you," Claire said.

They took off. The room was quiet now. Erik chewed quietly.

"Is there any more coffee?" he asked.

She poured some. He crossed his legs, careful not to crease his trousers. They had been married for nineteen years, but the passion had slipped out the window in under two. They were treading water now, had been treading for so long that it no longer seemed that difficult. Oldest cliché in the book was about how fast time went by, but it was true. It didn't seem like the passion had been gone that long. Sometimes, like right now, she could look at him and remember a time when just seeing him would take her breath away.

Still not glancing up, Erik asked, "Have you heard from Aimee?"

"No."

He straightened his arm to pull back the sleeve, checked his watch, arched an eyebrow. "Two in the afternoon."

"She's probably just waking up."

"We might want to call."

He didn't move.

"By we," Claire said, "do you mean me?"

"I'll do it if you want."

She reached for the phone and dialed their daughter's cell phone. They'd gotten Aimee her own phone last year. Aimee had brought them an advertisement showing them that they could add a third line for ten dollars a month. Erik was unmoved. But, Aimee whined, all her friends—everyone!—had one, an argument that always *always* led Erik to remark, "We are not everyone, Aimee."

But Aimee was ready for that. She quickly changed tracks and plucked on the parental-protection heart-strings: "If I had my own phone, I could always stay in touch. You could find me twenty-four-seven. And if there was ever an emergency . . . "

That had closed the sale. Mothers understood this basic truism: Sex and peer pressure may sell, but nothing sells like fear.

The call went to voice mail. Aimee's enthusiastic voice—she had taped her message almost immediately after getting the phone—told Claire to, like, leave a message. The sound of her daughter's voice, familiar as it was, made her ache, though she wasn't sure for what exactly.

When the beep came, Claire said, "Hey, honey, it's Mom. Just give me a call, okay?"

She hung up.

Erik still read his paper. "She didn't answer?"

"Gee, what gave it away? Was it the part where I asked her to give me a call?"

He frowned at the sarcasm. "Her phone probably went dead."

"Probably."

"She always forgets to charge it," he said, with a shake of his head. "Whose house was she sleeping over? Steffi's, right?"

"Stacy."

"Right, whatever. Maybe we should call Stacy."

"Why?"

"I want her home. She has that project due on Thursday."

"It's Sunday. She just got into college."

"So you think she should slack off now?"

Claire handed him the portable. "You call."

"Fine."

She gave him the number. He pressed the digits and put the phone to his ear. In the background, Claire heard her younger daughters giggle. Then one shouted, "I do not!" When the phone was picked up, Erik cleared his throat. "Good afternoon, this is Erik Biel. I'm Aimee Biel's father. I was wondering if she was there right now."

His face didn't change. His voice didn't change. But Claire saw his grip on the phone tighten and she felt something deep in her chest give way.

Chapter 12

Myron had two semicontradictory thoughts about Miami. One, the weather was so beautiful he should move down here. Two, sun—there was too much sun down here. Everything was too bright. Even in the airport Myron found himself squinting.

This was not a problem for Myron's parents, the beloved Ellen and Al Bolitar, who wore those oversize sunglasses that looked suspiciously like welder's goggles, though without the style. They both waited for him at the airport. Myron had told them not to, that he would get a taxi, but Dad had insisted. "Don't I always pick you up from the airport? Remember when you came back from Chicago after that big snowstorm?"

"That was eighteen years ago, Dad."

"So? You think I forgot how to go?"

"And that was Newark Airport."

"Eighteen minutes, Myron."

Myron's eyes closed. "I remember."

"Exactly eighteen minutes."

"I remember, Dad."

"That's how long it took me to get from the house to Terminal A at Newark Airport. I used to time it, remember?"

"I do, yes."

So here they were, both of them, at the airport with dark suntans and fresh liver spots. When Myron came down the escalator, Mom ran over and wrapped her arms around her boy as if this were a POW homecoming in 1974. Dad stayed in the background with that satisfied smile. Myron hugged her back. Mom felt smaller. That was how it was down here. Your parents withered and got smaller and darker, like giant shrunken heads.

Mom said, "Let's get your luggage."

"I have it here."

"That's it? Just that one bag?"

"I'm only down for a night."

"Still."

Myron watched her face, checked her hands. When he saw the shake was more pronounced, he felt the thud in his chest.

"What?" she said.

"Nothing."

Mom shook her head. "You've always been the worst liar. Remember that time I walked in on you and Tina Ventura and you said nothing was going on? You think I didn't know?"

Junior year of high school. Ask Mom and Dad what they did yesterday, they won't remember. Ask them about anything from his youth, and it's like they studied replays at night.

He held up his hands in mock surrender. "Got me."

"Don't be such a smart guy. And that reminds me."

They reached Dad. Myron kissed him on the cheek.

He always did. You never outgrow that. The skin felt loose. The smell of Old Spice was still there, but it was fainter than usual. There was something else there, some other smell, and Myron thought it was the smell of the old. They started for the car.

"Guess who I ran into?" Mom said.

"Who?"

"Dotte Derrick. Remember her?"

"No."

"Sure you do. She had that thing, that what-you-call-it, in her yard."

"Oh, right. Her. With that thing."

He had no idea what she was talking about, but this was easier.

"So anyway, I saw Dotte the other day and we start talking. She and Bob moved down here four years ago. They have a place in Fort Lauderdale, but Myron, it's really run-down. I mean, it hasn't been kept up at all. Al, what's the name of Dotte's place? Sunshine Vista, something like that, right?"

"Who cares?" Dad said.

"Thanks, Mr. Helpful. Anyway, that's where Dotte lives. And this place is awful. So run-down. Al, isn't Dotte's place run-down?"

"The point, El," Dad said. "Get to the point."

"I'm getting there, I'm getting there. Where was I?"

"Dotte Something," Myron said.

"Derrick. You remember her, right?"

"Very well," Myron said.

"Right, good. Anyway, Dotte still has cousins up north. The Levines. Do you remember them? No reason you should, forget it. Anyway, one of the cousins lives in Kasselton. You know Kasselton, right? You used to play them in high school—"

"I know Kasselton."

"Don't get snappy."

Dad spread his arms to the sky. "The point, El. Get to the point."

"Right, sorry. You're right. When you're right, you're right. So to make a long story short—"

"No, El, you've never made a long story short," Dad said. "Oh, you've made plenty of short stories long. But never, ever, have you made a long story short."

"Can I talk here, Al?"

"Like anyone could stop you. Like a large gun or big army tank—like even that could stop you."

Myron couldn't help but smile. Ladies and gents, meet Ellen and Alan Bolitar or, as Mom liked to say, "We're El Al—you know, like the Israeli airline?"

"So anyway, I was talking to Dotte about this and that. You know, the usual. The Ruskins moved out of town. Gertie Schwartz had gall stones. Antonietta Vitale, such a pretty thing, she married some millionaire from Montclair. That kind of thing. And then Dotte told me—Dotte told me this, by the way, not you—Dotte said you're dating someone."

Myron closed his eyes.

"Is it true?"

He said nothing.

"Dotte said you were dating a widow with six children."

"Two children," Myron said.

Mom stopped and smiled.

"What?"

"Gotcha."

"Huh?"

"If I said two children, you might have just denied it." Mom pointed an aha finger up in the air. "But I knew if I said six, you'd react. So I caught you."

Myron looked at his father. His father shrugged.

"She's been watching a lot of *Matlock* lately."

"Children, Myron? You're dating a woman with children?"

"Mom, I'm going to say this as nicely as I can: Butt out."

"Listen to me, Mr. Funny Guy. When children are involved, you can't just go on your merry way. You need to think about the repercussions on them. Do you understand what I'm telling you?"

"Do you understand the meaning of 'butt out'?"

"Fine, do what you want." Now she did the mock surrender. Like mother, like son. "What do I care?"

They continued walking—Myron in the middle, Dad on his right, Mom on his left. That was how they always walked. The pace was slower now. That didn't bother him much. He was more than willing to slow down so they could keep up.

They drove to the condo and parked in the designated spot. Mom purposely took the long path past the swimming pool, so she could introduce Myron to a dizzying array of condo owners. Mom kept saying, "You remember meeting my son?" and Myron faked remembering them back. Some of the women, many in their upper seventies, were too-well built. As Dustin Hoffman had been advised in *The Graduate*, "Plastics." Just a different kind. Myron had nothing against cosmetic surgery, but past a certain age, discriminatory or not, it creeped him out.

The condo was also too bright. You'd think as you got older you'd want less light, but no. His parents actually kept on the welder sunglasses for the first five minutes. Mom asked if he was hungry. He was smart enough to answer yes. She had already ordered a sloppy joe platter—Mom's cooking would be deemed inhumane at Guantánamo Bay—from a place called

Tony's, which was "just like the old Eppes Essen's" at home.

They ate, they talked, Mom kept trying to wipe the small bits of cabbage that got stuck in the corners of Dad's mouth, but her hand shook too badly. Myron met his father's eye. Mom's Parkinson's was getting worse, but they wouldn't talk to Myron about it. They were getting old. Dad had a pacemaker. Mom had Parkinson's. But their first duty was still to shield their son from all that.

"When do you have to leave for your meeting?" Mom asked.

Myron checked his watch. "Now."

They said good-byes, did the hug-n-kiss thing again. When he pulled away, he felt as if he were abandoning them, as if they were going to hold off the enemy on their own while he drove to safety. Having aging parents sucked; but as Esperanza, who lost both parents young, often pointed out, it was better than the alternative.

Once in the elevator, Myron checked his cell phone. Aimee had still not called him back. He tried her number again and was not surprised when it went to voice mail. Enough, he thought. He would just call her house. See what's what.

Aimee's voice came to him: "You promised . . ."

He dialed Erik and Claire's home number. Claire answered. "Hello?"

"Hey, it's Myron."

"Hi."

"What's happening?"

"Not much," Claire said.

"I saw Erik this morning"—man, was it really the same day?—"and he told me about Aimee getting accepted to Duke. So I wanted to offer up my congratulations."

"Yeah, thanks."

"Is she there?"

"No, not right now."

"Can I call her later?"

"Yeah, sure."

Myron changed gears. "Everything okay? You sound a little distracted."

He was about to say more but again Aimee's words—"*You promised you wouldn't tell my parents*"—floated down to him.

"Fine, I guess," Claire said. "Look, I gotta go. Thanks for writing that recommendation letter."

"No big deal."

"Very big deal. The kids ranked four and seven in her class both applied and didn't get in. You were the difference."

"I doubt it. Aimee's a great candidate."

"Maybe, but thanks anyway."

There was a grumbling noise in the background. Sounded like Erik.

In his mind, there was Aimee's voice again: "*Things aren't so great with them right now.*" Myron was trying to think of something else to say, a follow-up question maybe, when Claire hung up the phone.

Loren Muse had landed a fresh homicide case—double homicide, actually, two men shot outside a nightclub in East Orange. Rumor was that the killings were a hit carried out by John "The Ghost" Asselta, a notorious hitman who'd actually been born and raised in the area. Asselta had been quiet for the past few years. If he was back, they were about to be very busy.

Loren was reviewing the ballistics report when her

private line rang. She picked up and said, "Muse."

"Guess who?"

She smiled. "Lance Banner, you old dog. Is that you?"

"It is."

Banner was a police officer in Livingston, New Jersey, the suburb where they'd both grown up.

"To what do I owe the pleasure?"

"You still investigating Katie Rochester's disappearance?"

"Not really," she said.

"Why not?"

"For one thing, there's no evidence of violence. For another, Katie Rochester is over eighteen."

"Just barely."

"In the eyes of the law, eighteen might as well be eighty. So officially we don't even have an investigation going on."

"And unofficially?"

"I met with a doctor named Edna Skylar." She recounted Edna's story, using almost the same words she'd used when she'd told her boss, county prosecutor Ed Steinberg. Steinberg had sat there for a long while before predictably concluding: "We don't have the resources to go after such a maybe."

When she finished, Banner asked, "How did you get the case in the first place?"

"Like I said, there was no case, really. She's of age, no signs of violence, you know the drill. So no one was assigned. Jurisdiction is questionable anyway. But the father, Dominick, he made a lot of noise with the press, you probably saw it, and he knew someone who knows someone, and that led to Steinberg. . . ."

"And that led to you."

"Right. The key word being *led*. As in past tense."

Lance Banner asked, "Do you have ten minutes to spare?"

"Did you hear about that double homicide in East Orange?"

"I did."

"I'm the lead."

"As in the present tense of *led*?"

"You got it."

"I figured that," Banner said. "It's why I'm only asking for ten minutes."

"Important?" she asked.

"Let's just say"—he stopped, thinking of the word—"very odd."

"And it involves Katie Rochester's disappearance?"

"Ten minutes max, Loren. That's all I'm asking for. Heck, I'll take five."

She checked her watch. "When?"

"I'm in the lobby of your building right now," he said. "Can you get us a room?"

"For five minutes? Sheesh, your wife wasn't kidding about your bedroom stamina."

"Dream on, Muse. Hear that ding? I'm stepping into the elevator. Get the room ready."

Livingston police detective Lance Banner had a crew cut. He was big with features and a build that made you think of right angles. Loren had known him since elementary school and she still couldn't get that image out of her head, of what he looked like back then. That's how it is with kids you grew up with. You always see them as second-graders.

Loren watched him hesitate when he entered, unsure how to greet her—a kiss on the cheek or a more professional handshake. She took the lead and pulled him toward her and kissed his cheek. They were in an interrogation room, and they both headed for the interrogator seat. Banner pulled up, raised both hands, sat across from her.

"Maybe you should Mirandize me," he said.

"I'll wait until I have enough for an arrest. So what have you got on Katie Rochester?"

"No time for chitchat, eh?"

She just looked at him.

"Okay, okay, let's get to it then. Do you know a woman named Claire Biel?"

"No."

"She lives in Livingston," Banner said. "She would have been Claire Garman when we were kids."

"Still no."

"She was older than us anyway. Four, five years probably." He shrugged. "I was just checking."

"Uh-huh," Loren said. "Do me a favor, Lance. Pretend I'm your wife and skip the foreplay."

"Fine, here it is. She called me this morning. Claire Biel. Her daughter went out last night and hasn't come home."

"How old is she?"

"She just turned eighteen."

"Any sign of foul play?"

He made a face suggesting an inner debate. Then: "Not yet."

"So?"

"So normally we wait a little. Like you said on the phone—over eighteen, no signs of violence."

"Like with Katie Rochester."

"Right."

"But?"

"I know the parents a little. Claire was in school with my older brother. They live in the neighborhood.

They're concerned, of course. But on the face of it, well, you figure the kid is just messing around. She got accepted to college the other day. Made Duke. Her first choice. She goes out partying with her friends. You know what I'm saying."

"I do."

"But I figure, what's the harm in doing a little checking, right? So I do the easiest thing. Just to satisfy the parents that their girl—her name is Aimee, by the way—that Aimee is okay."

"So what did you do?"

"I ran her credit card number, see if Aimee made any charges or used an ATM."

"And?"

"Sure enough. She took out a thousand dollars, the max, at an ATM machine at two in the morning."

"You get the video from the bank?"

"I did."

Loren knew that this was done in seconds now. You didn't have an old-fashioned tape anymore. The videos are digital and could be e-mailed and downloaded almost instantaneously.

"It was Aimee," he said. "No question about it. She didn't try to hide her face or anything."

"So?"

"So you figure it's a runaway, right?"

"Right."

"A slam dunk," he went on. "She took the money and is doing a little partying, whatever. Blowing off steam at the end of her senior year." Banner looked off.

"Come on, Lance. What's the problem?"

"Katie Rochester."

"Because Katie did the same thing? Used an ATM before disappearing?"

He tilted his head back and forth in a maybe-yes,

maybe-no gesture. His eyes were still far away. "It's not just that she did the same thing as Katie," he said. "It's that she did the *exact* same thing."

"I'm not following."

"The ATM machine Aimee Biel used was located in Manhattan—more specifically"—he slowed his words now—"at a Citibank on Fifty-second Street and Sixth Avenue."

Loren felt the chill begin at the base of her skull and travel south.

Banner said, "That's the same one Katie Rochester used, right?"

She nodded and then she said something truly stupid: "Could be a coincidence."

"Could be," he agreed.

"You got anything else?"

"We're just starting, but we pulled the logs on her cell phone."

"And?"

"She made a phone call right after she took out the money."

"To whom?"

Lance Banner leaned back and crossed his legs. "Do you remember a guy a few years ahead of us—big basketball star named Myron Bolitar?"

Chapter 13

own in Miami, Myron dined with Rex Storton, a new client, at some super-huge restaurant Rex had picked out because a lot of people walked by. The restaurant was one of those chains like Bennigans or TGI Fridays or something equally universal and awful.

Storton was an aging actor, a one-time superstar who was looking for the indie role that would launch him out of Miami's Loni Anderson Dinner Theater and back into the upper echelon of La-La Land. Rex was resplendent in a pink polo with the collar turned up, white pants that a man his age just shouldn't involve himself with, and a shiny gray toupee that looked good when you weren't sitting directly across the table from it.

For years Myron had represented professional athletes only. When one of his basketball players wanted to cross over and do movies, Myron started meeting actors. A new branch of the business took root, and now he handled the Hollywood clients almost exclusively, leaving the sports management stuff to Esperanza.

It was strange. As an athlete himself, one would think that Myron would relate more to those in a similar profession. He didn't. He liked the actors more. Most athletes are singled out right away, at fairly young ages, and elevated to godlike status from the get-go. Athletes are in the lead clique at school. They get invited to all the parties. They nab all the hot girls. Adults fawn. Teachers let them slide.

Actors are different. Many of them had started out at the opposite end of the spectrum. Athletics rule in most towns. Actors were often the kids who couldn't make the team and were looking for another activity. They were often too small—ever meet an actor in real life and notice that they're tiny?—or uncoordinated. So they back into acting. Later, when stardom hits them, they are not used to the treatment. They're surprised by it. They're somewhat more appreciative. In many cases—no, not all—it makes them more humble than their athletic counterparts.

There were other factors, of course. They say that actors take to the stage to fill a void of emptiness only applause can fill. Even if true, it made thespians somewhat more anxious to please. While athletes were used to people doing their bidding and came to believe it was their due in life, actors came to that from a position of insecurity. Athletes need to win. They need to beat you. Actors need only your applause and thus your approval.

It made them easier to work with.

Again this was a complete generalization—Myron was an athlete, after all, and did not consider himself difficult—but like most generalizations, there was something to it.

He told Rex about the indie role as, to quote the

pitch, "a geriatric, cross-dressing car thief, but with a heart." Rex nodded. His eyes continuously scanned the room, as if they were at a cocktail party and he was waiting for someone more important to come in. Rex always kept one eye toward the entrance. This was how it was with actors. Myron repped one guy who was world-renowned for detesting the press. He had battled with photographers. He had sued tabloids. He had demanded his privacy. Yet whenever Myron ate dinner with him, the actor always chose a seat in the center of the room, facing the door, and whenever someone would enter, he'd look up, just for a second, just to make sure he was recognized.

His eyes still moving, Rex said, "Yeah, yeah, I get it. Do I have to wear a dress?"

"For some scenes, yes."

"I've done that before."

Myron arched an eyebrow.

"Professionally, I mean. Don't be a wiseass. And it was tastefully done. The dress must be something tasteful."

"So, what, nothing with a plunging neckline?'

"Funny, Myron. You're a scream. Speaking of which, do I have to do a screen test?"

"You do."

"Chrissakes, I've made eighty films."

"I know, Rex."

"He can't look at one of them?"

Myron shrugged. "That's what he said."

"You like the script?"

"I do, Rex."

"How old is this director?'

"Twenty-two."

"Jesus. I was already a has-been by the time he was born."

"They'll pay for a flight to L.A."

"First class?"

"Coach, but I think I can get you a business upgrade."

"Ah, who am I kidding? I'd sit on the wing in only my girdle if the role was right."

"That's the spirit."

A mother and daughter came over and asked Rex for his autograph. He smiled grandly and puffed out his chest. He looked at the obvious mother and said, "Are you two sisters?"

She giggled as she left.

"Another happy customer," Myron said.

"I aim to please."

A buxom blonde came by for an autograph. Rex kissed her a little too hard. After she sashayed away, Rex held up a piece of paper. "Look."

"What is it?"

"Her phone number."

"Terrific."

"What can I say, Myron? I love women."

Myron looked up and to his right.

"What?"

"I'm just wondering," Myron said, "how your prenup will hold up."

"Very funny."

They ate some chicken from a deep fryer. Or maybe it was beef or shrimp. Once in the deep fryer, it all tasted the same. Myron could feel Rex's eyes on him.

"What?" Myron said.

"It's sort of tough to admit this," Rex said, "but I'm only alive when I'm in the spotlight. I've had three wives and four kids. I love them all. I enjoyed my time with them. But the only time I feel really myself is when I'm in the spotlight."

Myron said nothing.

"Does that sound pathetic to you?"

Myron shrugged.

"You know what else?"

"What?"

"In their heart of hearts, I think most people are like that. They crave fame. They want people to recognize them and stop them on the streets. People say it's a new thing, what with the reality TV crap. But I think it's always been that way."

Myron studied his pitiful food.

"You agree?"

"I don't know, Rex."

"For me, the spotlight has dimmed a touch, you know what I'm saying? It's faded bit by bit. I was lucky. But I've met some one-hit wonders. Man, they're never happy. Not ever again. But me, with the slow fade, I could get used to it. And even now, people still recognize me. It's why I eat out every night. Yeah, that's awful to say, but it's true. And even now, when I'm in my seventies, I still dream about clawing my way back to that brightest of spotlights. You know what I'm saying?"

"I do," Myron said. "It's why I love you."

"Why's that?"

"You're honest about it. Most actors tell me it's just about the work."

Rex made a scoffing noise. "What a load of crap. But it's not their fault, Myron. Fame is a drug. The most potent. You're hooked, but you don't want to admit it." Rex gave him the twinkly smile that used to melt the girls' hearts. "And what about you, Myron?"

"What about me?"

"Like I said, there's this spotlight, right? For me it faded slowly. But for you, top college basketball player in the country, on your way to a big pro career . . ."

Myron waited.

"... and then, *flick*"—Rex snapped his fingers—"lights out. When you're only, what, twenty-one, twenty-two?"

"Twenty-two," Myron said.

"So how did you cope? And I love you too, sweet-ums. So tell me the truth."

Myron crossed his legs. He felt his face flush. "Are you enjoying the new show?"

"What, the dinner theater gig?"

"Yes."

"It's dog crap. It's worse than stripping on Route 17 in Lodi, New Jersey."

"And you know this from personal experience?"

"Stop trying to change the subject. How did you cope?"

Myron sighed. "Most would say I coped amazingly well."

Rex lifted his palm to the sky and curled his fingers as if to say, *Come on, come on.*

"What exactly do you want to know?"

Rex thought about it. "What did you do first?"

"After the injury?"

"Yes."

"Rehab. Lots of rehab."

"And once you realized that your basketball days were over ... ?"

"I went back to law school."

"Where?"

"Harvard."

"Very impressive. So you went to law school. Then what?"

"You know what, Rex. I got my JD, opened up a sports agency, grew into a full-service agency that now represents actors and writers too." He shrugged.

"Myron?"

"What?"

"I asked for the truth."

Myron picked up his fork, took a bite, chewed slowly. "The lights didn't just go out, Rex. I had a full-fledged power outage. A lifetime blackout."

"I know that."

"So I needed to push past it."

"And?"

"And that's it."

Rex shook his head and smiled.

"What?"

"Next time," Rex said. He picked up his fork. "You'll tell me next time."

"You're a pain in the ass."

"But you love me, remember?"

By the time they finished dinner and drinks, it was late. Drinking for a second night in a row. Myron Bolitar, lush of the stars. He made sure that Rex was safely back in his residence before heading to his parents' condo. He had a key. He slipped it in quietly so as to not awaken Mom and Dad. He knew that it would do no good.

The TV was on. His father sat in the living room. When Myron entered, Dad faked like he was just waking up. He wasn't. Dad always stayed awake until Myron came home. Didn't matter what time Myron returned. Didn't matter that Myron was now in his fourth decade.

Myron came up behind his father's chair. Dad turned around and gave him the smile, the one he saved only for Myron, the one that told Myron that he was the single greatest creation in this man's eyes and how could you beat that?

"Have fun?"

"Rex is a pretty cool guy," Myron said.

"I used to like his movies." His father nodded a few times too many. "Sit for a second."

"What's up?"

"Just sit, okay?"

He did. Myron folded his hands and put them in his lap. Like he was eight. "Is this about Mom?"

"No."

"Her Parkinson's is getting worse."

"That's how it is with Parkinson's, Myron. It gets worse."

"Is there anything I can do?"

"No."

"I think I should say something, at least."

"Don't. It's better. And what would you say that your mother doesn't already know?"

Now it was Myron's turn to nod a few times too many. "So what do you want to talk about?"

"Nothing. I mean, your mother wants us to have a heart-to-heart."

"What about?"

"Today's *New York Times*."

"Excuse me?"

"There was something in it. Your mother thinks you'll be upset and that we should talk. But I don't think I'm going to do that. I think what I'm going to do instead is hand you the newspaper and let you read it for yourself and leave you alone for a while. If you want to talk, you come and get me, okay? If not, I'll give you your space."

Myron frowned. "Something in *The New York Times*?"

"Sunday Styles section." Dad stood and pointed with his chin toward the pile of Sunday papers. "Page sixteen. Good night, Myron."

"Good night, Dad."

His father moved down the hall. No need to tiptoe. Mom could sleep through a Judas Priest concert. Dad was the night watchman, Mom the sleepy princess. Myron stood. He picked up the Sunday Styles section, turned to page sixteen, saw the photo, and felt the stiletto pierce his heart.

The New York Times Sunday Styles was upscale gossip. The most well-read pages were for wedding announcements. And there, on page sixteen, in the top left-hand corner, was a photograph of a man with Ken-doll good looks and teeth that were too perfect to be capped. He had a Republican senator's cleft chin, and his name was Stone Norman. The article said Stone ran and operated the BMV Investment Group, a highly successful financial enterprise specializing in major institutional trades.

Snore.

The engagement announcement said that Stone Norman and his wife-to-be would be married next Saturday at Tavern on the Green in Manhattan. A reverend would preside over the ceremony. Then the newlyweds would begin their lives together in Scarsdale, New York.

More snore. Stone Snore.

But none of that was what had pierced his heart. No, what did that, what really hurt and made the knees buckle, was the woman ol' Stone was marrying, the one smiling with him in that photograph, a smile Myron still knew far too well.

For a moment Myron just stared. He reached out and brushed the bride-to-be's face with his finger. Her biography stated that she was a best-selling writer who'd been nominated for both the PEN/Faulkner and National Book Award. Her name was Jessica Culver, and though it didn't say so in the article, for more than a decade she had been the love of Myron Bolitar's life.

He just sat and stared.

Jessica, the woman he'd been sure was his soul mate, was getting married to someone else.

He had not seen her since they broke up seven years ago. Life had gone on for him. It had, of course, gone on for her. Why should he be surprised?

He put down the paper, then picked it up again. A lifetime ago Myron had asked Jessica to marry him. She had said no. They stayed together on and off for the next decade. But in the end Myron wanted to get married, and Jessica didn't. She pretty much scoffed at the bourgeois idea of it all—the suburbs, the picket fence, the children, the barbecues, the Little League games, the life Myron's parents had led.

Except now Jessica was marrying big Stone Norman and moving to the über-suburb of Scarsdale, New York.

Myron carefully folded the paper and put it on the coffee table. He stood with a sigh and headed down the corridor. He flicked off the lights as he went. He passed his parents' bedroom. The reading lamp was still on. His father faked a cough to let Myron know he was there.

"I'm fine," he said out loud.

His father did not respond, and Myron was grateful. The man was like a master on the tightrope, managing the nearly impossible feat of showing he cared without butting in or interfering.

Jessica Culver, the love of his life, the woman he'd always believed was his destined soul mate, was getting married.

Myron wanted to sleep on that one. But sleep would not come.

Chapter 14

Time to talk to Aimee Biel's parents.

It was six in the morning. County investigator Loren Muse sat on her floor cross-legged. She wore shorts, and the quasi-shag carpeting made her legs itch. Police files and reports were spread out everywhere. In the center was the timetable she'd made up.

A harsh snoring came from the other room. Loren had lived alone in this same crappy apartment for more than a decade now. They called them "garden" apartments, though the only thing that seemed to grow was a monotonous red brick. They were sturdy structures with the personality of prison cells, way stations for people on the way up or on the way down, or, for a very few, stuck in a sort of personal-life purgatory.

The snoring did not come from a boyfriend. Loren had one—a total loser named Pete—but her mother, the multimarried, once-desirable, now-flabby Carmen Valos Muse Brewster Whatever was between men and thus living with her. Her snoring had the phlegm of a lifelong smoker, mixed with a few too many years of cheap wine and tacky song.

Cracker crumbs dominated the counter. An open jar of peanut butter, the knife sticking out like Excalibur, stood in the middle like a watchtower. Loren studied the phone logs, the credit card charges, the E-ZPass reports. They painted an interesting picture.

Okay, Loren thought, let's map this out.

- 1:56 A.M.: Aimee Biel uses the 52nd Street Citibank ATM machine—the same one used by Katie Rochester three months ago. Weird.
- 2:16 A.M.: Aimee Biel places a call to the Livingston residence of Myron Bolitar. The call lasts only seconds.
- 2:17 A.M.: Aimee places a call to a mobile phone registered to Myron Bolitar. The call lasts three minutes.

Loren nodded to herself. It seemed logical that Aimee Biel had first tried Bolitar's home and when he didn't answer—that would explain the brevity of the first call—she called his mobile.

Back to it:

- 2:21 A.M.: Myron Bolitar calls Aimee Biel. This call lasts one minute.

From what they'd been able to dig up, Bolitar often stayed in New York City at the Dakota apartment of a friend named Windsor Horne Lockwood III. Lockwood was known to police; despite a ritzy, Main Line upbringing, he was a suspect in several assaults and, yes, even a couple of homicides. The man had the craziest reputation Loren had ever seen. But again, that did not seem relevant to the case at hand.

The point here was, Bolitar was probably staying at

Lockwood's apartment in Manhattan. He kept his car in a nearby lot. According to the night attendant, Bolitar had taken the car out sometime around 2:30 A.M.

They had no proof yet, but Loren was fairly sure Bolitar had gone to midtown and picked up Aimee Biel. They were working on getting surveillance videos from the nearby businesses. Maybe Bolitar's car would be on one. But for now, it seemed like a fairly likely conclusion.

More from the time line:

- 3:11 A.M.: There was a credit card charge on Bolitar's Visa account from an Exxon gas station on Route 4 in Fort Lee, New Jersey, right off the George Washington Bridge.
- 3:55 A.M.: the E-ZPass on Bolitar's car showed him heading south on the Garden State Parkway, crossing the Bergen County tolls.
- 4:08 A.M.: the E-ZPass hit the Essex County tolls, showing that Bolitar was still traveling south.

That was it on the tolls. He could have gotten off at Exit 145, which would lead him to his residence in Livingston. Loren drew the route out. It made no sense. You wouldn't go up over the George Washington Bridge and then down the parkway. And even if you did, it wouldn't take forty minutes to get to the Bergen toll. It would take at most, that time of night, twenty minutes.

So where had Bolitar gone?

She went back to her time line. There was a gap of more than three hours, but at 7:18 A.M., Myron Bolitar placed a call to Aimee Biel's cell phone. No answer. He tries twice more that morning. No answer. Yesterday he called the Biels' home number. That was the only call that lasted more than a few seconds. Loren wondered if he talked to the parents.

She picked up her phone and dialed Lance Banner.

"What's up?" he asked.

"Did you tell Aimee's parents about Bolitar?"

"Not yet."

"I think," Loren said, "that now might be the time."

Myron had a new morning routine. The first thing he did was grab the newspaper and check for war casualties. He looked at the names. All of them. He made sure that Jeremy Downing wasn't listed. Then he went back and took the time to read every name again slowly. He read the rank and hometown and age. That was all they put. But Myron imagined that every dead kid listed was another Jeremy, was like that terrific nineteen-year-old kid who lives down your street, because, simple as it sounded, they were. For just a few minutes Myron imagined what that death meant, that this young, hopeful, dream-filled life was gone forever, what the parents must be thinking.

He hoped that our leaders did something similar. But he doubted it.

Myron's cell phone rang. He checked the caller ID. It read SWEET CHEEKS. That was Win's unlisted number. Myron clicked it on and said hello.

Without preamble, Win said, "Your flight arrives at one P.M."

"You work for the airlines now?"

"Work for the airlines," Win repeated. "Good one."

"So what's up?"

"Work for the airlines," Win said again. "Wait, just let me savor that line for a moment. Work for the airlines. Hilarious."

"You done?"

"Hold on, let me get a pen so I can write that one down. Work. For. The. Airlines."

Win.

"You done now?"

"Let me try again: Your flight arrives at one P.M. I will meet you at the airport. I have two tickets to the Knicks game. We will sit courtside, probably next to Paris Hilton or Kevin Bacon. Personally, I'm pulling for Kevin."

"You don't like the Knicks," Myron said.

"True."

"In fact, you don't like going to basketball games. So why . . . ?" Myron saw it. "Damn."

Silence.

"Since when do you read the Styles Section, Win?"

"One o'clock. Newark Airport. See you then."

Click.

Myron hung up the phone and couldn't help but smile. That Win. What a guy.

He headed into the kitchen. His father was up and making breakfast. He said nothing about Jessica's upcoming nuptials. Mom, however, jumped from her chair, rushed over to him, gave him a look that suggested a terminal illness, asked if he was all right. He assured her that he was fine.

"I haven't seen Jessica in seven years," he said. "It's no big deal."

His parents both nodded in a way that suggested that they were humoring him.

A few hours later he took off for the airport. He had tossed and turned, but in the end he really was all right with it. Seven years. They had been over for seven years. And while Jessica had been the one with the upper hand throughout most of their time together, Myron had been the one who'd finally put an end to it.

Jessica was the past. He took out his cell phone and called Ali—the present.

"I'm at Miami airport," he said.

"How was your trip?"

Hearing Ali's voice filled him with warmth. "It was good."

"But?"

"But nothing. I want to see you."

"How about around two? The kids will be out, I promise."

"What have you got in mind?" he asked.

"The technical term would be—hold on, let me check my thesaurus—'a nooner.' "

"Ali Wilder, you little vixen."

"That I am."

"I can't make it at two. Win is taking me to see the Knicks."

"How about immediately following the game?" she asked.

"Man, I hate it when you play hard to get."

"I'll take that as yes."

"Very much so."

"You okay?" she asked.

"I'm fine."

"You sound a little funny."

"I'm trying to sound very funny."

"Then don't try so hard."

There was an awkward moment. He wanted to tell her that he loved her. But it was too soon. Or maybe, with what he'd learned about Jessica, the timing was wrong. You don't want to say something like that for the first time for the wrong reason.

So instead he said, "They're boarding my flight."

"See you soon, handsome."

"Wait, if I get there in the evening, will it still be a 'nooner'? Wouldn't it be an 'evening-er'?"

"That would take too long to say. I don't want to waste any time."

"And on that note . . ."

"Stay safe, handsome."

Erik Biel sat alone on the couch while his wife, Claire, chose a chair. Loren noticed that. One would think that a couple in a situation like this would sit next to each other, draw comfort from each other. The body language here suggested that both wanted to be as far away from the other as possible. It could mean a rift in the relationship. Or it could mean that this experience was so raw that even tenderness—especially tenderness—would sting like hell.

Claire Biel had served them tea. Loren really hadn't wanted any, but she learned that most people relaxed if you allow them to be in control of something, of anything, if you allow them to do something mundane or domestic. So she had accepted. Lance Banner, who remained standing behind her, had declined.

Lance was letting her take the lead. He knew them. That might help for some questioning, but she'd get the ball rolling. Loren took a sip of the tea. She let the silence work them a little—let them be the first to speak. Some might view it as cruel. It wasn't, if it helped find Aimee. If Aimee were found okay, it would be quickly forgotten. If she weren't, the discomfort from silence would be nothing compared to what they would then endure.

"Here," Erik Biel said, "we made a list of her close friends and their phone numbers. We've already called all of them. And her boyfriend, Randy Wolf. We spoke to him too."

Loren took her time looking over the names.

"Have there been any developments?" Erik asked.

Erik Biel was, Loren thought, the poster boy for uptight. The mother, Claire, well, you could see the missing kid etched into her face. She hadn't slept. She was a mess. But Erik, with his starched dress shirt and tie and recently shaved face, somehow looked more harried. He was trying so hard to keep it together that you just knew that there would be no slow fray here. When it came apart, it would be ugly and maybe permanent.

Loren handed the paper to Lance Banner. She turned and sat up straight. She kept her eyes on Erik's face as she dropped the bomb: "Do either of you know a man named Myron Bolitar?"

Erik frowned. Loren moved her gaze toward the mother. Claire Biel looked as if Loren had asked if she could lick their toilet.

"He's a family friend," Claire Biel said. "I've known him since junior high."

"Did he know your daughter?"

"Of course. But what does—"

"What sort of relationship did they have?"

"Relationship?"

"Yes. Your daughter and Myron Bolitar. What sort of relationship did they have?"

For the first time since they'd entered the house, Claire slowly turned and looked to her husband for guidance. Erik too turned toward his wife. They both wore the faces of someone who'd been smacked in the gut by a two-by-four.

Erik finally spoke. "What are you suggesting?"

"I'm not suggesting anything, Mr. Biel. I'm asking you a question. How well did your daughter know Myron Bolitar?"

Claire: "Myron is a family friend."

Erik: "He wrote Aimee a recommendation letter for her college application."

Claire nodded with vigor. "Right. Like that."

"Like what?"

They didn't respond.

Loren kept her voice even. "Do they ever see each other?"

"See each other?"

"Yes. Or talk on the phone. Or maybe e-mail." Then Loren added: "Without you two present."

Loren wouldn't have thought it possible, but Erik Biel's spine got even straighter. "What the hell are you saying?"

Okay, Loren thought. They didn't know. This was no act. It was time to shift gears, check their honesty. "When was the last time either of you spoke to Mr. Bolitar?"

"Yesterday," Claire said.

"What time?"

"I'm not sure. Early afternoon, I think."

"Did you call him or did he call you?"

"He called here," Claire said.

Loren glanced at Lance Banner. Score one for the mom. That matched up with the phone records.

"What did he want?"

"To congratulate us."

"What about?"

"Aimee got accepted to Duke."

"Anything else?"

"He asked if he could speak to her."

"To Aimee?"

"Yes. He wanted to congratulate her."

"What did you say?"

"That she wasn't home. And then I thanked him for

writing the recommendation."

"What did he say?"

"He said he'd call her back."

"Anything else?"

"No."

Loren let that sit.

Claire Biel said, "You can't think Myron has anything to do with this."

Loren just stared at her, letting the silence soak in, giving her a chance to keep talking. She didn't disappoint.

"You have to know him," Claire went on. "He's a good man. I'd trust him with my life."

Loren nodded and then looked at Erik. "And you, Mr. Biel?"

His eyes were out of focus.

Claire said, "Erik?"

"I saw Myron yesterday," he said.

Loren sat up. "Where?"

"At the middle school gym." His voice was a dull ache. "There's pickup basketball there on Sundays."

"What time would this have been?"

"Seven thirty. Maybe eight."

"In the morning?"

"Yes."

Loren glanced back at Lance. He nodded slowly. He'd caught it too. Bolitar couldn't have gotten home much before five, six in the morning. A few hours later, he goes off to play basketball with the missing girl's father?

"Do you play with Mr. Bolitar every Sunday?"

"No. I mean, he used to play a bit. But he hadn't been there in months."

"Did you talk to him?"

Erik's nod was slow.

"Wait a second," Claire said. "I want to know why you're asking us so many questions about Myron. What does he have to do with any of this?"

Loren ignored her, keeping her gaze on Erik Biel. "What did you two talk about?"

"Aimee, I guess."

"What did he say?"

"He tried to be subtle about it."

Erik explained that Myron Bolitar had approached him and that they started talking about exercising and waking up early and then he segued into asking about Aimee, about where she was, about how troublesome teenagers could often be. "His tone was strange."

"How so?"

"He wanted to know *how* she was trouble. I remember he asked if Aimee was sullen, if she spent too much time on the Internet, things like that. I remember thinking it was a little odd."

"How did he look?"

"Like hell."

"Tired? Unshaven?"

"Both."

"Okay, that's enough," Claire Biel said. "We have a right to know why you're asking all these questions."

Loren looked up at her. "You're a lawyer, aren't you, Mrs. Biel?"

"I am."

"So help me out here: Where in the law does it say I have to tell you anything?"

Claire opened her mouth, closed it. Unduly harsh, Loren thought, but playing good cop/bad cop—it's not just for the perps. Witnesses too. She didn't like it, but it was damn effective.

Loren looked back at Lance. Lance picked up his cue. He coughed into his fist. "We have some information linking Aimee with Myron Bolitar."

Claire's eyes narrowed. "What sort of information?"

"The night before last, at two a.m., Aimee called him. First at home. Then on his cell phone. We know Mr. Bolitar then picked up his car from a garage in the city." Lance continued to explain the time line. Claire's face drained of color. Erik's hands tightened into fists.

When Lance finished, when they were still too dazed to ask follow-up questions, Loren leaned forward. "Is there any way that there may have been more between Myron and Aimee than family friends?"

"Absolutely not," Claire said.

Erik closed his eyes. "Claire . . ."

"What?" she snapped. "You can't possibly believe that Myron would get involved—"

"She called him right before . . ." He shrugged. "Why would Aimee call him? Why wouldn't he say something about that when I saw him at the gym?"

"I don't know, but the idea"—she stopped, snapped her fingers—"wait, Myron's dating a friend of mine, as a matter of fact. Ali Wilder. An adult woman, thank you very much. A lovely widow with two kids of her own. The idea that Myron could possibly . . ."

Erik squeezed his eyes shut.

Loren said, "Mr. Biel?"

His voice was soft. "Aimee hasn't been herself lately."

"How so?"

Erik's eyes were still shut. "We both dismissed it as normal teenage stuff. But the last few months, she's been secretive."

"That is normal, Erik," Claire said.

"It's gotten worse."

Claire shook her head. "You still think of her as your little girl. That's all it is."

"You know it's more than that, Claire."

"No, Erik, I don't."

He closed his eyes again.

"What is it, Mr. Biel?" Loren asked.

"Two weeks ago I tried to access her computer."

"Why?"

"Because I wanted to read her e-mail."

His wife glared at him, but he didn't see it—or maybe he didn't care. Loren pushed ahead.

"So what happened?"

"She changed her password. I couldn't get on."

"Because she wanted privacy," Claire said. "You think that's unusual? I had a diary when I was a kid. I kept it locked with a key and still hid it. So what?"

Erik went on. "I called our Internet provider. I'm the bill payer with the master account. So they gave me the new password. Then I went online to check her e-mails."

"And?"

He shrugged. "They were gone. All of them. She'd deleted every one of them."

"She knew you'd snoop," Claire said. Her tone was a blend of anger and defensiveness. "She was just guarding against it."

Erik spun toward her. "Do you really believe that, Claire?"

"Do you really believe that she's having an affair with Myron?"

Erik did not reply.

Claire spun back toward Loren and Lance. "Have you asked Myron about the calls?"

"Not yet."

"So what are we waiting for?" Claire started for her purse. "Let's go now. He'll straighten this out."

"He's not in Livingston," Loren said. "In fact, he flew down to Miami, not long after he played ball with your husband."

Claire was about to ask something else, but she stopped. For the first time, Loren could see the doubt crawl into her face. Loren decided to use that. She rose.

"We'll be in touch," Loren said.

Chapter 15

Myron sat on the plane and thought about his old love, Jessica.

Shouldn't he be happy for her?

She had always been fiery to the point of a pain in the ass. His mother and Esperanza hadn't liked her. His father, like a great TV anchor, played it neutral. Win yawned. In Win's eyes, women were either doable or they weren't. Jessica was most definitely doable, but after that . . . so what?

The women thought that Myron was blinded by Jessica's beauty. She could write like a dream. She was two steps beyond passionate. But they were different. Myron wanted to live like his parents. Jessica sneered at that idyllic nonsense. It was a constant tension that both kept them apart and drew them to each other.

Now Jessica was marrying some Wall Street dude named Stone. Big Stone, Myron thought. Rolling Stone. The Stoner. Smokin' Stone. The Stone Man.

Myron hated him.

What had become of Jessica?

Seven years, Myron. It changes a person.

But that much?

The plane landed. He checked his phone while the plane taxied toward the terminal. There was a text message from Win:

YOUR PLANE JUST LANDED.
PLEASE FILL IN YOUR OWN WITTICISM ABOUT MY WORKING FOR THE AIRLINES. I'M WAITING BY THE LOWER LEVEL CURB.

The plane slowed as it approached the gate. The pilot asked everybody to stay in their seats with their belts fastened. Almost everybody ignored that request. You could hear the belts clack open. Why? What did people gain from that extra second? Was it that we just liked to defy rules?

He debated calling Aimee's cell phone again. That might be overkill. How many calls could he make, after all? The promise had also been pretty clear. He would drive her anywhere. He would not ask questions. He would not tell her parents. It should hardly surprise him that after such a venture, Aimee would not want to talk to him for a few days.

He got off the plane and was starting toward the exit when he heard someone call out, "Myron Bolitar?"

He turned. There were two of them, a man and a woman. The woman had been the one who called his name. She was small, not much over five feet. Myron was six-four. He towered over her. She did not seem intimidated. The man with her sported a military cut. He also looked vaguely familiar.

The man had a badge out. The woman did not.

"I'm Essex County investigator Loren Muse," she said. "This is Livingston police detective Lance Banner."

"Banner," Myron said automatically. "You Buster's brother?"

Lance Banner almost smiled. "Yeah."

"Good guy, Buster. I played hoops with him."

"I remember."

"How's he doing?"

"Good, thanks."

Myron did not know what was going on, but he'd had experience with law enforcement. Out of habit more than anything else, he reached for his cell phone and pressed the button. It was his speed dial. It would reach Win. Win would hit the mute button and listen in. This was an old trick of theirs, one Myron hadn't employed in years, and yet there he was, with police officers, falling into the old routines.

From his past run-ins with the law, Myron had learned a few basic truisms that could be summed up thusly: Just because you haven't done anything wrong doesn't mean you're not in trouble. Best to play it with that knowledge.

"We'd like you to come with us," Loren Muse said.

"May I ask what this is about?"

"We won't take much of your time."

"I got Knicks tickets."

"We'll try not to interfere with your plans."

"Courtside." He looked at Lance Banner. "Celebrity row."

"Are you refusing to come with us?"

"Are you arresting me?"

"No."

"Then before I agree to go with you, I'd like you to tell me what it's about."

Loren Muse did not hesitate this time. "It's about Aimee Biel."

Whack. He should have seen it coming, but he didn't. Myron staggered back a step. "Is she all right?"

"Why don't you come with us?"

"I asked you—"

"I heard you, Mr. Bolitar." She turned away from him now and started heading down toward the exit. "Why don't you come with us so we can discuss this further?"

Lance Banner drove. Loren Muse rode shotgun. Myron sat in the backseat.

"Is she okay?" Myron asked.

They would not reply. He was being played, Myron knew that, but he didn't much care. He wanted to know about Aimee. The rest was irrelevant.

"Talk to me, for crying out loud."

Nothing.

"I saw her Saturday night. You know that already, right?"

They did not respond. He knew why. The ride was mercifully short. That explained their silence. They wanted his admissions on record. It was probably taking all of their willpower not to say anything, but soon they would have him in an interrogation room and put it all on tape.

They drove into the garage and led him to an elevator. They got off on the eighth floor. They were in Newark, the county courthouse. Myron had been here before. They brought him into an interrogation room. There was no mirror and thus no one-way glass. That meant a camera was doing the surveillance.

"Am I under arrest?" he asked.

Loren Muse tilted her head. "What makes you say that?"

"Don't play these games with me, Muse."

"Please have a seat."

"Have you done any checking on me yet? Call Jake Courter, the sheriff in Reston. He'll vouch for me. There are others."

"We'll get to that in a moment."

"What happened to Aimee Biel?"

"You mind if we film this?" Loren Muse asked.

"No."

"Do you mind signing a waiver?"

It was a Fifth Amendment waiver. Myron knew better than to sign it—he was a lawyer, for Chrissake—but he pushed past that. His heart hammered in his chest. Something had happened to Aimee Biel. They must think he either knew something or was involved. The faster this moved along and they eliminated him, the better for Aimee.

"Okay," Myron said. "Now what happened to Aimee?"

Loren Muse spread her hands. "Who said anything happened to her?"

"You did, Muse. When you braced me at the airport. You said, 'It's about Aimee Biel.' And because, while I don't like to brag, I have amazing powers of deduction, I deduced that two police officers didn't stop me and say it was about Aimee Biel because she sometimes pops her gum in class. No, I deduced that something must have happened to her. Please don't shun me because I have this gift."

"You finished?"

He was. He got nervous, he started talking.

Loren Muse took out a pen. There was already a notebook on her desk. Lance Banner stood and remained silent. "When was the last time you saw Aimee Biel?"

He knew better than to ask what happened again.

Muse was going to play it her way.

"Saturday night."

"What time?"

"I guess between two and three a.m."

"So this would have been Sunday morning rather than Saturday night?"

Myron bit back the sarcastic rejoinder. "Yes."

"I see. Where did you last see her?"

"In Ridgewood, New Jersey."

She wrote that down on a legal pad. "Address?"

"I don't know."

Her pen stopped. "You don't know?"

"That's right. It was late. She gave me directions. I just followed them."

"I see." She sat back and dropped the pen. "Why don't you start at the beginning?"

The door behind them flew open. All heads spun to the door. Hester Crimstein stomped in as though the very room had whispered an insult and she wanted to call it out. For a moment no one moved or said anything.

Hester waited a beat, spread her arms, put her right foot forward, and shouted, "Ta-da!"

Loren Muse raised an eyebrow. "Hester Crimstein?"

"We know each other, sweetie?"

"I recognize you from TV."

"I'll be happy to sign autographs later. Right now I want the camera off and I want you two"—Hester pointed at Lance Banner and Loren Muse—"out of here, so I can chat with my client."

Loren stood. They were eye-to-eye, both about the same height. Hester had the frizzy hair. Loren tried to stare her down. Myron almost laughed. Some would call famed criminal attorney Hester Crimstein as mean as a snake, but most would consider that slanderous to the snake.

"Wait," Hester said to Loren. "Wait for it. . . ."

"Excuse me?"

"Any second now, I'm going to pee in my pants. From fear, I mean. Just wait. . . ."

Myron said, "Hester . . ."

"Shh, you." Hester shot him a glare and made a *tsk-tsk* noise. "Signing a waiver and talking without your lawyer. What kind of dope are you?"

"You're not my lawyer."

"Shh again, you."

"I'm representing myself."

"You know the expression 'A man who represents himself has a fool for a client'? Change 'fool' to 'total brain-dead numbskull.' "

Myron wondered how Hester had gotten there so quickly, but the answer was obvious. Win. As soon as Myron had hit his cell phone, as soon as Win heard the voices of the cops, he would have found Hester and gotten her there.

Hester Crimstein was one of the country's top defense attorneys. She had her own cable show called *Crimstein on Crime*. They'd become friends when Hester had helped Esperanza with a murder rap a few years back.

"Hold up." Hester looked back at Loren and Lance. "Why are you two still here?"

Lance Banner took a big step forward. "He just said you're not his lawyer."

"Your name again, handsome?"

"Livingston police detective Lance Banner."

"Lance," she said. "Like in what I use to get rid of a boil? Okay, Lance, here's some advice: The step forward was a nice move, very commanding, but you need to stick out your chest more. Make your voice a little deeper and add a scowl. Like this: 'Yo, chickie, he just said you're not his lawyer.' Try it."

Myron knew that Hester wouldn't simply go away. He also knew that he probably didn't want her to. He wanted to cooperate, of course, get this over with, but he also wanted to know what the hell had happened to Aimee.

"She's my lawyer," Myron said. "Please give us a minute."

Hester gave them a satisfied smirk that you know they both wanted to slap off her face. They turned for the doors. Hester gave them a five-finger toodle-oo wave. When they were both out the door, she closed it and looked up at the camera. "Turn it off now."

"It probably is," Myron said.

"Yeah, sure. Cops never play games with that."

She took out her cell phone.

"Who are you calling?" he asked.

"Do you know why they have you in here?"

"It has something to do with a girl named Aimee Biel," Myron said.

"That much I know already. But you don't know what happened to her?"

"No."

"That's what I'm trying to find out. I got my local investigator working on it. She's the best, knows everybody in this office." Hester put the phone to her ear. "Yeah, Hester here. What's up? Uh-huh. Uh-huh." Hester listened without taking notes. A minute later, she said, "Thanks, Cingle. Keep digging and see what they got."

Hester hung up. Myron shrugged a *well*? at her.

"This girl—her last name is Biel."

"Aimee Biel," Myron said. "What about her?"

"She's missing."

Myron felt the thump again.

"It seems she never came home on Saturday night. She was supposed to sleep at a friend's house. She never arrived. Nobody knows what happened to her. Apparently there are phone records linking you to the girl. Other stuff too. My investigator is trying to find out what exactly."

Hester sat down. She looked across the table at him. "So okay, bubbe, tell Aunt Hester everything."

"No," Myron said.

"What?"

"Look, you have two choices here. You can stay while I talk to them right now or I can fire you."

"You should talk to me first."

"We can't waste the time. You have to let me tell them everything."

"Because you're innocent?"

"Of course I'm innocent."

"And the police never ever *ever* arrest the wrong man."

"I'll risk it. If Aimee is in trouble, I can't have them wasting time on me."

"I disagree."

"Then you're fired."

"Don't get all Trump on me. I'm advising you, that's all. You're the client."

She rose, opened the door, called them back in. Loren Muse moved past her and sat back down. Lance took his post in the corner. Muse was red-faced, probably upset with herself for not questioning him in the car before Hester's arrival.

Loren Muse was about to say something, but Myron stopped her by raising his palm.

"Let's get to it," Myron said to them. "Aimee Biel is missing. I know that now. You've probably pulled our phone logs, so you know she called me around two in the morning. I'm not sure what else you have so far, so let me help you out. She asked for a ride. I picked her up."

"Where?" Loren asked.

"Midtown Manhattan. Fifty-second and Fifth, I think. I took the Henry Hudson to the GWB. Do you have the credit card charge for the gas station?"

"Yes."

"Then you know we stopped there. We continued down Route 4 to Route 17 and then to Ridgewood." Myron saw a change in their posture. He had missed something, but he pressed on. "I dropped her off at a house on the end of a cul-de-sac. Then I drove home."

"And you don't remember the address, is that correct?"

"That's correct."

"Anything else?"

"Like?"

"Like why did Aimee Biel call you in the first place?"

"I'm a friend of the family."

"You must be a close friend."

"I am."

"So why you? I mean, first she called your house in Livingston. Then she went to your cell phone. Why did she call you and not her parents or an aunt or an uncle or even a school friend?" Loren lifted her palms to the sky. "Why you?"

Myron's voice was soft. "I made her promise."

"Promise?"

"Yes."

He explained about the basement, about hearing the girls talk about driving with a drunk kid, about making them promise—and as he did, he could see their faces change. Even Hester's. The words, the rationale, rang hollow in his own ears now, and yet he couldn't put his finger on why. His explanation went on a little too long. He could hear the defensiveness in his voice.

When he was done, Loren asked, "Have you ever made this promise before?"

"No."

"Never?"

"Never."

"No other helpless or inebriated girls you volunteered to chauffeur around?"

"Hey!" Hester wouldn't let that pass. "That's a total mischaracterization of what he said. And the question was already asked and answered. Move on."

Loren shifted in her seat. "How about young boys? You ever make any boys promise to call you?"

"No."

"So just girls?"

"Just *these* two girls," Myron said. "It wasn't like I planned it."

"I see." Loren rubbed her chin. "How about Katie Rochester?"

Hester said, "Who's that?"

Myron ignored that. "What about her?"

"Did you ever make Katie Rochester promise to call you when she was drunk?"

"Again that's a total mischaracterization of what he said," Hester jumped in. "He was trying to prevent them from drinking and driving."

"Right, sure, he's a hero," Loren said. "Ever do anything like that with Katie Rochester?"

"I don't even know Katie Rochester," Myron said.

"But you've heard the name."

"Yes."

"In what context?"

"On the news. So what's the deal, Muse—I'm a suspect in every missing persons case?"

Loren smiled. "Not every."

Hester leaned toward Myron and whispered in his ear. "I don't like this, Myron."

Neither did he.

Loren continued: "So you've never met Katie Rochester?"

He couldn't help his lawyer training. "Not to my knowledge."

"Not to your knowledge. Then whose knowledge would it be?"

"Objection."

"You know what I mean," Myron said.

"How about her father, Dominick Rochester?"

"No."

"Or her mother, Joan? Ever meet her?"

"No."

"No," Loren repeated, "or not to your knowledge?"

"I meet lots of people. I don't remember them all. But the names ring no bells."

Loren Muse looked down at the table. "You said you dropped Aimee off in Ridgewood?"

"Yes. At her friend Stacy's."

"At her friend's?" That got Loren's attention. "You didn't mention that before."

"I'm mentioning it now."

"What's Stacy's last name?"

"Aimee didn't say."

"I see. Did you meet this Stacy?"

"No."

"Did you walk Aimee to the front door?"

"No, I stayed in the car."

Loren Muse faked a puzzled look. "Your promise to protect her didn't extend from the car to the front door?"

"Aimee asked me to stay in the car."

"Who opened the door to the house then?"

"Nobody."

"Aimee just let herself in?"

"She said that Stacy was probably asleep and that she always lets herself in the back door."

"I see." Loren rose. "Let's go then."

"Where are you taking him?" Hester asked.

"To Ridgewood. Let's see if we can find this cul-de-sac."

Myron stood with her. "Can't you just find Stacy's address from Aimee's parents?"

"We already know Stacy's address," Loren said. "The problem is, Stacy doesn't live in Ridgewood. She lives in Livingston."

Chapter 16

When Myron headed out of the interrogation room, he spotted Claire and Erik Biel in an office down the corridor. Even from the distance and through the reflection in the plate glass window, Myron could see the strain. He stopped.

"What's the problem?" Loren Muse asked.

He gestured with his chin. "I want to talk to them."

"And say what exactly?"

He hesitated.

"Do you want to waste time explaining yourself," Loren Muse asked, "or do you want to help us find Aimee?"

She had a point. What would he say right now anyway? "I didn't harm your daughter? I just drove her to some house in Ridgewood because I didn't want her to drive with a drunk kid"? What good would that do?

Hester kissed him good-bye. "Keep your trap shut."

He looked at her.

"Fine, whatever. Just call me if they arrest you, okay?"

"Okay."

Myron took the elevator to the garage with Lance Banner and Loren Muse. Banner took one car and started out. Myron looked a question at Loren.

"He's going ahead to get a local to accompany us."

"Oh."

Loren Muse moved over to a squad car, complete with the perp cage in the back. She opened the back door for Myron. He sighed and slid in. She took the driver's seat. There was a laptop attached to the console. She started typing into it.

"So what now?" Myron asked.

"Can I have your mobile phone?"

"Why?"

"Just give it to me."

He handed it to her. She scanned through the call log and then dropped it on the front passenger's seat.

"When exactly did you call Hester Crimstein?" she asked.

"I didn't."

"Then how—"

"Long story."

Win would not want his name mentioned.

"It doesn't look good," she said. "Calling a lawyer so quickly."

"I don't much care how it looks."

"No, I guess you don't."

"So what's next?"

"We drive to Ridgewood. We try to figure out where you purportedly dropped off Aimee Biel."

They started moving.

"I know you from somewhere," Myron said.

"I grew up in Livingston. When I was a kid, I went to some of your high school basketball games."

"That's not it," he said. He sat up. "Wait, did you

handle that Hunter case?"

"I was"—she paused—"involved."

"That's it. The Matt Hunter case."

"You know him?"

"I went to school with his brother Bernie. I was at his funeral." He sat back. "So what's next? Are you getting a warrant for my house, my car, what?"

"Both." She checked her watch. "They're being served now."

"You'll probably find evidence that Aimee was in both. I told you about the party, about being in my basement. And I told you I drove her the night before."

"All very neat and convenient, yes."

Myron closed his eyes. "Are you going to take my computer too?"

"Of course."

"I have a lot of private correspondence on it. Client information."

"They'll be careful."

"No, they won't. Do me a favor, Muse. Inspect the computer yourself, okay?"

"You trust me? I'm almost flattered."

"Okay, look, cards on the table," Myron said. "I know I'm a good suspect."

"Really? Why? Because you were the last person who saw her? Because you're a single ex-jock who lives alone in his childhood home and picks up teenage girls at two in the morning?" She shrugged. "Why would you be a suspect?"

"I didn't do it, Muse."

She kept her eyes focused on the road.

"What is it?" Myron asked.

"Tell me about the gas station."

"The . . ." And then he saw it. "Oh."

"Oh what?"

"What do you have—a surveillance video or the attendant's testimony?"

She said nothing.

"Aimee got mad at me because she thought I'd tell her parents."

"Why would she think that?"

"Because I kept asking her questions—where she'd been, who she'd been with, what happened."

"And you'd promised to take her wherever she wanted, no questions asked."

"Right."

"So why were you reneging?"

"I wasn't reneging."

"But?"

"She didn't look right."

"How's that?"

"She wasn't in a part of the city where kids would go to drink at that hour. She didn't look drunk. I didn't smell booze on her. She looked more upset than anything else. So I thought I'd try to find out why."

"And she didn't like that?"

"Right. So at the gas station, Aimee jumped out of the car. She wouldn't get back in until I promised I wouldn't ask any more questions or tell her parents. She said"—Myron frowned, hating to betray this sort of confidence—"she said that there were problems at home."

"With Mom and Dad?"

"Yes."

"What did you say?"

"That that was normal."

"Man," Loren said, "you are good. What other nuggets did you offer? 'Time heals all wounds'?"

"Give me a break, Muse, will you?"

"You're still my prime suspect, Myron."

"No, I'm not."

She lowered her eyebrows. "Excuse me?"

"You're not this stupid. Neither am I."

"What's that supposed to mean?"

"You've known about me since last night. So you made some calls. Who did you talk to?"

"You mentioned Jake Courter earlier."

"You know him?"

Loren Muse nodded.

"And what did Sheriff Courter say about me?"

"That in the tri-state area, you've caused more ass discomfort than hemorrhoids."

"But that I didn't do it, right?"

She said nothing.

"Come on, Muse. You know I couldn't be this stupid. Phone records, credit card charges, E-ZPass, an eyewitness at the gas station . . . it's overkill. Plus you know my story will pan out. The phone records show that Aimee called me first. That fits in with what I'm telling you."

They drove in silence for a while. The car radio buzzed. Loren picked it up. Lance Banner said, "I got a local with me. We're good to go."

"I'm almost there," she said. Then to Myron: "What exit did you take—Ridgewood Avenue or Linwood?"

"Linwood."

She repeated it into the microphone. She pointed at the green sign through the windshield. "Linwood Avenue West or East?"

"Whichever one says Ridgewood."

"That would be west."

He sat back. She took the ramp. "Do you remember how far away from here?"

"I'm not sure. We drove straight for a while. Then we started making a lot of turns. I don't remember."

Loren frowned. "You don't hit me as the forgetful type, Myron."

"Then I got you fooled."

"Where were you before she called?"

"At a wedding."

"Drink much?"

"More than I should have."

"Were you drunk when she called?"

"I probably would have passed a Breathalyzer."

"But you were, shall we say, feeling it?"

"Yes."

"Ironic, don't you think?"

"Like an Alanis Morissette song," he said. "I have a question for you."

"I'm not really into answering your questions, Myron."

"You asked me if I knew Katie Rochester. Was that just routine—two missing girls—or do you have a reason to believe that their disappearances are related?"

"You're kidding, right?"

"I just need to know—"

"Squat. You need to know squat. Now walk me through it again. Everything. What Aimee said, what you said, the phone calls, the drop-off, everything."

He did. On the corner of Linwood Avenue, Myron noticed a Ridgewood police car slide in behind them. Lance Banner sat in the passenger seat.

"They coming along for jurisdiction?" Myron asked.

"More like protocol. Do you remember where you drove from here?"

"I think we turned right by that big pool."

"Okay. I have a map up on the computer. We'll try to find the cul-de-sacs and see what happens."

Myron's hometown of Livingston was nouveau and

Jewish-y, former farmland converted into look-alike clusters of split-levels, with one big mall. Ridgewood was old Victorians and WASPy, lusher landscapes, and a true town center with restaurants and shops. The houses in Ridgewood were built in a variety of eras. Trees lined both sides of the streets, age tilting them toward the center to form a protective canopy. There was less sameness here.

Was this street familiar?

Myron frowned. He couldn't say. Not much sameness during the day, but at night, it all looked woodsy. Loren headed down a cul-de-sac. Myron shook his head. Then another and another. The roads twisted seemingly without reason or plan, like something in an abstract painting.

More dead ends.

"You said before that Aimee didn't seem drunk," Loren said.

"That's right."

"How did she seem?"

"Distraught." He sat up. "I was thinking that maybe she'd broken up with her boyfriend. I think his name is Randy. Have you talked to him yet?"

"No."

"Why not?"

"I need to explain myself to you?"

"It's not that, but a girl vanishes, you investigate—"

"There wasn't an investigation. She's of age, no signs of violence, missing only a few hours . . ."

"Enter me."

"Exactly. Claire and Erik called her friends, of course. Randy Wolf, the boyfriend, wasn't supposed to see her last night. He stayed home with his parents."

Myron frowned. Loren Muse spotted it in the rearview mirror. "What?" she asked.

"Saturday night at the end of his senior year," he said, "and Randy stays home with his mommy and daddy?"

"Do me a favor, Bolitar. Just look for the house, will you?"

As soon as she made the turn, Myron felt the pang of déjà vu. "On the right. At the end of the cul-de-sac."

"That's it?"

"I'm not sure yet." Then: "Yeah. Yeah, this is it."

She pulled up to it and parked. The Ridgewood police car parked behind them. Myron looked out the window. "Move up a few yards."

Loren did as he asked. Myron kept his eyes on the house.

"Well?"

He nodded. "This is it. She opened that gate on the side of the house." He almost added *That was the last time I saw her*, but he held back.

"Wait in the car."

She got out. Myron watched. She headed over and talked to Banner and a cop with Ridgewood police logos on his uniform. They chatted and gestured toward the house. Then Loren Muse started up the walk. She rang the doorbell. A woman answered it. Myron couldn't see her at first. Then she stepped outside. Nope, not familiar. She was slim. Her blond hair peeked out from a baseball cap. She looked like she'd just finished a workout.

The two women talked for a full ten minutes. Loren kept glancing back at Myron as if she feared he'd try to escape. Another minute or two passed. Loren and the woman shook hands. The woman went back inside and closed the door. Loren walked back to the car and opened the back door.

"Show me where Aimee walked."

"What did she say?"

"What do you think she said?"

"That she never heard of Aimee Biel."

Loren Muse touched her index finger to her nose and then pointed at him.

"This is the place," Myron said. "I'm sure of it."

Myron traced her path. He stopped at the gate. He remembered how Aimee had stood here. He remembered her wave, that there was something there, something that bugged him.

"I should have . . ." He stopped. No point. "She went in here. She disappeared from sight. Then she came back and waved that I should leave."

"And you did?"

"Yes."

Loren Muse looked in the backyard before she walked him back to another squad car. "They'll drive you home."

"Can I have my cell phone?"

She tossed it to him. Myron got into the back of the car. Banner started it up. Myron took hold of the door handle.

"Muse?"

"What?"

"There was a reason she picked this house," Myron said.

He closed the door. They drove off in silence. Myron watched that gate, watched it grow smaller until finally it, like Aimee Biel, was gone.

Chapter 17

Dominick Rochester, the father of Katie, sat at the head of the dining-room table. His three boys were there too. His wife, Joan, was in the kitchen. That left two empty chairs—hers and Katie's. He chewed his meat and stared at the chair, as if willing Katie to appear.

Joan came out of the kitchen. She had a platter of sliced roast beef. He gestured toward his near-empty plate, but she was already on it. Dominick Rochester's wife stayed home and took care of the house. None of that working-woman crap. Dominick wouldn't have it.

He grunted a thank-you. Joan returned to her seat. The boys were all chowing down in silence. Joan smoothed her skirt and picked up her fork. Dominick watched her. She used to be so damned beautiful. Now she was glassy-eyed and meek. She hunched over in a permanent cower. She drank too much during the day, although she thought he didn't know. No matter. She was still the mother of his children and kept in line. So he let it slide.

The phone rang. Joan Rochester leaped to her feet, but Dominick signaled her to sit with a wave of his hand. He wiped his face as though it were a windshield and rose from his seat. Dominick was a thick man. Not fat. Thick. Thick neck, thick shoulders, thick chest, thick arms and thighs.

The last name Rochester—he hated that. His father had changed it because he wanted to sound less ethnic. But his old man was a weakling and a loser. Dominick thought about changing it back, but that would look weak too. Like maybe he worried too much about what other people would think. In Dominick's world, you never showed weakness. They had walked all over his father. Made him shut down his barbershop. Poked fun at him. His father thought he could rise above it. Dominick knew better.

You bust heads or you get your head busted. You don't ask questions. You don't reason with them—at least, not at first. At first, you bust heads. You bust heads and take licks until they respect you. Then you reason with them. You show them you're willing to take a hit. You let them see you're not afraid of blood, not even your own. You want to win, you smile right through your blood. That gets their attention.

The phone rang again. He checked the caller ID. The number was blocked, but most people who called here didn't like people to know their business. He was still chewing when he lifted the receiver.

The voice on the other end said, "I have something for you."

It was his contact at the county prosecutor's office. He swallowed the meat. "Go ahead."

"There's another missing girl."

That got his attention.

"She's from Livingston too. Same age, same class."

"Name?"

"Aimee Biel."

The name didn't mean anything to him, but he really didn't know Katie's friends very well. He put his hand over the mouthpiece. "Any of you know a girl named Aimee Biel?"

No one said anything.

"Hey, I asked a question here. She'd be Katie's year."

The boys shook their heads. Joan didn't move. His eyes met hers. She shook her head slowly.

"There's more," his contact said.

"Like what?"

"They found a link to your daughter."

"What kind of link?"

"I don't know. I've just been eavesdropping. But I think it has something to do with where they both went missing. Do you know a guy named Myron Bolitar?"

"The old basketball star?"

"Yeah."

Rochester had seen him a few times. He also knew that Bolitar had had run-ins with some of Rochester's nastier colleagues.

"What about him?"

"He's involved."

"How?"

"He picked up the missing girl in midtown Manhattan. That's the last time she was seen. She used the same ATM as your Katie."

He felt a jolt. "He what?"

Dominick's contact explained a bit more, about how this Bolitar guy had driven Aimee Biel back over to Jersey, how a gas station attendant saw them arguing, and how she just disappeared.

"The police talk to him?"

"Yeah."

"What did he say?"

"I don't think very much. He lawyered up."

"He . . ." Dominick felt a red swirl build in his head. "Son of a bitch. Did they arrest him?"

"No."

"Why not?"

"Not enough yet."

"So, what, they just let him walk?"

"Yeah."

Dominick Rochester didn't say anything. He got very quiet. His family noticed. They all went very still, afraid to move. When he finally spoke again, his voice was so calm, his family held their breaths.

"Anything else?"

"That's it for now."

"Keep digging."

Dominick hung up the phone. He turned toward the table. His whole family was watching him.

Joan said, "Dom?"

"It was nothing."

He felt no need to explain. This didn't involve them. It was his job to handle stuff like this. The father was the soldier, the one who kept vigil so that his family could sleep untroubled.

He headed to the garage. Once inside, he closed his eyes and tried to smother the rage. It wouldn't happen.

Katie . . .

He eyed the metal baseball bat. He remembered reading about Bolitar's injured knee. If he thought that hurt, if he thought a mere knee injury was pain . . .

He made some calls, did a little background. In the past, Bolitar had gotten in trouble with the Ache brothers, who ran New York. Bolitar was supposedly a tough guy, good with his fists, who hung out with a psycho named Windsor Something.

Taking on Bolitar would not be easy.

But it wouldn't be all that difficult either. Not if Dominick got the best.

His cell phone was a throwaway, the kind you can buy in cash with a false name and toss away after you use up your minutes. No way to trace it back to him. He grabbed a fresh one off the shelf. For a moment he just held it and debated his next move. His breathing was labored.

Dominick had busted his share of heads in his day, but if he dialed this number, if he did indeed call the Twins, he was crossing a line he'd never gone near before.

He thought about his daughter's smile. He thought about how she had to wear braces when she was twelve and how she wore her hair and the way she used to look at him, a long time ago, when she was a little girl and he was the most powerful man in the world.

Dominick pressed the digits. After this call, he would have to get rid of the phone. That was one of the Twins' rules, and when it came to those two, it didn't matter who you were, didn't matter how tough or how hard you'd scraped to buy this fancy house in Livingston, you don't mess around with the Twins.

The phone was answered on the second ring. No hello. No greeting at all. Just silence.

Dominick said, "I'm going to need both of you."

"When?"

Dominick picked up the metal bat. He liked the weight of it. He thought about this Bolitar guy, this guy who drove off with a missing girl and then lawyered up, who was free now and probably watching TV or enjoying a nice meal.

No way you let that slide. Even if you gotta bring in the Twins.

"Now," Dominick Rochester said. "I need you both now."

Chapter 18

When Myron arrived back at his house in Livingston, Win was already there.

Win was sprawled out in a chaise longue on the front lawn. His legs were crossed. He wore khakis sans socks, a blue shirt, a Lilly Pulitzer tie of dizzying green. Some people could wear anything and make it work. Win was one of those people.

He had his face tilted to the sun, eyes closed. He did not open them as Myron approached.

"Do you still want to go to the Knicks game?" Win asked.

"I think I'll pass."

"You mind if I take someone else then?"

"No."

"I met a girl at Scores last night."

"She's a stripper?"

"Please." Win held up a finger. "She's an erotic dancer."

"Career woman. Nice."

"Her name is Bambi, I think. Or maybe Tawny."

"Is that her real name?"

"Nothing about her is real," Win said. "By the way, the police were here."

"Searching the place?"

"Yes."

"They take my computer?"

"Yes."

"Damn."

"Fret not. I arrived before them and backed up your personal files. Then I erased the hard drive."

"You," Myron said. "You're good."

"The best," Win said.

"Where did you back it up?"

"USB hard drive on my key chain," he said, dangling it, his eyes still closed. "Kindly move to the right a little. You're blocking my sun."

"Has Hester's investigator learned anything new?"

"There was an ATM charge on young Ms. Biel's card," Win said.

"Aimee took out cash?"

"No, a library book. Yes, cash. Apparently, Aimee Biel picked up a thousand dollars at an ATM machine a few minutes before she called you."

"Anything else?"

"Like?"

"They're linking this to another disappearance. A girl named Katie Rochester."

"Two girls disappearing from the same area. Of course they're going to link them."

Myron frowned. "I think there's something else."

Win opened one eye. "Trouble."

"What?"

Win said nothing, just kept staring. Myron turned and followed his gaze and felt his stomach drop.

It was Erik and Claire.

For a moment no one moved.

Win said, "You're blocking my sun again."

Myron saw Erik's face. There was rage there. Myron started toward them, but something made him stop. Claire put her hand on her husband's arm. She whispered something in his ear. Erik closed his eyes. She stepped toward Myron, her head high. Erik stayed back.

Claire walked toward Myron's door. He slid toward her.

Myron said, "You know I didn't—"

"Inside." Claire kept walking toward his front door. "I want you to tell me everything when we're inside."

Essex County prosecutor Ed Steinberg, Loren's boss, was waiting for her when she got back to the office.

"Well?"

She filled him in. Steinberg was a big man, soft in the middle, but he had that wanna-squeeze-him, teddy-bear thing going on. Of course he was married. It had been so long since Loren had met a desirable man who wasn't.

When she finished, Steinberg said, "I did a little more checking up on Bolitar. Did you know he and his friend Win used to do some work with the feds?"

"There were rumors," she said.

"I spoke to Joan Thurston." Thurston was the U.S. Attorney for the State of New Jersey. "A lot of it is hush-hush, I guess, but in sum, everyone thinks Win is several fries short of a Happy Meal—but that Bolitar is pretty straight."

"That's the vibe I got too," Loren said.

"You believe his story?"

"Overall, yeah, I guess I do. It's just too crazy. Plus,

as he sort of pointed out himself, would a guy with his experience be dumb enough to leave so many clues behind?"

"You think he's being framed?"

Loren made a face. "That doesn't jibe much either. Aimee Biel called him herself. She'd have to be in on it, I guess."

Steinberg folded his hands on his desk. His sleeves were rolled up. His forearms were big and covered with enough hair to count as fur. "Then odds are, what, she's a runaway?"

"Odds are," Loren said.

"And the fact that she used the same ATM as Katie Rochester?"

She shrugged. "I don't think it's a coincidence."

"Maybe they know each other."

"Not according to either set of parents."

"That doesn't mean anything," Steinberg said. "Parents don't know *bupkus* about their kids. Trust me here, I had teenage daughters. The moms and dads who claim they know everything about their kids usually know the least." He shifted in his chair. "Nothing found in the search of Bolitar's home or car?"

"They're still going through it," Loren said. "But what can they find? We know she was in the house and in the car."

"The locals handled the search?"

She nodded.

"Then let's let the locals handle the rest of it. We really don't even have a case yet anyway—the girl is of age, right?"

"Right."

"Good, then it's settled. Give it to the locals. I want you concentrating on these homicides in East Orange."

Steinberg told her more about the case. She listened

153

and tried to focus. This was a biggie, no doubt about it. A double murder. Maybe a major hit man back in the area. It was the kind of case she loved. It would take up all her time. She knew that. And she knew the odds. Aimee Biel had withdrawn cash before she called Myron. That meant that she had probably not been abducted, that she was probably just fine—and that either way, Loren Muse really shouldn't be involved anymore.

They say worrying and grief make you age, but with Claire Biel it was almost the opposite. Her skin was drawn tight around her cheekbones—so tight the blood seemed to stop flowing. There were no lines on her face. She was pale and almost skeletal.

Myron flashed back to an ordinary memory. Study hall, senior year. They would sit and talk and he would make her laugh. Claire was normally quiet, often subdued. She spoke with a soft voice. But when he got her going, when he worked in all her favorite routines from stupid movies, Claire would laugh so hard she'd start to cry. Myron wouldn't stop. He loved her laugh. He loved to see the pure joy when she let go like that.

Claire stared at him. Every once in a while you try to trace your life back to a time like that, when everything was so good. You try to go back and figure out how it started and the path you'd taken and how you ended up here, if there was a moment you could go back to and somehow alter and *poof*, you wouldn't be here, you'd be someplace better.

"Tell me," Claire said.

He did. He started with the party at his house, overhearing Aimee and Erin in the basement, the promise, the late-night phone call. He went through it all. He told her about the stop at the gas station. He even told her about Aimee talking about how things weren't great with her parents.

Claire's posture stayed rigid. She said nothing. There was a quake near her lips. Every once in a while she would close her eyes. There would be a slight wince, as if she spotted a coming blow but was unwilling to defend herself from it.

Neither spoke when he finished. Claire did not ask any follow-up questions. She just stood there and looked very frail. Myron took a step toward her, but he could see right away it was the wrong move.

"You know I'd never hurt her," he said.

She did not reply.

"Claire?"

"Do you remember that time we met up at Little Park by the circle?"

Myron waited a beat. "We met up there a lot, Claire."

"At the playground. Aimee was three years old. The Good Humor truck came along. You bought her a Toasted Almond Fudge."

"Which she hated."

Claire smiled. "You remember?"

"I do."

"Do you remember what I was like that day?"

He thought about it. "I don't know what you're trying to get at."

"Aimee didn't know her limits. She would try everything. She wanted to go on that high slide. There was a big ladder. She was too young for it. Or at least that's what I thought. She was my first child. I was so afraid all the time. But I couldn't stop her. So I let her climb the ladder, but I would stay right behind her, remember? You made a crack about it."

He nodded.

"Before she was born, I swore I'd never be one of those overprotective parents. Swore it. But Aimee is climbing up this ladder and I'm right behind her, my hands poised behind her butt. Just in case. Just in case she slipped because wherever you are, even someplace as innocent as a playground, all a parent imagines is the worst. I kept picturing her tiny foot missing a step. I kept seeing her fingers slipping off those rails and her little body tipping back and then she'd land on her head wrong and her neck would be at a bad angle . . ."

Her voice faded away.

"So I stayed behind her. And I was ready for anything."

Claire stopped and stared at him.

"I'd never hurt her," Myron said.

"I know," she said softly.

He should have felt relief at that. He didn't. There was something in her tone, something that kept him on the hook.

"You wouldn't harm her, I know that." Her eyes flared up. "But you're not blameless either."

He had no idea what to say to that.

"Why aren't you married?" she asked.

"What the hell does that have to do with anything?"

"You're one of the nicest, sweetest men I know. You love kids. You're straight. So why aren't you married yet?"

Myron held back. Claire was in shock, he told himself. Her daughter was missing. She was just lashing out.

"I think it's because you bring destruction, Myron. Wherever you go, people get hurt. I think that's why you've never been married."

"You think—what?—that I'm cursed?"

"No, nothing like that. But my little girl is gone."
Her voice was slow now, one weighted word at a time.
"You were the last to see her. You promised that you
would protect her."

He just stood there.

"You could have told me," she said.

"I promised—"

"Don't," she said, holding up her hand. "That's no
excuse. Aimee wouldn't have ever known. You could
have pulled me aside and said, 'Look, I told Aimee that
she could call me if she had a problem.' I'd have understood that. I'd have even liked it, because then I would
have still been there for her, like with the ladder. I would
have been able to protect her because that's what a parent does. A parent, Myron, not a family friend."

He wanted to defend himself, but the arguments
wouldn't come.

"But you didn't do that," she went on, her words
raining down on him. "Instead you promised that you
wouldn't tell her parents. Then you drove her somewhere and dropped her off, but you didn't watch out for
her like I would have. Do you understand that? You
didn't take care of my baby. And now she's gone."

He said nothing.

"What are you going to do about that?" she asked.

"What?"

"I asked you what you're going to do about it."

He opened his mouth, closed it, tried again. "I don't
know."

"Yeah, you do." Suddenly Claire's eyes seemed
focused and clear. "The police are going to do one of
two things. I can see it already. They're backing away.
Aimee took money out of an ATM machine before she
called you. So they're either going to dismiss her as a
runaway or they're going to think you were involved.

Or both. You helped her run maybe. You're her boyfriend. Either way, she's eighteen. They're not going to look hard. They're not going to find her. They'll have other priorities."

"What do you want me to do?"

"Find her."

"I don't save people. You yourself pointed that out."

"Then you better start now. My daughter is gone because of you. I hold you accountable."

Myron shook his head. But she was having none of it.

"You made her promise. Right here in this house. You made her promise. Now you do the same, dammit. Promise me you'll find my baby. Promise me you'll bring her home."

And a moment later—the truly final what-if?— Myron did.

Chapter 19

Ali Wilder had finally stopped thinking long enough about Myron's impending visit to call her editor, a man she generously referred to as Caligula.

"I just don't get this paragraph, Ali."

She bit back a sigh. "What about it, Craig?" Craig was the name her editor used when he introduced himself, but Ali was sure his real name was Caligula.

Before 9/11, Ali had a solid job with a major magazine in the city. After Kevin's death, there was no way she could keep it. Erin and Jack needed her home. She took a sabbatical and then became a freelance journalist, mostly writing for magazines. At first, everyone offered her jobs. She refused them out of what she now saw as stupid pride. She hated getting the "pity" assignments. She felt above it. She now regretted that.

Caligula cleared his throat, making a production about it, and read her paragraph out loud: "The closest town is Pahrump. Picture Pahrump, rhymes with dump, as what's left on the road if a buzzard ate Las Vegas and spit out the bad parts. Tackiness as art form. A bordello is made to look like a White Castle restaurant, which seems like a bad pun. Signs with giant cowboys compete with signs for fireworks stores, casinos, trailer parks, and beef jerky. All the cheese is American singles."

After a meaningful pause, Caligula said, "Let's start with the last line."

"Uh-huh."

"You say that the only cheese in the town is American singles?"

"Yes," Ali said.

"Are you sure?"

"Pardon me?"

"I mean, did you go to the supermarket?"

"No." Ali started gnawing on a fingernail. "It's not a statement of fact. I'm trying to give you a feel for the town."

"By writing untruths?"

Ali knew where this was going. She waited. Caligula did not disappoint.

"How do you know, Ali, they don't have some other kind of cheese in this town? Did you check all the super-market shelves? And even if you did, did you consider the fact that maybe someone shops in a neighboring town and brings other cheese into Pahrump? Or that maybe they order by mail service? Do you understand what I'm saying?"

Ali closed her eyes.

"We print that, about the American singles being the only cheese in town, and suddenly we get a call from the mayor and he says, 'Hey, that's not true. We have tons of varieties here. We have Gouda and Swiss and ched-dar and provolone—' "

"I get the point, Craig."

" 'And Roquefort and blue and mozzarella—' "

"Craig . . ."

"—and heck, what about cream?"

"Cream?"

"Cream cheese, for crying out loud. That's a kind of cheese, right? Cream cheese. Even a hickville place would have cream cheese. You see?"

"Right, uh-huh." More gnawing on the nail. "I see."

"So that line has to go." She could hear his pen go through it. "Now let's talk about the line before that, the one about trailer parks and beef jerky."

Caligula was short. Ali hated short editors. She used to joke about it with Kevin. Kevin had always been her first reader. His job was to tell her that whatever she had scribbled out was brilliant. Ali, like most writers, was insecure. She needed to hear his praise. Any criticism while she wrote paralyzed her. Kevin understood. So he would rave. And when she battled with her editors, especially those short of sight and stature like Caligula, Kevin always took her side.

She wondered if Myron would like her writing.

He had asked to see some of her pieces, but she'd been putting it off. The man had dated Jessica Culver, one of the top novelists in the country. Jessica Culver had been reviewed on the front page of *The New York Times Book Review*. Her books had been short-listed for every major literary award. And as if that weren't enough, as if Jessica Culver didn't have it all over Ali Wilder professionally, the woman was ridiculously gorgeous.

How could Ali possibly stack up against that?

The doorbell rang. She checked her watch. Too early for Myron.

"Craig, can I call you back?

Caligula sighed. "Fine, okay. In the meantime I'll just tweak this a bit."

She winced when he said that. There was an old joke about being left on a deserted island with an editor. You are starving. All you have left is a glass of orange juice. Days pass. You are near death. You are about to drink the juice when the editor grabs the glass from your hand and pees into it. You look at him, stunned. "There," the editor says, handing you the glass. "It just needed a little tweaking."

The bell rang again. Erin galloped down the stairs and yelled, "I'll get it."

Ali hung up. Erin opened the door. Ali saw her go rigid. She hurried her step.

There were two men at the door. They both held police badges.

"May I help you?" Ali said.

"Are you Ali and Erin Wilder?"

Ali's legs went rubbery. No, this wasn't a flashback of how she learned about Kevin. But there was still some sort of déjà vu here. She turned to her daughter. Erin's face was white.

"I'm Livingston police detective Lance Banner. This is Kasselton detective John Greenhall."

"What's this about?"

"We'd like to ask you both a few questions, if we might."

"What about?"

"Can we come in?"

"I'd like to know why you're here first."

Banner said, "We'd like to ask a few questions about Myron Bolitar."

Ali nodded, trying to figure this through. She turned to her daughter. "Erin, head upstairs for a little while and let me talk to the officers, okay?"

"Actually, uh, ma'am?"

It was Banner.

"Yes?"

"The questions we want to ask," he said, stepping through the door and motioning with his head toward Erin. "They're for your daughter, not you."

Myron stood in Aimee's bedroom.

The Biel house was walking distance from his. Claire and Erik had driven ahead of him. Myron talked to Win a few minutes, asked him if he could help track down whatever the police had on both Katie Rochester and Aimee. Then he followed on foot.

When Myron entered the house, Erik was already gone.

"He's driving around," Claire said, leading him down the corridor. "Erik thinks if he goes to where she hangs out, he can find her."

They stopped in front of Aimee's door. Claire opened it.

"What are you looking for?" she asked.

"Damned if I know," Myron said. "Did Aimee know a girl named Katie Rochester?"

"That's the other missing girl, right?"

"Yes."

"I don't think so. In fact, I asked her about it, you know, when she was on the news?"

"Right."

"Aimee said she'd seen her around but she didn't know her. Katie went to middle school at Mount Pleasant. Aimee went to Heritage. You remember how it is."

He did. By the time they both got to high school, their cliques were solidified.

"Do you want me to call around and ask her friends?"

"That might be helpful."

Neither of them moved for a moment.

Claire asked, "Should I leave you alone in here?"

"For now, yeah."

She did. She closed the door behind her. Myron looked around. He had told the truth—he didn't have a clue what he was looking for here—but he figured that it would be a good first step. This was a teenage girl. She had to keep secrets in her room, right?

It also felt right, being here. From the moment he'd made the promise to Claire, his entire perspective began to shift. His senses felt strangely attuned. It had been a while since he'd done this—investigate—but the memory muscle jumped in and took effect. Being in the girl's room brought it all back to him. In basketball, you need to get into the zone to do your best. Doing this kind of thing, there was a similar feel. Being here, in the victim's room, did that. Put him in the zone.

There were two guitars in the room. Myron didn't know anything about instruments, but one was clearly electric, the other acoustic. There was a poster of Jimi Hendrix on the wall. Guitar picks were encased in Lucite blocks. Myron read through them. They were collector's picks. One belonged to Keith Richards—others to Nils Lofgren, Eric Clapton, Buck Dharma.

Myron almost smiled. The girl had good taste.

The computer was already on, a screen saver of a fish tank rolling by. Myron wasn't a computer expert, but he knew enough to get started. Claire had given him Aimee's password and told him about Erik going through the e-mail. He checked it anyway. He brought up AOL and signed on.

Yep, all the e-mail had been deleted.

He hit Windows Explorer and put her files in date order, to see what she had worked on most recently.

Aimee had been writing songs. He thought about that, about this creative young woman, about where she was now. He scanned through the most recent word processing documents. Nothing special. He tried checking her downloads. There were some recent photographs. He opened them. Aimee with a bunch of school pals, he guessed. Nothing obviously special about them either, but maybe he'd have Claire take a look.

Teens, he knew, were huge with instant messaging online. From the relative calm of their computers, they had conversations with dozens of people sometimes at the same time. Myron knew plenty of parents who whined about this, but in his day, they'd spent hours tying up the phone gossiping with one another. Was IMing any worse?

He brought up her buddy list. There were at least fifty screen names like SpazaManiacJack11, MSG Watkins, and YoungThangBlaine742. Myron printed them out. He'd let Claire and Erik go through them with one of Aimee's friends, see if there was a name that didn't belong, that none of them knew about. It was a long shot, but it would keep them busy.

He let go of the computer mouse and started to search the old-fashioned way. The desk came first. He went through her drawers. Pens, papers, note cards, spare batteries, a smattering of computer software CDs. Nothing personal. There were several receipts from a place called Planet Music. Myron checked the guitars. They had Planet Music stickers on the back.

Big wow.

He moved to the next drawer. More nothing.

In the third drawer, Myron saw something that made him stop. He reached down and gently lifted it into view. He smiled. Protected in a plastic sleeve . . . it was Myron's rookie basketball card. He stared at his younger self. Myron remembered the photo shoot. He had done several dumb poses—taking a jump shot, pretending to pass, the old-fashioned triple-threat position—but they'd settled for one of him bending down and dribbling. The background was an empty arena. In the picture he wore his green Boston Celtics jersey—one of maybe five times he got to wear it in his entire life. The card company had printed up several thousand before his injury. They were collector's items now.

It was nice to know Aimee had one, though he wondered what the police might make of it.

He put it back in the drawer. His fingerprints would be on it now, but then again they would be all over the room. Didn't matter. He pressed on. He wanted to find a diary. That was what you always saw in the movies. The girl writes a diary, and it talks about her secret boyfriend and double life and all that. That worked in fiction. It wasn't happening for him in reality.

He hit an undergarments drawer. He felt yucky but he persevered. If she was going to hide anything, this could be the place. But there was nothing. Her tastes seemed on the wholesome side for a teenage girl. Tank tops were as bad as it got. Near the bottom, however, he found something particularly racy. He pulled it into view. There was a tag on it from a mall lingerie store called Bedroom Rendezvous. It was white, sheer, and looked like something out of a nurse fantasy. He frowned and wondered what to make of it.

There was a smattering of bobble-head dolls. An iPod with white earbuds was lounged out on the bed. He checked the tunes. She had Aimee Mann on there. He took that as a small victory. He'd given her Aimee Mann's *Lost in Space* a few years back, thinking the first name might pique her interest. Now he could see that she had five of Aimee Mann's CDs. He liked that.

There were photographs stuck onto a mirror. They were all group pictures—Aimee with a slew of girlfriends. There were two of the volleyball team, one in classic team pose, another a celebration shot taken after they'd won the counties. There were several pictures of her high school rock band, Aimee playing lead guitar. He looked at her face while she played. Her smile was heartbreaking, but what girl that age doesn't have a heartbreaking smile?

He found her yearbook. He started paging through it. Yearbooks had come a long way since he'd graduated. For one thing, they included a DVD. Myron would watch it, he guessed, if he had the time. He looked up Katie Rochester's entry. He'd seen that photograph before, on the news. He read about her. She'd miss hanging with Betsy and Craig and Saturday nights at the Ritz Diner. Nothing significant. He turned to Aimee Biel's page. Aimee mentioned a whole bunch of her friends; her favorite teachers, Miss Korty and Mr. D; her volleyball coach, Mr. Grady; and all the girls on the team. She ended with, "Randy, you've made the past two years so special. I know we'll be together always."

Good ol' Randy.

He checked out Randy's entry. He was a good-looking kid with wild, almost Rastafarian curls. He had a soul patch and a big white smile. He talked mostly about sports in his write-up. He mentioned Aimee too, how much she'd "enriched" his time in high school.

Hmm.

Myron thought about that, looked again at the mirror, and for the first time wondered if perhaps he'd stumbled across a clue.

Claire opened the door. "Anything?"

Myron pointed to the mirror. "This."

"What about it?"

"How often do you come in this room?"

She frowned. "A teenager lives here."

"Would that mean rarely?"

"Pretty much never."

"Does she do her own laundry?"

"She's a teenager, Myron. She does nothing."

"So who does it?"

"We have a live-in. Her name is Rosa. Why?"

"The photographs," he said.

"What about them?"

"She has a boyfriend named Randy, right?"

"Randy Wolf. He's a sweet kid."

"And they've been together awhile?"

"Since sophomore year. Why?"

Again he gestured to the mirror. "There are no pictures of him. I looked all over the room. No photos of him anywhere. That's why I was asking about when you were last in the room." He looked back at her. "Did there used to be?"

"Yes."

He pointed to several blank spots on the bottom of the mirror. "This all looks out of sequence, but I bet she removed the pictures from here."

"But they just went to the prom together, what, three nights ago."

Myron shrugged. "Maybe they had a big fight there."

"You said Aimee looked emotional when you picked her up, right?"

"Right."

"Maybe they'd just broken up," Claire said.

"Could be," Myron said. "Except she hasn't been home since then, and the photographs on the mirror are gone. That would imply that they broke up at least a day or two before I picked her up. One more thing."

Claire waited. Myron showed her the lingerie from Bedroom Rendezvous. "Have you seen this before?"

"No. You found it in here?"

Myron nodded. "Bottom of the drawer. It looks unworn. The tag is still on it."

Claire went quiet.

"What?"

"Erik was telling the police how Aimee's been acting strangely lately. I fought him on it, but the truth is, she has. She's grown very secretive."

"Do you know what else struck me about this room?"

"What?"

"Forgetting this lingerie—which might be relevant and might be nothing—the opposite of what you just said: There is almost nothing secretive in here. I mean, she's a high school senior. There should be something, right?"

Claire considered that. "Why do you think that is?"

"It's like she's working hard to hide something. We need to check other places where she might have kept personal stuff, someplace that you and Erik wouldn't think to snoop. Like her school locker maybe."

"Should we do that now?"

"I think it'd be better to talk to Randy first."

She frowned. "His father."

"What about him?"

"His name is Jake. Big Jake, everyone calls him. He's bigger than you. And the wife is a flirt. Last year Big Jake got into a fight at one of Randy's football games. Beat this poor guy senseless in front of his kids. He's a total putz."

"Total?"

"Total."

"Whew." Myron pantomimed wiping the sweat off his brow. "A partial putz, I mind. A total putz—that's my bag."

Chapter 20

Randy Wolf lived in the new Laurel Road section. The brand-new estates of brushed brick had more square footage than Kennedy Airport. There was a faux wrought-iron gate. The gate was open enough for Myron to walk through. The grounds were over-landscaped, the lawn so green it looked like someone had gone overboard with spray paint. There were three SUVs parked in the driveway. Next to them, gleaming from a fresh waxing and seemingly perfect sun placement, sat a little red Corvette. Myron started humming the matching Prince tune. He couldn't help it.

The familiar whack of a tennis ball drifted in from the backyard. Myron headed toward the sound. There were four lithe ladies playing tennis. They all wore ponytails and tight tennis whites. Myron was a big fan of women in tennis whites. One of the lithe ladies was about to serve when she noticed him. She had great legs, Myron observed. He checked again. Yep, great.

Ogling tan legs probably wasn't a clue, but why chance it?

Myron waved and gave the woman serving his best smile. She returned it and signaled to the ladies to excuse her for a moment. She jogged toward him. Her dark ponytail bounced. She stopped very close to him. Her breathing was deep. Sweat made the tennis whites cling. It also made them a little see-through—again Myron was just being observant—but she didn't seem to care.

"Something I can do for you?"

She had one hand on her hip.

"Hi, my name is Myron Bolitar."

Commandment Four from the Bolitar Book on Smoothness: Wow the ladies with a dazzling first line.

"Your name," she said. "It rings a bell."

Her tongue moved around a lot when she talked.

"Are you Mrs. Wolf?"

"Call me Lorraine."

Lorraine Wolf had that way of speaking where everything sounded like a double entendre.

"I'm looking for your son, Randy."

"Wrong reply," she said.

"Sorry."

"You were supposed to say that I looked too young to be Randy's mother."

"Too obvious," Myron said. "An intelligent woman like you would have seen right through that."

"Nice recovery."

"Thanks."

The other ladies gathered by the net. They had towels draped around their necks and were drinking something green.

"Why are you looking for Randy?" she asked.

"I need to talk to him."

"Well, yes, I figured that out. But maybe you could tell me what this is about?"

The back door opened with an audible bang. A large man—Myron was six-four, two-fifteen and this guy had at least two inches and thirty pounds on him—stepped out the door.

Big Jake Wolf, Myron deducted, was in da house.

His black hair was slicked back. He had a mean squint going.

"Wait, isn't that Steven Seagal?" Myron asked, sotto voce.

Lorraine Wolf smothered a giggle.

Big Jake stomped over. He kept glaring at Myron. Myron waited a few seconds, then he winked and gave Big Jake the Stan Laurel, five-finger wave. Big Jake did not look pleased. He marched to Lorraine's side, put his arm around her, tugged her tight against his hip.

"Hi, honey," he said, his eyes still on Myron.

"Well, hi, back!" Myron said.

"I wasn't talking to you."

"Then why were you looking at me?"

Big Jake frowned and pulled his wife closer. Lorraine cringed a little, but she let him. Myron had seen this act before. Raging insecurity, he suspected. Jake released his glare long enough to kiss his wife's cheek before retightening his grip. Then he started glaring again, holding his wife firmly against his side.

Myron wondered if Big Jake was going to pee on her to mark his territory.

"Go back to your game, honey. I'll handle this."

"We were just finishing anyway."

"Then why don't you ladies go inside and have a drink, hmm?"

He let her go. She looked relieved. The ladies walked down the path. Myron again checked their legs. Just in case. The women smiled at him.

"Hey, what are you looking for?" Big Jake snapped.

"Potential clues," Myron said.

"What?"

Myron turned back to him. "Never mind."

"So what do you want here?"

"My name is Myron Bolitar."

"So?"

"Good comeback."

"What?"

"Never mind."

"You some kind of comedian?"

"I prefer the term 'comic actor.' Comedians are always typecast."

"What the . . . ?" Big Jake stopped, got his bearings. "You always do this?"

"Do what?"

"Stop by uninvited?"

"It's the only way people will have me," Myron said.

Big Jake squinted a little more. He wore tight jeans and a silk shirt that had one too many buttons open. There was a gold chain enmeshed in chest hair. "Stayin' Alive" wasn't playing in the background, but it should have been.

"Wild stab in the dark here," Myron said. "The red Corvette. It's yours, right?"

He glared some more. "What do you want?"

"I'd like to speak to your son, Randy."

"Why?"

"I'm here on behalf of the Biel family."

That made him blink. "So?"

"Are you aware that their daughter is missing?"

"So?"

"That 'so' line. It never gets old, Jake, really. Aimee Biel is missing and I'd like to ask your son about it."

"He has nothing to do with that. He was home Saturday night."

"Alone?"

"No. I was with him."

"How about Lorraine? Was she there too? Or was she out for the evening?"

Big Jake didn't like Myron using his wife's first name. "None of your business."

"Be that as it may, I'd still like to talk to Randy."

"No."

"Why not?"

"I don't want Randy mixed up in this."

"In what?"

"Hey," he pointed at Myron, "I don't like your attitude."

"You don't?" Myron gave him the wide game-show-host smile and waited. Big Jake looked confused. "Is this better? Rosier, am I right?"

"Get out."

"I would say, 'Who's going to make me,' but really, that would be sooo expected."

Big Jake smiled and stepped right up to Myron. "You wanna know who's going to make you?"

"Wait, hold on, let me check the script." Myron mimed flipping pages. "Okay here it is. I say, 'No, who?' Then you say, 'I am.' "

"Got that straight."

"Jake?"

"What?"

"Are any of your children home?" Myron asked.

"Why? What's that gotta do with anything?"

"Lorraine, well, she already knows you're a little man," Myron said, not moving an inch, "but I'd hate to beat your ass in front of your kids."

Jake's breathing turned into a snort. He didn't back up, but he was having trouble holding the eye contact. "Ah, you ain't worth it."

Myron rolled his eyes, but he bit back the that's-the-next-line-in-the-script rejoinder. Maturity.

"Anyway, my son broke up with that slut."

"By slut, you mean . . . ?"

"Aimee. He dumped her."

"When?"

"Three, four months ago. He was done with her."

"They went to the prom together last week."

"That was for show."

"For show?"

He shrugged. "I'm not surprised any of this happened."

"Why do you say that, Jake?"

"Because Aimee was no good. She was a slut."

Myron felt his blood tick. "And why do you say that?"

"I know her, okay? I know the whole family. My son has a bright future. He's going to Dartmouth in the fall, and I want nothing getting in the way of that. So listen to me, Mr. Basketball. Yeah, I know who you are. You think you're such hot stuff. Big, tough basketball stud who never made it to the pros. Big-time All-American who crapped out in the end. Who couldn't hack it once the going got tough."

Big Jake grinned.

"Wait, is this the part where I break down and cry?" Myron asked.

Big Jake put his finger on Myron's chest. "You just stay the hell away from my son, you understand me? He has nothing to do with that slut's disappearance."

Myron's hand shot forward. He grabbed Jake by the balls, and squeezed. Jake's eyes flew open. Myron positioned his body so that nobody could see what he was doing. Then he leaned in so he could whisper in Jake's ear.

"We're not going to call Aimee that anymore, are we, Jake? Feel free to nod."

Big Jake nodded. His face was turning purple. Myron closed his eyes, cursed himself, let go. Jake sucked in a deep breath, staggered back, dropped to one knee. Myron felt like a dope, losing control like that.

"Hey, look, I'm just trying to—"

"Get out," Jake hissed. "Just . . . just leave me alone."

And this time, Myron obeyed.

From the front seat of a Buick Skylark, the Twins watched Myron walk down the Wolfs' driveway.

"There's our boy."

"Yep."

They weren't really twins. They weren't even brothers. They didn't look alike. They did share a birthday, September 24, but Jeb was eight years older than Orville. That was part of how they got the name—having the same birthday. The other was how they met: at a Minnesota Twins baseball game. Some would claim that it was a sadistic turn of fate or ridiculously bad star alignment that brought them together. Others would claim that there was a bond there, two lost souls that recognized a kindred spirit, as if their streak of cruelty and psychosis were some kind of magnet that drew them to each other.

Jeb and Orville met in the bleachers at the Dome in Minneapolis when Jeb, the older Twin, got into a fight with five beer-marinated head cases. Orville stepped in and together they put all five in the hospital. That was eight years ago. Three of the guys were still in comas.

Jeb and Orville stayed together.

These two men, both life-loners, neither married,

never in a long-term relationship, became inseparable. They moved around from city to city, town to town, always leaving havoc in their wake. For fun, they would enter bars and pick fights and see how close they could come to killing a man without actually killing him. When they destroyed a drug-dealing motorcycle gang in Montana, their rep was cemented.

Jeb and Orville did not look dangerous. Jeb wore an ascot and smoking jacket. Orville had the Woodstock thing going on—a ponytail, scruffy facial hair, pink-tinted glasses, and a tie-dyed shirt. They sat in the car and watched Myron.

Jeb began singing, as he always did, mixing English songs with his own Spanish interpretation. Right now he was singing the Police's "Message in a Bottle."

"I hope that someone gets my, I hope that someone gets my, I hope that someone gets my, *mensaje en una botella* . . ."

"I like that one, dude," Orville said.

"Thank you, *mi amigo*."

"Man, you were younger, you should do that *American Idol*. That Spanish thing. They'd love that. Even that Simon judge who hates everything."

"I love Simon."

"Me too. The dude is far out."

They watched Myron get into his car.

"So, like, what do you think he was doing at this house?" Orville asked.

Singing: "You ask me if our love would grow, *yo no se, yo no se*."

"The Beatles, right?"

"Bingo."

"And *yo no se*. I don't know."

"Right again."

"Groovy." Orville checked the car's clock. "Should

we call Rochester and tell him what's shaking?"

Jeb shrugged. "Might as well."

Myron Bolitar started driving. They followed. Rochester picked up on the second ring.

"He, like, left that house," Orville said.

Rochester said, "Keep following him."

"Your dollars," Orville said with a shrug. "But I think it's a waste, man."

"He may give you a clue where he stashed the girls."

"If we, like, snatch his ass now, he'll give us all the clues he knows."

There was a moment of hesitation. Orville smiled and gave Jeb a thumbs-up sign.

"I'm at his house," Rochester said. "That's where I want you to take him."

"Are you at or in?"

"At or in what?"

"His house."

"I'm outside. In my car."

"So you don't know if he's got a plasma TV."

"What? No, I don't know."

"If we're going to be working him awhile, it'd be righteous if he had one. In case it gets to be a drag, you know what I'm saying? The Yankees are playing against Boston. Jeb and me dig watching in HD. That's why I'm asking."

There was another moment of hesitation.

"Maybe he has one," Rochester said.

"That would be groovy. That DLP technology is good too. Anything with high-def, I guess. By the way, do you, like, got a plan or anything?"

"I'm going to wait until he comes back home," Dominick Rochester said. "I'll tell him I want to talk to him. We go inside. You go inside."

"Radical."

"Where is he going now?"

Orville checked the navigator on the car. "Hey, like, unless I'm mistaken, we're heading back to Bolitar's crib right now."

Chapter 21

Myron was two blocks from home when the cell rang.

Win asked, "Did I ever tell you about Cingle Shaker?"

"No."

"She's a private eye. If she were any hotter, your teeth would melt."

"That's swell, really."

"I've had her," Win said.

"Good for you."

"I went back for seconds. And we still talk."

"Yikes," Myron said.

Win still talking to a woman he'd slept with more than once—in human terms, that was like a marriage celebrating its silver anniversary.

"Is there a reason you're sharing this warm moment with me right now?" Then Myron remembered something. "Wait, a private eye named Cingle. Hester Crimstein called her when I was being interrogated, right?"

"Exactly. Cingle has gathered some new information on the disappearances."

"You set up a meet?"

"She's waiting for you at Baumgart's."

Baumgart's, long Myron's favorite restaurant serving both Chinese and American dishes, had recently opened a branch in Livingston.

"How will I recognize her?"

"Hot enough to make your teeth melt," Win said. "How many women at Baumgart's fit that description?"

Win hung up. Five minutes later Myron entered the restaurant. Cingle didn't disappoint. She was curvy to the max, built like a Marvel comic drawing come to life. Myron walked up to Peter Chin, the owner, to say hello. Peter frowned at him.

"What?"

"She's not Jessica," Peter said.

Myron and Jessica used to go to Baumgart's, albeit the original in Englewood, all the time. Peter had never gotten over the breakup. The unspoken rule was that Myron was not allowed to bring other women here. For seven years he had kept that rule, more for himself than Peter.

"It's not a date."

Peter looked at Cingle, looked at Myron, made a face that said *Who are you kidding?*

"It's not." Then: "You realize, of course, I haven't even seen Jessica in years."

Peter put a finger in the air. "Years fly by, but the heart stays in the same place."

"Damn."

"What?"

"You've been reading fortune cookies again, haven't you?"

"There is much wisdom there."

"Tell you what. Read Sunday's *New York Times* instead. Styles section."

"I already did."

"And?"

Again Peter raised his finger. "You can't ride two horses with one behind."

"Hey, I told you that one. It's Yiddish."

"I know."

"And it doesn't apply."

"Just sit down." Peter dismissed him with a wave. "And order for yourself. I'm not helping you."

When Cingle stood to greet him, necks didn't so much turn in her direction as snap. They exchanged hellos and sat down.

"So you're Win's friend," Cingle said.

"I am."

She studied him for a moment. "You don't look psychotic."

"I like to think of myself as the counterbalance."

There were no papers in front of her.

"Do you have the police file?" he asked.

"There is none. There isn't even an official investigation yet."

"So what have you got?"

"Katie Rochester started taking money out at ATMs. Then she ran away. There is no evidence, other than parental protestations, to suggest anything other than that."

"The investigator who grabbed me at the airport—" Myron began.

"Loren Muse. She's good, by the way."

"Right, Muse. She asked me a lot about Katie Rochester. I think they have something solid linking me to her."

"Yes and no. They have something solid linking Katie to Aimee. I'm not sure it links directly to you."

"That being?"

"Their last ATM charges."

"What about them?"

"Both girls used the exact same Citibank in Manhattan."

Myron stopped, tried to absorb that one.

The waiter came over. New guy. Myron didn't know him. Usually Peter had the waiter bring over a few free appetizers. Not today.

"I'm used to men staring at me," Cingle said. "But the owner keeps glaring at me like I urinated on the floor."

"He misses my old girlfriend."

"That's sweet."

"Adorable."

Cingle met Peter's eye, wiggled her fingers to show a wedding band, and yelled in Peter's direction, "He's safe. I'm already married."

Peter turned away.

Cingle shrugged, explained about the ATM charge, about Aimee's face being clear in the security camera. Myron tried to figure it through. Nothing came to him.

"There's one more thing you might want to know about."

Myron waited.

"There's a woman named Edna Skylar. She's a doctor over at St. Barnabas. The cops are keeping this under heavy wraps because Rochester's father is a nutjob, but apparently, Dr. Skylar spotted Katie Rochester on the street in Chelsea."

She told him the story, about how Edna Skylar had followed the girl into the subway, that she was with a man, what Katie said about not telling anyone.

"Did the police look into it?"

"Look into what?"

"Did they try to figure out where Katie was, who the guy was, anything?"

"Why? Katie Rochester is eighteen years old. She gathered money before she ran. She's got a connected father who was probably abusive in some fashion. The police have other things to worry about. Real crimes. Muse is handling a double homicide in East Orange. Manpower is short. And what Edna Skylar saw confirmed what they already knew."

"That Katie Rochester ran away."

"Right."

Myron sat back. "And the fact that they both used the same ATM?"

"Either a startling coincidence . . ."

Myron shook his head. "No way."

"I agree. No way. So either that or they both planned to run away. There was a reason they both chose that ATM. I don't know what. But maybe they planned this together. Katie and Aimee went to the same high school, right?"

"Right, but I haven't found any other connection between them."

"Both eighteen, both graduating high school, both from the same town." Cingle shrugged. "There has to be something."

She was right. He'd need to speak to the Rochesters, see what they knew. He'd have to be careful. He didn't want to open that side of things up. He also wanted to talk to the doctor, Edna Skylar, get a good description of the man Katie Rochester was with, see exactly where she was, what subway she was riding, what direction she was heading in.

"Thing is," Cingle said, "if Katie and Aimee are runaways, there might be a reason they ran."

"I was just thinking the same thing," Myron said.

"They might not want to be found."

"True."

"What are you going to do?"

"Find them anyway."

"And if they want to stay hidden?"

Myron thought about Aimee Biel. He thought about Erik and he thought about Claire. Good people. Reliable, solid. He wondered what could possibly make Aimee run away from them, what could have been so bad that she'd pull something like this.

"Guess I'll cross that bridge when I get to it," he said.

Win sat by himself in the corner of the dimly lit strip club. No one bothered him. They knew better. If he wanted someone near him, he'd let them know.

The song on the jukebox was one of the most putrid songs from the eighties, Mr. Mister's "Broken Wings." Myron claimed that it was the worst song of the decade. Win countered that "We Built This City on Rock-n-Roll" by Starship was worse. The argument lasted an hour without resolution. So, as they often did in situations like this, they went to Esperanza to end the tie-breaker, but she sided with "Too Shy" by Kajagoogoo.

Win liked to sit in this corner booth and look out and think.

There was a major-league baseball team in town. Several of the players had come to the "gentlemen's club," a truly inspired euphemism for strip joint, to unwind. The working girls went crazy. Win watched a stripper of questionably legal age hit on one of the team's top pitchers.

"How old did you say you were?" the stripper asked.

"Twenty-nine," the pitcher said.

"Wow." She shook her head. "You don't look *that* old."

A wistful smile played on Win's lips. Youth.

Windsor Horne Lockwood III was born to great wealth. He did not pretend otherwise. He did not like multibillionaires who bragged about their business acumen when they'd started out with Daddy's billions. Genius is almost irrelevant in the pursuit of enormous riches anyway. In fact, it can be a hindrance. If you are smart enough to see the risks, you might try to avoid them. That type of thinking—safe thinking—never led to great wealth.

Win started life in the lush Main Line of Philadelphia. His family had been on the board of the stock exchange since its inception. He had a direct descendant who'd been this country's first secretary of the treasury. Win was born with not only a silver spoon in his mouth, but an entire silver place setting at his feet.

And he looked the part.

That had been his problem. From his earliest years, with his tow-head blond hair and ruddy complexion and delicate features, with his face naturally set in an expression that looked smug, people detested Win on sight. You looked at Windsor Horne Lockwood III and you saw elitism, undeserved wealth, someone who would always look down his porcelain-sculpted nose at you. All your own failures rose up in a wave of resentment and envy—just by gazing upon this seemingly soft, coddled, privileged boy.

It had led to ugly incidents.

At the age of ten Win had gotten separated from his mother at the Philadelphia Zoo. A group of students from an inner-city school had found him in his little blue blazer with the crest on the pocket and beaten the hell out of him. He'd been hospitalized and nearly lost a kidney. The physical pain was bad. The shame of being a scared little boy was far worse.

Win never wanted to experience that again.

People, Win knew, made snap judgments based on appearances. No great insight there. And yes, there were the obvious prejudices against African-Americans or Jews or what-have-you. But Win was more concerned with the more garden-variety prejudices. If, for example, you see an overweight woman eating a doughnut, you are repulsed. You make snap judgments—she is undisciplined, lazy, sloppy, probably stupid, definitely lacking in self-esteem.

In a strange way, the same thing happened when people saw Win.

He had a choice. Stay behind the hedges, safe in the cocoon of privilege, live a protected albeit fearful life. Or do something about it.

He chose the latter.

Money makes everything easier. Oddly enough, Win always considered Myron to be a real-life Batman, but the Caped Crusader had started off as Win's childhood role model. Bruce Wayne's only superpower was tremendous wealth. He used it to train himself to be a crime fighter. Win did something similar with his money. He hired former squad leaders from both Delta Force and the Green Berets to train him as if he were one of their most elite. Win also found the world's top instructors on firearms, on knives, on hand-to-hand combat. He secured the services of martial artists from a wide variety of countries and either flew them to the family estate in Bryn Mawr or traveled overseas. He spent a full year with a reclusive martial-arts master in

Korea, high in the hills in the southern part of the country. He learned about pain, how to inflict it without leaving marks. He learned about intimidation tactics. He learned about electronics, about locks, about the underworld, about security procedures.

It all came together. Win was a sponge when it came to picking up new techniques. He worked hard, ridiculously hard, training at least five hours every day. He had naturally fast hands, the hunger, the desire, the work ethic, the coldness—all the ingredients.

The fear went away.

Once he was sufficiently trained, Win started hanging out in the most drug-infested, crime-ridden corners of the city. He would go there wearing blue blazers with crests or pink polos or loafers without socks. The bad people would see him and lick their lips. There would be hate in their eyes. They would attack. And Win would answer.

There may be better fighters out there, Win assumed, especially now that he was growing older.

But not many.

His cell phone rang. He picked it up and said, "Articulate."

"We got a wiretap on a guy named Dominick Rochester."

The call was from an old colleague Win hadn't heard from in three years. No matter. This was how it worked in their world. The wiretap did not surprise him. Rochester was supposedly connected. "Go on."

"Someone leaked to him your friend Bolitar's connection to his daughter."

Win waited.

"Rochester has a more secure phone. We're not sure. But we think he called the Twins."

There was silence.

"Do you know them?"

"Just by reputation," Win said.

"Take what you heard and put it on steroids. One of them has some kind of weird condition. He doesn't feel pain, but man, does he like to inflict it. The other one, his name is Jeb—and yeah, I know how this is going to sound—he likes to bite."

"Do tell," Win said.

"We once found some guy the Twins worked over with just Jeb's teeth. The body . . . I mean, it was a red puddle. He bit out the guy's eyes, Win. I still don't sleep when I think about it."

"Maybe you should buy a night-light."

"Don't think I haven't thought of it. They scare me," the voice on the phone said, "like you scare me."

Win knew that in this man's world, that was about as big a compliment as he could pay the Twins. "And you believe that Rochester called them right after he heard about Myron Bolitar?"

"Within minutes, yeah."

"Thank you for the information."

"Win, listen to what I'm saying. They're absolutely nuts. We know about this one guy, a big old mafia don from Kansas City. He hired them. Anyway, it didn't work out. The mafia don pisses them off, I don't know how. So the don, no fool, he tries to buy them off, make peace. Nothing doing. The Twins get a hold of his four-year-old grandson. Four years old, Win. They send him back in chewed-up pieces. Then—get this—*after* they're done, then they accept the don's money. The *same* amount of money he'd already offered. They didn't ask for a penny more. Do you understand what I'm telling you?"

Win hung up. There was no need to reply. He understood perfectly.

Chapter 22

M yron had his cell phone in hand, preparing to call Ali for a much-needed hello, when he noticed a car parked in front of his house. Myron pocketed the cell and pulled into his driveway. A husky man sat on the curb in front of Myron's yard. He stood when Myron approached. "Myron Bolitar?"

"Yes."

"I'd like to talk to you."

Myron nodded. "Why don't we go inside?"

"You know who I am?"

"I know who you are."

It was Dominick Rochester. Myron recognized him from the news reports on TV. He had a ferocious face with pores big enough to get your foot caught in. The smell of cheap musk came off him in squiggly line waves. Myron held his breath. He wondered how Rochester had learned about Myron's connection to the case, but no matter. This would work well, Myron figured. He had wanted to talk to Rochester anyway.

Myron was not sure when the feeling came upon

him. It could have been when the other car made the turn. It could have been something in Dominick Rochester's walk. Myron could see right away that Rochester was the real deal—a bad guy you did not want to mess with, as opposed to that poser, Big Jake Wolf.

But again it was a bit like basketball. There were moments when Myron was so in the game, where he would be rising on his jump shot, his fingers finding the exact grooves on the ball, his hand cocked in front of his forehead, his eyes locked on the rim, only the rim, when time would slow down, as if he could stop in midair and readjust and see the rest of the court.

Something was wrong here.

Myron stopped at the door, keys in hand. He turned and looked back at Rochester. Rochester had those black eyes, the kind that view everything with an equal lack of emotion—a human being, a dog, a file cabinet, a mountain range. They never changed no matter what they saw, no matter what horror or delight played out in front of them.

"Why don't we talk out here?" Myron said.

Rochester shrugged. "If you want."

The car, a Buick Skylark, slowed.

Myron felt his cell phone vibrate. He looked down at it. Win's SWEET CHEEKS was displayed. He put the phone to his ear.

Win said, "There are two very bad hombres—"

That was when Myron was jarred by the blow.

Rochester had thrown a punch.

The fist skimmed across the top of Myron's head. The instincts were rusty, but Myron still had his peripheral vision. He'd seen Rochester launch the fist at the last second. He ducked in time to take away the brunt. The blow ended up glancing across the top of Myron's skull. There was pain, but Rochester's knuckles probably felt worse.

The phone fell to the ground.

Myron was down on one knee. He grabbed Rochester's extended arm by the wrist. He curled the fingers of his free hand. Most people hit with fists. That was necessary at times, but in reality you should avoid doing it. You hit something hard with a fist, you'll break your hand.

The palm strike, especially to vulnerable areas, was usually more effective. With a punch, you need to flick or jab. You can't power straight through, because the small bones in the hand can't handle the stress. But if the palm strike is delivered correctly, fingers curled and protected, the wrist tilted back, the blow landing on the meaty bottom of the palm, you put the pressure on the radius, the ulna, the humerus—in short, the larger arm bones.

That was what Myron did. The obvious place to aim right now was the groin, but Myron figured that Rochester had been in plenty of scrapes before. He'd be looking for that.

And he was. Rochester raised a knee for protection.

Myron went for the diaphragm instead. When the shot landed just below the sternum, the air burst out of the big man. Myron pulled on Rochester's arm and threw him in what looked like an awkward judo throw. Truth was, in real fights, all throws look pretty awkward.

The zone. He was in it now. Everything slowed down.

Rochester was still in the air when Myron saw the car stop. Two men came out. Rochester landed like a sack of rocks. Myron stood. The two men were moving toward him now.

They were both smiling.

Rochester rolled through the throw. He'd be up in no time. Then there would be three of them. The two men in the car did not approach slowly. They did not look wary or worried. They charged toward Myron with the abandon of children playing a game.

Two very bad hombres . . .

Another second passed.

The man who'd been on the passenger side wore his hair in a ponytail and looked liked that hip, middle-school art teacher who always smelled like a bong. Myron ran through his options. He did this in tenths of a second. That was how it worked. When you're in danger, time either slows down or the mind races. Hard to say which.

Myron thought about Rochester lying on the ground, about the two men charging, about Win's warning, about what Rochester might be after here, about why he might attack unprovoked, about what Cingle had said about Rochester being a nutjob.

The answer was obvious: Dominick Rochester thought that Myron had something to do with his daughter's disappearance.

Rochester probably knew that Myron had been questioned by the police, and that nothing had come of it. A guy like Rochester wouldn't accept that. So he'd do his best, his damned best, to see if he could shake something loose.

The two men were maybe three steps away now.

Another point: They were willing to attack him right here, on the street, where anyone could see. That suggested a certain level of desperation and recklessness and, yes, confidence—a level Myron wanted no part of.

So Myron made his choice: He ran.

The two men had the advantage. They were already

accelerating. Myron was starting from a standing position.

This was where pure athleticism would help.

Myron's knee injury had not really affected his speed much. It was more a question of lateral movement. So Myron faked a step to the right, just to get them to lean. They did. Then he broke left toward his driveway. One of the men—the other one, not the hippy art teacher—lost his footing but only for a split second. He was back up. So was Dominick Rochester.

But it was the hippy art teacher who was causing the most trouble. The man was fast. He was almost close enough to make a diving tackle.

Myron debated taking him on.

But no. Win had called in a warning. If it had reached that level, this was probably indeed a very bad hombre. He wouldn't go down with one blow. And even if he did, the delay would give the other two the chance to catch up. There was no way to eliminate the art teacher and keep moving.

Myron tried to accelerate. He wanted to gain enough distance to get Win on the cell phone and tell him—

The cell phone. Damn, he didn't have it. He'd dropped it when Rochester hit him.

They kept chasing him. Here they were, on a quiet suburban street, four adults running all-out. Was anybody watching? What would they think?

Myron had another advantage: He knew the neighborhood.

He didn't look over his shoulder, but he could hear the art teacher panting behind him. You don't become a professional athlete—and brief as his career was, he did play professional ball—without having a million things go right internally and externally. Myron had grown up in Livingston. His high school class had six hundred people in it. There had been zillions of great athletes going through the doors. None had made the pros. Two or three had played minor league baseball. One, maybe two, had been drafted for one sport or another. That was it. Every kid dreams about it, but the truth is, none make it. None. You think your kid is different. He's not. He won't make it to the NBA or NFL or MLB. Won't happen.

The odds are that long.

The point here, as Myron began to increase his lead, was that, yes, he had worked hard, shot baskets by himself for four to five hours a day, had been frighteningly competitive, had the right mind frame, had and did all those things, but none of that would have helped him reach the level he'd gotten to if he hadn't been blessed with extraordinary physical gifts.

One of those gifts was speed.

The panting was falling behind him.

Someone, maybe Rochester, shouted: "Shoot him in the leg!"

Myron kept accelerating. He had a destination in mind. His knowledge of the neighborhood would help now. He hit the hill up Coddington Terrace. As he reached the top, he prepared. He knew that if he got there enough ahead of them, there'd be a blind spot on the curve back down.

When he reached that down-curve, he didn't look back. There was a somewhat hidden path between two houses on the left. Myron had used it to go to Burnet Hill Elementary School. All the kids did. It was the strangest thing—a paved walking path between two houses—but he knew it was still there.

The very bad hombres would not.

The paved walk was public enough, but Myron had

another idea. The Horowitzes used to live in the house on the left. Myron had built a fort in the woods there with one of them a lifetime ago. Mrs. Horowitz had been furious about it. He veered into that area now. There used to be a crawling path under the bush, one that led from the Horowitzes' backyard on Coddington Terrace to the Seidens' on Ridge Road.

Myron pushed the first bush to the side. It was still there. He got down on his hands and knees and scrambled through the opening. Brown branches whipped his face. It didn't hurt so much as bring him back to a more innocent time.

As he emerged on the other side, in the old Seidens' backyard, he wondered if the Seiden family still lived here. The answer came to him fast.

Mrs. Seiden was in the backyard. She wore a kerchief and gardening gloves.

"Myron?" There was no hesitation or even much surprise in her voice. "Myron Bolitar, is that you?"

He had gone to school with her son, Doug, although he had not crawled through this path or even been in this backyard since he was maybe ten years old. But that didn't matter in towns like this. If you were friends in elementary school, there was always some kind of link.

Mrs. Seiden blew the strands of hair out of her face. She started toward him. Damn. He hadn't wanted to involve anyone else. She opened her mouth to say something, but Myron silenced her with a finger to his lips.

She saw the look on his face and stopped. He gestured for her to get in the house. She gave a slight nod and moved toward it. She opened the back door.

Someone shouted, "Where the hell did he go?"

Myron waited for Mrs. Seiden to disappear from view. But she didn't go inside.

Their eyes met. Now it was Mrs. Seiden's turn to

gesture. She motioned for him to come inside too. He shook his head. Too dangerous.

Mrs. Seiden stood there, her back rigid.

She would not move.

A sound came from the brush. Myron snapped his head toward it. It stopped. Could have been a squirrel. No way they could have found him already. But Win had called them "very bad" meaning, of course, very good at what they did. Win was never one for overstatement. If he said these guys were very bad . . .

Myron listened. No sound now. That scared him more than noise.

He did not want to put Mrs. Seiden in further danger. He shook his head one more time. She just stood there, holding the door open.

There was no sense in arguing. There are few creatures more stubborn than Livingston mothers.

Keeping low, he sprinted across the yard and through the open door, dragging her in with him.

She closed the door.

"Stay down."

"The phone," Mrs. Seiden said, "is over there."

It was a kitchen wall unit. He dialed Win.

"I'm eight miles away from your house," Win said.

"I'm not there," Myron said. "I'm on Ridge Road." He looked back at Mrs. Seiden for more information.

"Seventy-eight," she said. "And it's Ridge Drive, not Road."

Myron repeated what she'd said. He told Win there were three of them, including Dominick Rochester.

"Are you armed?" Win asked.

"No."

Win didn't lecture him, but Myron knew that he wanted to. "The other two are good and sadistic," Win said. "Stay hidden until I get there."

"We're not moving," Myron said.

And that was when the back door burst open.

Myron turned in time to see Hippy Art Teacher fly through it.

"Run!" Myron shouted at Mrs. Seiden. But he didn't wait to see if she obeyed. Art Teacher was still off balance. Myron leapt toward him.

But Art Teacher was fast.

He sidestepped Myron's lunge. Myron saw that he was going to miss. He stuck out his left arm, clothesline style, hoping to get under Art's chin. The blow touched down on the back of Art's head, cushioned by the ponytail. Art staggered. He turned and hit Myron a short shot to the rib cage.

The man was very fast.

Everything slowed down again. In the distance, Myron could hear footsteps. Mrs. Seiden making a run for it. Art Teacher smiled at Myron, breathing hard. The speed of that punch told Myron that he probably shouldn't stand and trade blows. Myron had the size advantage. And that meant taking him to the floor.

Art Teacher revved up to throw another punch. Myron crowded in. It was tougher to hit someone hard, especially someone bigger, when you crowded in. Myron grabbed Art Teacher's shirt by the shoulders. He twisted to take him down, raising a forearm at the same time.

Myron hoped to put the forearm against the man's nose. Myron weighed two hundred fifteen pounds. That kind of size, you land full force with your forearm resting on someone's nose, the nose is going to snap like a dried-out bird's nest.

But again Art Teacher was good. He saw what Myron intended to do. He tucked down just a little. The forearm was now resting on the rose-tinted glasses. Art

Teacher closed his eyes and pulled them both down harder. He also raised a knee up to Myron's midsection. Myron had to curve in his belly to protect himself. That took a good part of the power away from his forearm blow.

When they landed, the wire-framed glasses bent, but there was no serious power behind the shot. Art Teacher had the momentum now. He shifted his weight. His knee hadn't landed with much force either because of the way Myron had rounded his back. But the knee was still there. And the momentum.

He threw Myron over his head. Myron took it with a roll. In less than a second they were both on their feet.

The two men faced each other.

Here was what they don't tell you about fighting: You always feel crippling, paralyzing fear. The first few times, when Myron felt that stress-induced tingle in his legs, the kind that got so bad you wondered if you'd be able to stay on your feet, he felt like the worst sort of coward. Men who only get into a scrape or two, who get that leg tingle when they argue with a drunk lout at a bar, feel awash with shame. They shouldn't. It is not cowardice. It is a natural biological reaction. Everyone feels that way.

The question is, what do you do with that? What you learn with experience is that it can be controlled, harnessed even. You need to breathe. You need to relax. If you get hit when you're tensed up, it'll cause more damage.

The man threw off his bent glasses. He met Myron's eye. This was part of the game. The staring down. The guy was good. Win had said so.

But so was Myron.

Mrs. Seiden screamed.

To both men's credit, neither of them turned away at

the sound. But Myron knew that he had to get to her. He faked a charge, just enough so that Art would back up, and then he darted toward the front of the house, where the scream had originated.

The front door was open. Mrs. Seiden was standing there. And next to her, with his fingers digging into her upper arm, was the other man who'd chased him from the car. This guy was a few years older than Art Teacher and wore an ascot. An ascot, for crying out loud. He looked like Roger Healey from the old *I Dream of Jeannie* show.

No time.

Art Teacher was behind him. Myron slid to the side and threw a roundhouse right. Art Teacher ducked it, but Myron was ready. He stopped mid-punch and looped his arm around the man's neck.

Myron had him in a headlock.

But now, with a grotesque rebel yell, Ascot leapt toward Myron.

Tightening his grip on the neck, Myron aimed a mule kick. Ascot let it land on his chest. He made his body soft and rolled with the blow, holding on to Myron's leg.

Myron lost his balance.

Art Teacher managed to free himself then. He threw a knife hand, aiming for Myron's throat. Myron tucked so that the blow hit his chin. It rattled his teeth.

Ascot held on to Myron's leg. Myron tried to kick him off. Art Teacher was laughing now. The front door burst open again. Myron prayed it was Win.

It wasn't.

Dominick Rochester arrived. He was out of breath.

Myron wanted to call out a warning to Mrs. Seiden, but that was when a pain unlike any other he had felt ripped through him. Myron let loose a blood-curdling howl. He looked down at his leg. Ascot had his head lowered.

He was biting Myron's leg.

Myron screamed again, the sound mixing in with the laughter and cheers coming from Art Teacher.

"Go, Jeb! Woo-hoo!"

Myron kept kicking, but Ascot dug in deeper, holding on, growling like a terrier.

The pain was excruciating, all-encompassing.

Panic filled Myron. He stamped down with his free leg. Ascot held on with his teeth. Myron kicked harder, finally landing a kick on top of the man's head. He pushed hard. His flesh ripped off as he finally pried himself free. Ascot sat up and spit something out of his mouth. Myron realized with horror that it was a meaty chunk of leg.

Then they were on him. All three. Piled on.

Myron ducked his head and started swinging. He connected with somebody's chin. There was a grunt and a curse. But someone else hit him in the stomach.

He felt the teeth on his leg again, the same spot, opening up the wound.

Win. Where the hell was Win . . . ?

He bucked up in pain, wondering what to do next, when he heard a singsong voice say, "Oh, Mr. Bolitar . . . ?"

Myron looked. It was Art Teacher. He had a gun in one hand. In the other, he had Mrs. Seiden by the hair.

Chapter 23

They moved Myron to a large cedar closet on the second floor. Myron was flat on the floor. His hands were duct-taped behind his back, his feet bound together too. Dominick Rochester stood over him, a gun in his hand.

"Did you call your friend Win?"

Myron said, "Who?"

Rochester frowned. "You think we're stupid?"

"If you know about Win," Myron said, meeting his eye, "about what he can do, then the answer is yes. I think you're very stupid."

Rochester sneered. "We'll see about that," he said.

Myron quickly assessed the situation. No windows, one entrance. That was why they'd brought him up here: no windows. So Win couldn't attack from the outside or at a distance. They had realized that, considered it, been smart enough to bind him and bring him up here.

This was not good.

Dominick Rochester was armed. So was Art

Teacher. It would indeed be nearly impossible to get in here. But he knew Win. Myron just needed to give him time.

On the right, Ascot Bite was still smiling. There was blood—Myron's blood—on his teeth. Art Teacher was on the left.

Rochester bent down so his face was close to Myron's. The cologne smell was still on him, worse than ever. "I'm going to tell you what I want," he said. "Then I'm going to leave you alone with Orville and Jeb. See, I know you had something to do with that girl disappearing. And if you had something to do with her, you had something to do with my Katie. Makes sense, doesn't it?"

"Where's Mrs. Seiden?"

"No one is interested in hurting her."

"I didn't have anything to do with your daughter," Myron said. "I just gave Aimee a ride. That's all. The police will tell you."

"You lawyered up."

"I didn't lawyer up. My lawyer arrived. I answered every question. I told them that Aimee called me for a ride. I showed them where I dropped her off."

"And what about my daughter?"

"I don't know her. I've never met her in my life."

Rochester looked back at Orville and Jeb. Myron didn't know which was which. His leg was throbbing from the bite.

Art Teacher was redoing his ponytail, making it tight and wrapping it with the band. "I believe him."

"But," Ascot Bite added, "we got to be, got to be certain, *tengo que estar seguro.*"

Art Teacher frowned. "Who was that?"

"Kylie Minogue."

"Whoa, pretty obscure, dude."

Rochester stood upright. "You guys do your thing. I'll keep watch downstairs."

"Wait," Myron said. "I don't know anything."

Rochester looked at him for a moment. "It's my daughter. I can't take that chance. So what's going to happen here is, the Twins are going to work you over. You still telling the same story after that, I know you had nothing to do with it. But if you did, maybe I save my kid. You understand what I'm saying?"

Rochester moved to the door.

The Twins crept closer. Art Teacher pushed Myron back. Then he sat on Myron's legs. Ascot straddled Myron's chest. He looked down and bared his teeth. Myron swallowed. He tried to buck him off, but with his hands taped behind him, it was impossible. His stomach did flips of fear.

"Wait," Myron said again.

"No," Rochester said. "You'll stall. You'll sing, you'll dance, you'll make up stories—"

"No, that's not—"

"Let me finish, okay? It's my daughter. You have to understand that. You need to crack before I'll believe you. The Twins. They're good at making a man crack."

"Just hear me out, okay? I'm trying to find Aimee Biel—"

"No."

"—and if I find her, there's an excellent chance I'll find your daughter too. I'm telling you. Look, you checked me out, right? That's how you know about Win."

Rochester stopped, waited.

"You must have heard this is what I do. I help people when they're in trouble. I dropped that girl off and now she's gone. I owe it to her parents to find her."

Rochester looked at the Twins. In the distance

Myron heard a car radio, the song fading in and then fading out. The song was "We Built This City on Rock-n-Roll" by Starship.

The *second* worst song in the world, Myron thought.

Ascot Bite started singing along, "We built *este ciudad*, we built *este ciudad*, we built *este ciudad* . . ." Hippy Art Teacher, still holding Myron's legs, started bobbing his head, clearly digging his colleague's vocals.

"I'm telling the truth," Myron said.

"Either way," Rochester said, "if you're telling the truth or not, the Twins here. They'll find out. See? You can't lie to them. Once they hurt you some, you'll tell us everything we need to know."

"But by then it's too late," Myron said.

"They won't take long." Rochester looked at Art Teacher.

Art Teacher said, "Half an hour, hour max."

"That's not what I meant. I'll be too hurt. I won't be able to function."

"He has a point," Art Teacher said.

"We leave marks," Ascot added, flashing his teeth.

Rochester thought about it.

"Orville, where did you say he was before he came home?"

Art Teacher—Orville—gave him Randy Wolf's address and told him about the diner. They'd been tailing him, and Myron hadn't picked up on it. Either they were very good or Myron was awfully rusty—or both. Rochester asked Myron why he visited both places.

"The house is where her boyfriend lives," Myron said. "But he wasn't home."

"You think he has something to do with it?"

Myron knew better to answer in the positive. "Just talking to Aimee's friends, see what was up with her.

Who better than her boyfriend?"

"And the diner?"

"I met a source. I wanted to see what they had on your daughter and Aimee. I'm trying to find a connection between them."

"So what have you learned so far?"

"I'm just starting."

Rochester thought some more. Then he shook his head slowly. "Way I heard it, you picked up the Biel girl at two A.M."

"That's right."

"At two A.M.," he repeated.

"She called me."

"Why?" His face reddened. "Is it because you like picking up high school girls?"

"That's not it."

"Oh, I suppose you gonna tell me it was innocent?"

"It was."

Myron could see the anger mounting. He was losing him.

"You watch that trial with that perv Michael Jackson?"

The question confused Myron. "A little, I guess."

"He sleeps with little boys, right? He admits it. But then he says, 'Oh but it's innocent.' "

Now Myron saw where this was going.

"And here you are, just like that, telling me you pick up pretty high school girls, late at night. At two A.M. And then you say, 'Oh, but it's innocent.' "

"Listen to me—"

"Nah, I think I listened enough."

Rochester nodded for the Twins to go ahead.

Enough time had passed. Win was, Myron hoped, in place. He was probably waiting for one last distraction. Myron couldn't move, so he tried something else.

Without warning, Myron let loose a scream.

He screamed as long and as loud as he could, even after Orville the Art Teacher snapped a fist into his teeth.

But the scream had the desired effect. For a second, everyone looked at him. Just for a second. No more.

But that was enough.

An arm snaked around Rochester's neck as a gun appeared at his forehead. Win's face materialized next to Rochester's.

"Next time," Win said, crinkling his nose, "please refrain from buying your cologne at your local Exxon station."

The Twins were greased lightning. They were off Myron in under a second. Art Teacher took to the far corner. Ascot Bite flipped behind Myron and pulled him up, using Myron as a shield. He had a gun out now too. He put it against the back of Myron's neck.

Stalemate.

Win kept his arm around Rochester's neck. He squeezed the windpipe. Rochester's face darkened red as the oxygen drained away. His eyes rolled back. A few seconds later, Win did something a little surprising: He released his grip on the throat. Rochester retched and sucked in a deep breath. Using him as a shield, Win's gun stayed near the back of the man's head but now angled toward Art Teacher.

"Cutting off his air supply, what with that awful cologne," Win said, by way of an explanation. "It was too merciful."

The Twins studied Win as though he were something little and cute they'd stumbled across in the forest. They did not appear to be afraid of him. As soon as Win had come upon the scene, they'd coordinated their movements as if they'd done this before.

"Sneaking up like that," Hippy Art Teacher said, smiling at Win. "Dude, that was one radical move."

"Far out," Win said. "Like, dig it."

He frowned. "Are you mocking me, man?"

"Tripping. Groovy. Flower power."

Art Teacher looked at Ascot Bite as if to say, *Do you believe this guy?*

"Man oh man, dude, you don't know who you're messing with."

"Put your weapons down," Win said, "or I'll kill you both."

The Twins smiled some more, enjoying this.

"Dude, you ever do, like, math?"

Win gave Art Teacher the flat eyes. "Like, yah."

"See, we got two guns. You got one."

Ascot Bite rested his head on Myron's shoulder. "You," he said to Win, excited, licking his lips. "You shouldn't threaten us."

"You're right," Win said.

All eyes were on the gun pressed near Rochester's temple. That was the mistake. It was like a classic magician's trick. The Twins had not wondered why Win had released his grip on Rochester's throat. But the reason was simple:

It was so that Win—using Rochester's body to block their view—could ready his second gun.

Myron tilted his head a little to the left. The bullet from the second gun, the one that had been hidden behind Rochester's left hip, struck Ascot Bite square in the forehead. He was dead instantly. Myron felt something wet splash on his cheek.

At the same time, Win fired the first gun, the one that had been at Rochester's head. That bullet slammed into Art Teacher's throat. He went down, his hands clawing at what had been his voice box. He may have been dead or at least bleeding to death. Win didn't chance it.

The second bullet hit the man square between the eyes.

Win turned back to Rochester. "Breathe funny and you end up like them."

Rochester made himself stay impossibly still. Win bent down next to Myron and started ripping off the duct tape. He looked down at Ascot Bite's dead body.

"Chew on that," Win said to the corpse. He turned back to Myron. "Get it? The biting, chew on that?"

"Hilarious. Where's Mrs. Seiden?"

"She's safe, out of the house, but you'll need to make up a cover story for her."

Myron thought about that.

"Did you call the police?" Myron asked.

"Not yet. In case you wanted to ask some questions."

Myron looked at Rochester.

"Talk to him downstairs," Win said, handing Myron a gun. "I'll pull the car into the garage and start the cleanup."

Chapter 24

The cleanup.

Myron had some idea of what Win meant, though they wouldn't discuss it directly. Win had holdings all over the place, including a tract of land in a secluded section of Sussex County, New Jersey. The property was eight acres. Most of it was undeveloped woods. If you ever tried to trace down ownership, you'd find a holding company from the Cayman Islands. You would find no names.

There was a time when Myron would have been upset over what Win had done. There was a time when he would have mustered up all his moral outrage. He would give his old friend long, complicated musings about the sanctity of life and the dangers of vigilantism and all that. Win would look at him and utter three words:

Us or them.

Win probably could have given the "stalemate" another minute or two. He and the Twins might have come to an understanding. You go, we go, no one gets hurt. That sort of thing. But that wasn't meant to be.

The Twins were as good as dead the moment Win entered the scene.

The worst part was that Myron no longer felt bad about it. He would shrug it off. And when he'd started doing that, when he knew that killing them was the prudent thing to do and that their eyes would not haunt his sleep . . . that was when he knew it was time to stop doing this. Rescuing people, playing along that flimsy line between good and bad—it robbed a little sliver of your soul.

Except maybe it didn't.

Maybe playing along that line—seeing the other side of it—just grounded you in awful reality. The fact is this: A million Orville the Art Teachers or Jeb the Ascots aren't worth the life of even one innocent, of one Brenda Slaughter or one Aimee Biel or one Katie Rochester or, as in the case overseas, the life of his soldier son, Jeremy Downing.

It might seem amoral to feel this way. But there it was. He applied this thinking to the war too. In his most honest moments, the ones he dare not speak out loud, Myron didn't care that much about the civilians trying to scrape by in some dump-hole desert. He didn't care if they got democracy or not, if they experienced freedom, if their lives were made better. What he did care about were the boys like Jeremy. Kill a hundred, a thousand, on the other side, if need be. But don't let anyone hurt my boy.

Myron sat across from Rochester. "I wasn't lying before. I'm trying to find Aimee Biel."

Rochester just stared.

"You know that both girls used the same ATM?"

Rochester nodded.

"There has to be a reason why. It's not a coincidence.

Aimee's parents don't know your daughter. They don't think Aimee knew her either."

Rochester finally spoke. "I asked my wife and kids," he said, his voice soft. "None of them think Katie knew Aimee."

"But the two girls went to the same school," Myron said.

"It's a big school."

"There's a connection. There has to be. We're just missing it. So what I need you and your family to do is start searching for that connection. Ask Katie's friends. Look through her stuff. Something links your daughter and Aimee. We find it, we'll be that much closer."

Rochester said, "You're not going to kill me."

"No."

His eyes traveled upstairs. "Your guy made the right move. Killing the Twins, I mean. You let them go, they'd have tortured your mother until she cursed the day you were born."

Myron chose not to comment.

"I was stupid to hire them," Rochester said. "But I was desperate."

"If you're looking for forgiveness, go to hell."

"I'm just trying to make you understand."

"I don't want to understand," Myron said. "I want to find Aimee Biel."

Myron had to go to the emergency room. The doctor looked at the bite on his leg and shook his head.

"Jesus, you get attacked by a shark?"

"A dog," Myron lied.

"You should put it down."

Win took that one: "Already done."

The doctor used sutures and then bandaged it up. It

213

hurt like hell. He gave Myron some antibiotics and pills for the pain. When they left, Win made sure Myron still had the gun. He did.

"You want me to stay around?" Win said.

"I'm fine." The car accelerated down Livingston Avenue. "Are those two guys taken care of?"

"Gone forever."

Myron nodded. Win watched his face.

"They're called the Twins," Win said. "The older one with the ascot, he would have bitten off your nipples first. That's how they warm up. One nipple, then the other."

"I understand."

"No lecture on overreacting?"

Myron's fingers touched down on his chest. "I really like my nipples."

It was late by the time Win dropped him off. Near his front door, Myron found his cell phone on the ground where he'd dropped it. He checked the caller ID. There were a bunch of missed calls, mostly business related. With Esperanza in Antigua on her honeymoon, he should have stayed in touch. Too late to worry about that now.

Ali had also called him.

A lifetime ago he had told her that he'd come by tonight. They had joked about him stopping by for a late-night "nooner." Man, was that really today?

He debated waiting until morning, but Ali might be worried. Plus, it would be nice, *really* nice, to hear the warmth in her voice. He needed that, in this crazy, exhausting, hurting day. He was sore. His leg throbbed.

Ali answered on the first ring. "Myron?"

"Hey, hope I didn't wake you."

"The police were here."

There was no warmth in her voice.

"When?"

"A few hours ago. They wanted to talk to Erin. About some promise the girls made in your basement."

Myron closed his eyes. "Damn. I never meant to involve her."

"She backed your story, by the way."

"I'm sorry."

"I called Claire. She told me about Aimee. But I don't understand. Why would you make the girls promise something like that?"

"To call me, you mean?"

"Yes."

"I overheard them talking about driving with someone who was drunk. I just didn't want that to happen to them."

"But why you?"

He opened his mouth but nothing came out.

"I mean, you just met Erin that day. That was the first time you ever talked to her."

"I didn't plan it, Ali."

There was a silence. Myron didn't like it.

"We okay?" he asked.

"I need a little time with this," she said.

He felt his stomach clench.

"Myron?"

"Sooo," he said, stretching out the word, "I guess there's no rain check on that nooner?"

"This isn't the time for jokes."

"I know."

"Aimee is missing. The police came around and questioned my daughter. This might be routine for you, but this isn't my world. I'm not blaming you, but . . ."

"But?"

"I just . . . I just need time."

" 'Need time,' " Myron repeated. "That sounds a whole lot like 'need space.' "

"You're making a joke again."

"No, Ali, I'm not."

Chapter 25

There was a reason Aimee Biel wanted to be dropped off on that cul-de-sac.

Myron showered and threw on a pair of sweats. His pants had blood on them. His own. He remembered that old Seinfeld routine about laundry detergent commercials that talk about getting out bloodstains, how if you have bloodstains on your clothes, maybe laundry wasn't your biggest worry.

The house was silent, except for those customary house noises. When he was a kid, alone at night, those noises would scare him. Now they were just there—neither soothing nor alarming. He could hear the slight echo as he walked across the kitchen floor. The echo only happened when you were alone. He thought about that. He thought about what Claire had said, about him bringing violence and destruction, about him still not being married.

He sat alone at the kitchen table of his empty house. This was not the life he'd planned.

Man plans, God laughs.

He shook his head. Truer words.

Enough wallowing, Myron thought. The "plans" part got his mind back on track. To wit: What had Aimee Biel been planning?

There was a reason she chose that ATM. And there was a reason she chose that cul-de-sac.

It was almost midnight when Myron got back in his car and started north to Ridgewood. He knew the way now. He parked at the end of the cul-de-sac. He turned off the car. The house was dark, just like two nights ago.

Okay, now what?

Myron went through the possibilities. One, Aimee actually went into that house at the end of the cul-de-sac. The woman who'd answered the door before, the slim blonde with the baseball cap, had lied to Loren Muse. Or maybe the woman didn't know. Maybe Aimee was having a fling with her son or was a friend of her daughter's, and this woman didn't know about it.

Doubtful.

Loren Muse was no idiot. She had been at that door a fair amount of time. She would have checked into those angles. If they existed, she would have followed up.

So Myron ruled that out.

That meant that this house had been a diversion.

Myron opened the car door and stepped out. The road was silent. There was a hockey goal at the end of the cul-de-sac. This was probably a neighborhood with kids. There were only eight houses and almost no traffic. The kids probably still played on the street. Myron spotted one of those roll-out basketball hoops in one of the driveways. They probably did that too. The cul-de-sac was a little neighborhood playground.

A car turned down the block, just like when he'd dropped Aimee off.

Myron squinted toward the headlights. It was midnight now. Only eight houses on the street, all with lights out, all tucked in for the evening.

The car pulled up behind his and came to a stop. Myron recognized the silver Benz even before Erik Biel, Aimee's father, got out. The light was dim, but Myron could still see the rage on his face. It made him look like an annoying little boy.

"What the hell are you doing here?" Erik shouted.

"Same thing as you, I guess."

Erik came closer. "Claire may buy your story about why you drove Aimee here but . . ."

"But what, Erik?"

He didn't reply right away. He was still in the tailored shirt and trousers, but the look wasn't as crisp. "I just want to find her," he said.

Myron said nothing, letting him talk his way down.

"Claire thinks you can help. She says you're good at stuff like this."

"I am."

"You're like Claire's knight in shining armor," he said with more than a trace of bitterness. "I don't know why you two didn't end up together."

"I do," Myron said. "Because we don't love each other that way. In fact, in all the time I've known Claire, you're the only man she ever really loved."

Erik shifted his feet, pretending the words didn't matter, not quite pulling it off. "When I made the turn, you were getting out of your car. What were you going to do?"

"I was going to try to retrace Aimee's footsteps. See if I can figure out where she really went."

"What do you mean, 'really went'?"

"There was a reason she picked this spot. She used this house as a diversion. It wasn't her real destination."

"You think she ran away, don't you?"

"I don't think it was a random abduction or anything like that," Myron said. "She led me to this specific spot. The question is, why?"

Erik nodded. His eyes were wet. "You mind if I tag along?"

He did, but Myron shrugged and started toward the house. The occupants might wake up and call the police. Myron was willing to risk that. He opened the gate. This was where Aimee had gone in. He made the same turn she made, went behind the house. There was a sliding glass door. Erik stayed silent behind him.

Myron tried the glass door. Locked. He ducked down and ran his fingers along the bottom. Some kind of crud had accumulated. Same with the door frame going up.

The door had not been opened in a while.

Erik whispered, "What?"

Myron signaled him to keep quiet. The curtains were pulled closed. Myron stayed low and cupped his hands around his eyes. He looked into the room. He couldn't see much, but it looked like a standard family den. It was not a teen's bedroom. He moved toward the back door. That led to a kitchen.

Again no teen bedroom.

Of course Aimee might have misspoken. She might have meant that she went through a back door to get to Stacy's room, not that the bedroom was right there. But heck, Stacy didn't even live here. So either way, Aimee had clearly lied. This other stuff—the fact that the door hadn't been opened and didn't lead to a bedroom. That was just the icing.

So where had she gone?

He got on all fours and took out his penlight. He shined it on the ground. Nothing. He hoped for footprints, but there hadn't been much rain lately. He put his cheek flat on the grass, tried to look not so much for prints as any sort of ground indentation. More nothing.

Erik started looking too. He didn't have a penlight. There was almost no other illumination back here. But he looked anyway and Myron didn't stop him.

A few seconds later Myron stood. He kept the penlight low. The backyard was half an acre, maybe more. There was a pool with a whole other fence surrounding it. This gate was six feet high and kept locked. It would be hard, though not impossible, to scale. But Myron doubted Aimee had come here for a swim.

The backyard disappeared into woods. Myron followed the property line into the trees. The nice wooden picket fence ran around the side property lot, but once you got into the wooded area, the barrier became wire mesh. It was cheaper and less aesthetic, but back here, mixed in with branches and thicket, what did it matter?

Myron was pretty sure what he would find now.

It was not unlike the Horowitz–Seiden border near his own home. He put his hand on top of the fence and kept moving through the brush. Erik followed. Myron wore Nikes. Erik had on tasseled loafers without socks.

Myron's hand dipped down near an overgrown pine bush.

Bingo, this was the spot. The fence had caved in here. He shined the penlight. From the rusted-out look of it, the post had buckled years ago. Myron pulled down on the mesh a little and stepped over. Erik did likewise.

The cut-through was easier to find. It ran no more than five, six yards. It had probably been a longer path years ago, but with the value of land, only the thinnest clump of brush was now used for privacy. If your land could be made usable, you made sure that it was.

He and Erik ended up between two backyards on another cul-de-sac.

"You think Aimee went this way?"

Myron nodded. "I do."

"So what now?"

"We find out who lives on this street. We try to see if there's a connection to Aimee."

"I'll call the police," Erik said.

"You can try that. They might care, they might not. If someone she knows lives here, it might just further back up the theory that she's a runaway."

"I'll try anyway."

Myron nodded. If he were in Erik's shoes, he would do that too. They moved through the yard and stood on the cul-de-sac. Myron studied the homes as if they might give him answers.

"Myron?"

He looked at Erik.

"I think Aimee ran away," he said. "And I think it's my fault."

There were tears on his cheek.

"She's changed. Claire and I, we've both seen that. Something happened with Randy. I really like that boy. He was so good with her. I tried to talk to her about it. But she wouldn't tell me. I . . . this is going to sound so stupid. I thought maybe Randy had tried to pressure her. You know. Sexually."

Myron nodded.

"But what decade do I think we're living in? They'd been together two years already."

"So you don't think that was it?"

"No."

"Then what?"

"I don't know." He went silent.

"You said it was your fault."

Erik nodded.

"When I drove Aimee here," Myron said, "she begged me not to say anything to you and Claire. She said that things weren't good with you two."

"I started spying on her," Erik said.

That wasn't a direct answer to the question, but Myron let it go. Erik was working up to something. Myron would need to give him room.

"But Aimee . . . she's a teenage girl. Remember those years? You learn how to hide things. So she was careful. I guess that she was more practiced than I was. It's not that I didn't trust her. But it's part of a parent's job to keep tabs on their children. It doesn't do much good because they know it."

They stood in the dark, staring at the houses.

"But what you don't realize is that even while you're spying on them, maybe every once in a while, they turn the tables on you. Maybe they suspect something's wrong and they want to help. And maybe the child ends up keeping tabs on the parent."

"Aimee spied on you?"

He nodded.

"What did she find, Erik?"

"That I'm having an affair."

Erik almost collapsed with relief when he said it. Myron felt blank for a second, totally empty. Then he thought about Claire, about how she was in high school, about the way she'd nervously pluck her bottom lip in the back of Mr. Lampf's English class. A surge of anger coursed through him.

"Does Claire know?"

"I don't know. If she does, she's never said anything."

"This affair. Is it serious?"

"Yes."

"How did Aimee find out?"

"I don't know. I don't even know for sure that she did."

"Aimee never said anything to you?"

"No. But . . . like I said. There were changes. I would go to kiss her cheek and she'd pull back. Almost involuntarily. Like I repulsed her."

"That might be normal teenage stuff."

Erik hung his head, shook it.

"So when you were spying on her, trying to check her e-mails, besides wanting to know what she was up to . . ."

"I wanted to see if she knew, yes."

Again Myron flashed to Claire, this time to her face on her wedding day, starting a new life with this guy, smiling like Esperanza had on Saturday, no doubts about Erik even though Myron had never warmed to him.

As if reading his mind, Erik said, "You've never been married. You don't know."

Myron wanted to punch him in the nose. "You say so."

"It doesn't just happen all at once," he said.

"Uh-huh."

"It just starts to slip away. All of it. It happens to everyone. You grow apart. You care but in a different way. You're about your job, your family, your house. You're about everything but the two of you. And then one day you wake up and you want that feeling back. Forget the sex. That's not really it. You want the passion. And you know you're never going to get it from the woman you love."

"Erik?"

"What?"

"I really don't want to hear this."

He nodded. "You're the only one I've told."

"Yeah, well, I must live under a lucky star then."

"I just wanted . . . I mean, I just needed . . ."

Myron held up a hand. "You and Claire are none of my business. I'm here to find Aimee, not play marriage counselor. But let me just make something clear because I want you to know exactly where I stand: If you hurt Claire, I'll . . . "

He stopped. Stupid to go that far.

"You'll what?"

"Nothing."

Erik almost smiled. "Still her knight in shining armor, eh, Myron?"

Man, Myron *really* wanted to punch him in the nose. He turned away instead, turned toward a yellow house with two cars in the driveway. And that was when he saw it.

Myron froze.

"What?" Erik said.

He quickly averted his gaze. "I need your help."

Erik was all over that. "Name it."

Myron started walking back toward the path, cursing himself. He was still rusty. He should have never let that show. The last thing he needed was Erik going off half-cocked. He needed to hash it out without Erik.

"Are you good with a computer?"

Erik frowned. "I guess so."

"I need you to go online. I need you to put all the addresses on this street into a search engine. We need a list of who lives here. I need you to go home right away and do that for me."

"But shouldn't we do something now?" Erik asked.

"Like what?"

"Knock on doors."

"And say what? Do what?"

"Maybe someone is holding her hostage right here, right on this very block."

"Very, very doubtful. And even so, knocking on doors will probably get them to panic. And once we knock on one door at this hour, that person will call the police. The neighbors will be warned. Listen to me, Erik. We need to figure out what's what first. This could all be a dead end. Aimee might not have taken that path."

"You said you thought she did."

"Thought. That doesn't mean much. Plus maybe she walked five blocks after that. We can't just stumble around. If you want to help, go home. Look those addresses up. Get me some names."

They were through the path now. They moved past the gate and walked back to their cars.

"What are you going to do?" Erik asked.

"I have a few other leads I want to follow up on."

Erik wanted to ask more, but Myron's tone and body language cut him off. "I'll call you as soon as I've finished the search," Erik said.

They both got in their cars. Myron watched Erik drive off. Then he picked up the cell phone and hit Win's speed dial.

"Articulate."

"I need you to break into a house."

"Goody. Please explain."

"I found a path where I dropped Aimee off. It leads to another cul-de-sac."

"Ah. Do we have a thought then about where she ended up?"

"Sixteen Fernlake Court."

"You sound fairly certain."

"There's a car in the driveway. On the back windshield is a sticker. It's for teacher parking at Livingston High School."

"On my way."

Chapter 26

Myron and Win met up three blocks away near an elementary school. A parked car here would be less conspicuous. Win was dressed in black, including a black skull cap that hid his blond locks.

"I didn't see an alarm system," Myron said.

Win nodded. Alarms were minor nuisances anyway, not deal breakers. "I'll be back in thirty minutes."

He was. On the dot.

"The girl isn't inside the house. Two teachers live there. His name is Harry Davis. He teaches English at Livingston High School. His wife is Lois. She teaches at a middle school in Glen Rock. They have two daughters, college age, judging by the pictures and the fact that they weren't home."

"This can't be a coincidence."

"I put a GPS tracker on both cars. Davis also has a well-worn briefcase, stuffed with term papers and lesson plans. I put one on that too. You go home, get some sleep. I'll let you know when he wakes up and starts to move. I'll follow. And then we'll be on him."

Myron crawled into bed. He figured sleep would never come to him. But it did. He slept deep until he heard a metallic click coming from downstairs.

His father had been a light sleeper. In his youth, Myron would wake up at night and try to walk past his parents' room without stirring Dad. He had never made it. His father did not wake up slowly either. He woke with a start, like someone had poured ice water down his drawstring bottoms.

So that was how it was when he heard the click. He shot up in the bed. The gun was on the night table. He grabbed it. His cell phone was there too. He hit Win's speed dial, the line that rang for Win to mute and eavesdrop.

Myron sat very still and listened.

The front door opened.

Whoever it was, they were trying to keep quiet. Myron crept to the wall next to his bedroom door. He waited, listened some more. The intruder had gone through the front door. That was odd. The lock was old. It could be picked. But to be that silent about it— just one quick click—it meant whoever it was, or whoever they were, they were good.

He waited.

Footsteps.

They were light. Myron pressed his back against the wall. The gun tightened in his hand. His leg ached from the bite. His head pounded. He tried to swim through it, tried to focus.

He calculated the best place to stand. Pressed against the wall next to the door, where he was now—that was good for listening, but it wouldn't be ideal, despite what you see in the movies, if someone entered his room. In the first place, if the guy was good, he'd be looking for that. In the second place, if there were more than one of them, jumping someone from behind the door would be the worst place to be. You're forced to attack right away and thus expose your location. You might nail the first guy, but the second one would lay you to waste.

Myron padded toward the bathroom door. He stood behind it, kept low, the door almost closed. He had a perfect angle. He could see the intruder enter. He could shoot or call out—and if he did shoot, he'd still be in a good position if someone else either charged in or retreated.

The footsteps stopped outside his bedroom door.

He waited. His breath rang in his ears. Win was good at this, the patience part. That had never been Myron's forte. But he calmed himself. He kept his breathing deep. His eyes stayed on the open doorway.

He saw a shadow.

Myron aimed his gun at the middle of it. Win might go for the head, but Myron zeroed in on the center of the chest, the most forgiving target.

When the intruder stepped through the doorway and into a bit of light, Myron nearly gasped out loud. He stepped out from behind the door, still holding the gun.

"Well, well," the intruder said. "After seven years, is that a gun in your hand or are you just happy to see me?"

Myron did not move.

Seven years. After seven years. And within seconds, it was like those seven years had never happened.

Jessica Culver, his former soul mate, was back.

Chapter 27

They were downstairs in the kitchen.

Jessica opened up the refrigerator. "No Yoo-hoo?"

Myron shook his head. Chocolate Yoo-hoo had been his favorite beverage. When they lived together, he'd always had plenty on hand.

"You don't drink it anymore?"

"Not much."

"I guess one of us should note that everything changes."

"How did you get in?" he asked.

"You still keep the key in the gutter. Just like your father did. We used it once. Do you remember?"

He did. They'd sneaked down to the basement, giggling. They'd made love.

Jessica smiled at him. The years showed, he guessed. There were more lines around the eyes. Her hair was shorter and more stylized. But the effect was still the same.

She was knock-you-to-your-knees beautiful.

Jessica said, "You're staring."

He said nothing.

"Good to know I still have it."

"Yeah, that Stone Norman is a lucky man."

"Right," she said. "I figured you'd see that."

Myron said nothing.

"You'd like him," she said.

"Oh, I bet."

"Everyone does. He has lots of friends."

"Do they call him Stoner?"

"Only his old frat buddies."

"I should have guessed."

Jessica studied him for a moment. Her gaze made his face warm. "You look like hell, by the way."

"I took something of a beating today."

"Some things don't change then. How's Win?"

"Speaking of things that don't change."

"Sorry to hear that."

"We going to keep this up," Myron said, "or are you going to tell me why you're here?"

"Can we keep this up for a few more minutes?"

Myron shrugged a *suit-yourself* at her.

"How are your parents?" she asked.

"Fine."

"They never liked me."

"No, I don't suppose they did."

"And Esperanza? Does she still refer to me as Queen Bitch?"

"She hasn't so much as mentioned your name in seven years."

That made her smile. "Like I'm Voldemort. In the Harry Potter books."

"Yep, you're She-who-must-not-be-named."

Myron shifted in his chair. He turned away for a few seconds. She was just so damn beautiful. It was like looking into an eclipse. You need to look away every once in a while.

"You know why I'm here," she said.

"One last fling before you marry Stoner?"

"Would you be willing?"

"No."

"Liar."

He wondered if she was right, so he took the mature route. "Are you aware that 'Stoner' rhymes with 'boner'?"

"Making fun of someone's name," Jessica said, "when yours is Myron."

"Throwing stones, glass houses, yeah, I know." Her eyes were red. "Are you drunk?"

"Tipsy maybe. I had enough to get my courage up."

"To break into my house?"

"Yes."

"So what is it, Jessica?"

"You and I," she said. "We're not really through."

He said nothing.

"I pretend we're done, you pretend we're done. But we both know better." Jessica turned to the side and swallowed. He watched her neck. He saw hurt in her eyes. "What was the first thing that went through your mind when you read I was getting married?"

"I wished you and Stoner nothing but the best."

She waited.

"I don't know what I thought," he said.

"It hurt?"

"What do you want me to say, Jess? We were together a long time. Of course there was a pang."

"It's like"—she paused, thought about it—"it's like, despite the fact I haven't talked to you in seven years, it was always just a question of time before we got back together. Like this was all part of the process. Do you know what I mean?"

He said nothing, but he felt something deep inside him start to fray.

"And then today, I saw my announcement in print—the announcement I wrote—and suddenly it was like, 'Wait, this is for real. Myron and I don't end up together.'" She shook her head. "I'm not saying this right."

"Nothing to say, Jessica."

"Just like that?"

"You being here," he said. "It's just prewedding jitters."

"Don't patronize me."

"What do you want me to say?"

"I don't know."

They sat there for a while. Myron held out his hand. She took it. He felt something course through him.

"I know why you're here," Myron said. "I don't even think I'm surprised."

"There's still something between us, isn't there?"

"I don't know. . . ."

"I hear a 'but.'"

"You go through what we went through—the love, the breakups, my injuries, all that pain, all that time together, the fact that I wanted to marry you—"

"Let me address that part, okay?"

"In a second. I'm on a roll here."

Jessica smiled. "Sorry."

"You go through all that, your lives become so entwined with one another. And then one day, you just end it. You just sever it off like with a machete. But you're so entwined, stuff is still there."

"Our lives are enmeshed," she said.

"Enmeshed," he repeated. "That sounds so precious."

"But it's somewhat accurate."

234

He nodded.

"So what do we do?"

"Nothing. That's just part of life."

"Do you know why I didn't marry you?"

"It's irrelevant, Jess."

"I don't think it is. I think we need to play through this."

Myron let go of her hand and signaled, *fine, go ahead.*

"Most people hate their parents' lives. They rebel. But you wanted to be just like them. You wanted the house, the kids—"

"And you didn't," he interrupted. "We know all this."

"That's not it. I might have wanted that life too."

"Just not with me."

"You know that's not it. I just wasn't sure. . . ." She tilted her head. "You wanted that life. But I didn't know if you wanted that life more than me."

"That," Myron said, "is the biggest load of crap I've ever heard."

"Maybe, but that's how I felt."

"Great, I didn't love you enough."

She looked at him, shook her head. "No man has ever loved me like you did."

Silence. Myron held back the "what-about-Stoner" remark.

"When you blew out your knee—"

"Not that again. Please."

Jessica pushed ahead. "When you blew out your knee, you changed. You worked so hard to move past it."

"You'd have preferred the self-pity route," Myron said.

"That might have worked better. Because what you did instead, what you ended up doing, was running

235

scared. You grabbed so tight to everything you had that it was suffocating. All of a sudden you were mortal. You didn't want to lose anything else and suddenly—"

"This is all great, Jess. Hey, I forget. At Duke, who taught your Intro to Psychology class? Because he'd be proud as punch right about now."

Jessica just shook her head at him.

"What?" he said.

"You're still not married, are you, Myron?'

"Neither," he said, "are you."

"Touché. But have you had a lot of serious relationships over the past seven years?"

He shrugged. "I'm involved right now."

"Really?"

"What, that's such a surprise?"

"No, but think about it. You, Mr. Commitment, Mr. Long-Term Relationship—why is it taking you so long to find anybody else?"

"Don't tell me." He held up a hand. "You spoiled me for all other women?"

"Well, that would be understandable." Jessica arched an eyebrow. "But no, I don't think so."

"Well, I'm all ears. Why? Why aren't I happily married by now?"

Jessica shrugged. "I'm still working on it."

"Don't work on it. It doesn't involve you anymore."

She shrugged again.

They both sat there. It was funny how comfortable he was with all this.

"You remember my friend Claire?" Myron said.

"She married that uptight guy, right? We went to their wedding."

"Erik." He didn't want to go into it all, so he started with something else. "He told me tonight that he and Claire are having troubles. He says it's inevitable, that eventually it all dims and fades and that it becomes something else. He says he misses the passion."

"Is he messing around?" Jessica asked.

"Why do you ask that?"

"Because it sounds like he's trying to justify his actions."

"So you don't think there's anything to that dimming passion stuff?"

"Of course there's something to it. Passion can't stay at that fevered pitch."

Myron thought about that. "It did for us."

"Yes," she said.

"There was no fade."

"None. But we were young. And maybe that's why, in the end, we blew up."

He considered that. She took his hand again. There was a charge. Then Jessica gave him a look. *The* look, to be more specific. Myron froze.

Uh-oh.

"You and this new woman," Jessica said. "Are you exclusive?"

"You and Stoner-Boner," he countered. "Are you exclusive?"

"Low blow. But it's not about Stone. It's not about your new missus. It's about us."

"And you think, what, a quick boink will help clarify things?"

"Still a wordsmith with the ladies, I see."

"Here's another word from the wordsmith: no."

Jessica toyed with the top button of her blouse. Myron felt his mouth go a little dry. But she stopped.

"You're right," she said.

He wondered if he was disappointed that she hadn't pushed it further. He wondered what he would have done if she had.

They started talking then, just catching up on the years. Myron told her about Jeremy, about his serving overseas. Jessica told him about her books, her family, her time working out on the West Coast. She didn't talk about Stoner. He didn't talk about Ali.

Morning came. They were still in the kitchen. They'd been talking for hours, but it didn't feel like it. It just felt good. At seven A.M., the phone rang. Myron picked it up.

Win said, "Our favorite schoolteacher is heading to work."

Chapter 28

Myron and Jessica hugged good-bye. The hug lasted a long time. Myron could smell Jessica's hair. He didn't remember the name of her shampoo, but it had lilacs and wildflowers and was the same one she'd used when they'd been together.

Myron called Claire. "I have a quick question," he said to her.

"Erik said he saw you last night."

"Yeah."

"He's been on the computer all night."

"Good. Look, do you know a teacher named Harry Davis?"

"Sure. Aimee had him for English last year. He's also a guidance counselor now, I think."

"Did she like him?"

"Very much." Then: "Why? Does he have something to do with this?"

"I know you want to help, Claire. And I know Erik wants to help. But you have to trust me on this, okay?"

"I do trust you."

"Erik told you about the cut-through we found?"

"Yes."

"Harry Davis lives on the other side of it."

"Oh my God."

"Aimee is not in his house or anything. We already checked."

"What do you mean, you checked? How did you check?"

"Please, Claire, just listen to me. I'm working on this, but I need to do it without interference. You have to keep Erik off my back, okay? Tell him I said to search all the surrounding streets online. Tell him to drive around that area, but not on that cul-de-sac. Or better yet, have him call Dominick Rochester—that's Katie's father—"

"He called us."

"Dominick Rochester?"

"Yes."

"When?"

"Last night. He said he met with you."

Met, Myron thought. Nice euphemism.

"We're getting together this morning—the Rochesters and us. We're going to see if we can find a connection between Katie and Aimee."

"Good. That'll help. Listen, I have to go."

"You'll call?"

"As soon as I know something."

Myron heard her sob.

"Claire?"

"It's been two days, Myron."

"I know. I'm on it. You might want to try to pressure the police more too. Now that we've crossed the forty-eight-hour mark."

"Okay."

He wanted to say something like *Be strong*, but it

sounded so stupid in his head that he let it go. He said good-bye and hung up. Then he called Win.

"Articulate," Win said.

"I can't believe you still answer the phone that way. 'Articulate.' "

Silence.

"Is Harry Davis still heading to the high school?"

"He is."

"On my way."

Livingston High School, his alma mater. Myron started up the car. The total ride would be maybe two miles, but whoever was tailing him either wasn't very good at it or didn't care. Or maybe, after the debacle with the Twins, Myron was being more wary. Either way, a gray Chevy, maybe a Caprice, had been on him since he made the first turn.

He called Win and got the customary "Articulate."

"I'm being followed," Myron said.

"Rochester again?"

"Could be."

"Make and license plate?"

Myron gave it to him.

Win said, "We're still on Route 280, so stall a little. Take them down past Mount Pleasant Avenue. I'll get in behind them, meet you back at the circle."

Myron did as Win suggested. He turned into Harrison School for the U-turn. The Chevy following him kept going straight. Myron started back down the other way on Livingston Avenue. By the time he hit the next traffic light, the gray Chevy was back on his tail.

Myron hit the big circle in front of the high school, parked, and got out of his car. There were no stores here, but this was the nerve center of Livingston—a plethora of identical brick. There was the police station, the courthouse, the town library, and there, the large crown jewel, Livingston High School.

The early morning joggers and walkers were on the circle. Most were on the elderly side and moved slowly. But not all. A group of four hotties, all hard-bodied and maybe twenty-ish, were jogging in his direction.

Myron smiled at them and arched an eyebrow. "Hello, ladies," he said as they passed.

Two of them snickered. The other two looked at him as though he'd just announced that he had a poopie in his pants.

Win sidled up next to him. "Did you give them the full-wattage smile?"

"I'd say a good eighty, ninety watts."

Win studied the young women before making a declaration: "Lesbians," he said.

"Must be."

"A lot of that going around, isn't there?"

Myron did the math in his head. He probably had fifteen to twenty years on them. When it comes to young girls, you just never want to feel it.

"The car following you," Win said, keeping his eyes on the young joggers, "is an unmarked police vehicle with two uniforms inside. They're parked in the library lot watching us through a telephoto lens."

"You mean they're taking our picture right now?"

"Probably," Win said.

"How's my hair?"

Win made an *eh* gesture with his hand.

Myron thought about what it meant. "They probably still see me as a suspect."

"I would," Win said. He had what looked like a Palm Pilot in his hand. It was tracking the car's GPS. "Our favorite teacher should be arriving now."

The teachers' lot was on the west side of the school. Myron and Win walked over. They figured that it would be better to confront him here, outside, before class started.

As they headed over, Myron said, "Guess who stopped by my house at three A.M.?"

"Wink Martindale?"

"No."

"I love that guy."

"Who doesn't? Jessica."

"I know."

"How . . ." Then he remembered. He'd called Win's cell when he heard the click at the door. He'd hung up as they headed down to the kitchen.

Win said, "Did you do her?"

"Yes. Many times. But not in the last seven years."

"Good one. Pray tell, did she stop by to shag for old times' sake?"

"'Shag?'"

"My Anglo ancestry. Well?"

"A gentleman never kisses and tells. But yes."

"And you refused?"

"I remain chaste."

"Your chivalry," Win said. "Some would call it admirable."

"But not you."

"No, I'd call it—and I'm breaking out the big words here so pay attention—really, really moronic."

"I'm involved with someone else."

"I see. So you and Miss Six-Point-Eight have promised to shag only one another?"

"It's not like that. It's not like one day you turn to the other and say, 'Hey, let's not sleep with anybody else.' "

"So you didn't specifically promise?"

"No."

Win held up both hands, totally lost. "I don't understand then. Did Jessica have BO or something?"

Win. "Just forget it."

"Done."

"Sleeping with her would only complicate things, okay?"

Win just stared.

"What?"

"You're a very big girl," Win said.

They walked a little more.

Win said, "Do you still need me?"

"I don't think so."

"I'll be in the office then. If there's trouble, hit the cell."

Myron nodded as Win headed off. Harry Davis got out of his car. There were clusters of cliques in the lot. Myron shook his head. Nothing changed. The Goths wore only black with silver studs. The Brains had heavy backpacks and dressed in short-sleeved button-down shirts of one hundred percent polyester like a bunch of assistant managers at a chain drugstore convention. The Jocks took up the most space, sitting on car hoods and wearing leather-sleeved varsity jackets, even though it was too hot for them.

Harry Davis had the easy walk and carefree smile of the well-liked. His looks landed him smack in the average category, and he dressed like a high school teacher, which was to say poorly. All the cliques greeted him, which said something. First, the Brains shook his hand and called out, "Hey, Mr. D!"

Mr. D?

Myron stopped. He thought back to Aimee's yearbook, her favorite teachers: Miss Korty . . .

. . . and Mr. D.

Davis kept moving. The Goths were next. They gave him small waves, much too cool to do more than that.

244

When he approached the Jocks, several offered up high-fives and "Yo, Mr. D!"s.

Harry Davis stopped and started talking to one of the Jocks. The two moved a few feet away from the cluster. The conversation appeared more animated. The jock had a varsity jacket with a football on the back of it and the letters *QB* for *quarterback* on the sleeve. Some of the guys were calling to him. They yelled out, "Hey, Farm." But the quarterback was focused on the teacher. Myron moved closer for a better look.

"Well, hello," Myron said to himself.

The boy talking with Harry Davis—Myron could see him clearly now, the soul patch on his chin, the Rastafarian hair—was none other than Randy Wolf.

Chapter 29

Myron considered his next move—let them keep talking or confront them now? He checked his watch. The bell was about to sound. Both Harry Davis and Randy Wolf would probably head inside then, lost to him for the day.

Showtime.

When Myron was about ten feet away from them, Randy spotted him. The boy's eyes widened with something akin to recognition. Randy stepped away from Harry Davis. Davis turned to see what was going on.

Myron waved. "Hi, guys."

Both froze as though caught in headlights.

"My father said I shouldn't talk to you," Randy said.

"But your father never got to know the real me. I'm actually quite a sweetheart." Myron waved to the confused teacher. "Hi, Mr. D."

He was almost on them when he heard a voice behind him.

"That's far enough."

Myron turned around. Two cops in full uniform stood in front of them. One was tall and lanky. The other was short with long, dark, curly hair and a bushy mustache. The shorter one looked like he'd just stepped out of a VH1 special on the eighties.

The tall one said, "Where do you think you're going?"

"This is public property. I'm walking on it."

"Are you smarting off to me?"

"You think that's smarting off?"

"I'll ask you again, wise guy. Where do you think you're going?"

"To class," Myron said. "There's a bitch of an algebra final coming up."

The tall one looked at the short one. Randy Wolf and Harry Davis stared without saying a word. Some of the students began to point and gather. The bell rang. The taller officer said, "Okay, nothing to see here. Break it up, get to class now."

Myron pointed at Wolf and Davis. "I need to talk to them."

The taller officer ignored him. "Get to class." Then looking at Randy, he added: "All of you."

The crowd thinned and then vanished. Randy Wolf and Harry Davis were gone too. Myron was alone with the two officers.

The tall one came up close to Myron. They were about the same height, but Myron had at least twenty or thirty pounds on him. "You stay away from this school," he said slowly. "You don't talk to them. You don't ask questions."

Myron thought about that. Don't ask questions? That was not the kind of thing you say to a suspect. "Don't ask who questions?"

"Don't ask anybody anything."

"That's pretty vague."

"You think I should be more specific?"

"That would help, yes."

"Are you being a smart guy again?"

"Just looking for clarification."

"Hey, asswipe." It was the shorter cop with the VH1-eighties look. He took out his nightstick and held it up. "This clarification enough for you?"

Both cops smiled at Myron.

"What's the matter?" The shorter cop with the bushy mustache was slapping the nightstick against his palm. "Cat got your tongue?"

Myron looked first at the tall cop, then back at the short one with the mustache. Then he said: "Darryl Hall called. He wants to know if the reunion tour is still on."

That made the smiles vanish.

The taller officer said, "Put your hands behind your back."

"What, are you going to tell me he doesn't look like John Oates?"

"Hands behind your back now!"

"Hall and Oates? 'Sarah Smile'? 'She's Gone'?"

"Now!"

"It's not an insult. Many chicks dug John Oates, I'm sure."

"Turn around now!"

"Why?"

"I'm cuffing you. We're taking you in."

"On what charge?"

"Assault and battery."

"On whom?"

"Jake Wolf. He told us you trespassed on his residence and attacked him."

Bingo.

His cop-needling had worked. Now he knew why these guys were on him. It wasn't about him being a suspect in Aimee's disappearance. It was the pressure brought upon them by one Big Jake Wolf.

Of course, the plan hadn't gone perfectly. They were arresting him now.

The John Oates cop snapped on the cuffs, making the obvious move of having them pinch his skin. Myron checked out the taller one. He looked a little nervous now, his eyes darting about. Myron figured that was a good thing.

The shorter one dragged him by the cuffs back to the same gray Chevy that had been tailing him since he'd left his house. He pushed Myron into the backseat, trying to hit his head on the doorframe, but Myron was ready and ducked it. In the front seat, Myron spotted a camera with a telephoto lens, just as Win had said.

Hmm. Two cops taking pictures, following him from his house, stopping him from talking to Randy, cuffing him—Big Jake had some juice.

The taller one stayed outside and paced. This was all going a little too fast for him. Myron decided that he could play that. The short one with the bushy mustache and dark curly hair slid into the seat next to Myron and grinned.

"I really liked 'Rich Girl,' " Myron said to him. "But 'Private Eyes'—I mean, what was up with that song? 'Private eyes, they're watching you.' I mean, don't all eyes watch you? Public, private, whatever?"

The short guy's fuse blew faster than anticipated. He took a swing at Myron's gut. Myron was still ready. One of the lessons Myron had learned over the years was how to take a punch. It was crucial if you were going to get into any physical confrontation. In a real fight, you almost always get hit, no matter how good you are. How you reacted psychologically often decided the outcome. If you don't know what to expect, you shrivel up and cower. You get too defensive. You let the fear conquer you.

If the blow is a headshot, you need to play the angles. Don't let the punch land square, especially on the nose. Even slight head tilts can help. Instead of four knuckles landing, maybe it will only be two or one. That makes a huge difference. You also have to relax your body, let it go. You should turn away from the strike, literally roll with the punch. When a blow is aimed at your abdomen, especially when your hands are cuffed behind your back, you need to clench the stomach muscles, shift, and bend at the waist so it doesn't wallop the bread-basket. That was what Myron did.

The blow didn't hurt much. But Myron, noting the taller guy's nervousness, put on a performance that would have made De Niro take notes.

"Aarrrgggggghhh!"

"Damn, Joe," the tall one said, "what the hell are you doing?"

"He was making fun of me!"

Myron stayed bent over and faked loss of breath. He wheezed, he retched, he started coughing uncontrollably.

"You hurt him, Joe!"

"I just knocked the wind out of him. He'll be fine."

Myron coughed more. He faked like he couldn't breathe. Then he added convulsions. He rolled back his eyes and started bucking like a fish on the dock.

"Calm down, dammit!"

Myron stuck his tongue out, gagged some more. Somewhere, a casting agent was speed-dialing Scorsese.

"He's choking!"

"Medicine!" Myron managed.

"What?"

"Can't breathe!"

"Dammit, get the cuffs off him!"

"Can't breathe!" Myron gasped and made his body wrack. "Heart medicine! In my car!"

The taller one opened the door. He grabbed the keys from his partner and unlocked the cuffs. Myron kept up with the convulsions and eye rolls.

"Air!"

The tall one was wide-eyed. Myron could see what he was thinking: out of hand. This was getting too out of hand.

"Air!"

The tall one stepped aside. Myron rolled out of the car. He got up and pointed to his car. "Medicine!"

"Go," the taller one said.

Myron ran to his car. The two officers, dumbfounded, just watched. Myron had expected that. They were just here to scare him off. They had not expected any back talk. They were town cops. The citizens of this happy suburb obeyed them without question. But this guy hadn't bowed to them. They'd lost their cool and assaulted a man. This could mean huge trouble. They both just wanted it to end. So did Myron. He had learned what he needed to—Big Jake Wolf was scared and trying to hide something.

So when Myron reached his car, he slid into the driver's seat, put the key in the ignition, started it up, and simply drove off. He glanced in his rearview mirror. He figured that the odds were on his side, that the two cops would not chase him.

They didn't. They just stood there.

In fact, they looked relieved to just let him go.

He had to smile. Yep, there was no question about it now.

Myron Bolitar was baaack.

Chapter 30

Myron was trying to figure out what to do next when his cell phone rang. The caller ID read OUT OF AREA. He picked it up. Esperanza said, "Where the hell are you?"

"Hey, how's the honeymoon going?"

"Like crap. Do you want to know why?"

"Is Tom not putting out?"

"Yeah, you men are so tough to seduce. No, my problem is that my business partner is not answering calls from our clients. My business partner is also not in the office to cover my absence."

"I'm sorry."

"Oh, well, that covers it."

"I'll have Big Cyndi transfer all the calls directly to my cell. I'll be in as soon as I can."

"What's wrong?" Esperanza asked.

Myron didn't want to disrupt her honeymoon any more than he already had, so he said, "Nothing."

"You so lie."

"I'm telling you. It's nothing."

"Fine, I'll ask Win."

"Wait, okay."

He briefly filled her in.

"So," Esperanza said, "you feel obligated because you did a good deed?"

"I was the last to see her. I dropped her off and let her go."

"Let her go? What kind of crap is that? She's eighteen, Myron. That makes her an adult. She asked you for a ride. You gallantly—and stupidly, I might add—gave her one. That's it."

"That's not it."

"Look, if you gave, say, Win a ride home, would you make sure he got all the way into the house safely?"

"Good analogy."

Esperanza snickered. "Yeah, well. I'm coming home."

"No, you're not."

"You're right, I'm not. But you can't handle both on your own. So I'll tell Big Cyndi to transfer the calls down here. I'll take them. You go play superhero."

"But you're on your honeymoon. What about Tom?"

"He's a man, Myron."

"Meaning?"

"As long as a man gets some, he's happy."

"That's such a cruel stereotype."

"Yeah, I know I'm awful. I could be talking on the phone at the same time or, hell, breast-feeding Hector, Tom wouldn't blink. Plus this will give him more time to play golf. Golf and sex, Myron. It'll pretty much be Tom's dream honeymoon."

"I'll make it up to you."

There was a moment of silence.

"Esperanza?"

"I know it's been a while since you've done something like this," she said. "And I know I made you promise you wouldn't again. But maybe . . . maybe it's a good thing."

"How do you figure?"

"Damned if I know. Christ, I got more important things to worry about. Like stretch marks when I wear a bikini. I can't believe I have stretch marks now. The kid's fault, you know."

They hung up a minute later. Myron drove around, feeling conspicuous in his car. If the police decided to keep an eye on him or if Rochester decided another tail might be in order, this car would be inconvenient. He thought about it and called Claire. She answered on the first ring.

"Did you learn something?"

"Not really, but do you mind if I switch cars with you?"

"Of course not. I was about to call you anyway. The Rochesters just left."

"And?"

"We talked for a while. Trying to find a connection between Aimee and Katie. But something else came up. Something I need to run by you."

"I'm two minutes from your house."

"I'll meet you in the front yard."

As soon as Myron stepped out of the car, Claire tossed him her car keys. "I think Katie Rochester ran away."

"What makes you say that?"

"Have you met that father?"

"Yes."

"Says it all, doesn't it?"

"Maybe."

"But more than that, have you met the mother?"

"No."

"Her name is Joan. She has this wince—like she's waiting for him to smack her."

"Did you find a connection between the girls?"

"They both liked to hang out at the mall."

"That's it?"

Claire shrugged. She looked like hell. The skin was pulled even tighter now. She looked like she'd lost ten pounds in the last day. Her body teetered as she walked, as though a strong gust would knock her all the way to the ground. "They ate lunch at the same time. They had one class together in the past four years—PE with Mr. Valentine. That's it."

Myron shook his head. "You said something else came up?"

"The mother. Joan Rochester."

"What about her?"

"You might miss it because like I said, she cowers and looks scared all the time."

"Miss what?"

"She's scared of him. Her husband."

"So? I met him. I'm scared of him."

"Right, okay, but here's the thing. She's scared of him, sure, but she's *not* scared about her daughter. I have no proof, but that's the vibe I'm getting. Look, you remember when my mom got cancer?"

Sophomore year of high school. The poor woman died six months later. "Of course."

"I met with other girls going through the same thing. A support group for cancer families. We had this picnic once, where you could bring other friends too. But it was weird—you knew exactly who was really going through the torment and who was just a friend. You'd meet a fellow sufferer and you'd just know. There was a vibe."

255

"And Joan Rochester didn't have a vibe?"

"She had a vibe, but not the 'my daughter is missing' vibe. I tried to get her alone. I asked her to help me make some coffee. But I didn't get anywhere. I'm telling you, she knows something. The woman is scared, but not like I am."

Myron thought about that. There were a million explanations, especially the most obvious—people react differently to stress—but he wanted to trust Claire's intuition on this. The question was, what did it mean? And what could he do about it?

"Let me think this through," he said at last.

"Did you talk to Mr. Davis?"

"Not yet."

"How about Randy?"

"I'm on it. That's why I need your car. The police ran me off the high school campus this morning."

"Why?"

He didn't want to get into Randy's father so he said, "I'm not sure yet. Look, let me get going, okay?"

Claire nodded, closed her eyes.

"She'll be okay," Myron said, stepping toward her.

"Please." Claire held up a hand to stop him. "Don't waste time handing me platitudes, okay?"

He nodded, slipped into her SUV. He wondered about his next destination. Maybe he'd head back to school. Talk to the principal. Maybe the principal could call Randy or Harry Davis into his office. But then what?

The cell phone sounded. Again the caller ID gave him no information. Caller ID technology was fairly useless. The people you wanted to avoid just blocked the service anyway.

"Hello?"

"Hey, handsome, I just got your message."

It was Gail Berruti, his contact from the phone company. He had forgotten all about the crank calls referring to him as a "bastard." It seemed unimportant now, just some sort of childish prank, except that maybe, just maybe, there was a connection. Claire had noted that Myron brought destruction. Maybe someone from his past was out to get him. Maybe somehow Aimee had gotten tangled up in that.

It was the longest of long shots.

"I haven't heard from you in forever," Berruti said.

"Yeah, I've been busy."

"Or not busy, I guess. How are you?"

"I'm pretty good. Were you able to trace the number?"

"It's not a trace, Myron. You said that in your phone message. 'Trace the number.' It's not a trace. I just had to look it up."

"Whatever."

"Not whatever. You know better. It's like on TV. You ever watch a phone trace on TV? They always say to keep the guy on the line so they can trace the call. That's nonsense, you know. You trace it right away. It's immediate. It doesn't take time. Why do they do that?"

"It's more suspenseful," Myron said.

"It's dumb. They do everything ass-backward on TV. I'm watching some cop show the other night, and it takes five minutes to do a DNA test. My husband works in the crime lab at John Jay. They're lucky if they get a DNA confirmation in a month. Meanwhile the phone stuff—all of which can be done in minutes with the touch of a computer—that takes them forever. And the bad guy always hangs up just before they get the location. Have you ever seen the trace work? Never. Pisses me off, you know?"

Myron tried to get Berruti back on track. "So you looked up the number?"

"I got it here. Curious though: Why do you need it?"

"Since when do you care?"

"Good point. Okay, let's get to it then. First off, whoever it was wanted to be anonymous. The call was from a pay phone."

"Where?"

"The location is near one-ten Livingston Avenue in Livingston, New Jersey."

The center of town, Myron thought. Near his local Starbucks and his dry cleaner. Myron thought about that. A dead end? Maybe. But he had a thought.

"I need you to do me two more favors, Gail," Myron said.

"Favor implies nonpayment."

"Semantics," Myron said. "You know I'll take care of you."

"Yeah, I know. So what do you need?"

Harry Davis taught a lesson on *A Separate Peace* by John Knowles. He tried to concentrate, but the words were coming out as if he were reading off a prompter in a language he didn't quite understand. The students took notes. He wondered if they noticed that he wasn't really there, that he was going through the motions. The sad part was, he suspected that they didn't.

Why did Myron Bolitar want to talk to him?

He did not know Myron Bolitar personally, but you don't walk around the corridors of this school for more than two decades without knowing who he was. The guy was a legend here. He held every basketball record the school ever had.

So why had he wanted to talk to him?

Randy Wolf had known who he was. His father had warned him not to talk to Myron. Why?

"Mr. D? Yo, Mr. D?"

The voice fought through the fog in his head.

"Yes, Sam."

"Can I, like, go to the bathroom?"

"Go."

Harry Davis stopped then. He put down the chalk and looked over the faces in front of him. No, they weren't beaming. Most of them were eyes-down in their notebooks. Vladimir Khomenko, a new exchange student, had his head down on his desk, probably asleep. Others looked out the window. Some sat so low in their chairs, with spines seemingly created from Jell-O, Davis was surprised that they didn't slip to the floor.

But he cared about them. Some more than others. But he cared about all of them. They were his life. And for the first time, after all these years, Harry Davis was starting to feel it all slip away.

Chapter 31

Myron had a headache, and quickly realized why. He hadn't had coffee yet that day. So he headed over to Starbucks with two thoughts in mind—caffeine and pay phone. The caffeine was taken care of by a grunge barista with a soul patch and long frontal hair that looked like a giant eyelash. The pay phone problem would take a little more work.

Myron sat at an outdoor table and eyed the offending pay phone. It was awfully public. He walked over to it. There were stickers on the phone advertising 800 numbers to call for discount calls. The most prominent one was offering "free night calls" and had a picture of a quarter moon in case you didn't know what night was.

Myron frowned. He wanted to ask the pay phone who had dialed his number and called him a bastard and said that he'd pay for what he'd done. But the phone wouldn't talk to him. It had been that kind of day.

He sat back down and tried to figure out what he

needed to do. He still wanted to talk to Randy Wolf and Harry Davis. They probably wouldn't tell him much—they probably wouldn't talk to him at all—but he would figure a way to get a run at them. He also needed to interview that doctor who worked at St. Barnabas, Edna Skylar. She had purportedly seen Katie Rochester in New York. He wanted some details on that.

He called St. Barnabas's switchboard and after two brief explanations, Edna Skylar got on the phone. Myron explained what he wanted.

Edna Skylar sounded annoyed. "I asked the investigators to keep my name out of this."

"They have."

"So how do you know it?"

"I have good contacts."

She thought about that. "What's your standing in this, Mr. Bolitar?"

"Another girl has gone missing."

No response.

"I think there may be a connection between this girl and Katie Rochester."

"How?"

"Could we meet? I can explain everything then."

"I really don't know anything."

"Please." There was a pause. "Dr. Skylar?"

"When I saw the Rochester girl, she indicated that she didn't want to be found."

"I understand that. I just need a few minutes."

"I have patients for the next hour. I can see you at noon."

"Thank you," he said, but Edna Skylar had already hung up.

Lithium Larry Kidwell and the Medicated Five shuffled into Starbucks. Larry headed right for his table.

"Fourteen hundred eighty-eight planets on creation

day, Myron. Fourteen hundred eighty-eight. And I haven't seen a penny. You know what I'm saying?"

Larry looked as awful as always. Geographically, they were so close to their old high school, but what had his favorite restaurateur, Peter Chin, said about years flying by but the heart staying the same? Well, only the heart then.

"Good to know," Myron said. He looked back at the pay phone and a thought struck him hard and fast: "Wait."

"Huh?"

"Last time I saw you there were fourteen hundred eighty-seven planets, right?"

Larry looked confused. "Are you sure?"

"I am." Myron's mind started racing. "And if I'm not mistaken, you said the next planet was mine. You said it was out to get me and something about stroking the moon."

Larry's eyes lit up. "Stroking the moon sliver. He hates you bad."

"Where is that moon sliver?"

"In the Aerolis solar system. By Guanchomitis."

"Are you sure, Larry? Are you sure it's not . . ." Myron rose and walked him to the pay phone. Larry cringed. Myron pointed to the sticker, to the image of the quarter moon on the ad for free night calls. Larry gasped.

"Is this the moon sliver?"

"Oh please, oh my god, oh please . . ."

"Calm down, Larry. Who else wants that planet? Who hates me enough to stroke the moon sliver?"

Twenty minutes later, Myron headed into Chang's Dry Cleaning. Maxine Chang was there, of course. There were three people in line. Myron didn't get behind them. He stood to the side and crossed his arms. Maxine kept sneaking glances at him. Myron waited until the customers were gone. Then he approached.

"Where's Roger?" he asked.

"He has school."

Myron met her eye. "Do you know he's been calling me?"

"Why would he call you?"

"You tell me."

"I don't know what you're talking about."

"I have a friend at the phone company. Roger called me from that booth over there. I have reliable witnesses who can place him there at the right time." That was more than an exaggeration, but Myron went with it. "He threatened me. He called me a bastard."

"Roger wouldn't do that."

"I don't want to get him in trouble, Maxine. What's going on?"

Another customer came in. Maxine shouted something out in Chinese. An elderly woman came out of the back and took over. Maxine gestured with her head for Myron to follow her. He did. They walked past the tracks of moving hangers. When he was a kid, the metallic whir of the tracks had always amazed him, like something out of a cool sci-fi movie. Maxine kept walking until they were out in the back alley.

"Roger is a good boy," she said. "He works so hard."

"What's going on, Maxine? When I was in here the other day, you were acting funny."

"You don't understand how hard it is. To live in a town like this."

He did—he had lived here his whole life—but he held his tongue.

"Roger worked so hard. He got good grades. Number four in his class. These other kids. They're spoiled. All have private tutors. They don't work a real job. Roger, he works here every day after school. He studies in the back room. He doesn't go to parties. He doesn't have a girlfriend."

"What does any of this have to do with me?"

"Other parents hire people to write their children's essays. They pay for classes to improve their boards. They donate money to the big schools. They do other things, I don't even know. It's so important, where you go to college. It can decide your whole life. Everyone is so scared, they do anything, *anything* to get their kid in the right school. This town, you see it all the time. Nice people maybe, but you can justify any evil as long as you can say, 'It's for my child.' You understand?"

"I do, but I don't see what that has to do with me."

"I need you to understand. That's what we have to compete with. With all that money and power. With people who cheat and steal and will do anything."

"If you're telling me that college acceptance is competitive in this town, I know that. It was competitive when I graduated."

"But you had basketball."

"Yes."

"Roger is such a good student. He works so hard. And his dream is to go to Duke. He told you that. You probably don't remember."

"I remember him saying something about applying there. I don't remember him saying it was his dream or anything. He just listed a bunch of schools."

"It was his first choice," Maxine Chang said firmly. "And if Roger makes it, there is a scholarship waiting for him. He'd have his tuition paid for. That was so important to us. But he didn't get in. Even though he was number four in his class. Even though he had very good boards. Better boards—and better grades—than Aimee Biel."

Maxine Chang looked at Myron with heavy eyes.

"Wait a second. Are you blaming me because Roger didn't get into Duke?"

"I don't know much, Myron. I'm just a dry cleaner. But a school like Duke almost never takes more than one student from a specific high school in New Jersey. Aimee Biel made it. Roger had better grades. He had better board scores. He had great teacher recommendations. Neither of them are athletes. Roger plays the violin, Aimee plays guitar." Maxine Chang shrugged.

"So you tell me: Why did she get in and not Roger?"

He wanted to protest, but the truth stopped him. He had written a letter. He had even called his friend in admissions. People do stuff like that all the time. It doesn't mean that Roger Chang was denied admission. But simple math: When one person gets a spot, someone else doesn't.

Maxine's voice was a plea. "Roger was just so angry."

"That's no excuse."

"No, it's not. I will talk to him. He will apologize to you, I promise."

But another thought came to Myron. "Was Roger just mad at me?"

"I don't understand."

"Was he mad at Aimee too?"

Maxine Chang frowned. "Why would you ask that?"

"Because the next call on that pay phone was to Aimee Biel's cell phone. Was Roger angry with her? Resentful maybe?"

"Not Roger, no. He's not like that."

"Right, he'd only call me and make threats."

"He didn't mean anything. He was just lashing out."

"I need to talk to Roger."

"What? No, I forbid it."

"Fine, I'll go to the police. I'll tell them about the threatening calls."

Her eyes widened. "You wouldn't."

He would. Maybe he should. But not yet. "I want to talk to him."

"He'll be here after school."

"Then I'll be back at three. If he's not here, I'm going to the police."

Chapter 32

D r. Edna Skylar met Myron in the lobby of St. Barnabas Medical Center. She had all the props—a white coat, a name tag with the hospital logo, a stethoscope dangling across her neck, a clipboard in her hand. She had that impressive doctor bearing too, complete with the enviable posture, the small smile, the firm-but-not-too-firm handshake.

Myron introduced himself. She looked him straight in the eye and said, "Tell me about the missing girl."

Her voice left no room for arguments. Myron needed her to trust him, so he launched into the story, keeping Aimee's last name out of it. They both stood in the middle of the lobby. Patients and visitors walked on either side of them, some coming very close.

Myron said, "Maybe we could go somewhere private."

Edna Skylar smiled, but there was no joy in it. "These people are preoccupied with things much more important to them than us."

Myron nodded. He saw an old man in a wheelchair

with an oxygen mask. He saw a pale woman in an ill-fitted wig checking in with a look both resigned and bewildered, as if she was wondering if she'd ever check out and if it even mattered anymore.

Edna Skylar watched him. "A lot of death in here," she said.

"How do you do it?" Myron asked.

"You want the standard cliché about being able to detach the personal from the professional?"

"Not really."

"The truth is, I don't know. My work is interesting. It never gets old. I see death a lot. That never gets old either. It hasn't helped me to accept my own mortality or any of that. Just the opposite. Death is a constant outrage. Life is more valuable than you can ever imagine. I've seen that, the real value of life, not the usual platitudes we hear about it. Death is the enemy. I don't accept it. I fight it."

"And that never gets tiring?"

"Sure it does. But what else am I going to do? Bake cookies? Work on Wall Street?" She looked around. "Come on, you're right—it's distracting out here. Walk with me, but I'm on a tight schedule so keep talking."

Myron told her the rest of the story of Aimee's disappearance. He kept it as short as possible—kept his own name out of it—but he made sure to hit upon the fact that both girls used the same ATM. She asked a few questions, mostly small clarifications. They reached her office and sat down.

"Sounds like she ran away," Edna Skylar said.

"I'm aware of that."

"Someone leaked you my name, is that correct?"

"More or less."

"So you have some idea what I saw?"

"Just the basics. What you said convinced the

investigators that Katie was a runaway. I'm just wondering if you saw something that makes you think differently."

"No. And I've gone over it a hundred times in my head."

"You're aware," Myron said, "that kidnap victims often identify with their abductors."

"I know all that. The Stockholm syndrome and all its bizarre offshoots. But it just didn't seem that way. Katie didn't look particularly exhausted. The body language was right. There wasn't panic in her eyes or any kind of cult-like zealousness. Her eyes were clear, in fact. I didn't see signs of drugs there, though granted I only got a brief look."

"Where exactly did you first see her?'

"On Eighth Avenue near Twenty-first Street."

"And she was heading into the subway?"

"Yes."

"A couple of trains go through that station."

"She was taking the C train."

The C train basically ran north–south through Manhattan. That wouldn't help.

"Tell me about the man she was with."

"Thirty to thirty-five. Average height. Nice looking. Long, dark hair. Two-day beard."

"Scars, tattoos, anything like that?"

Edna Skylar shook her head and told him the story, how she'd been walking on the street with her husband, how Katie looked different, older, more sophisticated, different hair, how she wasn't even positive it was Katie until Katie uttered those final words: "*You can't tell anybody you saw me.*"

"And you said she seemed scared?"

"Yes."

"But not of the man she was with?"

"That's right. May I ask you something?"

"Sure."

"I know something about you," she said. "No, I'm not a basketball fan, but Google works wonders. I use it all the time. With patients too. If I'm seeing someone new, I check them out online."

"Okay."

"So my question is, why are you trying to find the girl?"

"I'm a family friend."

"But why you?"

"It's hard to explain."

Edna Skylar gave that a second, seemingly unsure if she should accept his vague response. "How are her parents holding up?"

"Not well."

"Their daughter is most likely safe. Like Katie."

"Could be."

"You should tell them that. Offer them some comfort. Let them know she'll be okay."

"I don't think it'll do any good."

She looked off. Something crossed her face.

"Dr. Skylar?"

"One of my children ran away," Edna Skylar said. "He was seventeen. You know the nature versus nurture question? Well, I was a crappy mother. I know that. But my son was trouble from day one. He got into fights. He shoplifted. He got arrested when he was sixteen for stealing a car. He was heavily into drugs, though I don't think I knew it at that time. This was in the days before we talked about ADD or put kids on Ritalin or any of that. If that was a serious option, I probably would have done it. I reacted instead by withdrawing and hoping he'd outgrow it. I didn't get involved in his life. I didn't give him direction."

She said it all matter-of-factly.

"Anyway, when he ran away, I didn't do anything. I almost expected it. A week passed. Two weeks. He didn't call. I didn't know where he was. Children are a blessing. But they also rip your heart out in ways you could never imagine."

Edna Skylar stopped.

"What happened to him?" Myron asked.

"Nothing overly dramatic. He eventually called. He was out on the West Coast, trying to become a big star. He needed money. He stayed out there for two years. Failed at everything he did. Then he came back. He's still a mess. I try to love him, to care about him, but"— she shrugged—"doctoring comes natural to me. Mothering does not."

Edna Skylar looked at Myron. He could see that she wasn't finished, so he waited.

"I wish . . ." Her throat caught. "It's a horrible cliché, but more than anything, I wish I could start over again. I love my son, I really do, but I don't know what to do for him. He may be beyond hope. I know how cold that sounds, but when you make professional diagnoses all day, you tend to make them in your personal life too. My point is, I've learned that I can't control those I love. So I control those I don't."

"I'm not following," Myron said.

"My patients," she explained. "They are strangers, but I care a great deal about them. It's not because I'm a generous or wonderful person, but because in my mind, they are still innocent. And I judge them. I know that's wrong. I know that I should treat every patient the same, and in terms of treatment, I think I do. But the fact is, if I Google the person and see that they spent time in jail or seem like a lowlife, I try to get them to go to another doctor."

"You prefer the innocents," Myron said.

"Precisely. Those whom—I know how this will sound—those whom I deem pure. Or at least, purer."

Myron thought about his own recent reasoning, how the life of the Twins held no value to him, about how many civilians he'd sacrifice to save his own son. Was this reasoning that much different?

"So what I'm trying to say is, I think about this girl's parents, the ones you said aren't doing well, and I worry about them. I want to help."

Before Myron could respond, there was a light rap on the door. It opened, and a head of gray hair popped through. Myron rose. The gray-haired man stepped all the way in and said, "I'm sorry, I didn't know you were with someone."

"It's okay, honey," Edna Skylar said, "but maybe you could come back later?"

"Of course."

The gray-haired man wore a white coat too. He spotted Myron and smiled. Myron recognized the smile. Edna Skylar wasn't a basketball fan, but this guy was. Myron stuck out his hand. "Myron Bolitar."

"Oh, I know who you are. I'm Stanley Rickenback. Better known as Mr. Dr. Edna Skylar."

They shook hands.

"I saw you play at Duke," Stanley Rickenback said. "You were something else."

"Thank you."

"I didn't mean to interrupt. I just wanted to see if my blushing bride wanted to join me for the lunchtime culinary delight that is our hospital cafeteria."

"I was just leaving," Myron said. Then: "You were with your wife when she saw Katie Rochester, weren't you?"

"Is that why you're here?"

"Yes."

"Are you a police officer?"

"No."

Edna Skylar was already up. She kissed her husband's cheek. "Let's hurry. I have patients in twenty minutes."

"Yes, I was there," Stanley Rickenback said to Myron. "Why, what's your interest?"

"I'm looking into the disappearance of another girl."

"Wait, another girl ran away?"

"Could be. I'd like to hear your impressions, Dr. Rickenback."

"Of what?"

"Did Katie Rochester seem like a runaway to you too?"

"Yes."

"You seem pretty sure," Myron said.

"She was with a man. She made no move to escape. She asked Edna not to tell anybody and—" Rickenback turned to his wife. "Did you tell him?"

Edna made a face. "Let's just go."

"Tell me what?"

"My darling Stanley is getting old and senile," Edna said. "He imagines things."

"Ha, ha, very funny. You have your expertise. I have mine."

"Your expertise?" Myron said.

"It's nothing," Edna said.

"It's not nothing," Stanley insisted.

"Fine," Edna said. "Tell him what you think you saw."

Stanley turned to Myron. "My wife told you about how she studies faces. That was how she recognized the girl. She looks at people and tries to make a diagnosis. Just for fun. I don't do that. I leave my work at the office."

"What is your specialty, Dr. Rickenback?"

He smiled. "That's the thing."

"What is?"

"I'm an ob-gyn. I didn't really think about it then. But when we got home, I looked up pictures of Katie Rochester on the Web. You know, the ones released to the media. I wanted to see if it was the same girl we saw in the subway. And that was why I'm fairly certain of what I saw."

"Which is?"

Stanley suddenly seemed unsure of himself.

"See?" Edna shook her head. "This is such total nonsense."

"It might be," Stanley Rickenback agreed.

Myron said, "But?"

"But either Katie Rochester put on some weight," Stanley Rickenback said, "or maybe, just maybe, she's pregnant."

Chapter 33

Harry Davis gave his class a phony-baloney read-this-chapter-now assignment and headed out. His students were surprised. Other teachers played that card all the time, the do-busy-silent-work-so-I-can-catch-a-smoke card. But Mr. D, Teacher of the Year four years running, never did that.

The corridors at Livingston High were ridiculously long. When he was alone in one, like right now, looking down to the end made him dizzy. But that was Harry Davis. He didn't like it quiet. He liked it lively, when this artery was loaded with noise and kids and back-packs and adolescent angst.

He found the classroom, gave the door a quick knock, and stuck his head in. Drew Van Dyne taught mostly malfeasants. The room reflected that. Half the kids had iPods in their ears. Some sat on top of their desks. Others leaned against the window. A beefy guy was making out with a girl in the back corner, their mouths open wide. You could see the saliva.

Drew Van Dyne had his feet on the desk, his hands

275

folded on his lap. He turned toward Harry Davis.

"Mr. Van Dyne? May I speak with you a moment?"

Drew Van Dyne gave him the cocky grin. Van Dyne was probably thirty-five, ten years younger than Davis. He'd come in as a music teacher eight years ago. He looked the part, the former rock 'n' roller who woulda-shoulda made it to the top except the stupid record companies could never understand his true genius. So now he gave guitar lessons and worked in a music store where he scoffed at your pedestrian taste in CDs.

Recent cutbacks in the music department had forced Van Dyne into whatever class was closest to babysitting.

"Why of course, Mr. D."

The two teachers stepped into the hallway. The doors were thick. When it closed, the corridor was silent again.

Van Dyne still had the cocky grin. "I'm just about to start my lesson, Mr. D. What can I do for you?"

Davis whispered because every sound echoed out here. "Did you hear about Aimee Biel?"

"Who?"

"Aimee Biel. A student here."

"I don't think she's one of mine."

"She's missing, Drew."

Van Dyne said nothing.

"Did you hear me?"

"I just said I don't know her."

"Drew—"

"And," Van Dyne interrupted, "I think we'd be notified if a student had gone missing, don't you?"

"The police think she's a runaway."

"And you don't?" Van Dyne held on to the grin, maybe even spread it a bit. "The police will want to know why you feel that way, Mr. D. Maybe you should go to them. Tell them all you know."

"I might just do that."

"Good." Van Dyne leaned closer and whispered. "I think the police would definitely want to know when you last saw Aimee, don't you?"

Van Dyne leaned back and waited for Davis's reaction.

"You see, Mr. D," Van Dyne went on, "they'll need to know everything. They'll need to know where she went, who she talked to, what they talked about. They'll probably look into all that, don't you think? Maybe open up a full investigation into the wonderful works of our Teacher of the Year."

"How do you . . . ?" Davis felt the quake start in his legs. "You have more to lose than I do."

"Really?" Drew Van Dyne was so close now that Davis could feel the spittle in his face. "Tell me, Mr. D. What exactly do I have to lose? My lovely house in scenic Ridgewood? My sterling reputation as a beloved teacher? My perky wife who shares my passion for educating the young? Or maybe my lovely daughters who look up to me so?"

They stood there for a moment, still in each other's face. Davis couldn't speak. Somewhere in the distance, another world maybe, he heard a bell ring. Doors flew open. Students poured out. The arteries filled with their laughter and angst. It all grabbed hold of Harry Davis. He closed his eyes and let it, let it sweep him away to someplace far away from Drew Van Dyne, someplace he'd much rather be.

The Livingston Mall was aging and trying hard not to show it, but the improvements came across more like a bad face-lift than true youth.

Bedroom Rendezvous was located on the lower

level. To some, the lingerie store was like Victoria's Secret's trailer-park cousin, but the truth was, the cousins were really a lot alike. It was all about presentation. The sexy models on the big posters were closer to porno stars, with wagging tongues and suggestive hand placement. The Bedroom Rendezvous slogan, which was centered across the buxom models' cleavage, read: *what kind of woman do you want to take to bed?*

"A hot one," Myron said out loud. It was again not that different from Victoria's Secret commercials, the one where Tyra and Frederique are all oiled up and ask, "What is sexy?" Answer: Really hot women. The clothing seems beside the point.

The saleswoman wore a tight tiger print. She had big hair and chewed gum, but there was a confidence there that somehow made it work. Her tag read SALLY ANN.

"Looking to make a purchase?" Sally Ann asked.

"I doubt you have anything in my size," Myron said.

"You'd be surprised. So what's the deal?" She motioned toward the poster. "You just like staring at the cleavage?"

"Well, yes. But that's not why I'm here." Myron pulled out a photograph of Aimee. "Do you recognize this girl?"

"Are you a cop?"

"I might be."

"Nah."

"What makes you say that?"

Sally Ann shrugged. "So what are you after?"

"This girl is missing. I'm trying to find her."

"Let me take a look."

Myron handed her the photograph. Sally Ann studied it. "She looks familiar."

"A customer maybe?"

"No. I remember customers."

Myron reached into a plastic bag and pulled out the white outfit he'd found in Aimee's drawer. "This look familiar?"

"Sure. It's from our Naughty-pout line."

"Did you sell this one?"

"It could be. I've sold a few."

"The tag is still on it. Do you think you could trace down who purchased it?"

Sally Ann frowned and pointed at the picture of Aimee. "You think your missing girl bought it?"

"I found it in her drawer."

"Yeah, but still."

"Still what?"

"It's too slutty and uncomfortable."

"And, what, she looks classy?"

"No, not that. Women rarely buy this one. Men do. The material is itchy. It rides up the crotch. This is a man's fantasy, not a woman's. It's a bit like porno videos." Sally Ann cocked her head and worked the gum. "Have you ever watched a porno flick?"

Myron kept his face blank. "Never, ever, never," he said.

Sally Ann laughed. "Right. Anyway, when a woman picks out the film, it's totally different. It usually has a story or maybe a title with the word 'sensuous' or 'loving' in it. It might be raunchy or whatever, but it usually isn't called something like *Dirty Whore 5*. You know what I mean?"

"Let's assume I do. And this outfit?"

"It's the equivalent."

"Of *Dirty Whore Whatever*?"

"Right. No woman would pick it out."

"So how do I find out who bought it for her?"

"We don't keep records or anything like that. I could ask some of the other girls, but . . ." Sally Ann shrugged.

Myron thanked her and headed out. As a young boy, Myron had come here with his dad. They had frequented Herman's Sporting Goods back then. The store was now out of business. But as he exited Bedroom Rendezvous, he still looked down the corridor, to where Herman's used to be. And two doors down, he spotted a store with a familiar name.

PLANET MUSIC.

Myron flashed back to Aimee's room. Planet Music. The guitars had been from Planet Music. There had been receipts in Aimee's drawer from there. And here it was, her favorite music shop, located two stores down from Bedroom Rendezvous.

Another coincidence?

In Myron's youth, the store in this spot had sold pianos and organs. Myron had always wondered about that. Piano-organ stores at malls. You go to the mall to buy clothes, a CD, a toy, maybe a stereo. Who goes to the mall to buy a piano?

Clearly not many people.

The pianos and organs were gone. Planet Music sold CDs and smaller instruments. They had signs for rentals. Trumpets, clarinets, violins—probably did a big business with the schools.

The kid behind the counter was maybe twenty-three, wore a hemp poncho, and looked like a seedier version of the average Starbucks barista. He had a dusty knit hat atop a shaved head. He sported the now seemingly prerequisite soul patch.

Myron gave him the stern eye and slapped the picture down on the counter. "You know her?"

The kid hesitated a second too long. Myron jumped in.

"You answer my questions, you don't get busted."

"Busted for what?"

"Do you know her?"

He nodded. "That's Aimee."

"She shops here?"

"Sure, all the time," he said, his eyes darting every-where but on Myron. "And she understands music too. Most people come in here, they ask for boy bands." He said *boy bands* the way most people say *bestiality*. "But Aimee, she rocks."

"How well do you know her?"

"Not very. I mean, she doesn't come here for me."

The poncho kid stopped then.

"Who does she come here for?"

"Why do you want to know?"

"Because I don't want to make you empty your pockets."

He raised his hands. "Hey, I'm totally clean."

"Then I'll plant something on you."

"What the . . . You serious?"

"Cancer serious." Myron worked the stern eye again. He wasn't great at the stern eye. The strain was giving him a headache. "Who does she come here to see?"

"My assistant manager."

"He have a name?"

"Drew. Drew Van Dyne."

"Is he here?"

"No. He comes in this afternoon."

"You got an address for him? A phone number?"

"Hey," the kid said, suddenly wise. "Let me see your badge."

"Bye now."

Myron headed out of the store. He found Sally Ann again.

She clacked the gum. "Back so soon?"

"Couldn't stay away," Myron said. "Do you know

a guy who works at Planet Music named Drew Van Dyne?"

"Oh," she said, nodding as though it all made sense now. "Oh yes."

Chapter 34

Claire jumped at the sound of the phone.

She had not slept since Aimee had gone missing. In the past two days Claire had imbibed enough coffee, and thus the caffeine, to be wired for sound. She kept going back to the Rochesters' visit, the father's anger, the mother's meekness. The mother. Joan Rochester. Something was definitely up with that woman.

Claire spent the morning going through Aimee's room while wondering about how to get Joan Rochester to talk. A mother-to-mother approach, maybe. Aimee's room held no new surprises. Claire started going through old boxes, stuff she'd saved from what seemed like two weeks ago. The pencil holder Aimee made Erik in preschool. Her first-grade report card—all As, plus Mrs. Rohrbach's comment that Aimee was a gifted student, fun to have in class, and had a bright future. She stared at the words *bright future*, letting them mock her.

The phone jangled a nerve. She dove for it, hoping

once again that it was Aimee, that this was all some silly misunderstanding, that there was a perfectly reasonable explanation for where she was.

"Hello?"

"She's fine."

The voice was robotic. Neither male nor female. Like an edgier version of the one who tells you that your call is valued and to hold for the next available representative.

"Who is this?"

"She's fine. Just let it be. You have my word."

"Who is this? Let me speak to Aimee."

But the only response was a dial tone.

Joan Rochester said, "Dominick isn't home right now."

"I know," Myron said. "I want to talk to you."

"Me?" As if the very idea of someone wanting to talk to her was a shock on par with a Mars landing. "But why?"

"Please, Mrs. Rochester, it's very important."

"I think we should wait for Dominick."

Myron pushed past her. "I don't."

The house was neat and orderly. It was all straight lines and right angles. No curves, no surprising splashes of color, everything standing upright, as if the very room didn't want to draw attention to itself.

"Can I fix you some coffee?"

"Where is your daughter, Mrs. Rochester?"

She blinked maybe a dozen times in rapid succession. Myron knew men who blinked like that. They were always the guys who were bullied in school as kids and never got over it. She managed to stammer out the word, "What?"

"Where is Katie?"

"I . . . I don't know."

"That's a lie."

More blinking. Myron did not let himself feel sorry for her. "Why . . . I'm not lying."

"You know where Katie is. I assume you have a reason for keeping quiet about it. I assume it involves your husband. That isn't my concern."

Joan Rochester tried to straighten her back. "I'd like you to leave this house."

"No."

"Then I'm going to call my husband."

"I have phone records," Myron said.

More blinking. She put up her hand like she was warding off a blow.

"For your mobile. Your husband wouldn't check that. And even if he did, an incoming call from a pay phone in New York City probably wouldn't mean much. But I know about a woman named Edna Skylar."

Confusion replaced the fear. "Who?"

"She's a doctor at St. Barnabas. She spotted your daughter in Manhattan. More specifically, near Twenty-third Street. You've received several phone calls at seven P.M. from a phone booth four blocks away, which is close enough."

"Those calls weren't from my daughter."

"No?"

"They were from a friend."

"Uh-huh."

"My friend shops in the city. She likes to call when she finds something interesting. To get my opinion."

"On a pay phone?"

"Yes."

"Her name?"

"I'm not going to tell you that. And I insist you leave this very instant."

Myron shrugged, threw up his hands. "I guess this is a dead end for me then."

Joan Rochester was blinking again. She was about to start blinking some more.

"But maybe your husband will have more luck."

All color drained from her face.

"I might as well tell him what I know. You can explain about your friend who likes to shop. He'll believe you, don't you think?"

Terror widened her eyes. "You have no idea what he's like."

"I think I do. He had two goons try to torture me."

"That's because he thought you knew what happened to Katie."

"And you let him, Mrs. Rochester. You'd have let him torture and maybe kill me, and you knew that I had nothing to do with it."

She stopped blinking. "You can't tell my husband. Please."

"I have no interest in harming your daughter. I'm only interested in finding Aimee Biel."

"I don't know anything about that girl."

"But your daughter might."

Joan Rochester shook her head. "You don't understand."

"Don't understand what?"

Joan Rochester walked away, just leaving him there. She crossed the room. When she turned back to him, her eyes were filled with tears. "If he finds out. If he finds her . . ."

"He won't."

She shook her head again.

"I promise," he said.

His words—yet another seemingly empty promise—echoed in the still room.

"Where is she, Mrs. Rochester? I just need to talk to her."

Her eyes started moving around the room as if she suspected her breakfront might overhear them. She stepped toward the back door and opened it. She signaled for him to go outside.

"Where is Katie?" Myron asked.

"I don't know. That's the truth."

"Mrs. Rochester, I really don't have time—"

"The calls."

"What about them?"

"You said they came from New York?"

"Yes."

She looked off.

"What?"

"Maybe that's where she is."

"You really don't know?"

"Katie wouldn't tell me. I didn't ask either."

"Why not?"

Joan Rochester's eyes were perfect circles. "If I don't know," she said, finally meeting his eye, "then he can't make me tell."

Next door a lawn mower started up, shattering the silence. Myron waited a moment. "But you've heard from Katie?"

"Yes."

"And you know she's safe."

"Not from him."

"But in general, I mean. She wasn't kidnapped or anything like that."

She nodded slowly.

"Edna Skylar spotted her with a dark-haired man. Who is he?"

"You're underestimating Dominick. Please don't do that. Just let us be. You're trying to find another girl.

Katie has nothing to do with her."

"They both used the same ATM machine."

"That's a coincidence."

Myron did not bother arguing. "When is Katie calling again?"

"I don't know."

"Then you're not much use to me."

"What's that supposed to mean?"

"I need to talk to your daughter. If you can't help me, I'll have to take the chance that your husband can."

She just shook her head.

"I know she's pregnant," Myron said.

Joan Rochester groaned.

"You don't understand," she said again.

"Then tell me."

"The dark-haired man . . . His name is Rufus. If Dom finds out, he'll kill him. It is that simple. And I don't know what he'll do to Katie."

"So what's their plan? Hide forever?"

"I doubt they have a plan."

"And Dominick doesn't know about any of this?"

"He's not stupid. He thinks Katie probably ran away."

Myron thought about it. "Then I don't get something. If he suspects Katie ran away, why did he go to the press?"

Joan Rochester smiled then, but it was the saddest smile Myron had ever seen. "Don't you see?"

"No."

"He likes to win. No matter what the cost."

"I still don't—"

"He did it to put pressure on them. He wants to find Katie. He doesn't care about anything else. That's his strength. He doesn't mind taking hits. Big hits. Dom doesn't embarrass. He never feels shame. He's willing to lose or suffer to make you hurt and suffer more. That's the kind of man he is."

They fell quiet. Myron wanted to ask why she stayed married to him, but that wasn't his business. There were so many cases of abused women in this country. He'd like to help, but Joan Rochester wouldn't accept it—and he had more pressing matters on his mind. He thought back to the Twins, about not being bothered by their deaths, about Edna Skylar and the way she handled what she thought of as her purer patients.

Joan Rochester had made her choice. Or maybe she was just a little less innocent than the others.

"You should tell the police," Myron said.

"Tell them what?"

"That your daughter is a runaway."

She snorted. "You don't get it, do you? Dom would find out. He has sources in the department. How do you think he found out about you so fast?"

But, Myron realized, he hadn't learned about Edna Skylar. Yet. So his sources weren't infallible. Myron wondered if he could use that, but he didn't see how. He moved closer now. He took Joan Rochester's hands in his and made her look him in the eye.

"Your daughter will be safe. I guarantee it. But I need to talk to her. That's all. Just talk. Do you understand?"

She swallowed. "I don't have much choice, do I?"

Myron said nothing.

"If I don't cooperate, you'll go to Dom."

"Yes," Myron said.

"Katie is supposed to call me tonight at seven," she said. "I'll let you talk to her then."

Chapter 35

Win called Myron on the cell phone.

"Drew Van Dyne, your assistant Planet Music manager, is also a teacher at Livingston High."

"Well, well," Myron said.

"Indeed."

Myron was on his way to pick up Claire. She had told him about the "she's fine" phone call. Myron had immediately reached out for Berruti, who was, as the voice mail informed him, "away from her desk." He told her what he needed in the message.

Now Myron and Claire were going to Livingston High to check out Aimee's locker. Myron also hoped to catch up with her ex, Randy Wolf. And Harry "Mr. D" Davis. And now, most of all, Drew "Music Teacher–Lingerie Buyer" Van Dyne.

"You have anything else on him?"

"Van Dyne is married, no kids. He's had two DUIs in the past four years and one drug arrest. He has a juvie record but it's sealed. That's all I have so far."

"So what is he doing buying lingerie for a student like Aimee Biel?"

"Pretty obvious, I would say."

"I just talked to Mrs. Rochester. Katie got pregnant and ran away with her boyfriend."

"A not-uncommon story."

"No. But what—do we think Aimee did the same?"

"Ran away with her boyfriend? Not likely. No one has reported Van Dyne missing."

"He doesn't have to go missing. Katie's boyfriend is probably afraid of Dominick Rochester. That's why he's with her. But if no one knew about Aimee and Van Dyne . . ."

"Mr. Van Dyne would have little to fear."

"Exactly."

"So pray tell, why would Aimee run away?"

"Because she's pregnant."

"Bah," Win said.

"Bah what?"

"What precisely would Aimee Biel be afraid of?" Win asked. "Erik is hardly a Dominick Rochester type."

Win had a point. "Maybe Aimee didn't run away. Maybe she got pregnant and wanted to have it. Maybe she told her boyfriend, Drew Van Dyne . . ."

"Who," Win picked up the thread, "as a school-teacher, would be ruined if word got out."

"Yes."

It made awful sense. "There's still one big hole," Myron said.

"That being?"

"Both girls used the same ATM machine. Look, the rest doesn't even rise to the level of coincidence. Two girls getting pregnant in a school with almost a thousand girls? It is statistically insignificant. Even if you add two girls running away because of it, okay, the odds that there is a connection rise, but it's still more than plausible that they aren't related, wouldn't you say?"

"I would," Win agreed.

"But then you add in both using the same ATM machine. How do we explain that?"

Win said, "Your little statistical diagnosis goes through the roof."

"So we're missing something."

"We're missing everything. At this stage, this whole matter is too flimsy to label supposition."

Another point for Win. They might be theorizing too early, but they were getting close. There were other factors too, like Roger Chang's threatening "bastard" phone calls. That might be connected, might not be. He also didn't know how Harry Davis fit in. Maybe he was a liaison between Van Dyne and Aimee, but that seemed a stretch. And what should Myron make of Claire's "she's fine" phone call? Myron wondered about the timing and the motive—to comfort or terrorize; and either way, why?—but so far, nothing had come to him.

"Okay," Myron said to Win, "are we all set for tonight?"

"We are indeed."

"I'll talk to you later then."

Win hung up as Myron pulled into Claire and Erik's driveway. Claire was out the front door before Myron came to a complete stop.

"You okay?" he asked.

Claire didn't bother answering the obvious. "Did you hear from your phone contact?"

"Not yet. Do you know a teacher at Livingston High named Drew Van Dyne?"

"No."

"The name doesn't ring a bell?"

"I don't think so. Why?"

"You remember the lingerie I found in her room? I think he might have bought it for her."

Her face reddened. "A teacher?"

"He worked at that music store at the mall."

"Planet Music."

"Yes."

Claire shook her head. "I don't understand any of this."

Myron put a hand on her arm. "You have to stay with me, Claire, okay? I need you to be calm and focus."

"Don't patronize me, Myron."

"I don't mean to, but look, if you go off half-cocked when we get to the school—"

"We'll lose him. I know that. What else is going on?"

"You were dead-on about Joan Rochester." Myron filled her in. Claire sat there and stared at the window. She nodded every once in a while, but the nod didn't seem to be connected to anything he said.

"So you think Aimee might be pregnant?"

Her voice was indeed calm now, too matter-of-fact. She was trying to disengage. That might be a good thing.

"Yes."

Claire put her hand to her lip and started plucking. Like in high school. This was all so weird, driving this route they'd gone on a thousand times in their youth, Claire plucking her lip like the algebra final was coming up. "Okay, let's try to look at this rationally for a moment," she said.

"Right."

"Aimee broke up with her high school boyfriend. She didn't tell us. She was very secretive. She was erasing e-mails. She wasn't herself. She had lingerie in her drawer that was probably bought by a teacher who worked in a music store she used to frequent."

The words hung heavy in the air.

"I have another thought," Claire said.

"Go on."

"If Aimee was pregnant—God, I can't believe I'm talking like this—she would have gone to a clinic of some sort."

"Could be. Maybe she'd just buy a home pregnancy test though."

"No." Claire's voice was firm. "Not in the end. We talked about stuff like this. One of her friends got a false positive on one of those once. Aimee would get it checked. She'd probably find a doctor too."

"Okay."

"And around here, the only clinic is at St. Barnabas. I mean, that's the one everyone uses. So she might have gone there. We should call and see if someone could check the records. I'm the mother. That should count for something, right?"

"I don't know what the laws on that stuff are now."

"They keep changing."

"Wait." Myron picked up his mobile phone. He dialed the hospital's switchboard. He asked for Dr. Stanley Rickenback. Myron gave his name to the secretary. He pulled onto the circle in front of the high school and parked. Rickenback picked up the phone, sounding somewhat excited by the call. Myron explained what he wanted. The excitement vanished.

"I can't do that," Rickenback said.

"I have her mother right here."

"You just told me she's eighteen years old. It's against the rules."

"Listen, you were right about Katie Rochester. She was pregnant. We're trying to find out if Aimee was too."

"I understand that, but I can't help you. Her medical records are confidential. With all the new HIPAA rules, the computer system keeps track of everything, even who opens a patient's file and when. Even if I didn't think it was unethical, it would be too big a personal risk, I'm sorry."

He hung up. Myron stared out the window. Then he called the switchboard back.

"Dr. Edna Skylar, please."

Two minutes later, Edna said, "Myron?"

"You can access patient files from your computer, can't you?"

"Yes."

"All the patients in the hospital?"

"What are you asking?"

"Remember our talk about innocents?"

"Yes."

"I want you to help an innocent, Dr. Skylar." Then, thinking about it, he said, "In this case, maybe two innocents."

"Two?"

"An eighteen-year-old girl named Aimee Biel," Myron said, "and if we're correct, the baby she's carrying."

"My God. Are you telling me Stanley was right?"

"Please, Dr. Skylar."

"It's unethical."

He just let the silence wear on her. He had made his argument. Adding more would be superfluous. Better to let her think it through on her own.

It didn't take long. Two minutes later, he heard the computer keys clacking.

"Myron?" Edna Skylar said.

"Yes."

"Aimee Biel is three months pregnant."

Chapter 36

Livingston High School principal Amory Reid was dressed in Haggar slacks, an off-white short-sleeve dress shirt made of material flimsy enough to highlight the wife-beater tee beneath it, and thick-soled black shoes that might have been vinyl. Even when his tie was loosened, it looked as though it were strangling him.

"The school is, of course, very concerned."

Reid's hands were folded on his desk. On one hand he wore a college ring with a football insignia on it. He had uttered the line as though he'd been rehearsing in front of a mirror.

Myron sat on the right, Claire on the left. She was still dazed from the confirmation that her daughter, the one she knew and loved and trusted, had been pregnant for the past three months. At the same time there was a feeling akin to relief. It made sense. It explained recent behavior. It might provide an explanation for what had been, so far, inexplicable.

"You can, of course, check her locker," the principal

informed them. "I have a master key to all the locks."

"We also want to talk to two of your teachers," Claire said, "and a student."

His eyes narrowed. He looked toward Myron, then back to Claire. "Which teachers?"

"Harry Davis and Drew Van Dyne," Myron said.

"Mr. Van Dyne is already gone for the day. He leaves on Tuesdays at two P.M."

"And Mr. Davis?"

Reid checked a schedule. "He's in room B-202."

Myron knew exactly where that was. After all these years. The halls were still lettered from A to E. Rooms beginning with 1 were on the first floor, 2 on the second floor. He remembered one exasperated teacher telling a tardy student that he wouldn't know his E hall from his—get this—his A hall.

"I can see if I can pull Mr. D out of class. May I ask why you want to talk to these teachers?"

Claire and Myron exchanged a glance. Claire said, "We'd rather not say at this time."

He accepted that. His job was political. If he knew something, he'd have to report it. Ignorance, for a little while, might just be bliss. Myron had nothing big on either teacher yet, just innuendo. Until he had more, there was no reason to inform the school principal.

"We'd also like to talk to Randy Wolf," Claire said.

"I'm afraid I can't let you do that."

"Why not?"

"Off school grounds, you can do whatever you want. But here, I would need to get parental permission."

"Why?"

"That's the rules."

"If a kid is caught cutting class, you can talk to them."

"I can, yes. But you can't. And this isn't a case of cutting class." Reid shifted his gaze. "Furthermore, I'm a little confused why you, Mr. Bolitar, are here."

"He's my representative," Claire said.

"I understand that. But that doesn't give him much standing in terms of talking to a student—or, for that matter, a teacher. I can't make Mr. Davis talk to you either, but I can at least bring him into this office. He's an adult. I can't do that with Randy Wolf."

They started down the corridor to Aimee's locker.

"There is one more thing," Amory Reid said.

"What's that?"

"I'm not sure it relates, but Aimee got into a bit of trouble recently."

They stopped. Claire said, "How?"

"She was caught in the guidance office, using a computer."

"I don't understand."

"Neither did we. One of the guidance counselors found her in there. She was printing out a transcript. Turns out it was just her own."

Myron thought about that. "Aren't those computers password-protected?"

"They are."

"So how did she get in?"

Reid spoke a little too carefully. "We're not sure. But the theory is, someone in the administration made an error."

"An error how?"

"Someone may have forgotten to sign out."

"In other words, they were still logged on so she could gain access?"

"It's a theory, yes."

Pretty dumb one, Myron thought.

"Why wasn't I informed?" Claire asked.

"It wasn't really that big a deal."

"Breaking into school transcripts isn't a big deal?"

"She was printing out her own. Aimee, as you know, was an excellent student. She has never gotten in trouble before. We decided to let her go with a stern warning."

And save yourself some embarrassment, Myron thought. It wouldn't pay to let it out that a student had managed to break into the school computer system. More sweeping under the rug.

They arrived at the locker. Amory Reid used his master key to unlock it. When he opened the door, they all stood back for a moment. Myron was the first to step forward. Aimee's locker was frighteningly personal. Photographs similar to the ones he'd seen in her room adorned the metallic surface. Again no Randy. There were images of her favorite guitar players. On one hanger was a black Green Day American Idiot tour T-shirt; on the other, a New York Liberty sweatshirt. Aimee's textbooks were piled on the bottom, covered in protective sleeves. There were hair ties on the top shelf, a brush, a mirror. Claire touched them tenderly.

But there was nothing in here that seemed to help. No smoking gun, no giant sign reading THIS WAY TO FINDING AIMEE.

Myron felt lost and empty, and staring into the locker, at something so Aimee—it just made her absence that much more obscene.

The mood was broken when Reid's mobile phone buzzed. He picked it up, listened for a moment, and then he hung up.

"I found someone to cover Mr. Davis's class. He's waiting for you in the office."

Chapter 37

Drew Van Dyne was thinking about Aimee and trying to figure out his next step when he arrived at Planet Music. Whenever he did that, whenever he got too confused by life and the poor choices he'd often made, Van Dyne either self-medicated or, as he was doing now, he turned to music.

The iPod ear buds were jammed deep into the canals. He was listening to Alejandro Escovedo's "Gravity," enjoying the sound, trying to put together how Escovedo had written the song. That was what Van Dyne liked to do. He'd tear a song down in the best way possible. He'd come up with a theory about the origin, how the idea had come, the first bit of inspiration. Was that first seed a guitar riff, the chorus, a specific stanza or lyric? Had the writer been heartbroken or sad or filled with joy—and why specifically had he been feeling that way? And where, after that first step, did he go with the song? Van Dyne could see the songwriter at the piano or strumming the guitar, taking notes, altering it, tweaking it, whatever.

Bliss, man. Pure, simple bliss. Figuring out a song. Even if. Even if there was always a small voice, deep in the background, saying, "It should have been you, Drew."

You forget about the wife who looks at you like you're a dog turd and now wants a divorce. You forget about your father, who abandoned you when you were still a kid. You forget about your mother, who tries now to make up for the fact that she didn't give a rat's ass for too many years. You forget the mind-numbing, regular-Joe teaching job you hate. You forget that the job is no longer something you're doing while waiting for your big break. You forget that your big break, when you're honest with yourself, will never come. You forget that you're thirty-six years old and that no matter how hard you try to kill it, your damn dream will not die—no, that would be too easy. Instead the dream stays and taunts and lets you know that it will never, ever, come true.

You escape into the music.

What the hell should he do now?

That was what Drew Van Dyne was thinking as he walked past the Bedroom Rendezvous. He saw one of the salesgirls whisper to another. Maybe they were talking about him, but he didn't much care. He entered Planet Music, a place he both loved and loathed. He loved being surrounded by music. He loathed being reminded that none of it was his.

Jordy Deck, a younger, less talented version of himself, was behind the counter. Van Dyne could see from the young kid's face that something was wrong.

"What?"

"A big dude," the kid said. "He came in here looking for you."

"What was his name?"

The kid shrugged.

"What did he want?"

"He was asking about Aimee."

A lump of fear hardened in his chest. "What did you tell him?"

"That she comes in here a lot, but I think he already knew that. No big deal."

Drew Van Dyne stepped closer. "Describe this guy."

He did. Van Dyne thought about the warning call he'd received earlier today. It sounded like Myron Bolitar.

"Oh, one other thing," the kid said.

"What?"

"When he left, I think he went to Bedroom Rendezvous."

Claire and Myron decided to let Myron talk to Mr. Davis alone.

"Aimee Biel was one of my most gifted students," Harry Davis said.

Davis was pale and shaking and didn't have the same confident stride Myron had seen just that morning.

"Was?" Myron said.

"Pardon me?"

"You said 'was.' 'Was one of my most gifted students.' "

His eyes went wide. "She isn't in my class anymore."

"I see."

"That's all I meant."

"Right," Myron said, trying to keep him on the defensive. "When exactly was she your student?"

"Last year."

"Great." Enough with the prelims. Straight for the

knockout punch: "So if Aimee wasn't your student anymore, what was she doing at your house Saturday night?"

Beads of sweat popped up on his forehead like plastic gophers in one of those arcade games. "What makes you think she was?"

"I dropped her off there."

"That's not possible."

Myron sighed and crossed his legs. "There are two ways to play this, Mr. D. I can get the principal in here or you can tell me what you know."

Silence.

"Why were you talking to Randy Wolf this morning?"

"He's also a student of mine."

"Is or was?"

"Is. I teach sophomores, juniors, and seniors."

"I understand that the students here have voted you Teacher of the Year the past four years."

He said nothing.

Myron said, "I went here."

"Yes, I know." There was a small smile on his lips. "It would be hard to miss the lingering presence of the legendary Myron Bolitar."

"My point is, I know what an accomplishment winning Teacher of the Year is. To be that popular with your students."

Davis liked the compliment. "Did you have a favorite teacher?" he asked.

"Mrs. Friedman. Modern European History."

"She was here when I started." He smiled. "I really liked her."

"That's sweet, Mr. D, really, but there's a girl missing."

"I don't know anything about it."

"Yeah, you do."

Harry Davis looked down.

"Mr. D?"

He didn't look up.

"I don't know what's going on, but it's all coming apart now. All of it. You know that, I think. Your life was one thing before we had this chat. It's another thing now. I don't want to sound melodramatic, but I won't let go until I find out everything. No matter how bad it is. No matter how many people are hurt."

"I don't know anything," he said. "Aimee has never been to my house."

If asked right then, Myron would have said that he wasn't all that mad. In hindsight, that was the problem: a lack of warning. He had been talking in a measured voice. The threat had been there, sure, but it wasn't even worth checking. If he had felt it coming, he would have been able to prepare himself. But the fury just flooded in, snapping him into action.

Myron moved fast. He grabbed Davis from behind the neck, squeezed the pressure points near the base of the shoulders, and pulled him toward the window. Davis let out a little cry as Myron pushed his face hard against the one-way glass.

"Look out there, Mr. D."

In the waiting area Claire sat upright. Her eyes were closed. She thought that no one was watching. Tears ran down her cheeks.

Myron pushed harder.

"Ow!"

"You see that, Mr. D?"

"Let go of me!"

Damn. The fury spread, diffused. Reason bled back in. As with Jake Wolf, Myron scolded his loss of temper and released his grip. Davis stood back and rubbed the back of his neck. His face was scarlet now.

"You come anywhere near me," Davis said, "and I'll sue you. Do you understand?"

Myron shook his head.

"What?"

"You're done, Mr. D. You just don't know it yet."

Chapter 38

Drew Van Dyne headed back to Livingston High School.

How the hell had Myron Bolitar connected him to this mess?

He was in full panic mode now. He had assumed that Harry Davis, Mr. Friggin' Dedicated Teacher, wouldn't say anything. That would have been better, would have left Van Dyne to handle whatever arose. But now, somehow, Bolitar had ended up at Planet Music. He had been asking about Aimee.

Someone had talked.

As he pulled up to the school, he saw Harry Davis burst out the door. Drew Van Dyne was no student of body language, but man, Davis did not look like himself. His fists were clenched, his shoulders slumped, his feet in a fast shuffle mode. Usually he walked with a smile and a wave, sometimes even whistling. Not today.

Van Dyne drove through the lot, pulling the car into Davis's path. Davis saw him and veered to the right.

"Mr. D?"

"Leave me alone."

"You and me, we need to have a little chat."

Van Dyne was out of the car. Davis kept moving.

"You know what will happen if you talk to Bolitar, don't you?"

"I haven't talked," Davis said, teeth clenched.

"Will you?"

"Get in your car, Drew. Leave me the hell alone."

Drew Van Dyne shook his head. "Remember, Mr. D. You got a lot to lose here."

"As you keep pointing out."

"More than any of us."

"No." Davis had reached his car. He slid into the front seat and before he closed his door he said, "Aimee has the most to lose, wouldn't you say?"

That made Van Dyne pause. He tilted his head. "What do you mean by that?"

"Think about it," Davis said.

He closed the door and drove off. Drew Van Dyne took a deep breath and moved back to his car. Aimee had the most to lose. . . . It got him thinking. He started up the engine and began to pull out when he noticed the school's side door open again.

Aimee's mother came out the very same door that beloved educator Harry Davis had stormed out just minutes ago. And behind her was Myron Bolitar.

The voice on the phone, the one that had warned him earlier: *Don't do anything stupid. It's under control.*

It didn't feel under control. It didn't feel that way at all.

Drew Van Dyne reached for the car radio as though he were underwater and it held oxygen. The CD feature was on, the latest from Coldplay. He drove away, letting Chris Martin's gentle voice work on him.

The panic would not leave.

This, he knew, was where he usually made the wrong decision. This is where he usually messed up big-time. He knew that. He knew that he should just back up, think it through. But that was how he lived his life. It was like a car wreck in slow motion. You see what you're heading for. You know there is going to be an ugly collision. You can't stop or get out of the way.

You're powerless.

In the end, Drew Van Dyne made the phone call.

"Hello?"

"We may have a problem," Van Dyne said.

On the other end of the phone, Drew Van Dyne heard Big Jake Wolf sigh.

"Tell me," Big Jake said.

Myron dropped Claire off before heading to the Livingston Mall. He hoped to find Drew Van Dyne at Planet Music. No luck. The poncho kid wouldn't talk this time, but Sally Ann said that she'd seen Drew Van Dyne arrive, talk briefly to the poncho kid, and then sprint out. Myron had Van Dyne's home number. He tried it, but there was no answer.

He called Win. "We need to find this guy."

"We're spread a little thin right now."

"Who can we get to watch Van Dyne's house?"

Win said, "How about Zorra?"

Zorra was a former Mossad spy, an assassin for the Israelis, and a transvestite who wore stiletto heels—literally. Many transvestites are lovely. Zorra was not one of them.

"I'm not sure she'll blend into the suburbs, are you?"

"Zorra knows how to blend."

"Fine, whatever you think."

"Where are you headed?"

"Chang's Dry Cleaning. I need to talk to Roger."

"I'll call Zorra."

Business was brisk at Chang's. Maxine saw Myron enter and gestured with her head for him to come forward. Myron moved ahead of the line and followed her into the back. The smell of chemicals and lint was cloying. It felt like dust particles were clinging to his lungs. He was relieved when she opened the back door.

Roger sat on a crate in the alley. His head was down. Maxine folded her arms and said, "Roger, do you have something to say to Mr. Bolitar?"

Roger was a skinny kid. His arms were reeds with absolutely no definition. He did not look up as she spoke.

"I'm sorry I made those phone calls," he said.

It was like he was a kid who'd broken a neighbor's window with an errant baseball and his mother had dragged him across the street to apologize. Myron did not need this. He turned to Maxine. "I want to talk to him alone."

"I can't let you do that."

"Then I go to the police."

First Joan Rochester, now Maxine Chang—Myron was getting damn good at threatening terrified mothers. Maybe he'd start slapping them around too, really feel like a big man.

But Myron did not blink. Maxine Chang did. "I will be right inside."

"Thank you."

The alley reeked, as all alleys do, of past garbage and dried urine. Myron waited for Roger to look up at him. Roger didn't.

"You didn't just call me," Myron said. "You called Aimee Biel, right?"

He nodded, still not looking up.

"Why?"

"I was calling her back."

Myron made a skeptical face. Since the kid's head was still down, the effort was a bit of a waste. "Look at me, Roger."

He slowly raised his eyes.

"Are you telling me that Aimee Biel called you first?"

"I saw her in school. She said we needed to talk."

"About what?"

He shrugged. "She just said we needed to talk."

"So why didn't you?"

"Why didn't we what?"

"Talk. Right then and there."

"We were in the hall. There were people all around. She wanted to talk privately."

"I see. So you called her?"

"Yes."

"And what did she say?"

"It was weird. She wanted to know about my grades and extra-curricular activities. It was more like she wanted to confirm them. I mean, we know each other a little. And everyone talks. So she already knew most of that stuff."

"That's it?"

"We only talked for, like, two minutes. She said she had to go. But she also said she was sorry."

"About?"

"About my not making Duke." He put his head down again.

"You got a lot of anger stored up, Roger."

"You don't understand."

"Tell me then."

"Forget it."

"I wish I could, but see, you called me."

Roger Chang studied the alley as though he'd never really seen it before. His nose twitched, and his face twisted in disgust. Finally he found Myron's face. "I'm always the Asian geek, you know? I was born in this country. I'm not an immigrant. When I talk, half the time people expect me to sound like an old Charlie Chan movie. And in this town, if you don't have money or you're not good at sports . . . I see my mother sacrifice. I see how hard she works. And I think to myself: If I can just stick it out. If I can just work hard in high school, not worry about all that stuff I'm missing, just work hard, make the sacrifice, it will all be okay. I'll be able to move out of here. I don't know why I focused on Duke. But I did. It was, like, my one goal. Once I made it, I could relax a little. I'd be away from this store. . . ."

His voice drifted off.

"I wish you'd have said something to me," Myron said.

"I'm not good at asking for help."

Myron wanted to tell him he should do more than that, maybe get some therapy to deal with the anger, but he hadn't walked a mile in the kid's shoes. He didn't have the time either.

"Are you going to report me?" Roger asked.

"No." Then: "You could still get in on wait-list."

"They've already cleared it."

"Oh," Myron said. "Look, I know it seems like life and death now, but what school you make isn't that important. I bet you'll love Rutgers."

"Yeah, sure."

He didn't sound convinced. Part of Myron was angry, but another part—a growing part—remembered Maxine's accusation. There was a chance, a decent chance, that by helping Aimee, Myron had destroyed this young man's dream. He couldn't just walk away from that, could he?

"If you want to transfer after a year," Myron said, "I'll write a letter."

He waited for Roger to react. He didn't. So Myron left him alone in the stench of the alley behind his mother's dry cleaning store.

Chapter 39

Myron was on his way to meet up with Joan Rochester—she was afraid to be home when her daughter called in case her husband was around—when his mobile phone rang. He checked the caller ID and his heart skipped a beat when he saw the name ALI WILDER pop up.

"Hey," he said.

"Hey."

Silence.

"I'm sorry about before," Ali said.

"Don't apologize."

"No, I sounded hysterical. I know what you were trying to do with the girls."

"I didn't want to get Erin involved."

"It's all right. Maybe I should be concerned or whatever, but I just really want to see you."

"Me too."

"Come over?"

"I can't right now."

"Oh."

"And I'll probably be working on this until late."

"Myron?"

"Yes."

"I don't care how late."

He smiled.

"Whatever the time, come by," Ali said. "I'll be waiting. And if I fall asleep, throw pebbles at my window and wake me up. Okay?"

"Okay."

"Be careful."

"Ali?"

"Yes?"

"I love you."

There was a little intake of air. Then, with a little song in the voice: "I love you too, Myron."

And suddenly, it was as if Jessica were a wisp of smoke.

Dominick Rochester's office was a depot for school buses.

Outside his window was a plethora of yellow. This place was his cover. School buses could do wonders. If you transport kids in the seats, you could pretty much transport anything else in the undercarriage. Cops might stop and search a truck. They never do that with a school bus.

The phone rang. Rochester picked it up and said, "Hello?"

"You wanted me to watch your house?"

He did. Joan was drinking more than ever. It could have been from Katie's disappearance, but Dominick was no longer so sure. So he had one of his guys keep an eye. Just in case.

"Yeah, so?"

"Earlier today some guy stopped by to talk to your wife."

"Earlier today?"

"Right."

"How much earlier?"

"Couple of hours maybe."

"Why didn't you call then?"

"Didn't think much about it, I guess. I mean, I wrote it down. But I thought you only wanted me to call you if it was important."

"What does he look like?"

"His name is Myron Bolitar. I recognized him. He used to play ball."

Dominick pulled the receiver closer, pushing it against his ear as though he could travel through it. "How long did he stay?"

"Fifteen minutes."

"Just the two of them?"

"Yeah. Oh, don't worry, Mr. Rochester. I watched them. They stayed downstairs, if that's what you're wondering. There was no . . ." He stopped, not sure how to put it.

Dominick almost laughed. This dopey guy thought he was having his wife watched in case she was sleeping around. Man, that was rich. But now he wondered: Why had Bolitar come by and stayed so long?

And what had Joan told him?

"Anything else?"

"Well, that's the thing, Mr. Rochester."

"What's the thing?"

"There is something else. See, I wrote down about Bolitar's visit, but since I could see where he was, I didn't worry much, you know?"

"And now?"

"Well, I'm following Mrs. Rochester. She just drove

315

to some park in town here. Riker Hill. You know it?"

"My kids went to elementary school there."

"Good, okay. She's sitting on a bench. But she's not alone. See, your wife is sitting there with that same guy. With Myron Bolitar."

Silence.

"Mr. Rochester?"

"Get a man on Bolitar too. I want him followed. I want them both followed."

During the Cold War, the Riker Hill Art Park, located right smack in the bosom of suburbia, had been a military control base for air-defense missiles. The army called it Nike Battery Missile Site NY-80. For real. From 1954 until the end of the Nike air defense system in 1974, the site was operational for both Hercules and Ajax missiles. Many of the U.S. Army's original buildings and barracks now serve as studios where painting, sculpture, and crafts flourish in a communal setting.

Years ago, Myron had found this all somewhat poignant and oddly comforting—the war relic now housing artists—but the world was different now. In the eighties and nineties, it had all been cute and quaint. Now this "progress" felt like phony symbolism.

Near the old military radar tower, Myron sat on the bench with Joan Rochester. They hadn't done more than nod at each other. They were waiting. Joan Rochester cradled her mobile phone as if it were an injured animal. Myron checked his watch. Any minute now, Katie Rochester was supposed to call her mother.

Joan Rochester looked off. "You're wondering why I stay with him."

In truth, he wasn't. First off, awful as this situation

was, he was still feeling a little giddy from his phone call with Ali. He knew that was selfish, but this was the first time in seven years he had told a woman that he loved her. He was trying to push all that from his mind, trying to focus on the task at hand, but he couldn't help feeling a little high from her response.

Second—and maybe more relevant—Myron had long ago stopped trying to figure out relationships. He had read about battered woman syndrome and perhaps that was at play here and this was a cry for help. But for some reason, in this particular case, he didn't care enough to reach out and answer that call.

"I've been with Dom a long time. A very long time."

Joan Rochester went quiet. After a few more seconds, she opened her mouth to say more, but the phone in her hand vibrated. She looked down at it as though it had suddenly materialized in her hand. It vibrated again and then it rang.

"Answer it," Myron said.

Joan Rochester nodded and hit the green button. She brought the phone to her ear and said, "Hello?"

Myron leaned close to her. He could hear a voice on the other end of the line—sounded young, sounded female—but he couldn't make out any of the words.

"Oh, honey," Joan Rochester said, her face easing from the sound of her daughter's voice. "I'm glad you're safe. Yes. Yes, right. Listen to me a second, okay? This is very important."

More talking from the other end.

"I have someone here with me—"

Animated talk from the other end.

"Please, Katie, just listen. His name is Myron Bolitar. He's from Livingston. He means you no harm. How did he find . . . it's complicated. . . . No, of course I didn't say anything. He got phone records or something, I'm not really sure, but he said he would tell Daddy—"

Very animated talk now.

"No, no, he hasn't done that yet. He just needs to talk to you for a minute. I think you should listen. He says it's about the other missing girl, Aimee Biel. He's looking for her. . . . I know, I know, I told him that. Just . . . hold on, okay? Here he is."

Joan Rochester began to hand him the phone. Myron reached out and snatched it from her, afraid of losing this tenuous connection. He strapped on his calmest voice and said, "Hello, Katie. My name is Myron."

He sounded like a night host on NPR.

Katie, however, was a tad more hysterical. "What do you want with me?"

"I just have a few questions."

"I don't know anything about Aimee Biel."

"If you could just tell me—"

"You're tracing this, aren't you?" Her voice was cracking with hysteria. "For my dad. You're keeping me on the line so you can trace the call!"

Myron was about to launch into a Berruti-type explanation of how traces didn't really work that way, but Katie never gave him the chance.

"Just leave us alone!"

And then she hung up.

Like another dopey TV cliché, Myron said, "Hello? Hello?" when he knew that Katie Rochester had hung up and was gone.

They sat in silence for a minute or two. Then Myron slowly handed her back the phone.

"I'm sorry," Joan Rochester said.

Myron nodded.

"I tried."

"I know."

She stood. "Are you going to tell Dom?"

"No," Myron said.

"Thank you."

He nodded again. She walked away. Myron stood and headed in the opposite direction. He took out his cell phone and hit the speed-dial number one slot. Win answered it.

"Articulate."

"Was it Katie Rochester?"

He had expected something like this—Katie not cooperating. So Myron had prepared. Win was on the scene in Manhattan, ready to follow. It was, in fact, better. She would head back to wherever she was hiding. Win would tag along and learn all.

"Looked like her," Win said. "She was with a dark-haired paramour."

"And now?"

"After hanging up, she and said paramour began heading downtown by foot. By the way, the paramour is carrying a firearm in a shoulder holster."

That wasn't good. "You're on them?"

"I'll pretend you didn't ask me that."

"I'm on my way."

Chapter 40

Joan Rochester took a pull from the flask she kept under the car seat.

She was in her driveway now. She could have waited until she got inside. But she didn't. She was in a daze, had been in a daze for so long that she no longer remembered a time when she really felt truly clear-headed. Didn't matter. You get used to it. You get so used to it that it becomes normal, this daze, and it would be the clear head that would throw her out of whack.

She stayed in her car and stared at her house. She looked at it as though for the first time. This was where she lived. It sounded so simple, but there it was. This is where she was spending her life. It was unremarkable. It felt impersonal. She lived here. She had helped choose it. And now, as she looked at it, she wondered why.

Joan closed her eyes and tried to imagine something different. How had she gotten here? You don't just slip, she realized. Change was never dramatic. It was small shifts, so gradual that it becomes imperceptible to the human eye. That was how it had happened to Joan

Delnuto Rochester, the prettiest girl at Bloomfield High.

You fall in love with a man because he is everything your father isn't. He is strong and tough and you like that. He sweeps you off your feet. You don't even realize how much he takes over your life, how you start to become merely an extension of him, rather than a separate entity or, as you dream, one grander entity, two becoming one in love, like out of a romance novel. You acquiesce on small things, then large things, then everything. Your laugh starts to quiet before disappearing altogether. Your smile dims until it is only a facsimile of joy, something you apply like mascara.

But when had it turned the dark corner?

She couldn't find a spot on the time line. She thought back, but she couldn't locate a moment when she could have changed things. It was inevitable, she supposed, from the day they met. There wasn't a time when she could have stood up to him. There wasn't a battle she could have waged and won that would have altered anything.

If she could go back in time, would she walk away the first time he asked her out? Would she have said no then? Taken up with another boyfriend, like that nice Mike Braun, who lived in Parsippany now? The answer would probably be no. Her children wouldn't have been born. Children, of course, change everything. You can't wish it all never happened, because that would be the ultimate betrayal: How could you live with yourself if you wished your children never existed?

She took another swig.

The truth was, Joan Rochester wished her husband dead. She dreamed about it. Because it was her only escape. Forget that nonsense about abused women standing up to their man. It would be suicide. She could never leave him. He would find her and beat her and lock her up. He would do lord-knows-what to their children. He would make her pay.

Joan sometimes fantasized about packing up the children and finding one of those battered-women shelters in the city. But then what? She dreamed about turning state's evidence against Dom—she certainly had the knowledge—but even Witness Protection wouldn't do the trick. He'd find them. Somehow.

He was that kind of man.

She slipped out of her car. There was a wobble in her step, but again that had become almost the norm. Joan Rochester headed to her front door. She slipped the key in and stepped inside. She turned around to close it behind her. When she turned back around, Dominick stood in front of her.

Joan Rochester put her hand to her heart. "You startled me."

He stepped toward her. For a moment she thought that he wanted to embrace her. But that wasn't it. He bent low at the knees. His right hand turned into a fist. He swiveled into the roundhouse blow, using his hips for power. The knuckles slammed into her kidney.

Joan's mouth opened in a silent scream. Her knees gave way. She fell to the floor. Dominick grabbed her by the hair. He lifted her back up and readied the fist. He smashed it into her back again, harder this time.

She slid to the ground like a slit bag of sand.

"You're going to tell me where Katie is," Dominick said.

And then he hit her again.

Myron was in his car, talking on the phone to Wheat Manson, his former Duke teammate who now worked in the admissions office as assistant dean, when he realized yet again that he was being followed.

Wheat Manson had been a speedy point guard from the nasty streets of Atlanta. He had loved his years in Durham, North Carolina, and had never gone back. The two old friends started off exchanging quick pleasantries before Myron got to the point.

"I need to ask you something a little weird," Myron said.

"Go ahead."

"Don't get offended."

"Then don't ask me anything offensive," Wheat said.

"Did Aimee Biel get in because of me?"

Wheat groaned. "Oh no, you did *not* just ask me that."

"I need to know."

"Oh no, you did *not* just ask me that."

"Look, forget that for a second. I need you to fax me two transcripts. One for Aimee Biel. And one for Roger Chang."

"Who?"

"He's another student from Livingston High."

"Let me guess. Roger didn't get accepted."

"He had a better ranking, better SAT scores—"

"Myron?"

"What?"

"We are not going there. Do you understand me? It's confidential. I will not send you transcripts. I will not discuss candidates. I will remind you that acceptance is not a matter of scores or tests, that there are intangibles. As two guys who got in based much more on our ability to put a sphere through a metallic ring than rankings and test scores, we should understand that better than anyone. And now, only slightly offended, I will say good-bye."

"Wait, hold up a second."

"I'm not faxing you transcripts."

"You don't have to. I'm going to tell you something about both candidates. I just want you to look it up on the computer and make sure what I'm saying is true."

"What the hell are you talking about?"

"Just trust me here, Wheat. I'm not asking for information. I'm asking you to confirm something."

Wheat sighed. "I'm not in the office right now."

"Do it when you can."

"Tell me what you want me to confirm."

Myron told him. And as he did, he realized that the same car had been with him since he left Riker Hill. "Will you do it?"

"You're a pain in the ass, you know that?"

"Always was," Myron said.

"Yeah, but you used to have a sweet jumper from the top of the key. Now what do you got?"

"Raw animal magnetism and supernatural charisma?"

"I'm going to hang up now."

He did. Myron pulled the hands-free from his ear. The car was still behind him, maybe two hundred feet back.

What was up with all the car tails today? In the old days, a suitor would send flowers or candy. Myron pined for a brief moment, but now was hardly the time. The car had been on him since he left Riker Hill. That meant it was probably one of Dominick Rochester's goons again. He thought about that. If Rochester had sent a man to follow Myron, he'd probably at the very least known or seen that Myron was with his wife. Myron debated calling Joan Rochester, letting her know, but decided against it. As Joan had pointed out, she'd been with him a long time. She'd know how to handle it.

He was on Northfield Avenue heading to New York City. He didn't have time for this, but he needed to get rid of this tail as quickly as possible. In the movies, this would call for a car chase or a swift U-turn of some sort. That didn't really play in real life, especially when you need to get to a place in a hurry and don't want to attract the cops.

Still, there were ways.

The music store teacher, Drew Van Dyne, lived in West Orange, not far from here. Zorra should be in place now. Myron picked up his cell phone and called. Zorra picked up on the first ring.

"Hello, dreamboat," Zorra said.

"I assume there's been no activity at the Van Dyne house."

"You assume correctly, dreamboat. Zorra just sits and sits. So boring this, for Zorra."

Zorra always referred to herself in the third person. She had a deep voice, a thick accent, and lots of mouth phlegm. It was not a pleasant sound.

"I have a car following me," Myron said.

"And Zorra can help?"

"Oh yes," Myron said. "Zorra can definitely help."

Myron explained his plan—his frighteningly simple plan. Zorra laughed and started coughing.

"So Zorra like?" Myron asked, falling, as he often did when speaking to her, into Zorra-talk.

"Zorra like. Zorra like very much."

Since it would take a few minutes to set up, Myron took some unnecessary turns. Two minutes later, Myron took the right on Pleasant Valley Way. Up ahead, he saw Zorra standing by the pizzeria. She wore her '30s blond wig and smoked a cigarette in a holder and looked just like Veronica Lake after a real bad bender, if Veronica Lake was six feet tall and had a Homer Simpson five o'clock shadow and was really, really ugly.

Zorra winked as Myron passed and raised her foot just a little bit. Myron knew what was in that heel. The first time they met, she had sliced his chest with the hidden "stiletto" blade. In the end, Win had spared Zorra's life—something that surprised the heck out of Myron. Now they were all buddies. Esperanza compared it to her days in the ring when a famed bad-guy wrestler would all of a sudden turn good.

Myron used the left-turn signal and pulled to the side of the road, two blocks ahead of Zorra. He rolled down his window so he could hear. Zorra stood near an open parking spot. It was natural. The car following Myron's pulled into the spot to see where Myron was headed. Of course, he could have stopped anywhere on the street. Zorra had been ready for that.

The rest was, as already noted, frighteningly simple. Zorra strolled over to the back of the car. She had been wearing high heels for the past fifteen years, but she still walked like a newborn colt on bad acid.

Myron watched the scene in his rearview mirror.

Zorra unsheathed the dagger in her stiletto heel. She raised her leg and stomped on the tire. Myron heard the whoosh of air. She quickly circled to the other back tire and did the same thing. Then Zorra did something that was not part of the plan.

She waited to see if the driver would get out and accost her.

"No," Myron whispered to himself. "Just go."

He had been clear. Stomp the tires and run. Don't get into a fight. Zorra was deadly. If the guy got out of his car—probably some macho goon who was used to breaking heads—Zorra would slice him into pizza topping. Forget the morals for a moment. They didn't need that kind of police attention.

The goon driving the car yelled, "Hey! What the—?" and started getting out of the car.

Myron turned around and stuck his head out the window. Zorra had the smile. She bent her knees a little. Myron called out. Zorra looked up and met Myron's eye. Myron could see the anticipation, the itch to strike. He shook his head as firmly as he knew how.

Another second passed. The goon slammed his car door shut. "You dumb bitch!"

Myron kept shaking his head, more urgently now. The goon took a step. Myron held Zorra's gaze. Zorra reluctantly nodded.

And then she ran away.

"Hey!" The goon gave chase. "Stop!"

Myron started up his car. The goon looked back now, unsure what to do, and then he made a decision that probably saved his life.

He ran back to his car.

But with slashed back tires, he wouldn't go anywhere.

Myron pulled back onto the road, on his way to his encounter with the missing Katie Rochester.

Chapter 41

D rew Van Dyne sat in Big Jake Wolf's family room and tried to plan his next move.

Jake had given him a Corona Light. Drew frowned. A real Corona, okay, but light Mexican beer? Why not just pass out piss water? Drew sipped it anyway.

This room reeked of Big Jake. There was a deer head hanging above the fireplace. Golf and tennis trophies lined the mantel. The rug was some sort of bear skin. The TV was huge, at least seventy inches. There were tiny expensive speakers everywhere. Something classical drifted out from the digital player. A carnival popcorn machine with flashing lights sat in the corner. There were ugly gold statues and ferns. Everything had been selected not based on fashion or function, but by what would appear most ostentatious and overpriced.

On the side table was a picture of Jake Wolf's hot wife. Drew picked it up and shook his head. In the photograph, Lorraine Wolf wore a bikini. Another of Jake's trophies, he guessed. A picture of your own wife in a bikini on a side table in the family room—who the hell does that?

"I spoke to Harry Davis," Wolf said. He had a Corona Light too. There was a wedge of lime jammed into the top. Van Dyne rule of alcohol consumption: If a beer needs a fruit topping, choose another beer. "He's not going to talk."

Drew said nothing.

"You don't believe it?"

Drew shrugged, drank his beer.

"He has the most to lose here."

"You think?"

"You don't?"

"I reminded Harry of that. You know what he said?"

Jake shrugged.

"He told me that maybe Aimee Biel had the most to lose." Drew put down his beer, intentionally missing the coaster. "What do you think?"

Big Jake pointed his beefy finger at Drew. "Who the hell's fault would that be?"

Silence.

Jake walked over to the window. He gestured with his chin at the house next door. "You see that place over there?"

"What about it?"

"It's a friggin' castle."

"You're not doing too badly here, Jake."

A small smile played on his lip. "Not like that."

Drew would point out that it's all relative, that he, Drew Van Dyne, lived alone in a crap-hole that was smaller than Wolf's garage, but why bother? Drew could also point out that he didn't have a tennis court or three cars or gold statues or a theater room or even really a wife since the separation, much less one with a hot enough body to model in bikinis.

"He's a big-time lawyer," Jake droned on. "Went to Yale and never lets anyone forget it. He has a Yale decal on his car window. He wears Yale T-shirts when he takes his daily jog. He hosts Yale parties. He interviews Yale applicants in his big castle. His son is a dope, but guess what school still accepted him?"

Drew Van Dyne shifted in the chair.

"The world is not a level playing field, Drew. You need an in. Or you have to make one. You, for example, wanted to be a big rock star. The guys who make it—who sell a zillion CDs and fill up outdoor arenas—do you think they're more talented than you? No. The big difference, maybe the only difference, is that they were willing to take advantage of some situation. They exploited something. And you didn't. Do you know what the world's greatest truism is?"

Drew could see that there was no stopping him. But that was okay. The man was talking. He was revealing things in his own way. Drew was getting the picture now. He had a pretty good idea of where this was heading. "No, what?"

"Behind every great fortune is a great crime."

Jake stopped and let that sink in. Drew felt his breathing go a little funny.

"You see someone with beaucoup bucks," Jake Wolf went on, "a Rockefeller or Carnegie or someone. Do you want to know the difference between them and us? One of their great-grandpas cheated or stole or killed. He had balls, sure. But he understood that the playing field is never level. You want a break, you make it yourself. Then you peddle that hard-work, nose-to-the-grindstone fiction to the masses."

Drew Van Dyne remembered the warning call: *Don't do anything stupid. It's under control.*

"This Bolitar guy," Drew said. "You already had your cop friends lay into him. He didn't budge."

"Don't worry about him."

"That's not much of a comfort, Jake."

"Well," Jake said, "let's just remember whose fault this is."

"Your son's."

"Hey!" Again Jake pointed with the beefy finger. "Keep Randy out of it."

Drew Van Dyne shrugged. "You're the one who wanted to place blame."

"He's going to Dartmouth. That's a done deal. No one, especially not some dumb slut, is going to ruin that."

Drew took a long deep breath. "Still. The question is, if Bolitar keeps digging, what is he going to find?"

Jake Wolf looked at him. "Nothing," he said.

Drew Van Dyne felt a twinge start in the base of his spine.

"How can you be so sure?"

Wolf said nothing.

"Jake?"

"Don't worry about it. Like I said, my son is on his way to college. He's done with all this."

"You also said that behind every great fortune is a great crime."

"So?"

"She means nothing to you, does she, Jake?"

"It's not about her. It's about Randy. It's about his future."

Jake Wolf turned back to the window, to his Ivy League neighbor's castle. Drew gathered his thoughts, reined in his emotions. He looked at this man. He thought about what he had said, what it all meant. He thought again about the warning call.

"Jake?"

"What?"

"Did you know that Aimee Biel was pregnant?"

The room went quiet. The background music was between songs now. When it started up again, the beat had picked up a step, an old ditty from Supertramp. Jake Wolf slowly turned his head and looked back over his shoulder. Drew Van Dyne could see that the news was a surprise.

"That doesn't change anything," Jake said.

"I think maybe it does."

"How?"

Drew Van Dyne reached into his shoulder holster. He removed the gun and aimed it at Jake Wolf. "Take a wild guess."

Chapter 42

The storefront was a nail salon called Nail-R-Us in a not-yet-redeveloped section of Queens. The building had that decrepit thing going on, as if leaning against it would cause a wall to collapse. The rust on the fire escape was so thick that tetanus seemed a far greater threat than smoke inhalation. Every window was blocked by either a heavy shade or a plank of wood. The structure was four levels and ran almost the entire length of the block.

Myron said to Win, "The R on the sign is crossed out."

"That's intentional."

"Why?"

Win looked at him, waited. Myron did it in his head. Nail-R-Us had become Nail Us.

"Oh," Myron said. "Cute."

"They have two armed guards stationed at windows," Win said.

"They must do a mean manicure."

Win frowned. "Moreover, the two guards didn't

take up position until your Ms. Rochester and her beau returned."

"They're worried about her father," Myron said.

"That would be a logical deduction."

"You know anything about the place?"

"The clientele is below my level of expertise." Win nodded behind Myron. "But not hers."

Myron turned. The setting sun was blocked now as though by an eclipse. Big Cyndi was ambling toward them. She was dressed entirely in white spandex. Very tight white spandex. No undergarments. Tragically, you could tell. On a seventeen-year-old runway model, the spandex jumpsuit would be a fashion risk. On a woman of forty who weighed more than three hundred pounds . . . well, it took guts, lots of them, all of which were on full display, thank you very much. Everything jiggled as she trundled toward them; various body parts seemed to have lives of their own, moving of their own accord, as if dozens of animals were trapped in a white balloon and trying to squirm their way out.

Big Cyndi kissed Win on the cheek. Then she turned and said, "Hello, Mr. Bolitar." She hugged him, wrapping her arms around him, a feeling not unlike being wrapped in wet attic insulation.

"Hey, Big Cyndi," Myron said when she put him down. "Thanks for getting down here so quick."

"When you call, Mr. Bolitar, I run."

Her face remained placid. Myron never knew if Big Cyndi was putting him on or not.

"Do you know this place?" he asked.

"Oh yes."

She sighed. Elk within a forty-mile radius began to mate. Big Cyndi wore white lipstick like something out of an Elvis documentary. Her makeup had sparkles. Her fingernails were in a color she'd once told him was called Pinot Noir. Back in the day, Big Cyndi had been the bad-guy professional wrestler. She fit the bill. For those who have never watched professional wrestling, it is merely a morality play with good pitted against evil. For years, Big Cyndi had been the evil "warlordess" named Human Volcano. Then one night, after a particularly grueling match where Big Cyndi had "injured" the lovely and lithe Esperanza "Little Pocahontas" Diaz with a chair—"injured" her so badly that the fake ambulance came in and strapped on the neck brace and all that—an angry mob of fans waited outside the venue.

When Big Cyndi left for the night, the mob attacked. They might have killed her. The crowd was drunk and fired up and not really into the reality-versus-fiction equation at work here. Big Cyndi tried to run, but there was no escape. She fought hard and well, but there were dozens wanting her blood. Someone hit her with a camera, a cane, a boot. They moved in. Big Cyndi went down. People started stomping her.

Seeing the mayhem, Esperanza tried to intervene. The crowd would have none of it. Even their favorite wrestler could not halt their bloodlust. And then Esperanza did something truly inspired.

She jumped on a car and "revealed" that Big Cyndi had only been pretending to be a bad guy to gather information. The crowd almost paused. Furthermore, Esperanza announced, Big Cyndi was really Little Pocahontas's long lost sister, Big Chief Mama, a rather lame moniker but hey, she was making this stuff up on the fly. Little Pocahontas and her sister were now reuniting and would become tag-team partners.

The crowd cheered. Then they helped Big Cyndi to her feet.

Big Chief Mama and Little Pocahontas quickly became wrestling's most popular team. The same scenario played out weekly: Esperanza would start every match winning on skill, their opponents would do something illegal like throw sand in her eye or use the dreaded foreign object, the two baddies would team up on poor, helpless Pocahontas while someone distracted Big Chief Mama, they'd beat the sensuous beauty until the strap on Pocahontas's suede bikini ripped, and then Big Chief Mama would give out a war cry and ride in to the rescue.

Massively entertaining.

When she left the ring, Big Cyndi became a bouncer and sometimes stage performer for several lowlife sex clubs. She knew the seedier side of the streets. And that was what they were counting on now.

"So what is this place?" Myron asked.

Big Cyndi put on her totem-pole frown. "They do a lot of things, Mr. Bolitar. Some drugs, some Internet scamming, but mostly, these are sex clubs."

"Clubs," Myron repeated. "As in the plural?"

Big Cyndi nodded. "Six or seven different ones probably. Remember a few years ago when Forty-second Street was loaded with sleaze?"

"Yes."

"Well, when they forced them all out, where do you think the sleaze went?"

Myron looked at the nail salon. "Here?"

"Here, there, everywhere. You don't kill sleaze, Mr. Bolitar. It just moves to a new host."

"And this is the new host?"

"One of them. Here, in this very building, they offer specialty clubs catering to an international variety of tastes."

"When you say 'specialty clubs'—?"

"Let's see. If you care for flaxen-haired women, you go to On Golden Blonde. That's on the second floor, far right. If you're into African-American men, you head up to the third floor and visit a place called—you might like this, Mr. Bolitar—Malcolm Sex."

Myron looked at Win. Win shrugged.

Big Cyndi continued in her tour guide voice: "Those with an Asian fetish will enjoy the Joy Suck Club—"

"Yeah," Myron said, "I think I get the picture. So how do I get in and find Katie Rochester?"

Big Cyndi thought about that for a moment. "I can pose as a job applicant."

"Excuse me?"

Big Cyndi put her enormous fists on her hips. This meant that they were about two yards apart. "Not all men, Mr. Bolitar, have petite fetishes."

Myron closed his eyes and rubbed the bridge of his nose. "Right, okay, maybe. Any other thoughts?"

Win waited patiently. Myron had always thought that Win would be intolerant of Big Cyndi, but years ago, Win surprised him by pointing out what should have been obvious: "One of our worst and most accepted prejudices is against large women. We never, ever, see past it." And it was true. Myron had been deeply ashamed when Win pointed that out. So he started treating Big Cyndi as he should—like everyone else. That pissed Big Cyndi off. Once, when Myron smiled at her, she hit him hard on the shoulder—so hard he couldn't lift his arm for two days—and shouted, "Cut that out!"

"Perhaps you should try a more direct route," Win said. "I will stay out here. Keep your cell phone on. You and Big Cyndi try and talk your way in."

Big Cyndi nodded. "We can pretend we're a couple looking to try a threesome."

Myron was about to say something when Big Cyndi said, "Kidding."

"I knew that."

She arched a shiny eyebrow and leaned toward him. The mountain coming to Muhammad. "But now that I planted that most erotic seed, Mr. Bolitar, you may find performing with a petite difficult."

"I'll muddle through. Come on."

Myron stepped through the door first. A black man at the door sporting designer sunglasses told him to halt. He wore an earplug like someone in the Secret Service. He patted Myron down.

"Man," Myron said, "all this for a manicure?"

The man took away Myron's cell phone. "We don't allow pictures," he said.

"It's not a camera phone."

The black man grinned. "You'll get it back on the way out."

He held the grin until Big Cyndi filled the doorway. Then the grin fled, replaced with something akin to terror. Big Cyndi ducked inside like a giant entering a kid's clubhouse. She stood upright, stretched her arms over her head, and spread her legs apart. The white spandex cried out in agony. Big Cyndi winked at the black man.

"Frisk me, big boy," she said. "I'm packing."

The outfit was tight enough to double as skin. If Big Cyndi was indeed packing, the man didn't want to know where.

"You're okay, miss. Step through."

Myron thought again about what Win had said, about accepted prejudice. There was something personal in the words, but when Myron had tried to follow up, Win closed down on the subject. Still, about four years ago, Esperanza had wanted Big Cyndi to take on some clients. Outside of Myron and Esperanza, she had been with MB Reps the longest. It sort of made sense.

But Myron knew it would be a disaster. And it was. No one felt comfortable with Big Cyndi repping them. They blamed her outlandish clothes, her makeup, her manner of speech (she liked to growl), but even if she got rid of all that, would it have changed anything?

The black man cupped his ear. Someone was talking to him through the earpiece. He suddenly put an arm on Myron's shoulder.

"What can I do for you, sir?"

Myron decided to stick with the direct route. "I'm looking for a woman named Katie Rochester."

"There's no one here by that name."

"No, she's here," Myron said. "She walked in that very door twenty minutes ago."

The black man took a step closer to Myron. "Are you calling me a liar?"

Myron was tempted to snap his knee into the man's groin, but that wouldn't help. "Look, we can go through all the macho posturing, but really, what's the point? I know she came in. I know why she's hiding. I mean her no harm. We can play this one of two ways. One, she can talk to me quickly and that's the end of it. I say nothing about her whereabouts. Two, well, I have several men positioned outside. You throw me out the door and I call her father. He brings several more. It all gets ugly. None of us need that. I just want to talk."

The black man kept still.

"Another thing," Myron said. "If she's afraid I work for her father, ask her this: If her father knew she was here, would he be this subtle?"

More hesitation.

Myron spread his arms. "I'm in your place. I'm unarmed. What damage could I do?"

The man waited another second. Then he said, "You finished?"

"We might also be interested in a threesome," Big Cyndi said.

Myron hushed her with a look. She shrugged and kept quiet.

"Wait here."

The man headed to a steel door. It buzzed. The man opened it and went inside. It took about five minutes. A bald guy with spectacles entered the room. He was nervous. Big Cyndi started giving him the eye. She licked her lips. She cupped what might have been her breasts. Myron shook his head, afraid she'd drop to her knees and pantomime lord-knew-what when the door mercifully opened. The man with the sunglasses poked his head out.

"Come with me," he said, pointing to Myron. He turned toward Big Cyndi. "Alone."

Big Cyndi didn't like it. Myron calmed her with a look and stepped into the other room. The steel door closed behind him. Myron looked around and said, "Uh-oh."

There were four of them. Various sizes. Lots of tattoos. Some grinned. Some grimaced. All wore jeans and black T-shirts. None were clean-shaven. Myron tried to figure out who the leader was. In a group fight, most people mistakenly believe you look for the weakest link. Always the wrong move. Besides, if the guys were any good, it didn't matter what you did.

Four against one in a tight space. You were done.

Myron found a man who stood a little in front of the others. He had dark hair and more or less fit the description of Katie Rochester's beau given to him by both Win and Edna Skylar. Myron met his eye and held it.

Then Myron said, "Are you stupid?"

The dark-haired man frowned, surprised and insulted. "You talking to me?"

"If I say, 'Yeah, I'm talking to you,' will that be the end of it or will you come back with 'You talking to me' again or 'You better not be talking to me'? Because, really, neither one of us has the time."

The dark-haired man smiled. "You left one option off when you talked to my friend here."

"What's that?"

"Option three." He held up three fingers in case Myron didn't know what the word *three* meant. "We make sure you *can't* tell her father."

He grinned. The other men grinned.

Myron spread his arms and said, "How?"

That made the man frown again. "Huh?"

"How are you going to make sure of that?" Myron looked around. "You guys are going to jump me—that's the plan? So then what? The only way to shut me up would be to kill me. You willing to go that far? And what about my lovely associate out in the front room? Are you going to kill her too? And what about my other associates"—might as well exaggerate with the plural—"who are outside? Are you going to kill them too? Or is your plan, what, to beat me up and teach me a lesson? If so, one, I'm not a good learner. Not that way at least. And two, I'm looking at all of you and memorizing your faces, and if you do attack me, you better make sure I'm dead because if not, I'll come after you, at night, when you're sleeping, and I'll tie you down and pour kerosene on your crotch and set it on fire."

Myron Bolitar, Master of Melodrama. But he kept his eyes steady and looked at their faces carefully, one at a time.

"So," Myron said, "is that your option-three plan?"

One of the men shuffled his feet. A good sign. Another sneaked a glance at the third. The dark-haired man had something close to a smile on his face.

Someone knocked on the door on the far side of the room. The dark-haired man opened it a crack, talked to someone, closed it, turned back to Myron.

"You're good," he said to Myron.

Myron kept his mouth shut.

"Come this way."

He opened the door and swept his hand for Myron to go ahead. Myron stepped through it into a room with red walls. The walls were covered with pornographic pictures and XXX-rated movie posters. There was a black leather couch and two folding chairs and a lamp. And sitting on the couch, looking terrified but unharmed, was none other than Katie Rochester.

Chapter 43

Edna Skylar had been right, Myron thought. Katie Rochester looked older, more mature somehow. She twiddled a cigarette in her hand, but it remained unlit.

The dark-haired man stuck out his hand. "I'm Rufus."

"Myron."

They shook hands. Rufus sat down on the couch next to Katie. He took the cigarette from her hand.

"Can't smoke in your condition, honey," Rufus said. Then he put the cigarette between his lips, lit it up, threw his feet up on the coffee table, and let loose a long plume of smoke.

Myron stayed standing.

"How did you find me?" Katie Rochester asked.

"It's not important."

"That woman who spotted me in the subway. She said something, right?"

Myron did not reply.

"Damn." Katie shook her head and put a hand on

Rufus's thigh. "We're going to have to find a new place now."

"What," Myron said, pointing to a poster of a naked woman with her legs spread, "and leave all this behind?"

"That's not funny," Rufus said. "This is your fault, man."

"I need to know where Aimee Biel is."

"I told you on the phone," she said. "I don't know."

"Are you aware that she disappeared too?"

"I didn't disappear. I ran away. My choice."

"You're pregnant."

"That's right."

"So is Aimee Biel."

"So?"

"So you're both pregnant, both from the same school, both ran away or disappeared—"

"A million pregnant girls run away every year."

"Do they all use the same ATM machine?"

Katie Rochester sat up. "What?"

"Before you ran, you went to an ATM machine—"

"I went to a bunch of ATM machines," she said. "I needed money to run away."

"What, Rufus here couldn't spot you?"

Rufus said, "Go to hell, man."

"It was my money," Katie said.

"How far along are you anyhow?"

"That's none of your business. None of this is your business."

"The last ATM machine you visited was at a Citibank on Fifty-second Street."

"So?"

Katie Rochester sounded younger and more petulant with every response.

"So the last ATM machine Aimee Biel visited before

she disappeared was at the same Citibank on Fifty-second Street."

Now Katie looked genuinely puzzled. It wasn't faked. She hadn't known. She slowly swiveled her head toward Rufus. Her eyes narrowed.

"Hey," Rufus said. "Don't look at me."

"Rufus, did you . . . ?"

"Did I what?" Rufus threw the cigarette to the ground and jumped to his feet. He raised his hand as if about to slap her backhand. Myron slid between them. Rufus stopped, smiled, raised his palms in mock surrender.

"It's okay, baby."

"What was she talking about?" Myron asked.

"Nothing, it's over." Rufus looked at her. "I'm sorry, baby. You know I'd never hit you, right?"

Katie said nothing. Myron tried to read her face. She wasn't cowering, but there was something there, something he'd seen in her mother. Myron lowered himself to her level.

"Do you want me to get you out of here?" he asked.

"What?" Katie's head shot up. "No, of course not. We love each other."

Myron looked at her, again trying to read distress. He didn't see any.

"We're having a baby," she said.

"Why did you look at Rufus like that? When I mentioned the ATM?"

"It was stupid. Forget it."

"Tell me anyway."

"I thought . . . but I was wrong."

"You thought what?"

Rufus put his feet back on the coffee table, crossing them. "It's okay, baby. Tell him."

Katie Rochester kept her eyes down. "It was just, like, a reaction, you know?"

"Reaction to what?"

"Rufus was with me. That's all. It was his idea to use that last ATM. He thought it being midtown and all, it would be hard to trace to any spot, especially down here."

Rufus arched an eyebrow, proud of his ingenuity.

"But see, Rufus has lots of girls working for him. And if they have money I figure he takes them to an ATM and gets them to clear out the cash. He has one of the clubs in here. A place called Barely Legal. It's for men who want girls that are—"

"I think I can put together what they want. Go on."

"Legal," Rufus said, raising a finger. "The name is Barely *Legal*. The key word is *legal*. All the girls are over eighteen."

"I'm sure your mother must be the envy of her book group, Rufus." Myron turned back to Katie. "So you thought . . . ?"

"I didn't think. Like I said, I just reacted."

Rufus put his feet down and sat forward. "She thought maybe this Aimee was one of my girls. She's not. Look, that's the lie I sell. People think these girls run away from their farms or their homes in the burbs and come to the big city to become, I don't know, actresses or dancers or whatever and when they fail, they end up turning tricks. I sell that fantasy. I want the guys to think they're getting some farmer's daughter, if that gets his rocks off. But the fact is, these are just street junkies. The luckier ones work the flicks"—he pointed to a movie poster—"and the uglier ones work the rooms. That simple."

"So you don't recruit at high schools?"

Rufus laughed. "I wish. You want to know where I recruit?"

Myron waited.

"At AA meetings. Or rehab centers. Those places are like casting couches, you know what I'm saying? I sit in the back and drink that badass coffee and listen. Then I talk them up during the breaks and give them a card and wait until they fall off the wagon. They always do. And there I am, ready to scoop them up."

Myron looked at Katie. "Wow, he's terrific."

"You don't know the real him," she said.

"Yeah, I'm sure he's deep." Myron felt the itch in his fingers again, but he swallowed it down. "So how did you two meet?"

Rufus shook his head. "It ain't like that."

"We're in love," Katie said. "He knows my dad through business. He came to the house and once we saw each other . . ." She smiled and looked pretty and young and happy and dumb.

"Love at first sight," Rufus said.

Myron just looked at him.

"What," he said, "you don't think it's possible?"

"No, Rufus, you seem like quite the catch."

Rufus shook his head. "This here, this is just a job for me. That's all. Katie and that baby, they're my life. You understand?"

Myron still said nothing. He reached into his pocket and pulled out the picture of Aimee Biel. "Take a look at this, Rufus."

He did.

"Is she here?"

"Dude, I swear on my unborn child I've never seen this chick before and I don't know where she is."

"If you're lying—"

"Enough with the threats, okay? What you got there is a missing girl, right? The police want her. Her parents want her. You think I want that trouble?"

"You have a missing girl right here," Myron said.

"Her father will move heaven and earth to find her. And the police are interested too."

"But that's different," Rufus said, and his tone turned into a plea. "I love her. I'd walk through fire for Katie. Don't you see? But this girl . . . she'd never be worth it. If I had her here, I'd give her back. I don't need that kind of hassle."

It made sad, pathetic sense.

"Aimee Biel used the same ATM," Myron said again. "Do you have any explanation for that?"

They both shook their heads.

"Did you tell anyone?"

Katie said, "About the ATM machine?"

"Yes."

"I don't think so."

Myron kneeled down again. "Listen to me, Katie. I don't believe in coincidences. There has to be a reason why Aimee Biel went to that ATM. There has to be a connection between you two."

"I barely knew Aimee. I mean, yeah, we went to the same school, but we never hung out or anything. I'd see her at the mall sometimes, but we wouldn't even say hello. At school she was always with her boyfriend."

"Randy Wolf."

"Yeah."

"Do you know him?"

"Sure. The school's Golden Boy. Rich daddy who always got him out of trouble. Do you know Randy's nickname?'

Myron remembered something from the school parking lot. "Farmboy, something like that?"

"Pharm, not Farm Boy. It's with a *PH*, not *F*. You know how he got it?"

"No."

"It's short for *Pharmacist*. Randy is the biggest

348

dealer at Livingston High." Katie smiled then. "Wait, you want to know my connection to Aimee Biel? Here's the only one I can come up with: Her boyfriend sold me nickel bags."

"Hold up." Myron felt the room begin to spin ever so slowly. "You said something about his father?"

"Big Jake Wolf. Town hotshot."

Myron nodded, almost afraid to move now. "You said something about him getting Randy out of trouble." His own voice suddenly sounded very far away.

"Just a rumor."

"Tell me."

"What do you think? A teacher caught Randy dealing on campus. Reported him to the cops. His dad paid them off, the teacher too, I think. They all chuckled about not wanting to ruin the star quarterback's bright future."

Myron kept nodding. "Who was the teacher?"

"Don't know."

"Heard any rumors?"

"No."

But Myron thought that maybe he had an idea who it was.

He asked a few more questions. But there was nothing else here. Randy and Big Jake Wolf. It came back to them again. It came back to the teacher/guidance counselor Harry Davis and the musician/teacher/lingerie buyer Drew Van Dyne. It came back to that town, Livingston, and how the young rebelled, and how much pressure there was on all those kids to succeed.

At the end, Myron looked at Rufus. "Leave us alone for a minute."

"No way."

But Katie had some of her poise back. "It's okay, Rufus."

He stood. "I'll be right behind the door," Rufus said to Myron, "with my associates. You got me?"

Myron bit back the rejoinder and waited until they were alone. He thought about Dominick Rochester, how he was trying to find his daughter, how maybe he knew that Katie was in a place like this with a man like Rufus and how maybe his overreaction—his desire to find his daughter—was suddenly understandable.

Myron bent close to her ear and whispered, "I can get you out of here."

She leaned away and made a face. "What are you talking about?"

"I know you want to escape your father, but this guy isn't the answer."

"How do you know what the answer is for me?"

"He runs a brothel, for crying out loud. He almost hit you."

"Rufus loves me."

"I can get you out of here."

"I wouldn't go," she said. "I'd rather die than live without Rufus. Is that clear enough for you?"

"Katie . . ."

"Get out."

Myron rose.

"You know something," she said. "Maybe Aimee is more like me than you think."

"How's that?"

"Maybe she doesn't need rescuing either."

Or, Myron thought, maybe you both do.

Chapter 44

Big Cyndi stayed behind and flashed Aimee's photograph around the neighborhood, just in case. Those employed in these illicit fields wouldn't talk to cops or Myron, but they'd talk to Big Cyndi. She had her gifts.

Myron and Win headed back to their cars.

"Are you coming back to the apartment?" Win asked.

Myron shook his head. "I got more to do."

"I'll relieve Zorra."

"Thanks." Then looking back at the warehouse, Myron added: "I don't like leaving her here."

"Katie Rochester is an adult."

"She's eighteen."

"Exactly."

"So what are you saying? You turn eighteen, you're on your own? We only rescue adults?"

"No," Win said. "We rescue those we can. We rescue those in trouble. We rescue those who ask and need our help. We do not—repeat, not—rescue those who make choices we don't agree with. Bad choices are a part of life."

They kept walking. Myron said, "You know how I like to read the paper at Starbucks, right?"

Win nodded.

"Every teenager who hangs out there smokes. All of them. I sit there and watch them and when they light up, not even thinking about it, just as casual as you please, I think to myself, 'Myron, you should say something.' I think I should go up to them and excuse myself for interrupting and then beg them to stop smoking now because it'll only get harder. I want to shake them and make them understand how stupid they're being. I want to tell them about all the people I know, people who were living wonderful, happy lives like, say, Peter Jennings, a great guy from all I've heard, and how he was living this amazing life and how he lost it because he started smoking young. I want to shout at them the full litany of health problems they will inevitably face because of what they're so casually doing right now."

Win said nothing. He looked ahead and kept pace.

"But then I think I should mind my own business. They don't want to hear it. And who am I anyway? Just some guy. I'm not important enough to make them stop. They'd probably tell me to take a hike. So of course, I keep quiet. I look the other way and go back to my paper and coffee and meanwhile these kids are sitting near me, slowly killing themselves. And I let them."

"We pick and choose our battles," Win said. "That one would be a loser."

"I know, but here's the thing: If I said something to every kid, every time I saw them, maybe I'd perfect my antismoking pitch. And maybe I'd reach one. Maybe one would stop smoking. Maybe my prying would save just one life. And then I wonder if staying quiet is the right thing—or the easy thing."

"And then what?" Win asked.

"What do you mean?"

"Are you going to hang out at McDonald's and scold the people eating Big Macs? When you see a mother encouraging her overweight son to snarf down his second supersized order of fries, are you going to warn her about what the boy's horrible future will be like?"

"No."

Win shrugged.

"But okay, forget all that," Myron said. "In this specific case, right now, a few yards away from us, there is a pregnant girl sitting in that whorehouse—"

"—who has made up her own, adult mind," Win finished for him.

They kept walking.

"It's like what that Dr. Skylar told me."

"Who?" Win asked.

"The woman who spotted Katie near the subway. Edna Skylar. She talked about preferring the innocent patients. I mean, she took the Hippocratic oath and all and she follows it, but when push comes to shove, she'd rather work with someone more deserving."

"Human nature," Win said. "I assume you weren't comfortable with that?"

"I'm not comfortable with any of it."

"But it's not just Dr. Skylar. You do it too, Myron. Put aside Claire's guilt trip on you for a moment. Right now, you're choosing to help Aimee because you perceive her as an innocent. If she were a teenage boy who had a history of drug problems, would you be so apt to find her? Of course not. We all pick and choose, like it or not."

"It goes beyond that."

"How so?"

"How important is what college you make?"

"What does that have to do with anything?"

"We were lucky," Myron said. "We went to Duke."

"And your point is?"

"I got Aimee in. I wrote a letter, I made a phone call. I doubt she would have been accepted if it wasn't for me."

"So?"

"So where do I get off? As Maxine Chang pointed out to me, when one kid makes it, another is denied."

Win made a face. "Way of the world."

"Doesn't make it right."

"Someone makes the choice based on a fairly subjective set of criteria." Win shrugged. "Why shouldn't it be you?"

Myron shook his head. "I can't help but think that it's connected to Aimee's disappearance."

"Her college acceptance?"

Myron nodded.

"How?"

"I don't know yet."

They separated. Myron got into his car and checked his cell phone. One new message. He listened to it.

"Myron? Gail Berruti here. That call you asked about, the one that came to the residence of Erik Biel." There was noise behind her. "What? Damn, hold on a second."

Myron did. This was the call Claire had received from the robotic voice telling her that Aimee "is fine." A few seconds later, Berruti was back.

"Sorry about that. Where was I? Right, okay, here it is. The call was placed from a pay phone in New York City. More specifically, from a bank of pay phones in the Twenty-third Street subways. Hope that helps."

Click.

Myron thought about that. Right where Katie Rochester had been spotted. It made sense, he guessed. Or maybe, with what he'd just learned, it made no sense at all.

His cell phone buzzed again. It was Wheat Manson, calling back from Duke. He did not sound happy.

"What the hell is going on?" Wheat asked.

"What?"

"The ranking you gave me for that Chang kid. It matched."

"Fourth in the class, and he didn't get in?"

"Are we going there, Myron?"

"No, Wheat. We're not. What about Aimee's ranking?"

"There's the problem."

Myron asked a few follow-up questions before hanging up.

It was starting to fit.

Half an hour later Myron arrived at the home of Ali Wilder, the first woman in seven years he'd told that he loved. He parked and sat in the car for a moment. He looked out at the house. Too many thoughts ricocheted through his head. He wondered about her late husband, Kevin. This was the house they'd bought. Myron saw that day, Kevin and Ali coming here with a Realtor, both young, both choosing this vessel as the one where they would live their lives and raise their kids. Did they hold hands as they toured their future abode? What appealed to Kevin, or was it maybe his beloved's enthusiasm that won him over? And why the hell was Myron thinking about such things?

He had told Ali that he loved her.

Would he have done so—said "I love you" like that—if Jessica hadn't visited him last night?

Yes.

Are you sure about that, Myron?

His cell phone rang. "Hello?"

"Do you plan on sitting out in the car all night?"

He felt his heart soar at the sound of Ali's voice. "Sorry, just thinking."

"About me?"

"Yes."

"About what you'd like to do to me?"

"Well, not exactly," he said. "But I can start now, if you want."

"Don't bother. I got it all planned out already. You'll only interfere with what I've come up with."

"Do tell."

"I'd rather show. Come to the door. Don't knock. Don't talk. Jack is asleep and Erin is upstairs on her computer."

Myron hung up. He caught his reflection—the goofy smile—in the car's rearview mirror. He tried not to sprint to the door, but he couldn't help but do one of those run-walks. The front door opened as he approached. Ali had her hair down. Her blouse was clingy and red and shiny. It stretched at the top, just asking to be unbuttoned.

Ali put a finger to her lips. "Shh."

She kissed him. She kissed him hard and deep. He felt it in his fingertips. His body sang. She whispered in his ear, "The kids are upstairs."

"So you said."

"I'm usually not much of a risk-taker," she said. Then Ali licked his ear. Myron's entire body jerked in pleasure. "But I really, really want you."

Myron held back the quip. They kissed again. She

356

took his hand, quickly leading him down the hall. She closed the kitchen door. They went through the family room. She closed another door.

"How's the couch work for you?" she said.

"I don't care if we do it on a bed of nails at half court at Madison Square Garden."

They dropped to the couch. "Two closed doors," Ali said, her breathing heavy. They kissed again. Their hands began to wander. "No one can sneak up on us."

"My, haven't we been planning," Myron said.

"Pretty much all day."

"Worth it," he said.

She wiggled her eyebrows. "Oh, just you wait and see."

They kept their clothes on. That was the most amazing thing. Sure, buttons were undone and zippers were lowered. But they'd kept their clothes on. And now, as they panted in each other's arms, fully spent, Myron said the same thing that he said every time they finished.

"Wow."

"You've got quite the vocabulary."

"Never use a big word when a small one will suffice."

"I could make a crack here, but I won't."

"Thank you," he said. Then: "Can I ask you something?"

Ali snuggled closer. "Anything."

"Are we exclusive?"

She looked at him. "For real?"

"I guess."

"It sounds like you're asking me to go steady."

"What would you say if I did?"

"Asked me to go steady?"

"Sure, why not?"

"I'd exclaim, 'Oh yes!' Then I'd ask if I can doodle your name on my notebook and wear your varsity jacket."

He smiled.

Ali said, "Does your asking have anything to do with our earlier exchange of I-love-yous?"

"I don't think so."

Silence.

"We're adults, Myron. You can sleep with whomever you wish."

"I don't want to sleep with anyone else."

"So why are you asking me this right now?"

"Because, well, before? I don't, uh, think very clearly when I'm in a state of, you know . . ." He sort of gestured. Ali rolled her eyes.

"Men. No, I mean, why tonight. Why did you ask about exclusivity tonight?"

He debated what to say. He was all for honesty, but did he really want to get into Jessica's visit? "Just clarifying where we stand."

Footsteps suddenly began to pound down the stairs.

"Mom!"

It was Erin. A door—that first of two doors—banged open.

Myron and Ali moved with a speed that would intimidate NASCAR. Their clothes were on, but like a couple of teenagers, they made sure everything was fastened and tucked in by the time the second doorknob began to turn. Myron jumped to the other side of the couch as Erin threw open the door. They both tried to wipe the look of guilt off their faces with mixed results.

Erin burst into the room. She looked at Myron. "I'm glad you're here."

Ali finished adjusting her shirt. "What's wrong, honey?"

"You better come quick," Erin said.

"Why, what's up?"

"I was on the computer, instant messaging with my friends. And just now—I mean, like thirty seconds ago—Aimee Biel signed on and said hello to me."

Chapter 45

They all hurried up to Erin's room.

Myron took the stairs three at a time. The house shook. He didn't much care. The first thing that struck him when he entered the bedroom was how much it reminded him of Aimee's. The guitars, the photographs in the mirror, the computer on the desk. The colors were different, there were more pillows and stuffed animals, but you would have no doubt that both rooms belonged to high school girls with much in common.

Myron headed to the computer. Erin came in behind him, Ali after her. Erin sat at the computer and pointed to a word:

GuitarlovurCHC.

"CHC stands for Crazy Hat Care," Erin said, "the name of the band we were forming."

Myron said, "Ask Aimee where she is."

Erin typed: **WHERE ARE YOU?** Then she hit the return button.

Ten seconds passed. Myron noticed the icon on Aimee's profile. The band Green Day. Her wallpaper was for the New York Rangers. When she typed back a sliver of her "buddy sound," a song from Usher, came through the speakers:

I can't say. But I'm fine. Don't worry.

Myron said, "Tell her that her parents are upset. That she should call them."

Erin typed: **YOUR PARENTS ARE FREAKING OUT. YOU NEED TO CALL THEM.**

I know. But I'll be home soon. I'll explain everything then.

Myron thought how to approach this. "Tell her I'm here."

Erin typed: **MYRON IS HERE.**

Long pause. The cursor blinked.

I thought you were alone.

SORRY. HE'S HERE. NEXT TO ME.

I know I got Myron in trouble. Tell him I'm sorry, but I'm fine.

Myron thought about it. "Erin, ask her something only she would know."

"Like what?"

"You guys have private talks, right? Share secrets?"

"Sure."

"I'm not convinced it's Aimee. Ask her something only you and she would know."

Erin thought a moment. Then she typed: **WHAT IS THE NAME OF THE BOY I HAVE A CRUSH ON?**

The cursor blinked. She wasn't going to answer. Myron was pretty sure about that. Then GuitarLovur-CHC typed:

Did he finally ask you out?!?!

Myron said, "Insist on a name."

"Already on it," Erin said. She typed: **WHAT'S HIS NAME?**

I have to go.

Erin did not need prompting: **YOU'RE NOT AIMEE. AIMEE WOULD KNOW THE NAME.**

Long pause. The longest yet. Myron looked back at Ali. Her eyes were on the screen. Myron could hear his own breathing in his ears, as if he'd stuck seashells on them. Then finally an answer came:

Mark Cooper.

The screen name vanished. GuitarLovurCHC was gone.

For a moment, no one moved. Myron and Ali had their eyes on Erin. She stiffened.

"Erin?"

Something happened to her face. A quiet quake in the corner of her lip. It spread.

"Oh God," Erin said.

"What is it?"

"Who the hell is Mark Cooper?"

"Was it Aimee or not?"

Erin nodded. "It was Aimee. But . . ."

Her tone made the room drop ten degrees.

"But what?" Myron said.

"Mark Cooper is not the boy I have a crush on."

Myron and Ali both looked confused.

Ali said, "Then who is he?"

Erin swallowed. She looked back, first at Myron, then her mother. "Mark Cooper was this creepy guy who went to my summer camp. I told Aimee about him. He used to follow some of us around with this awful leer, you know. Whenever he'd walk by, we would laugh and whisper to one another. . . ." Her voice dropped off, came back, but lower now. "We'd whisper, 'Trouble.' "

They all watched the monitor now, all hoping that screen name would pop up again. But nothing happened. Aimee did not reappear. She had delivered her message. And now, once again, she was gone.

Chapter 46

Claire was on the phone in seconds. She dialed Myron's cell. When he answered, she said, "Aimee was just online! Two of her friends called!"

Erik Biel sat at the table and listened. His hands were folded. He had spent the past day or so online, searching per Myron's instructions for people who lived in the area of that cul-de-sac. Now, of course, he knew that he'd been wasting his time. Myron had spotted a car with a Livingston High School decal right away. He had traced it back to one of Aimee's teachers, a man named Harry Davis, that very night.

He had simply wanted to keep Erik out of the way.

So he gave him busywork.

Claire listened and then let out a little cry. "Oh no, oh my God. . . ."

"What?" Erik said.

She shushed him with her hand.

Erik felt the rage once more. Not at Myron. Not even at Claire. At himself. He stared down at the monogram on his French cuff. His clothes were tailor-made, a custom fit. Big deal. Who did he think he was impressing? He looked up at his wife. He had lied to Myron about the passion. He still longed for her. More than anything he wanted Claire to look at him the way she used to. Maybe Myron had been right. Maybe Claire had indeed loved him. But she had never respected him. She didn't need him.

She didn't believe in him.

When their family was in crisis, Claire had run to Myron. She had shut Erik out. And of course, he had taken it.

Erik Biel had done that his whole life. Taken it. His mistress, a mousy thing from his office, was pitiful and needy and treated him like royalty. That made him feel like a man. Claire didn't. It was that simple. And that pitiful.

"What?" Erik asked again.

She ignored him. He waited. Finally Claire asked Myron to hold on a second. "Myron says he saw her online too. He had Erin ask her a question. She answered in a way . . . it was her, but she's in trouble."

"What did she say?"

"I don't have time to go into details right now." Claire put the phone back to her ear and said to Myron—to Myron!—"We need to do something."

Do something.

The truth was, Erik Biel was not much of a man. He knew that early on. When he was fourteen, he backed out of a fight. The entire school was there. The bully was ready to pounce. Erik had walked away. His mother called him prudent. In the media, walking away is the "brave" thing to do. What a load of crap. No beating, no hospital stay, no concussion or broken bones could have hurt Erik Biel more than not standing up had. He had never forgotten it, never gotten over it. He had chickened out of a fight. The pattern continued. He abandoned his buddies when they got jumped at a fraternity party. At a Jets game, he let someone spill beer on his girlfriend. If a man looked at him wrong, Erik Biel always averted his gaze first.

You can couch it in all the psychological vernacular of modern civilization—all that garbage about strength coming from within and that violence never solved anything—but it was all a bunch of self-rationalization. You can live with fooling yourself like that, for a while anyway. And then a crisis hits, a crisis like this, and you realize what you really are, that nice suits and fancy cars and pressed pants make you nothing.

You're not a man.

But still, even with wimps like Erik, there was one line you don't cross. You cross it, you never come back. It had to do with your children. A man protects his family at all costs. No matter what the sacrifice. You will take any hit. You will go to the ends of the earth and risk everything to keep them from harm. You don't back away. Never. Not until your dying breath.

Someone had taken away his little girl.

You don't sit that fight out.

Erik Biel took out the gun.

It had been his father's. A Ruger .22. It was an old gun. Probably hadn't been fired in three decades. Erik had brought it to a gun shop this morning. He purchased ammunition and other sundries he might need. The man behind the counter had cleaned the Ruger for him, tested it out, smirking in disgust at the little man in front of him, so pitiful that he didn't even know how to load and use his own damn gun.

But the gun was loaded now.

Erik Biel was listening to his wife talk to Myron.

They were trying to figure out what to do next. Drew Van Dyne, he heard them say, wasn't home. They wondered about Harry Davis. Erik smiled. He was ahead of them on that count. He had used Call Block and dialed the teacher's number. He pretended to be a mortgage broker. Davis had answered and said he wasn't interested.

That was half an hour ago.

Erik started toward his car. The gun was tucked into his pants.

"Erik? Where are you going?"

He didn't answer. Myron Bolitar had confronted Harry Davis at the school. The teacher hadn't talked to Myron. But one way or the other, he sure as hell was going to talk to Erik Biel.

Myron heard Claire say, "Erik? Where are you going?"

His phone clicked.

"Claire, I have someone on the other line. I'll call you back." Myron clicked over to the other line.

"Is this Myron Bolitar?"

The voice was familiar. "Yes."

"This is Detective Lance Banner from the Livingston Police Department. We met yesterday."

Was it only yesterday? "Sure, Detective, what can I do for you?"

"How far are you from St. Barnabas Hospital?"

"Fifteen, twenty minutes, why?"

"Joan Rochester has just been rushed into surgery."

Chapter 47

M yron sped and made it to the hospital in ten minutes. Lance Banner was waiting for him. "Joan Rochester is still in surgery."

"What happened?"

"You want his story or hers?"

"Both."

"Dominick Rochester said she fell down the stairs. They've been here before. She falls down the stairs a lot, if you get my drift."

"I do. But you said there were his and her stories?"

"Right. She's always backed up his before."

"And this time?"

"She said he beat her up," Banner said. "And that she wants to press charges."

"That must have surprised him. How bad is it?"

"Pretty bad," Banner said. "Several broken ribs. A broken arm. He must have pounded the hell out of her kidneys, because the doctor is speculating about removing one."

"Jesus."

"And, of course, not a mark on her face. The guy's good."

"Comes with practice," Myron said. "Is he here?"

"The husband? Yeah. But we've got him in custody."

"For how long?"

Lance Banner shrugged. "You know the answer to that."

In short: not very.

"Why did you call me?" Myron asked.

"Joan Rochester was awake when she came in. She wanted to warn you. She said to be careful."

"What else?"

"That was it. It's a miracle she got that out."

Rage and guilt consumed him in equal measure. Joan Rochester could handle her husband, Myron had thought. She lived with him. She made her choices. Gee, what would be his next justification for not helping her—she'd been asking for it?

"Do you want to tell me how you're involved in the lives of the Rochesters?" Banner asked.

"Aimee Biel isn't a runaway. She's in trouble."

He filled him in as quickly as possible. When he finished, Lance Banner said, "We'll get an APB out on Drew Van Dyne."

"What about Jake Wolf?"

"I'm not sure how he fits in."

"Do you know his son?"

"You mean Randy?" Lance Banner shrugged a little too casually. "He's the high school quarterback."

"Has Randy ever gotten into any trouble?"

"Why are you asking?"

"Because I heard his father bribed you guys to get him off a drug charge," Myron said. "Care to comment?"

Banner's eyes turned black. "Who the hell do you think you are?"

"Save the indignation, Lance. Two of your fellow finest braced me on Jake Wolf's orders. They stopped me from talking to Randy. One punched me in the gut when I was cuffed."

"That's a load of crap."

Myron just looked at him.

"Which officers?" Banner demanded. "I want names, dammit."

"One was about my height, skinny. The other had a thick mustache and looked like John Oates from Hall and Oates."

The shadow hit Lance's face. He tried to cover it.

"You know who I'm talking about."

Banner tried to hold it back. He spoke through gritted teeth. "Tell me exactly what happened."

"We don't have the time. Just tell me what the deal with the Wolf kid is."

"No one got bribed."

Myron waited. A woman in a wheelchair headed toward them. Banner stepped aside and let her pass. He rubbed his face with his hand.

"Six months ago a teacher claimed that he caught Randy Wolf selling pot. He searched the kid and found two nickel bags on him. I mean, penny-ante stuff."

"This teacher," Myron said. "Who was he?"

"He asked us to keep his name out of it."

"Was it Harry Davis?"

Lance Banner didn't nod, but he might as well have.

"So what happened?"

"The teacher called us. I had two guys go in. Hildebrand and Peterson. They, uh, fit your description. Randy Wolf claimed that he was framed."

Myron frowned. "And your guys bought that?"

"No. But the case was weak. The constitutionality of the search was questionable. The amounts were small. And Randy Wolf. He was a good kid. No past record or anything."

"You didn't want to get him in trouble," Myron said.

"None of us did."

"Tell me, Lance. If he'd been a black kid from Newark caught selling at Livingston High, would you have felt the same way?"

"Don't start that hypothetical crap with me. We had a weak case to begin with and then, the next day, Harry Davis tells my officers he won't testify. Just like that. He backs out. So now it's over. My officers had no choice."

"My, how convenient," Myron said. "Tell me: Did the football team have a good season?"

"It was a nothing of a case. The kid had a bright future. He's going to Dartmouth."

"I keep hearing that," Myron said. "But I'm beginning to wonder if it'll happen."

Then a voice shouted, "Bolitar!"

Myron turned. Dominick Rochester stood at the end of the corridor. His hands were cuffed. His face was red. Two officers were on either side of him. Myron started toward him. Lance Banner jogged behind, calling out a soft warning.

"Myron . . . ?"

"I won't do anything, Lance. I just want to talk to him."

Myron stopped two feet in front of him. Dominick Rochester's black eyes burned. "Where is my daughter?"

"Proud of yourself, Dominick?"

"You," Rochester said. "You know something about Katie."

"Did your wife tell you that?"

"No." He grinned. It was one of the most frightening sights Myron had ever seen. "Just the opposite, in fact."

"What are you talking about?"

Dominick leaned in closer and whispered. "No matter what I did to her, no matter how much she suffered, my dearest wife wouldn't talk. See, that's why I'm sure you know something. Not because she talked—but because no matter how much hell I put her through, she wouldn't."

Myron was back in his car when Erin Wilder called him.

"I know where Randy Wolf is."

"Where?"

"There's a senior party at Sam Harlow's house."

"They're having a party? Aren't any of Aimee's friends concerned?"

"Everyone thinks she ran away," Erin said. "Some of them saw her online tonight, so they're even more sure."

"Wait, if they're at a party, how did they see her online?"

"They have BlackBerrys. They can IM from their phones."

Technology, he thought. Keeping people together by allowing them to be apart. Erin gave him the address. Myron knew the area. He hung up and started on his way. The ride did not take long.

There were a bunch of cars parked out on the Harlows' street. Someone had set up a big tent in the backyard. This was a real party, an invite party, as opposed to a few kids hanging out and sneaking beers.

Myron threw the car into park and entered the yard.

There were parents here—chaperones, he guessed. That would make this more difficult. But he didn't have time to worry about it. The police might be mobilizing, but they weren't anxious to look at the big picture. Myron was getting it now. It was coming into focus. Randy Wolf, he knew, was one of the keys.

The festivities were nicely partitioned. The parents hung out in the house's screened-in porch. Myron could see the adults in the dim light. They were laughing and had a keg. The men wore long shorts and loafers and smoked cigars. The women sported bright Lilly Pulitzer skirts and flip-flops.

The seniors gathered at the far end of the tent, as far away from adult supervision as possible. The dance floor was empty. The DJ played a song by the Killers, something about having a girlfriend who looked like a boyfriend that somebody had in February. Myron headed straight for Randy and put his hand on the boy's shoulder.

Randy shrugged Myron's hand away. "Get off me."

"We need to talk."

"My father said—"

"I know all about what your father said. We're talking anyway."

Randy Wolf was surrounded by about six guys. Some were huge. The quarterback and his offensive line, Myron figured.

"This butt-face bothering you, Pharm?"

The one who said that was huge. He grinned at Myron. The guy had spiky blond hair, but what you first noticed, what you couldn't help but notice, was that he wasn't wearing a shirt. Here they were at a party. There were girls and punch and music and dancing and even parents. And this guy wasn't wearing a shirt.

Randy didn't say anything.

Shirtless had barbed-wire tattoos around his bloated biceps. Myron frowned. The tattoos couldn't have been more wannabe without the word *wannabe* actually being stenciled in. The guy was slabs and slabs of beef. His chest was so smooth it looked like someone had taken a sander to it. He rippled. His forehead was sloped. His eyes were red, indicating that at least some of the beer had found its way to the under-aged. He wore calf-length pants that might have been capris, though Myron didn't know if guys wore those or not.

"What are you looking at, Butt-face?"

Myron said, "Absolutely—and I mean this sincerely—absolutely nothing."

There were several gasps from the crowd. One of them said, "Oh man, is this old dude gonna get a beating or what!"

Another said, "Bring it on, Crush!"

Shirtless aka Crush made his best tough-guy face. "Pharm ain't talking to you, you got me, Butt-face?"

That got a laugh from his friends.

"Butt-face," Myron repeated. "It's even funnier the third time you say it." He took a step toward the kid. Crush didn't budge. "This isn't your business."

"I'm making it my business."

Myron waited. Then he said, "Don't you mean, 'I'm making it my business, Butt-face'?"

There was another gasp. One of the other guys said, "Oh, mister, run and hide. Nobody wises off to Crush like that."

Myron looked at Randy. "We need to talk now. Before this gets out of hand."

Crush smiled, flexed his pecs, stepped forward. "It's already out of hand."

Myron didn't want to take out a kid, not with the

parents around. It would cause too many problems.

"I don't want trouble," Myron said.

"You already got it, Butt-face."

Some of the guys oooed at that one. Crush folded his massive arms across his chest. A stupid move. Myron needed to get this out of the way fast, before the parents started noticing. But Crush's friends were watching. Crush was the resident tough guy. He couldn't afford to back down.

Arms folded across the chest. How macho. How dumb.

Myron made the move. When you need to take out somebody with a minimum of fuss or mess, this technique was one of the most effective. Myron's hand started at his side. The natural resting spot. That was the key. You don't cock the wrist. You don't pull the arm back. You don't wind up or make a fist. The smallest distance between two points is a straight line. That's what you remember. Using his natural hand speed and the element of surprise, Myron shot the hand in that straight line, from the resting point near his hip to Crush's throat.

He didn't hit him hard. Myron used the knife edge below the pinky and found the neck's sweet spot. Few points on the human body are more vulnerable. If you hit someone in the throat, it hurts. It makes them gasp and cough and freeze. But you have to know what you're doing. You hit it too hard, you could do some serious damage. Myron's hand darted in and struck cobra-like.

Crush's eyes bulged. A choking sound got locked in his throat. With almost casual ease, Myron swept out Crush's legs with his instep. Crush went down. Myron did not wait. He grabbed Randy by the scruff of the neck and started dragging him away. If any kid so much as moved, Myron froze them with a stare-down, all the while hustling Randy into the neighbor's backyard.

Randy said, "Ow, let me go!"

Screw that. Randy was eighteen, an adult, right? No reason to go soft on him because he was a kid. He took him behind the garage two houses down. When Myron released him, Randy rubbed the back of his neck.

"What the hell is your problem, man?"

"Aimee is in trouble, Randy."

"She ran away. Everyone said so. People talked to her online tonight."

"Why did you two break up?"

"What?"

"I said—"

"I heard you." Randy thought about it, then shrugged. "We outgrew each other, that's all. We're both going to college. It was time to move on."

"Last week you went to the prom together."

"Yeah, so? We'd been planning for it all year. The tux, the dress, we rented a stretch Hummer with a bunch of friends. The whole group of us. We didn't want to ruin everyone's time. So we went together."

"Why did you two break up, Randy?"

"I just told you."

"Did Aimee find out you were dealing drugs?"

Randy smiled then. He was a handsome kid and he had a damn good smile. "You make it sound like I'm hanging in Harlem hooking kids on heroin."

"I'd get into a moral debate with you, Randy, but I'm a little pressed for time."

"Of course Aimee knew about it. She even partook on more than one occasion. No big deal. I was only providing for a few friends."

"One of those friends Katie Rochester?"

He shrugged. "She asked a few times. I helped her out."

"So again, Randy: Why did you and Aimee break up?"

He shrugged again and his tone quieted just enough. "You'd have to ask Aimee."

"She broke up with you?"

"Aimee changed."

"Changed how?"

"Why don't you ask her old man?"

That made Myron pull up. "Erik?" He frowned. "What does he have to do with it?"

He didn't reply.

"Randy?"

"Aimee found out her father was screwing around." He shrugged. "It made her change."

"Change how?"

"I don't know. It's like she wanted to do anything to piss him off. Her dad liked me. So all of a sudden"—another shrug—"she didn't."

Myron thought about it. He remembered what Erik had said last night, on the end of that cul-de-sac. It added up.

"I cared about her, man," Randy went on. "You have no idea how much. I tried to win her back, but it just backfired in my face. I'm over her now. Aimee's not a part of my life anymore."

Myron could hear the crowd gather. He reached to grab Randy again by the neck, drag him farther away, but Randy pulled back. "I'm fine!" Randy yelled out to his approaching friends. "We're just talking here."

Randy turned back to Myron. His eyes were suddenly clear. "Go ahead. What else do you want to know?"

"Your father called Aimee a slut."

"Right."

"Why?"

"Why do you think?"

"Aimee started seeing somebody else?"

Randy nodded.

"Was it Drew Van Dyne?"

"Doesn't matter anymore."

"Yeah, it does."

"Nah, not really. With all due respect, none of this does. Look, high school is over. I'm going to Dartmouth. Aimee is going to Duke. My mom, she told me something. She said that high school isn't important. The people who are happiest in high school end up being the most miserable adults. I'm lucky. I know that. And I know it won't last unless I take the next step. I thought . . . we talked about it. I thought Aimee understood that too. How important the next step was. And in the end, we both got what we wanted. We got accepted to our first choices."

"She's in danger, Randy."

"I can't help you."

"And she's pregnant."

He closed his eyes.

"Randy?"

"I don't know where she is."

"You said you did something to try to win her back, but it backfired. What did you do, Randy?"

He shook his head. He wouldn't say. But Myron thought that maybe he had an idea. Myron gave him his card. "If you think of anything . . ."

"Yeah."

Randy turned away then. He headed back to the party. The music still played. The parents kept laughing. And Aimee was still in trouble.

Chapter 48

When Myron got back to his car, Claire was there.

"It's Erik," she said.

"What about him?"

"He ran out of the house. With his father's old gun."

"Did you call his cell?"

"No answer," Claire said.

"Any idea where he went?"

"A few years ago I represented a company called KnowWhere," Claire said. "You heard of it?"

"No."

"They're like OnStar or LoJack. They put a GPS in your car for emergencies, that kind of thing. Anyway, we got one installed in both cars. I just called the owner at home and begged him to get me the location."

"And?"

"Erik is parked in front of Harry Davis's house."

"Jesus."

Myron jumped into his car. Claire slipped into the passenger seat. He wanted to argue, but there was no time.

"Call Harry Davis's home," he said.

"I tried," Claire said. "There was no answer."

Erik's car was indeed parked directly in front of the Davis residence. If he'd wanted to hide his approach, he hadn't done a very good job.

Myron stopped the car. He took out his own gun.

Claire said, "What the hell is that for?"

"Just stay here."

"I asked you—"

"Not now, Claire. Stay here. I'll call if I need you."

His voice left no room for argument and, for once, Claire just obeyed. He started up the path, keeping a low crouch. The front door was slightly ajar. Myron didn't like that. He ducked low and listened.

There were noises, but he couldn't make out what they were.

Using the barrel of the gun, he pushed the door open. There was no one in the foyer. The sounds were coming from the left. Myron crawled in. He turned the corner and there, lying on the floor, was a woman he assumed was Mrs. Davis.

She was gagged. Her hands were tied behind her back. Her eyes were wide with fear. Myron put a finger to his lips. She looked to her right, then back at Myron, then back to her right again.

He heard more noises.

There were other people in the room. On her right.

Myron debated his next move. He considered backing out and calling the police. They could surround the house, he guessed, start talking Erik down. But that might be too late.

He heard a slap. Someone cried out. Mrs. Davis squeezed her eyes shut.

There was no choice. Not really. Myron had the gun

at the ready. He was about to leap, preparing to turn and aim in the direction where Mrs. Davis had been looking. He bent his legs. And then he stopped.

Jumping in with a gun. Would that be the prudent move here?

Erik was armed. He might, of course, react by surrendering. He might also react by firing in a panic.

Fifty-fifty.

Myron tried something else.

"Erik?"

Silence.

Myron said, "Erik, it's me. Myron."

"Come on in, Myron."

The voice was calm. There was almost a lilt in it. Myron moved into the center of the room. Erik stood with a gun in his hand. He had on a dress shirt with no tie. There were splatters of blood across the chest.

Erik smiled when he saw Myron. "Mr. Davis is ready to talk now."

"Put the gun down, Erik."

"I don't think so."

"I said—"

"What? Are you going to shoot me?"

"Nobody is shooting anybody. Just put the gun down."

Erik shook his head. The smile remained. "Come all the way in. Please."

Myron stepped into the room, his gun still up. Now he could see Harry Davis in a chair. His back was to Myron. Nylon cuffs were around his wrists. Davis's head lolled on the neck, chin down.

Myron came around the front and took a look.

"Oh, man."

Davis had been beaten. There was blood on his face. A tooth was out and on the floor. Myron turned to Erik.

Erik's posture was different. He wasn't as ramrod as usual. He didn't look nervous or agitated. In fact, Myron had never seen him look more relaxed in his life.

"He needs a doctor," Myron said.

"He's fine."

Myron looked at Erik's eyes. They were placid pools.

"This isn't the way, Erik."

"Sure it is."

"Listen to me—"

"I don't think so. You're good at this stuff, Myron, no question. But you have to follow rules. A certain code. When your child is in danger, those niceties go out the window."

Myron thought about Dominick Rochester, how he had said something so very similar in the Seidens' house. You couldn't start off with two guys more different than Erik Biel and Dominick Rochester. Desperation and fear had rendered them near identical.

Harry Davis raised his bloodied face. "I don't know where Aimee is, I swear."

Before Myron could do much of anything, Erik aimed his gun at the ground and fired. The sound was loud in the small room. Harry Davis screamed. A groan came from behind Mrs. Davis's gag.

Myron's own eyes widened as he looked down at Davis's shoe.

There was a hole in it.

It was near the edge of the big toe. Blood began to run. Myron raised his gun and pointed it at Erik's head. "Put it down now!"

"No."

He said it simply. Erik looked at Harry Davis. The man was in pain, but his head was up now, his eyes more focused. "Did you sleep with my daughter?"

"Never!"

"He's telling the truth, Erik."

Erik turned to Myron. "How do you know?"

"It was another teacher. A guy named Drew Van Dyne. He works at the music store where she hung out."

Erik looked confused. "But when you dropped Aimee off, she came here, right?"

"Yes."

"Why?"

They both looked at Harry Davis. There was blood on his shoe now. It oozed out slowly. Myron wondered if the neighbors had heard the gunfire, if they'd call the police. Myron doubted it. People out here assume the sound is a car backfiring or fireworks, something explainable and safe.

"It's not what you think," Harry Davis said.

"What's not?"

And then Harry Davis's eyes darted toward his wife. Myron understood. He pulled Erik to the side. "You cracked him," Myron said. "He's ready to talk."

"So?"

"So he's not going to talk in front of his wife. And if he did something to Aimee, he's not going to talk in front of you."

Erik still had the small smile on his face. "You want to take over."

"It's not about taking over," Myron said. "It's about getting the information."

Erik surprised Myron then. He nodded. "You're right."

Myron just looked at him as if waiting for the punch line.

"You think this is about me," Erik said. "But it's not. It's about my daughter. It's about what I'd do to save her. I'd kill that man in a second. I'd kill his wife. Hell, Myron, I'd kill you too. But none of that will do any good. You're right. I cracked him. But if we want him to talk freely, his wife and I should leave the room."

Erik walked over to Mrs. Davis. She cowered.

Harry Davis shouted, "Leave her alone!"

Erik ignored him. He reached down and helped Mrs. Davis to her feet. Then Erik looked back at Harry. "Your wife and I will wait in the other room."

They moved into the kitchen and closed the door behind them. Myron wanted to untie Davis, but those nylon cuffs were tough to do by hand. He grabbed a blanket and stemmed the blood flow from the foot.

"It doesn't hurt much," Davis said.

His voice was far away. Strangely enough, he too looked more relaxed. Myron had seen that before. Confession is indeed good for the soul. The man was carrying a heavy load of secrets. It was going to feel good, at least temporarily, to unburden himself.

"I've been teaching high school for twenty-two years," Davis began without being prompted. "I love it. I know the pay isn't great. I know it's not prestigious. But I adore the students. I love to teach. I love to help them on their way. I love when they come back and visit me."

Davis stopped.

"Why did Aimee come here the other night?" Myron asked.

He didn't seem to hear. "Think about it, Mr. Bolitar. Twenty-plus years. With high-schoolers. I don't say high school kids. Because many of them aren't kids. They're sixteen, seventeen, and even eighteen. Old enough to serve in the military and vote. And unless you're blind, you know that those are women, not girls. You ever check out the *Sports Illustrated* swimsuit issue? You ever look on the runway at top fashion shows? Those models are the same age as the beautiful, fresh-faced ones that I'm with five days a week, ten months a year. Women, Mr. Bolitar. Not girls. This isn't about some sick attraction or pedophilia."

Myron said, "I hope you're not trying to justify sexual affairs with students."

Davis shook his head. "I just want to put what I'm about to say in context."

"I don't need context, Harry."

He almost laughed at that. "You understand what I'm saying more than you want to admit, I think. The thing is, I am a normal man—by that I mean, a normal heterosexual male with normal urges and desires. I'm surrounded year after year with mind-bogglingly beautiful women wearing tight clothes and low-cut jeans and plunging necklines and bare midriffs. Every day, Mr. Bolitar. They smile at me. They flirt with me. And we teachers are supposed to be strong and resist it every day."

"Let me guess," Myron said. "You stopped resisting?"

"I'm not trying to make you sympathize. What I'm telling you is, the position we're in is unnatural. If you see a sexy seventeen-year-old walking down the street, you look. You desire. You might even fantasize."

"But," Myron said, "you don't act."

"But why don't you? Because it's wrong—or because you don't really have a chance? Now imagine seeing hundreds of girls like that every day, for years on end. From the earliest times, man has striven to be powerful and wealthy. Why? Most anthropologists will tell you that we do it to attract more and better females. That's nature. Not looking, not desiring, not being attracted— that would make you a freak, wouldn't you say?"

"I don't have time for this, Harry. You know it's wrong."

"I do," he said. "And for twenty years I fought back those impulses. I stuck with the looking, the imagining, the fantasizing."

"And then?"

"Two years ago I had a wonderful, gifted, beautiful student. No, it wasn't Aimee. I won't tell you her name. There's no reason for you to know. She sat in the front of the class, this amazing bounty. She stared at me like I was a deity. She kept the top two buttons of her blouse undone. . . ."

Davis closed his eyes.

"You gave in to your natural urgings," Myron said.

"I don't know many men who could have resisted."

"And this has what to do with Aimee Biel?"

"Nothing. I mean, not directly. This young woman and I started an affair. I won't go into details."

"Thank you."

"But eventually we got found out. It was, as you might imagine, a disaster. Her parents went crazy. They told my wife. She still hasn't forgiven me. Not really. But Donna has family money. We paid them off. They wanted to keep it quiet too. They were worried about their daughter's reputation. So we all agreed to not say anything. She went on to college. And I went back to teaching. I'd learned my lesson."

"So?"

"So I put it behind me. I know you want to make me out a monster. But I'm not. I've had a lot of time to think about it. I know you think I'm just trying to rationalize, but there's more to it. I'm a good teacher. You pointed out how impressive winning Teacher of the Year was—and that I'd won it more than any other teacher in that school's history. That's because I care about the kids. It's not a contradiction—having these urges and caring about my students. And you know how perceptive teens are. They can spot a phony a mile away. They vote for me, they come to me when they have a problem, because they know I truly care."

Myron wanted to vomit, and yet the arguments, he knew, were not without some perverse merit. "So you went back to teaching," he said, trying to get him back on track. "You put it behind you and . . . ?"

"And then I made a second mistake," he said. He smiled again. There was blood on his teeth. "No, it's not what you think. I didn't have another affair."

"What then?"

"I caught a student selling pot. And I turned him in to both the principal and the police."

"Randy Wolf," Myron said.

Davis nodded.

"What happened?"

"His father. Do you know the man?"

"We've met."

"He did some digging. There were a few scant rumors about my liaison with the student. He hired a private eye. He also got another teacher, a man named Drew Van Dyne, to help him. Van Dyne, you see, was Randy's drug supplier."

"So if Randy was prosecuted," Myron said, "Van Dyne had a lot to lose too."

"Yes."

"So let me guess. Jake Wolf found out about your affair."

Davis nodded.

"And he blackmailed you into keeping quiet."

"Oh, he did more than that."

Myron looked down at the man's foot. The blood had let up. Myron should get him to a hospital, he knew that, but he didn't want to lose this momentum either. The odd thing was, Davis did not seem in pain. He wanted to talk. He had probably been thinking about these crazy justifications for years, rattling along in his brain, and now finally he was being given the chance to express them.

"Jake Wolf had me now," Davis went on. "Once you start down the blackmail road, you never really get off it. Yes, he offered to pay me. And yes, I took the money."

Myron thought about what Wheat Manson had told him on the phone. "You were not just a teacher. You were a guidance counselor."

"Yes."

"You had access to student transcripts. I've seen how far parents in this town will go to get their kids into the right college."

"You have no idea," Davis said.

"Yeah, I do. It wasn't that different when I was a kid. So Jake Wolf had you change his son's grades."

"Something like that. I just switched the academic part of his transcript. Randy wanted to go to Dartmouth. Dartmouth wanted Randy because of his football. But they needed him to be in the top ten percent. There are four hundred kids in his class. Randy was ranked fifty-third—not bad, but not top ten percent. There is another student, a bright kid named Ray Clarke. He's ranked fifth in the class. Clarke got into Georgetown early decision. So I knew he wouldn't be applying anywhere else. . . ."

"So you switched Randy's transcript with this Clarke kid's?"

"Yes."

Now Myron remembered something else, something Randy had said about trying to win Aimee back, about that backfiring, about having the same goal. "And you did the same thing for Aimee Biel. To make sure she got into Duke. Randy asked you to do that, didn't he?"

"Yes."

"And when Randy told Aimee what he'd done, he figured that she'd be grateful. Except she wasn't. She started investigating. She tried to break into the school computer and see what happened. She called Roger Chang, the number-four kid in the class, to see what his grades and extracurricular activities were. She was trying to put together what you guys had done."

"That I don't know," Davis said. He was losing the adrenaline flow. He was wincing in pain now. "I never talked to Aimee about it. I don't know what Randy said to her—that's what I was asking him about when you saw us in the school parking lot. He said he hadn't used my name, that he'd just told her he was going to help her get into Duke."

"But Aimee put it together. Or at least she was trying to."

"That could be."

He winced again. Myron didn't care.

"So now we're up to the big night, Harry. Why did Aimee have me drop her off here?"

The kitchen door swung open. Erik stuck his head into the room. "How are we doing?"

"We're doing okay," Myron said.

Myron expected an argument, but Erik just disappeared back into the kitchen.

"He's crazy," Davis said.

"You have daughters, don't you?"

"Yes." Then he nodded as if he suddenly understood.

"You're stalling, Harry. Your foot is bleeding. You need medical attention."

"I don't care about that."

"You've come this far. Let's get it done. Where is Aimee?"

"I don't know."

"Why did she stop by?"

He closed his eyes.

"Harry?"

His voice was soft. "God forgive me, but I don't know."

"You want to explain?"

"She knocked on the door. It was ridiculously late. Two, three in the morning. I don't know. Donna and I were asleep. She scared the hell out of us. We went to the window. We both saw her. I turned to my wife. You should have seen the look on her face. There was so much hurt. All the distrust, all that I'd been fighting to mend, it all ripped apart. She started to cry."

"So what did you do?"

"I sent Aimee away."

Silence.

"I opened the window. I said it was late. I told her we could talk Monday."

"What did Aimee do?"

"She just looked up at me. She didn't say a word. She was disappointed, I could tell that." Davis squeezed his eyes shut. "But I was also afraid that maybe she was angry."

"She just walked away?"

"Yes."

"And now she's missing," Myron said. "Before she could reveal what she knew. Before she could destroy you. And if the cheating scandal came out, well, it was like I said when we first talked. It's over for you. It would all come out."

"I know. I thought of that."

He stopped. Tears started running down his cheeks.

"What?" Myron said.

"My third big mistake," he said, his voice soft.

Myron felt a chill run down his spine. "What did you do?"

"I wouldn't hurt her. Not ever. I cared about her."

"What did you do, Harry?"

"I was confused. I didn't know what the situation was. So I got scared when she showed up. I knew what it could mean—like you said. Everything could come out. All of it. And I panicked."

"What did you do?" Myron asked again.

"I called someone. As soon as she left. I called someone I thought could help figure out what to do next."

"Who did you call, Harry?"

"Jake Wolf," he said. "I called Jake Wolf and told him that Aimee Biel was right outside my door."

Chapter 49

C laire met them as they ran out.

"What the hell happened in there?"

Erik did not break stride. "Go home, Claire. In case she calls."

Claire glanced at Myron, as though looking for help. Myron did not offer any. Erik was already in the driver's seat, figuratively and literally. Myron quickly slid to the passenger side before Erik zoomed off.

"You know the way to the Wolfs' house?" Myron asked.

"I dropped my daughter off there plenty of times," he said.

He hit the gas. Myron studied his face. Normally Erik's expression landed somewhere in the vicinity of disdainful. There'd be furrowed brows and deep lines of disapproval. None of that was there now. His face was smooth, untroubled. Myron half expected him to snap on the radio and start whistling along.

"You're going to get arrested," Myron said.

"Doubtful."

"You think they'll keep quiet?"

"Probably."

"The hospital will have to report the bullet wound."

Erik shrugged. "Even if they do talk, what would they say? I'm entitled to a jury of my peers. That would mean some parents with teenagers. I take the stand. I talk about how my daughter was missing and how the victim is a teacher who seduced a student and took bribes to change academic records. . . ."

He let his voice trail off as if the verdict was too obvious to mention. Myron was not sure what to say. So he sat back.

"Myron?"

"What?"

"I'm to blame, aren't I? My affair was the catalyst."

"I don't think it's that simple," Myron said. "Aimee is pretty strong willed. It may have contributed, but in a weird way, it sort of adds up. Van Dyne is a music teacher and works in her favorite music store. There would be some appeal there. She had probably outgrown Randy. Aimee has always been a good kid, right?"

"The best," he said softly.

"So maybe she just needed to rebel. That would be normal, right? And there was Van Dyne, at the ready. I mean, I don't know if that's how it worked. But I wouldn't put all of it on you."

He nodded, but he didn't seem to be buying it. Then again, Myron wasn't selling that hard either. Myron considered calling the police, but what exactly would he tell them? And what would they do? The local police could be in Jake Wolf's pocket. They might warn him. Either way, they'd have to respect his rights. He and Erik need not worry about that.

"So how do you figure this all played out?" Erik asked.

"We have two suspects left," Myron said. "Drew Van Dyne and Jake Wolf."

Erik shook his head. "It's Wolf."

"What makes you so sure?"

He cocked his head. "You still don't get the parental bond, do you, Myron?"

"I have a son, Erik."

"He's over in Iraq, right?"

Myron said nothing.

"And what would you give to save him?"

"You know the answer."

"I do. The same as me. And the same as Jake Wolf. He's already shown how far he'll go."

"There's a big difference between paying off a teacher to switch transcripts and . . ."

"Murder?" Erik finished for him. "It probably doesn't start that way. You start by talking to her, trying to make her see things your way. You explain how she could get in trouble too, what with her acceptance to Duke and all. But she won't back down. And suddenly you understand: It's a classic us-or-them scenario. She holds your son's future in her hands. It's either her future or your son's. Which are you going to choose?"

"You're speculating," Myron said.

"Perhaps."

"You have to keep your hopes up."

"Why?"

Myron turned toward him.

"She's dead, Myron. We both know that."

"No, we don't."

"Last night, when we were on that cul-de-sac, do you remember what you said?"

"I said a lot of things."

"You said you didn't think she'd been randomly abducted by a psycho."

393

"I still don't. So?"

"So think about it. If it was someone she knew—Wolf, Davis, Van Dyne, take your pick—why would they abduct her?"

Myron said nothing.

"They all had reasons to keep her quiet. But think it through. You said it could be either Van Dyne or Wolf. My money is on Wolf. But either way, they were all afraid of what Aimee could reveal, right?"

"Right."

"You don't simply abduct someone if that's what you're after. You kill them."

He said it all so calmly, his hands at ten and two o'clock on the steering wheel. Myron was not sure what to say. Erik had spelled it out in pretty convincing fashion. You don't kidnap if the goal is to silence. That doesn't work. That fear had been gnawing around in Myron too. He had tried to smother it, not let it free, but now here it was, excavated by the one man who'd want to paint the rosiest picture of what could have happened.

"And right now," Erik went on, "I'm fine. You see? I'm fighting. I'm battling to find out what happened. When we find her, if she's dead, it's over. Me, I mean. I'm done. I'll put on a façade. I'll move on for the sake of my other children. That's the only reason I won't just shrivel up and die. Because of my other kids. But trust me on this: My life will be over. You might as well bury me with Aimee. That's what this is about. I'm dead, Myron. But I'm not going out a coward."

"Hang on," Myron said. "We don't know anything yet."

Then Myron remembered something else. Aimee had been online tonight. He was going to remind Erik of this, give him some hope, but he wanted to play it through in his head first. It wasn't adding up. Erik had raised an interesting point. From what they had learned, there'd be no reason to abduct Aimee—only reason to kill her.

Had it really been Aimee online? Had she sent Erin a warning?

Something wasn't adding up.

They veered off Route 280 at a speed that put the car on two tires. Erik braked as they hit the Wolfs' street. The car crawled up the hill, stopping two houses away from the Wolfs'.

"What's our next move?" Erik asked.

"We knock on the door. We see if he's home."

They both got out of the car and started up the drive. Myron took the lead. Erik let him. He rang Wolf's doorbell. The sound was trilling and pretentious and droned on too long. Erik stood a few steps back, in the dark. Myron knew that Erik had the gun. He wondered how to play that. Erik had already shot one man tonight. He didn't seem disinclined to doing it again.

Lorraine Wolf's voice came over a speaker. "Who is it?"

"It's Myron Bolitar, Mrs. Wolf."

"It's very late. What do you want?"

Myron remembered the short white tennis dress and double-entendre tone. There was no double entendre now. The voice was drum-tight.

"I need to talk to your husband."

"He's not here."

"Mrs. Wolf, could you please open the door?"

"I'd like you to leave."

Myron wondered how to play this. "I spoke to Randy tonight."

Silence.

"He was at a party. We talked about Aimee. Then I

talked to Harry Davis. I know everything, Mrs. Wolf."

"I don't know what you're talking about."

"You either open this door or I go to the police."

More silence. Myron turned and looked at Erik. He was still at ease. Myron didn't like that.

"Mrs. Wolf?"

"My husband will be back in an hour. Come back then."

Erik Biel took that one. "I don't think so."

He took out the gun, put it against the lock, and fired. The door flew open. Erik rushed in, gun drawn. So did Myron.

Lorraine Wolf screamed.

Erik and Myron veered toward the sound. When they arrived in the family room, they both pulled up.

Lorraine Wolf was alone.

For a moment, no one moved. Myron just studied the situation. Lorraine Wolf stood in the center of the room. She wore rubber gloves. That was the first thing he noticed. Bright yellow rubber gloves. Then he looked at those hands more closely. In one of them, her right hand, she held a sponge. In the other—the left, obviously—she carried a yellow bucket that matched the gloves.

There was a wet spot on the carpet where she had just been cleaning.

Erik and Myron both took a step forward. Now they could see that there was water in the bucket. The water had an awful pink tinge.

Erik said, "Oh no . . ."

Myron turned to grab him, but he was too late. Something behind Erik's eyes exploded. He let out a howl and leapt toward the woman. Lorraine Wolf screamed. The bucket dropped to the carpet. The pink liquid poured out.

Erik tackled her. They both went over the back of

396

the couch. Myron was right behind, not sure how to play it. If he made too aggressive a move, Erik might just pull the trigger. But if he did nothing . . .

Erik had Lorraine Wolf now. He pressed the gun against her temple. She cried out, gripping his hand with her own. Erik did not move.

"What did you do to my daughter?"

"Nothing!"

Myron said, "Erik, don't."

But Erik wasn't listening. Myron raised his own gun. He pointed it at Erik. Erik saw it, but it was obvious he didn't care.

"If you kill her . . ." Myron began.

"What?" Erik shouted. "What do we lose, Myron? Look at this place. Aimee is already dead."

Lorraine Wolf shouted, "No!"

"Where is she then, Lorraine?" Myron asked.

She pressed her lips shut.

"Lorraine, where is Aimee?"

"I don't know."

Erik raised the gun. He was going to hit her with the butt end.

"Erik, don't."

He hesitated. Lorraine looked up, meeting Erik's eye. She was scared, but Myron could see that she was bracing herself, ready to take the blow.

"Don't," Myron said again. He took a step closer.

"She knows something."

"And we'll find out what, okay?"

Erik looked at him. "What would you do? If it was somebody you love?"

Myron inched closer. "I do love Aimee."

"Not like a father."

"No, not like that. But I've been there. I've pushed too hard. It doesn't work."

"It worked with Harry Davis."

"I know, but—"

"She's a woman. That's the only difference. I shot him in the foot and you asked him questions and let him bleed. Now we're face-to-face with someone who is cleaning up blood and all of a sudden you're squeamish?"

Even in this haze, even in this craziness, Myron could actually see his point. It was the guy–gal thing again. If Aimee was a boy. If Harry Davis had been a pretty, flirty woman.

Erik put the gun back against her temple. "Where is my daughter?"

"I don't know," she said.

"Whose blood are you cleaning up?"

Erik aimed the gun at her foot. But the control was gone. Myron could see that. Tears started streaming down Erik's face. His hand shook.

"If you shoot her," Myron said, "it contaminates the evidence. The blood will be mixed up. They'll never put together what happened here. The only one who will go to jail is you."

The argument didn't make full sense, but it was enough to slow Erik down. His entire face collapsed now. He was crying. But he held on to the gun. He kept it pointed at her foot.

"Just take a breath," Myron said.

Erik shook his head. "No!"

The air was still. Everything had stopped. Erik looked down at Lorraine Wolf. She looked up without a flinch. Myron could see Erik's finger on the trigger.

No choice now.

Myron had to make a move.

And then Myron's cell phone chirped.

It made everyone stop. Erik took his finger off the

trigger and wiped his face with his sleeve. "Check it," he said.

Myron took a quick glance at the caller ID. It was Win. He hit the answer button and put it to his ear.

"What?"

"Drew Van Dyne's car just pulled into his driveway," Win said.

Chapter 50

County homicide inspector Loren Muse was working on her new case, the one involving the two murders in East Orange, when her line rang. It was late, but Muse wasn't surprised. She often worked late. Her colleagues knew that.

"Muse."

The voice was muffled but sounded female. "I have some information for you."

"Who is this?"

"It's about that missing girl."

"Which missing girl?"

"Aimee Biel."

Erik was still holding the gun on Lorraine Wolf. "What is it?" he asked Myron.

"Drew Van Dyne. He's home."

"What does that mean?"

"It means we should talk to him."

Erik gestured at Lorraine Wolf with his gun. "We can't just leave her here."

"Agreed."

The smartest move, Myron realized, would be to get Erik to stay here and keep an eye on Lorraine Wolf, not let her warn anybody or clean up or whatever. But he didn't want to leave her alone with Erik. Not like this. Not in the state he was in.

"We should bring her with us," Myron said.

Erik pressed the gun against her head. "Get up," he said to her. She obeyed. They led her outside. Myron called Detective Lance Banner as they headed for the car.

"Banner."

"Get your best crime lab guys over to Jake Wolf's house," Myron said. "I don't have time to explain."

He hung up. In other circumstances, he might have asked for backup. But Win was at Drew Van Dyne's home. There would be no need.

Myron drove. Erik sat in the back with Lorraine Wolf. He kept the gun pointed at her. Myron glanced into the rearview mirror and met her eye.

"Where's your husband?" Myron asked, making a right turn.

"Out."

"Where?"

She did not reply.

"Two nights ago, you got a call," Myron said. "At three in the morning."

Her eyes found his in the mirror again. She didn't nod, but he thought that he could see agreement.

"The call came from Harry Davis. Did you answer it or did your husband?"

Her voice was soft. "Jake did."

"Davis told him that Aimee had been there, that he was worried. And then Jake ran to his car."

"No."

401

Myron paused, considered the answer. "What did he do then?"

Lorraine shifted in her seat again, looking straight at Erik. "We liked Aimee very much. For God's sake, Erik, she dated Randy for the past two years."

"But then she dumped him," Myron said.

"Yes."

"How did Randy react to that?"

"It broke his heart. He cared about her. But you can't think . . ." Her voice died off.

"I'll ask you again, Mrs. Wolf. After Harry Davis called your house, what did your husband do?"

She shrugged her shoulders. "What could he do?"

Myron paused.

"What, you think Jake drove up there and grabbed her? Come on. Even with no traffic it's half an hour from Livingston to Ridgewood. Do you think Aimee would just wait on the street for Jake to come along?"

Myron opened his mouth, closed it. He tried to picture it now. Harry Davis had just rejected her. Would she just stand there, on that dark street, for half an hour or more? Did that make sense?

"So what happened?" Myron asked.

She said nothing.

"You get this call from Harry Davis. He's in a panic about Aimee. What did you and Jake do?"

Myron made a left. They were on Northfield Avenue now, one of Livingston's bigger roads. He hit the accelerator harder.

"What would you have done?" she asked.

No one replied. Lorraine locked eyes on Myron's via the rearview.

"It's your son," she went on. "His entire future is on the line. He had this girlfriend. This wonderful sweet

402

girlfriend. Something happened to her. She changed. I don't know why."

Erik squirmed, but he kept the gun on her.

"All of a sudden she wants no part of him. She has an affair with a teacher. She goes knocking on doors at three in the morning. She's erratic and if she talks, she could bring your whole world down. So what would you have done, Mr. Bolitar?" She turned to look at Erik. "If the situation was reversed—if Randy had dumped Aimee and started acting like this, threatening to destroy her future—what would you have done, Erik?"

"I wouldn't have killed him," Erik said.

"We didn't kill her. All we did . . . We worried. Jake and I sat up and talked. We wondered how to handle it. We tried to plan it out. First, we'd have Harry Davis change the computer records. Put them back the way they were, if he could. Make it look like there'd been a computer glitch or something. People might suspect the truth, but if they couldn't prove it, maybe we'd be safe. We tried to think up other scenarios. I know you want to call Randy a drug dealer, but he was just a contact. Every school has a few. I won't defend it. I remember when I went to Middlebury, I won't mention his name, but a man who is a leading politician now, he was the supplier. You graduate, it's over and done with. But now we needed to make sure that it didn't come out. And mostly we wanted to figure out a way to reach Aimee. We were going to call you, Erik. We thought maybe you could reason with her. Because it wasn't just Randy's future. It was hers too."

They were getting close to Drew Van Dyne's house now.

"That's a nice story, Mrs. Wolf," Myron said. "But you left out one part."

She closed her eyes.

"Whose blood is on your carpet?"

No answer.

"You heard me call the police. They're on their way there now. There are tests. DNA and whatever. They'll find out."

Lorraine Wolf still said nothing. They were on Drew Van Dyne's street now. The homes were smaller and older. The lawns weren't quite as green. The shrubbery dipped and teetered. Win had told Myron exactly where he'd be standing, otherwise Myron would have never spotted him. He pulled to a stop and looked back at Erik.

"Stay here a second."

Myron put the car in park and moved behind the tree. Win was there.

Myron said, "I don't see Van Dyne's car."

"It's in the garage."

"How long has he been here?"

"How long ago did I call?"

"Ten minutes ago."

Win nodded. "There you go then."

Myron looked at the house. It was dark. "No lights on."

"I noticed that too."

"He backed into his garage ten minutes ago and he hasn't gone into the house yet?"

Win shrugged.

There was a grinding noise. The garage door opened. Headlights shone in their faces. The car zoomed out. Win took out his gun, preparing to shoot. Myron put his hand on his friend's arm.

"Aimee could be in there."

Win nodded.

The car flew down the drive and squealed right. It drove past the parked car, the one with Erik Biel and

Lorraine Wolf in the back. Van Dyne's Toyota Corolla hesitated and then accelerated.

Myron and Win sprinted back to the car. Myron got in the driver's side, Win the passenger's. In the backseat, Erik Biel still had the gun pointed at Lorraine Wolf.

Win turned and smiled at Erik. "Hi," he said.

Win reached back as though to shake Erik's hand. Instead, he quickly grabbed Erik's gun and pulled it away from him. Just like that. One second Erik Biel was holding a gun. The next he wasn't.

Myron threw the car into drive as Van Dyne's vehicle disappeared around the corner. Win looked at the gun, frowned, emptied it out.

The chase was on. But it wouldn't last long.

Chapter 51

It was not Drew Van Dyne driving the car.

It was Jake Wolf.

Jake drove fast. He made a few quick turns, but he only drove about a mile. He had a big enough lead. He hit the old Roosevelt Mall, sped around back, shifted into park. He walked across the dark soccer fields in the general direction of Livingston High School. He figured that Myron Bolitar was following him. But he also figured that he had enough of a head start.

He heard the party noises. After a few more steps, he could start to see the glow of lights. The night air felt good in his lungs. Jake tried to look at the trees, the houses, the cars in the driveways. He loved this town. He loved his life here.

As he came closer, he could hear the laughter. He thought about what he was doing here. He swallowed and moved behind a row of pine trees on the neighboring property. He found a spot between two of them and looked out at the tent.

Jake Wolf spotted his son right away.

It had always been like that with Randy. You never missed him. He stood out, no matter what the circumstance. Jake remembered going to Randy's first soccer program when the boy was in first grade. There must have been three, four hundred kids, all there, all running and bouncing around like molecules in heat. Jake had arrived late, but it took mere seconds to find his radiant boy in the waves of look-alike children. Like there was a spotlight coming down from above, illuminating his every step.

Jake Wolf just watched. His son was talking to a bunch of his pals. They were all laughing at something Randy said. Jake stared and felt his eyes well up. There was plenty of blame to go around, he guessed. He tried to think where it all started. With Dr. Crowley maybe. Damn history teacher calls himself *doctor*. What kind of pretentious crap was that anyhow?

Crowley was a small, meaningless man with a bad comb-over and slumped shoulders. He hated athletes. You could smell the envy a mile away. Crowley looked at someone like Randy, someone so good-looking and athletic and special, and he saw all his own adolescent failures.

That was how it all began.

Randy had written a wonderful essay on the Tet Offensive for Crowley's history class. Crowley had given him a C-minus. A goddamn C-minus. A friend of Randy's, a guy named Joel Fisher, had gotten an A. Jake read both essays. Randy's was better. It wasn't just Jake Wolf who thought so. He tried them both out on various people. He didn't let them know which essay was his son's and which was Joel's.

"Which is better?" he'd asked.

And almost all agreed. Randy's paper—the C-minus paper—was superior.

It might have seemed like a small thing, but it wasn't. That paper was three-quarters of the grade. Dr. Crowley gave Randy a C. It kept Randy off the honor roll for that semester, but more than that, more than anything else, it knocked him out of the class's top ten percent. Dartmouth had been clear. With Randy's SATs, he needed to be in the top ten percent. If that C had been a B, Randy would have been accepted.

That was the difference.

Jake and Lorraine had gone in to talk to Dr. Crowley. They had explained the situation. Crowley wouldn't budge. He had been dismissive, enjoying his power play, and it took all Jake's willpower not to put the man through a plate-glass window. But Jake was not about to give up that easy. He'd hired a private eye to dig into the man's past, but Crowley's life had been so pathetic, so nothing, so obviously unremarkable, especially next to the bright beacon that was Jake's son . . . There was nothing he could use against the man.

So if Jake Wolf had played by the rules, that would have been it. That would have kept his son out of an Ivy League education—the whim of a nothing like Crowley.

Uh-uh. No way.

And so it began.

Jake swallowed and stared. His son stood in the middle of the party, the sun with dozens of orbiting planets. He had a cup in his hand. Randy had such natural ease. Such poise in everything he did. Jake Wolf stood there, in the shadows, and wondered if there was any way to save it all. He didn't think so. It was like holding water in your hand. He had tried to sound confident for Lorraine. He thought that maybe he could dump the body in Drew Van Dyne's house. Lorraine would clean up the stain. It could have still worked.

But Myron Bolitar had showed up. Jake had spotted

him from the garage. He was trapped. Jake hoped to speed away, lose them, dump the body somewhere else. But when he made that first turn and saw that Lorraine was in the backseat, he knew that it was over.

He'd hire a good attorney. The best. He knew a guy in town, Lenny Marcus. Great defense lawyer. He'd call him, see what they could work out. But in his heart, Jake Wolf knew that it was over. For him, at least.

That was why he was here now. In the shadows. Watching his beautiful, perfect son. Randy was the only thing he had ever gotten right. His boy. His precious boy. But that was enough. From the first time he had laid eyes on the baby in the hospital, Jake Wolf was mesmerized. He went to every practice he could. He went to every game. It wasn't just to show support—often, during practices, Jake would stand behind a tree, almost hide, as he was doing now. He just liked to watch his son. That was all. He liked getting lost in this very simple bliss. And sometimes, when he did, he couldn't believe how lucky he was, how someone like Jake Wolf, also a nothing when you thought about it, could have been part of creating something so miraculous. The world was cruel and awful and you had to do all you could to get that edge, but then every once in a while, he'd look at Randy and realize that there was something other than the dog-eat-dog horror, that there had to be something better out there, some higher being, because here, in front of him, there was indeed perfection and beauty.

"Hey, Jake."

He turned at the sound of the voice. "Hi, Jacques."

It was Jacques Harlow, the father of one of Randy's closest friends and the party host. Jacques came up next to him. They both looked out at the party, at their sons, soaking it in for almost a full minute without speaking.

"Can you believe how fast it went by?" Harlow said.

Jake just shook his head, afraid to speak. His eyes never left his son.

"Hey, how about coming in for a drink?"

"I can't. I just had to drop something off for Randy. Thanks though."

Harlow slapped his back. "Sure." He headed back toward the porch.

It took another five minutes. Jake enjoyed every second. Then he heard the footsteps. He turned and saw Myron Bolitar. Myron had a gun in his hand. Jake Wolf smiled and turned back to his son.

"What are you doing here, Jake?"

"What's it look like?"

Jake Wolf did not want to move, but he knew that it was time. He soaked up one last look at his son. That was what this felt like. The last time he would see him like this. He wanted to say something to his son, offer some words of wisdom, but Jake wasn't good with words.

So instead he turned and raised his hands.

"In the trunk," Jake Wolf said. "The body is in the trunk."

Chapter 52

Win stood a few feet behind Myron. Just in case. But he could see right away that Jake Wolf was not about to make a move. He was surrendering. For now. There might be something else, something later. Win had dealt with men like Jake Wolf. They never really believe that it's over. They look for an out, an escape hatch, a loophole, a legal maneuver, something.

A few minutes earlier, they'd spotted Van Dyne's car in the Roosevelt Mall lot. Myron and Win had run ahead, leaving Lorraine Wolf and Erik Biel in the car. Erik still had a few nylon cuffs he'd bought at the same store where he'd picked up the ammunition. So they cuffed Lorraine's hands behind her back and hoped like hell that Erik wouldn't do something stupid.

Not long after Myron and Win disappeared into the dark, Erik got out of the backseat. He moved toward Van Dyne's car. He opened the front door. He didn't know what he was doing exactly. He just knew he had to do something. He slid into the driver's seat. There were guitar picks on the floor. He remembered his own daughter's collection, how much she loved them, how her eyes would close when she strummed the strings. He remembered Aimee's first guitar, a crappy thing he'd bought at a toy store for ten bucks. She'd been only four years old. She banged on it and did a wonderful rendition of "Santa Claus Is Coming to Town." More like Bruce Springsteen than something you'd see from a preschooler. He and Claire had clapped like mad when she finished.

"Aimee rocks," Claire had declared.

They had all been smiling. They had all been so happy.

Erik looked out the windshield, back toward his car, back toward Lorraine Wolf. Their eyes met. He had known Lorraine for two years now, since Aimee had first started dating her son. He liked her. Truth be told, he had even semi-fantasized about her. Not that he would have ever done anything about it. Not like that. Just a harmless fantasy for an attractive woman. Normal stuff.

He looked in the backseat now. There was sheet music, handwritten. He froze. His hand moved slowly. He saw the handwriting and realized that it was Aimee's. He picked it up, brought it closer, holding it as if it were porcelain.

Aimee had written this.

Something caught in his throat. His fingertips touched down on the words, the notes. His daughter had held this paper. She had scrunched up her face the way she always did and delved into her life experiences and produced this. It was a simple thought, really, but suddenly it meant the world to him. His anger was gone. It would be back. He knew that. But at that moment, his heart just felt heavy. There was no anger. Just pain.

That was when Erik decided to pop the trunk.

He looked back over at Lorraine Wolf. Something crossed her face. He didn't know what. He opened the car door and stepped back into the night. He moved toward the trunk, took hold of the hatch with one hand, began to lift it. He heard rustling from the field. He turned and saw Myron come flying into view.

"Erik, wait. . . ."

Erik opened the trunk then.

The black tarp. That was what he saw first. Something wrapped in black tarp. His knees buckled, but he held on. Myron started toward him, but Erik held up a hand as if telling him to stay back. He tried to rip the tarp. It wouldn't give. He pulled and tugged. The tarp held in place. Erik started to panic now. His chest heaved. His breath caught.

He took out his key chain and dug the end of a key into the plastic. It made a hole. There was blood. He slit the tarp and reached his hands in. They grew wet and sticky. Erik desperately pulled at the tarp, ripping at it as if he were trapped inside, running out of air.

He saw the dead face and fell back.

Myron was next to him now.

"Oh my God," Erik said. He collapsed. "Oh thank you. . . ."

It wasn't his daughter in the trunk. It was Drew Van Dyne.

Chapter 53

Lorraine Wolf said, "I shot him in self-defense."

In the distance Myron could hear the police sirens. Myron stood next to the trunk with Erik Biel and Lorraine Wolf. He had called the police. They'd be here soon. He looked across the field. He could see distant silhouettes of Win and Jake Wolf. Myron had run ahead. Win had taken care of securing their suspect.

"Drew Van Dyne was in the house," she went on. "He pulled a gun on Jake. I saw it. He was yelling all kinds of crazy stuff about Aimee—"

"What stuff?"

"He said that Jake didn't care about her. That she was just some dumb slut to him. That she was pregnant. He was ranting."

"So what did you do?"

"We keep guns in the house. Jake likes to hunt. So I got a rifle. I pointed it at Drew Van Dyne. I told him to put down the gun. He wouldn't. I could see that. So . . ."

"No!" It was Wolf who had said that. They were close enough to hear. "I shot Van Dyne!"

Everyone stared at him. The police sirens sounded.

"I shot him in self-defense," Jake Wolf insisted. "He pulled a gun on me."

"So why did you stick the body in the trunk?" Myron asked.

"I was afraid no one would believe that. I was going to bring him home, dump him in his own house. Then I realized that would be stupid."

"When did you realize that?" Myron said. "When you saw us?"

"I want a lawyer," Jake Wolf said. "Lorraine, don't say anything else."

Erik Biel stepped forward. "I don't care about any of this. My daughter. Where the hell is my daughter?"

No one moved. No one spoke. The night stayed silent except for the scream of sirens.

Lance Banner was the first cop out of his car, but dozens of squad cars descended on the Roosevelt Mall parking lot. They kept the flashing lights on. Everyone's face went from blue to red. The effect was dizzying.

"Aimee," Erik said softly. "Where is she?"

Myron tried to keep calm, tried to concentrate. He stepped to the side with Win. Win's face, as ever, remained unruffled.

"So," Win said, "where are we?"

"It's not Davis," Myron said. "We checked him out. It doesn't look like it was Van Dyne. He pulled a gun on Jake Wolf because he thought that he'd done it. And the Wolfs claim, somewhat convincingly, that it wasn't them."

"Any other suspects?"

"Not that I can think of."

Win said, "Then we need to look at them again."

"Erik thinks she's dead."

Win nodded. "That's what I mean," he said. "When I say we need to look at them again."

"You think one of them killed her and got rid of the body?"

Win did not bother replying.

"My God," Myron said. He looked back over at Erik. "Have we been looking at this wrong from the beginning?"

"I can't see how."

Myron's cell phone chirped. He looked down at the caller ID and saw the number was blocked.

"Hello?"

"It's Investigator Loren Muse. Do you remember me?"

"Of course."

"I just got an anonymous call," she said. "Someone claimed they spotted Aimee Biel yesterday."

"Where?"

"On Livingston Avenue. Aimee was in the passenger seat of a Toyota Corolla. The driver pretty much fits the description of Drew Van Dyne."

Myron frowned. "Are you sure?"

"That's what she said."

"He's dead, Muse."

"Who?"

"Drew Van Dyne."

Erik came over and stood next to Myron.

And that was when it happened.

Erik's cell phone rang.

He brought the phone up. When he saw the number on the caller ID, Erik nearly screamed.

"Oh my God. . . ."

Erik snapped the phone to his ear. His eyes were wet. His hand shook so badly he hit the wrong button to answer. He tried again and brought the phone back up. His voice was a panicked scream. "Hello?"

Myron leaned in close enough to hear. There was a moment of static. And then a voice, a teary voice, a familiar voice said, "Daddy?"

Myron's heart stopped.

Erik's face collapsed, but his voice was all father. "Where are you, honey? Are you all right?"

"I don't . . . I'm fine, I think. Daddy?"

"It's okay, honey. I'm here. Just tell me where you are."

And she did.

Chapter 54

Myron drove. Erik stayed in the passenger seat. The ride was not a long one.

Aimee had said that she was behind the Little Park near the high school—that same park that Claire had taken her to when she was only three. Erik would not let her off the line. "It's okay," he kept saying. "Daddy's on his way."

Myron cut time by taking the circle in the wrong direction. He drove over two curbs. He didn't care. Neither did Erik. Speed was the thing here. The lot was empty. The headlights danced through the night and then, as they made the final turn, the lights landed on a solitary figure.

Myron hit the brake.

Erik said, "Oh my God, oh my sweet dear God. . . ."

He was out of the car. Myron was out fast too. They both started sprinting. But somewhere along the way, Myron let up. Erik took the lead. That was how it should be. Erik swept his daughter into his arms. He took careful hold of her face, as though fearing it was only a dream, a puff of smoke, and that she might vanish again.

Myron stopped and watched. Then he picked up his own cell phone and called Claire.

"Myron? What the hell is going on?"

"She's okay," he said.

"What?"

"She's safe. We're bringing her home to you now."

In the car, Aimee was groggy.

"What happened?" Myron asked.

"I think," Aimee began. Her eyes went wide. Her pupils were dilated. "I think they drugged me."

"Who?"

"I don't know."

"You don't know who kidnapped you?"

She shook her head.

Erik sat in the back with Aimee. He held her. He stroked her hair. He told her over and over again that it was okay now, everything was okay.

Myron said, "Maybe we should take her to a doctor."

"No," Erik said. "She needs to go home first."

"Aimee, what happened?"

"She's been through hell, Myron," Erik said. "Give her a chance to catch her breath."

"It's okay, Daddy."

"Why were you in New York?"

"I was supposed to meet someone."

"Who?"

"About . . ." Her voice faded. Then she said, "This is tough to talk about."

"We know about Drew Van Dyne," Myron said. "We know you're pregnant."

419

She closed her eyes.

"Aimee, what happened?"

"I was going to get rid of it."

"The baby?"

She nodded. "I went to the corner of Fifty-second Street and Sixth. That's what they told me to do. They were going to help me out. They pulled up in a black car. They told me to get money from the ATM."

"Who?"

"I never saw them," Aimee said. "The windows were tinted. They were always in disguise."

"Disguise?"

"Yes."

"They. There was more than one?"

"I don't know. I know I heard a woman's voice. That much I'm sure."

"Why didn't you just go to St. Barnabas?"

Aimee hesitated. "I'm so tired."

"Aimee?"

"I don't know," she said. "Someone from St. Barnabas called. A woman. If I went there, my parents would find out. Something about shield laws. I just . . . I'd made so many mistakes. I just wanted to . . . But then I wasn't so sure. I got the money. I was going to get in the car. But then I panicked. That's when I called you, Myron. I wanted to talk to someone. It was going to be you, but, I don't know, I know you were trying, but I thought maybe it would be better to talk to someone else."

"Harry Davis?"

Aimee nodded. "I know this other girl," she said. "Her boyfriend got her pregnant. She said Mr. D was really helpful."

"That's enough," Erik said.

They were almost at Aimee's house. Myron did not

want to let this go. Not yet.

"So what happened then?"

"The rest is fuzzy," Aimee said.

"Fuzzy?"

"I know I got into a car."

"Whose?"

"The same one that was waiting for me in New York, I think. I felt so deflated after Mr. D sent me away. So I thought I might as well go with them. Get it over with. But . . ."

"But what?"

"It's all fuzzy."

Myron frowned. "I don't understand."

"I don't know," she said. "I was drugged almost the whole time. I only remember waking up for a few minutes at a time. Whoever it was, they held me in some kind of log cabin. That's all I remember. It had this fireplace with white and brown stone. And then suddenly I was in that field behind the playground. I called you, Daddy. I don't even know . . . how long was I gone?"

She started crying then. Erik put his arms around her.

"It's okay," Erik said. "Whatever happened, it's over now. You're safe."

Claire was in the yard. She sprinted up to the car. Aimee managed to get out, but she could barely stand. Claire let out a primordial cry and grabbed for her daughter.

They hugged, they cried, they kissed, the three of them. Myron felt like an intruder. They started toward the door then. Myron waited. Claire looked back. She caught Myron's eyes. She ran back to him.

Claire kissed him. "Thank you."

"The police are still going to need to talk to her."

"You kept your promise."

He said nothing.

"You brought her home."

Then she ran back to the house.

Myron stood there and watched them disappear inside. He wanted to celebrate. Aimee was home. She was healthy.

But he didn't feel in the mood.

He drove again to the cemetery that overlooked a schoolyard. The gate was open. He found Brenda's grave and sat next to it. The night closed in. He could hear the swishing of highway traffic. He thought about what had just happened. He thought about what Aimee had just said. He thought about her being home, safe and with her family, while Brenda lay in the ground.

Myron sat there until another car pulled up. He almost smiled as Win stepped into view. Win kept his distance for a moment. Then he approached the headstone. He looked down at it.

"Nice to have one in the win column, no?" Win said.

"I'm not so sure."

"Why not?"

"I still don't know what happened."

"She's alive. She's home."

"I'm not sure that's enough."

Win gestured toward the stone. "If you could go back in time, would you need to know everything that happened? Or would it be enough if she were alive and home?"

Myron closed his eyes, tried to imagine that bliss. "It would be enough if she were alive and home."

Win smiled. "There you go then. What else is there?"

He stood. He didn't know the answer. He only knew that he had spent enough time with ghosts, with the dead.

Chapter 55

The police took Myron's statement. They asked questions. They told him nothing. Myron slept in the house in Livingston that night. Win stayed with him. Win rarely did that. They both woke up early. They watched *SportsDesk* on TV and ate cold cereal.

It felt normal and right and rather wonderful.

Win said, "I've been thinking about your relationship with Ms. Wilder."

"Don't."

"No, no, I think I owe you an apology," Win continued. "I may have misjudged her. Her looks do grow on you. I'm thinking that perhaps her derriere is of a finer quality than I originally thought."

"Win?"

"What?"

"I don't much care what you think."

"Yes, my friend, you do."

At eight in the morning Myron walked over to the Biel house. He figured that they were awake by now. He knocked gently on the door. Claire answered it. She wore a bathrobe. Her hair was disheveled. She stepped outside and closed the door behind her.

"Aimee is still sleeping," Claire said. "Whatever drugs the kidnappers gave her, they really knocked her out."

"Maybe you should take her to the hospital."

"Our friend David Gold—do you know him? He's a doctor. He came by last night and checked her out. He said she'd be fine once the drugs wear off."

"What drugs did they give her?"

Claire shrugged. "Who knows?" They both stood there a moment. Claire took a deep breath and looked up and down the street. Then she said, "Myron?"

"Yes."

"I want you to let the police handle it from here."

He did not reply.

"I don't want you to ask Aimee about what happened."

There was just enough steel in her voice. Myron waited to see if she'd say more. She did. "Erik and I, we just want it to end. We hired an attorney last night."

"Why?"

"We're her parents. We know how to protect our daughter."

The implication being: Myron didn't. She hadn't needed to mention again that first night, how Myron had dropped Aimee off and hadn't looked out for her. But that was what she was saying here.

"I know how you are, Myron."

"How am I?"

"You want answers."

"You don't?"

"I want my daughter to be happy and healthy. That's more important than answers."

"You don't want whoever did this to pay?"

"It was probably Drew Van Dyne. And he's dead. So what's the point? We just want Aimee to be able to put this behind her. She's going to college in a few months."

"Everyone keeps talking about college like it's a great big do-over card," Myron said. "Like the first eighteen years of your life don't count."

"In a way, they don't."

"That's crap, Claire. What about her baby?"

Claire moved back to the door. "With all due deference—and no matter what you want to think about our decisions—that's not your concern."

Myron nodded to himself. She had him on that one.

"Your part in this is over," she said, and again he heard the steel. "Thank you for what you've done. I have to get back to my daughter now."

And then Claire closed the door on him.

Chapter 56

A week later, Myron sat at Baumgart's Restaurant with Livingston police detective Lance Banner and Essex County investigator Loren Muse. Myron had ordered the Kung Pao Chicken. Banner had ordered a Chinese fish special. Muse was having a grilled cheese sandwich.

"Grilled cheese at a Chinese restaurant?" Myron said.

Loren Muse shrugged mid-bite.

Banner used chopsticks. "Jake Wolf is pleading self-defense," he said. "He claims that Drew Van Dyne pulled a gun on him. Said that he made wild threats."

"What kind of threats?"

"Van Dyne was ranting that Wolf hurt Aimee Biel. Something like that. They're both a little vague on the specifics."

"Both?"

"Jake Wolf's star witness. His wife, Lorraine."

"That night," Myron said, "Lorraine told us she pulled the trigger."

"My guess is, she did. We did a powder residue check on Jake Wolf's hand. He was clean."

"Did you check his wife?"

"She refused," Banner said. "Jake Wolf forbade it."

"So he's taking the hit for his wife?"

Banner looked at Loren Muse. He nodded slowly.

"What?" Myron asked.

"We'll get to that."

"Get to what?"

"Look, Myron, I think you're right," Banner said. "Jake Wolf is trying to take the hit for the whole family. On the one hand, he's claiming self-defense. There is some evidence to back it up. Van Dyne had a bit of a history. He also had a gun on him—it's registered in his name. On the other hand, Jake Wolf is willing to do some time in exchange for giving his wife and kid a pass."

"His kid?"

"He wants a guarantee that his son still goes to Dartmouth. And that Randy will be cleared of all subsequent allegations, including anything related to the shooting, the cheating scandal, and his possible relationship with Van Dyne and drugs."

"Well," Myron said. But it added up. Jake Wolf was an ass, but Myron had seen the way he looked at his son at that graduation party. "He's still trying to salvage Randy's future."

"Yep."

"Will he be able to?"

"I don't know," Banner said. "The prosecutor has no jurisdiction over Dartmouth. If they want to rescind their acceptance, they can and probably will."

"What Jake is doing," Myron said. "It's almost admirable."

"If not twisted," Banner added.

Myron looked at Loren Muse. "You're awfully quiet."

"Because I think Banner has it wrong."

Banner frowned. "I don't have it wrong."

Loren put down the sandwich and brushed the crumbs off her hands. "For starters, you're going to put the wrong person in jail. The powder residue test proves that Jake Wolf didn't shoot Drew Van Dyne."

"He said he wore gloves."

Now Loren Muse frowned.

Myron said, "She has a point."

"Gee, Myron, thanks."

"Hey, I'm on your side here. Lorraine Wolf told me she shot Drew Van Dyne. Shouldn't she be the one on trial?"

Loren Muse turned to him. "I never said I thought it was Lorraine Wolf."

"Excuse me?"

"Sometimes the most obvious answer is the right one."

Myron shook his head. "I'm not following you."

"Go back a second," Loren Muse said.

"How far back?"

"All the way to Edna Skylar on the streets of New York City."

"Right."

"Maybe we had it right all along. From the moment she called us."

"I'm still not following."

"Edna Skylar confirmed what we already knew: that Katie Rochester was a runaway. And at first, that's what we all thought about Aimee Biel too, right?"

"So?"

Loren Muse said nothing.

"Wait a minute. Are you saying you think Aimee Biel ran away?"

429

"There are a lot of unanswered questions," Loren said.

"So ask them."

"Ask who?"

"What do you mean, who? Ask Aimee Biel."

"We tried." Loren Muse smiled. "Aimee's lawyer won't let us talk to her."

Myron sat back.

"Don't you find that odd?"

"Her parents want her to put it behind her."

"Why?"

"Because it was a traumatic experience for her," Myron said.

Loren Muse just looked at him. So did Lance Banner.

"That story she told you," Loren said. "About being drugged and held in some log cabin."

"What about it?"

"There are holes."

A cold pinprick started at the base of Myron's neck and slid south down his spine. "What holes?"

"First off, we have the anonymous source who called me. The one who saw her tooling around with Drew Van Dyne. If Aimee were kidnapped, how could that be exactly?"

"Your witness was wrong."

"Right. She happened to pick out the make of the car and described Drew Van Dyne to a tee. But hey, she's probably wrong."

"You can't trust anonymous sources," Myron tried.

"Fine, then let's move on to hole two. This late-night abortion story. We checked at St. Barnabas. Nobody told her anything about parental notification. More than that, it's not true. The laws might change on that subject, but either way, in her case—"

"She's eighteen," Myron interrupted. Eighteen. An adult. That age again.

"Exactly. And there's more."

Myron waited.

"Hole three: We found Aimee's fingerprints at Drew Van Dyne's house."

"They had an affair. Of course her prints were there. They could be weeks old."

"We found prints on a soda can. The can was still on the kitchen counter."

Myron said nothing, but he felt something deep inside of him start to give way.

"All your suspects—Harry Davis, Jake Wolf, Drew Van Dyne. We checked them all out thoroughly. None of them could have pulled off a purported kidnapping." Loren Muse spread her hands. "So it's like that old axiom in reverse. When you've eliminated all the other possibilities, you have to go back to your first, most obvious solution."

"You think Aimee ran away."

Loren Muse shrugged, shifted in her chair. "Here she is, a confused young woman. Pregnant with a teacher's child. Her dad is having an affair. She's caught up in this cheating scandal. She must have felt trapped, don't you think?"

Myron found himself almost nodding.

"There is no physical evidence—none at all—that Aimee was abducted. And think about it. Why would someone kidnap her anyway? What would be the motive in a case like this? The normal motives are, what, sexual assault, for one. We know that didn't happen. Her doctor told us that much. There was no physical or sexual trauma. Why else are people kidnapped? For ransom. Well, we know that didn't happen either."

Myron kept very still. It was almost exactly what

Erik had said. If you wanted to keep Aimee quiet, you didn't kidnap her. You killed her. But now she was alive. Ergo . . .

Loren Muse kept pounding at him. "Do you have a motive for a kidnapping, Myron?"

"No," he said. "But what about the ATM machine? How do you figure that in?"

"You mean both girls using the same one?"

"Yes."

"I don't know," she said. "Maybe it was a coincidence after all."

"Come on, Muse."

"Okay, fine, then let's turn it around." She pointed at him. "How does that ATM transaction fit into a kidnapping scenario? Would Wolf know about it? Davis, Van Dyne?"

Myron saw her point. "But there are other things too," he countered. "Like that phone call from a pay phone in the subway. Or the fact that she was online."

"All of which fit into her being a runaway," Loren said. "If someone did abduct her like she claims, why would they risk a call from a pay phone? Why would you put her on the Internet?"

Myron shook his head. He knew that she was making sense. He just refused to accept it. "So that's how this ends? It's not Davis. It's not Wolf or Van Dyne or anyone. Aimee Biel just ran away?"

Loren Muse and Lance Banner exchanged another glance.

Then Lance Banner said, "Yes, that's the working theory. And remember: There's no law against what she did. In the end a lot of people got hurt or even killed. But running away is not against the law."

Loren Muse kept quiet again. Myron didn't like it. "What?" he snapped at her.

"Nothing. What Banner said—the evidence all points that way. It might even explain why Aimee's parents don't want us talking to her. They don't want all that coming out—her affair, her pregnancy, heck, like it or not, she was helped in the cheating scandal too. So keeping it all quiet. Making her look like a victim instead of a runaway. It's the right move."

"But?"

She looked at Banner. He sighed and shook his head. Loren Muse started fiddling with her fork. "But both Jake and Lorraine Wolf wanted to take the blame for shooting Drew Van Dyne."

"So?"

"You don't find that odd?"

"No. We just explained why. Lorraine killed him. Jake wants to take the fall to protect her."

"And the fact that they were cleaning up the evidence and moving the body?"

Myron shrugged. "That would be the natural reaction."

"Even if you killed in self-defense?"

"In their case, yes. They were trying to protect it all. If Van Dyne is found dead in their house, even if they shot him in self-defense, all the stuff about Randy would come out. The drugs, the cheating, all of it."

She nodded. "That's the theory. That's what Lance here believes. And that's probably what happened."

Myron tried not to sound too impatient. "But?"

"But maybe that's not how it happened. Maybe Jake and Lorraine came home and found the body there."

Myron stopped breathing. There is something inside of you. It can bend. It can stretch. But then, every once in a while, you can feel it pulling too far. If you let it go there, you will break inside. You will snap in two. You know that. Myron had known Aimee his whole life.

433

And right now, if he was right about where Loren Muse was going, he was close to breaking. "What the hell are you talking about?"

"Maybe the Wolfs came home and saw a body. And maybe they assumed that Randy had done it." She leaned closer. "Van Dyne was Randy's drug supplier. He had also stolen Randy's girlfriend. So maybe Mom and Dad saw the body and figured that Randy shot him. Maybe they panicked and loaded the body in his car."

"What, you think Randy killed Drew Van Dyne?"

"No. I said that's what they thought. Randy has an alibi."

"So what's your point?"

"If Aimee Biel hadn't been kidnapped," Muse said, "if she ran away and stayed with Drew Van Dyne, maybe she was with him in the house. And maybe, just maybe, Aimee, our scared little girl, really did want to put it all behind her. Maybe she was ready for college, ready to move on and cut off all ties, except this guy, this Drew Van Dyne, wouldn't let go. . . ."

Myron closed his eyes. That little thing inside of him—it was being pulled hard. He stopped it, shook his head. "You're wrong."

She shrugged. "Probably."

"I've known this girl all my life."

"I know, Myron. She's a young, sweet girl, right? Young sweet girls can't be killers, can they?"

He thought about Aimee Biel, the way she laughed at him in his basement, the way she climbed up the jungle gym when she was three. He remembered her blowing out candles at her birthday party. He remembered watching her in a school play when she was in eighth grade. He remembered it all and he felt the anger starting to mount.

"You're wrong," Myron said again.

He waited on the sidewalk across the street from their house.

Erik came out first. His face was tight, grim. Aimee and Claire followed. Myron stood there and watched. Aimee spotted him first. She smiled at him and waved. Myron studied that smile. It looked the same to him. The same smile he'd seen on the playground when she was three. The same one he'd seen in the basement a few weeks ago.

There was nothing different.

Except now the smile gave him a chill.

He looked at Erik and then at Claire. Their eyes were hard, protective, but there was something else there, something beyond exhaustion and surrender, something primitive and instinctive. Erik and Claire walked with their daughter. But they did not touch her. That was what Myron noticed. They were not touching their own daughter.

"Hi, Myron!" Aimee shouted.

"Hi."

Aimee ran across the street. Her parents did not move. Neither did Myron. Aimee threw her arms around him, almost knocking him over. Myron tried to hug her back. But he couldn't quite do it. Aimee gripped him harder.

"Thank you," she whispered.

He didn't say anything. Her embrace, it felt the same. It felt warm and strong. No different than before.

And yet he wanted it to end.

Myron felt his heart drop and shatter. God help him, he just wanted her to let go, to get her away from him. He wanted this girl he'd loved for so long to be gone. He took hold of her shoulders and gently pushed her off.

Claire was behind her now. She said to Myron, "We're in a rush. We'll get together soon."

He nodded. The two women walked away. Erik waited by the car. Myron watched them. Claire was next to her daughter, but she still wouldn't touch her. Aimee got in the car. Erik and Claire glanced at each other. They did not speak. Aimee was in the back. They both sat in the front. Natural enough, Myron supposed, but it still seemed to him as if they were trying to keep their distance from Aimee, as if they wondered—or perhaps knew—about the stranger who now lived with them. Claire looked back at him.

They know, Myron thought.

Myron watched the car pull away. As it disappeared down the street, he realized something:

He hadn't kept his promise.

He hadn't brought home their baby.

Their baby was gone.

Chapter 57

Four Days Later

J essica Culver did indeed marry Stone Norman at Tavern on the Green.

Myron was in his office when he read about it in the paper. Esperanza and Win were both there too. Win was standing near a full-length mirror, checking out his golf swing. Win did that a lot. Esperanza watched Myron carefully.

"You okay?" she asked him.

"I am."

"You realize that her getting hitched is the greatest thing that's ever happened to you?"

"I do." Myron put the paper down. "I came to a realization that I wanted to share with both of you."

Win stopped his air swing midway. "My arm isn't straight enough."

Esperanza waved him quiet. "What?"

"I've always tried to run away from what I now see are my natural instincts," Myron said. "You know. Playing the hero. You both warn me against it. And I've listened. But I've figured something out. I'm supposed to do it. I'll have my defeats, sure, but I'll have more victories. I'm not going to run away from it anymore. I don't want to end up being cynical. I want to help people. And that's what I'm going to do."

Win turned toward him. "Are you done?"

"I am."

Win looked at Esperanza. "Should we applaud?"

"I think we should."

Esperanza stood and applauded wildly. Win put down his air club and offered up a polite golf clap.

Myron bowed and said, "Thank you so very much, you're a beautiful audience, don't forget your waitress on the way out, hey, try the veal."

Big Cyndi popped her head through the doorway. She'd gone heavy on the rouge this morning and looked like a traffic light.

"Line two, Mr. Bolitar." Big Cyndi batted her eyes. Picture two scorpions trapped on their backs. Then she added, "It's your new sweetie pie."

Myron picked up the phone. "Hey!"

Ali Wilder said, "What time are you coming over?"

"I should be there about seven."

"How about pizza and a DVD with the kids?"

Myron smiled. "Sounds great."

He hung up. He was smiling. Esperanza and Win exchanged a glance.

"What?" Myron said.

"You're so doofy when you're in love," Esperanza said.

Myron looked at his watch. "It's time."

"Good luck," Esperanza said.

Myron turned to Win. "You want to come along?"

"No, my friend. This one is all yours."

Myron stood. He kissed Esperanza on the cheek. He

hugged Win. Win was surprised by the gesture, but he took it. Myron drove back to New Jersey. It was a glorious day. The sun shone like it'd just been created. Myron fiddled with the radio dial. He kept hitting all his favorite songs.

It was that kind of day.

He did not bother stopping at Brenda's grave. He thought that she'd understand. Actions speak louder and all that.

Myron parked at St. Barnabas Medical Center. He headed up to Joan Rochester's room. She was sitting up when he got there, ready to leave.

"How are you feeling?" he asked.

"Fine," Joan Rochester said.

"I'm sorry about what happened to you."

"Don't be."

"Are you going home?"

"Yes."

"And you're not going to press charges?"

"That's right."

Myron figured as much. "Your daughter can't run forever."

"I know that."

"What are you going to do?"

"Katie came home last night."

So much for the happy ending, Myron thought. He closed his eyes. This was not what he'd wanted to hear.

"She and Rufus had a fight. So Katie came home. Dominick forgave her. It's all going to be okay."

They looked at each other. It wouldn't be okay. He knew that. She knew that.

"I want to help you," Myron said.

"You can't."

And maybe she was right.

You help those you can. That was what Win had

said. And you always, *always* keep a promise. That was why he had come today. To keep his promise.

He met up with Dr. Edna Skylar in the corridor outside the cancer ward. He had hoped to see her in her office, but this would be okay.

Edna Skylar smiled when she saw him. She wore very little makeup. The white coat was wrinkled. No stethoscope hung around her neck this time.

"Hello, Myron," she said.

"Hi, Dr. Skylar."

"Call me Edna."

"Okay."

"I was just on my way out." She pointed with her thumb toward the elevator. "What brings you here?"

"You, actually."

Edna Skylar had a pen tucked behind her ear. She took it out, made a note on a chart, put it back. "Really?"

"You taught me something when I was here last time," Myron said.

"What's that?"

"We talked about the virtuous patient, remember? We talked about the pure versus the sullied. You were so honest with me—about how you'd rather work with people who seemed more deserving."

"A lot of talk, yes," she said. "But at the end of the day, I took an oath. I treat those I don't like too."

"Oh I know. But you see, you got me thinking. Because I agreed with you. I wanted to help Aimee Biel because I thought she was . . . I don't know."

"Innocent?" Skylar said.

"I guess."

"But you learned that she's not."

"More than that," Myron said. "What I learned was, you were wrong."

"About?"

"We can't prejudge people like that. We become cynical. We assume the worst. And when we do that, we start to see only the shadows. You know that Aimee Biel is back home?"

"I heard that, yes."

"Everyone thinks she ran away."

"I heard that too."

"So nobody listened to her story. I mean, really listened. Once that assumption came about, Aimee Biel was no longer an innocent. You see? Even her parents. They had her best interests at heart. They wanted so much to protect her that even they couldn't see the truth."

"Which is?"

"Innocent until proven guilty. It's not just for the courtroom."

Edna Skylar made a production of checking her watch. "I'm not sure I see what you're getting at."

"I believed in that girl her whole life. Was I wrong? Was it a lie? But at the end of the day, it's like her parents said—it's their job to protect her, not mine. So I was able to be more dispassionate. I was willing to risk learning the truth. So I waited. When I finally got Aimee alone, I asked her to tell me the whole story. Because there were too many holes in the other one—the one where she ran away and maybe killed her lover. That ATM machine, for one. That call from the pay phone, for another. Stuff like that. I didn't want to just shove it all aside and help her get on with her life. So I talked to her. I remembered how much I loved and cared for her. And I did something truly strange."

"What?"

"I assumed that Aimee was telling the truth. If she was, then I knew two things. The kidnapper was a woman. And the kidnapper knew that Katie Rochester used the ATM machine on Fifty-second Street. The only people who fit that bill? Katie Rochester. Well, she didn't do it. Loren Muse. No way. And you."

"Me?" Edna Skylar began to blink. "Are you serious?"

"Do you remember when I called and asked you to look up Aimee's medical file?" Myron asked. "To see if she was pregnant?"

Again Edna Skylar checked her watch. "I really don't have time for this."

"I said it wasn't just about one innocent, it was about two."

"So?"

"Before I called you, I asked your husband to do the same thing. He worked in that department. I thought he'd have an easier time. But he refused."

"Stanley is a stickler for the rules," Edna Skylar said.

"I know. But you see, he told me something interesting. He told me that with all the new HIP laws nowadays, the computer date-stamps a patient's file every time you look into it. You can see the name of the doctor who viewed the file. And you get the time he or she viewed it."

"Right."

"So I checked Aimee's file. Guess what it shows?"

Her smile began to falter.

"You, Dr. Skylar, looked at that file two weeks *before* I asked you to. Why would you do that?"

She folded her arms across her chest. "I didn't."

"The computer is wrong?"

"Sometimes Stanley forgets his code. He probably used mine."

"I see. He forgets his own code but remembers yours." Myron tilted his head and edged closer. "You think he'll say that under oath?"

Edna Skylar did not reply.

"Do you know where you were really clever?" he went on. "Telling me about your son. The one who was trouble from day one and ran away to make it big. You said that he was still a mess, do you remember?"

A small, pain-filled sound escaped her lips. Her eyes filled with tears.

"But you never mentioned your son's name. No reason you should, of course. And there's no reason why anybody would know. Even now. It wasn't part of the investigation. I don't know the name of Jake Wolf's mother. Or Harry Davis's. But once I saw that you'd been in Aimee's medical file, I did a little checking. Your first husband, Dr. Skylar, was named Andrew Van Dyne, am I right? Your son's name was Drew Van Dyne."

She closed her eyes and took several deep breaths. When she opened them again, she shrugged, aiming for nonchalance but not even coming close. "So?"

"Odd, don't you think? When I asked you about Aimee Biel, you never mentioned that your son knew her."

"I told you that I was estranged from my son. I didn't know anything about him and Aimee Biel."

Myron grinned. "You have all the answers, don't you, Edna?"

"I'm just telling the truth."

"No, you're not. It was yet another coincidence. So many damn coincidences, don't you think? That's what I couldn't shake from the beginning. Two pregnant girls at the same high school? Okay, that one was no big deal. But all the rest—both girls running away, both using the same ATM, all that. Again, let's assume Aimee was telling the truth. Let's assume that someone—a woman—did indeed tell Aimee to wait on that corner.

443

Let's say that this mystery woman did tell Aimee to take money out of that ATM. Why? Why would someone do that?"

"I don't know."

"Sure you do, Edna. Because they weren't coincidences. None of them. You arranged them all. The two girls using the same ATM? Only one reason for that. The kidnapper—you, Edna—wanted to hook Aimee's disappearance with Katie Rochester's."

"And why would I want to do that?"

"Because the police were sure that Katie Rochester had run away—in part because of what you saw in the city. But Aimee Biel was different. She didn't have a Mob-connected, abusive daddy, for example. Her disappearance would cause commotion. The best way—the only way—to keep that heat from coming down was to make Aimee look like a runaway too."

For a moment they both just stood there. Then Edna Skylar shifted to the right as if preparing to pass him. Myron shifted with her, blocking the path. She looked up at him.

"Are you wearing a wire, Myron?"

He raised his arms. "Frisk me."

"No need. This is all nonsense anyway."

"Let's go back to that day on the street. You and Stanley are walking in Manhattan. Fate lends a hand here. You see Katie Rochester, just like you told the police. You realize that she's not missing or in serious trouble. She's a runaway. Katie begs you not to tell. And you listen. For three weeks, you say nothing. You go back to your regular life." Myron studied her face. "You with me so far?"

"I'm with you."

"So why the change? Why after three weeks do you suddenly call your old buddy Ed Steinberg?"

She folded her arms. "Why don't you tell me?"

"Because your situation changed, not Katie's."

"How?"

"You talked about your son being trouble from day one. That you'd given up on him."

"That's right."

"Maybe you did, I don't know. But you were in touch with Drew. At least somewhat. You knew that Drew fell in love with Aimee Biel. He told you about it. He probably told you that she was pregnant."

She crossed her arms. "You can prove that?"

"No. That part is speculation. The rest isn't. You looked up Aimee's medical files on the computer. That we know. You saw that yes, she was indeed pregnant. But more than that, you saw that she was going to terminate it. Drew didn't know about that. He thought that they were in love and going to get married. But Aimee just wanted out. Drew Van Dyne had been nothing but a foolish, albeit not uncommon, high school mistake. Aimee was on her way to college now."

"Sounds like motive for Drew to kidnap her," Edna Skylar said.

"It does, doesn't it? If that had been all. But again I kept wondering about all the coincidences. The ATM machine again. Who knew about it? You called your old buddy Ed Steinberg and pumped him for info on the case. He talked. Why not? Nothing was confidential. There wasn't really even a case. When he mentioned the Citibank ATM, you realized that would be the clincher. Everyone would assume Aimee was a runaway too. And that's exactly what happened. Then you called Aimee. You said you were from the hospital, which was true enough. You told her what she had to do to terminate the pregnancy in secret. You set up that meeting in New York. She's waiting at the corner. You drive by. You tell her to pick up some cash at the machine. Your clincher. Aimee does as she's told. And then she panics. She wants to think it through now. There you are, waiting to grab her, a syringe in your hand, and all of a sudden she runs off. She calls me. I get there. I drive her to Ridgewood. You follow—it was your car I saw that night follow us into the cul-de-sac. When she gets rejected by Harry Davis, you're waiting. Aimee doesn't remember much after that. She claims she was drugged. That fits—her memory would be fuzzy. Propofol would cause a lot of the symptoms. You're familiar with that drug, aren't you, Edna?"

"Of course I am. I'm a doctor. It's an anesthetic."

"You've used it in your practice?"

She hesitated. "I have."

"And that will be your downfall."

"Really? How's that."

"I have other evidence, but it's mostly circumstantial. Those medical records, for one. They show you not only viewed Aimee's medical records earlier than you indicated, but you didn't even bring them up again when I called. Why would you? You already knew she was pregnant. I'll also have phone records. Your son called you, you called your son."

"So?"

"Right, so. And I can even show how you called the school and spoke to your son right after I left you the first time. Harry Davis wondered how Drew knew something was up before he confronted him. That's how. You called and warned him. And you remember the call you made to Claire, the one from that pay phone near Twenty-third Street . . . first off, that was overkill. It was nice of you, trying to comfort the parents a little. But see, why would Aimee call from there— right where Katie Rochester had been spotted? She wouldn't know about that. Only you would. And we already checked your E-ZPass records. You went into Manhattan. Took the Lincoln Tunnel twenty minutes before the call was made."

"Hardly rock-solid," Edna said.

"No, probably not. But here's where you're going down. The Propofol. You can write prescriptions, sure, but you also had to order it. The police at my behest already checked with your office. You did purchase plenty of Propofol, but no one can explain where it went. Aimee was given a blood test. The stuff was still in her bloodstream. You see?"

Edna Skylar took a deep breath, held it, let it loose. "Do you have a motive for this purported kidnapping, Myron?"

"Are we really going to play this game?"

She shrugged. "We've played it this far."

"Fine, okay. The motive. That was the problem for everyone. Why would anyone kidnap Aimee? We all thought that someone wanted to keep her quiet. Your son could lose his job. Jake Wolf's son could lose everything. Harry Davis, well, he had a ton to lose too. But abducting her wouldn't help. There was also no ransom demand, no sexual assault, nothing like that. So I kept asking myself. Why would someone kidnap a young woman?"

"And?"

"You talked about the innocent."

"Right." There was resignation in her smile now. Edna Skylar knew what was coming next, Myron thought, but she won't move out of the way.

"Who was more innocent," Myron said, "than your unborn grandchild?"

She may have nodded. It was hard to tell. "Go on."

"You said it yourself when we talked about choosing patients. It's about prioritizing. It's about saving the innocents. Your motives were almost pure, Edna. You were trying to save your own grandchild."

Edna Skylar turned and looked down the corridor. When she faced Myron again, the sad smile was gone. Her face was oddly blank. "Aimee was already almost three months pregnant," she began. Her tone had changed. There was something gentle in it, something distant too. "If I could have held that girl for another month or two, it would have been too late to terminate. If I could just put off Aimee's decision for a little while longer, I would save my grandchild. Is that so wrong?"

Myron said nothing.

"And you're right. I wanted Aimee's disappearance to parallel Katie Rochester's. Part of it was already there for me, of course. They both went to the same school and both were pregnant. So I added the ATM. I did all I could to make it look like Aimee was a runaway. But not for the reasons you said—not because she was a nice girl with a nice family. Pretty much the opposite, in fact."

Myron nodded, seeing it now. "If the police started investigating," he said, "they may have found out about her affair with your son."

"Yes."

"None of the suspects owned a log cabin. But you do, Edna. It even has the brown and white fireplace like Aimee said."

"You've been a busy boy."

"Yes, I have."

"I had it pretty well planned out. I would treat her well. I would monitor the baby. I made that call to the parents hoping to offer some comfort. I would keep doing stuff like that—leaving hints that Aimee was a runaway and was okay."

"Like going online?"

"Yes."

"How did you get her password and screen name?"

"She gave it to me in a drug stupor."

"You wore a disguise when you were with her?"

"I kept my face covered, yes."

"And the name of Erin's boyfriend. Mark Cooper. How did you get that?"

Edna shrugged. "She gave me that too."

"It was the wrong answer. Mark Cooper was a boy nicknamed Trouble. That was another thing that bothered me."

"Clever of her," Edna Skylar said. "Still. I would have held her a few months. I would have kept leaving hints that she ran away. Then I would let her go. She would have told the same story about being abducted."

"And no one would have believed her."

"She would have the baby, Myron. That was all I was concerned with. The plan would have worked. Once that ATM charge came in, the police were certain that she was a runaway. So they were out of it. Her parents, well, they're parents. Their concerns were dismissed just like the Rochesters'." She met his eye. "Only one thing messed me up."

Myron spread his hands. "Modesty prevents me from saying it."

"Then I will. You, Myron. You messed me up."

"You're not going to call me a meddlesome kid, are you? Like on *Scooby-Doo*?"

"You think this is funny?"

"No, Edna. I don't think it's funny at all."

"I never wanted to hurt anyone. Yes, it would inconvenience Aimee. It might even be somewhat traumatic for her, though I'm pretty good at administering drugs. I could have kept her comfortable and the baby safe.

And her parents, of course they'd go through hell. I thought if I could convince them that she was a runaway—that she was all right—it might make it easier on them. But add up the pros and cons. Even if they all had to suffer a little, don't you see? I was saving a life. It was like I told you. I messed up with Drew. I didn't look out for him. I didn't protect him."

"And you weren't going to make those same mistakes with your grandchild," Myron said.

"That's right."

There were patients and visitors, doctor and nurses, all sorts of people moving to and fro. There were *ding*-ing noises from above. Someone walked by with a huge bouquet of flowers. Myron and Edna saw none of that.

"You said it to me on the phone," Edna went on. "When you asked me to look up Aimee's records. Protect the innocent. That's all I was trying to do. But when she vanished, you blamed yourself. You felt obligated to find her. You started digging."

"And when I got too close, you had to cut your losses."

"Yes."

"So you let her go."

"I had no choice. Everything went to hell. Once you got involved, people started dying."

"You're not blaming me for that, are you?"

"No, and I'm not blaming me either," she said, head high. "I never killed anyone. I never asked Harry Davis to switch transcripts. I never asked Jake Wolf to pay anybody off. I never asked Randy Wolf to sell drugs. I never told my son to sleep with a student. And I didn't tell Aimee Biel to get pregnant with his baby."

Myron said nothing.

"You want to take it another step?" Her voice edged up a notch. "I didn't tell Drew to pull a gun on Jake

Wolf. Just the opposite. I tried to keep my son calm, but I couldn't tell him the truth. Maybe I should have. But Drew had always been such a screw-up. So I just told him to relax. That Aimee would be okay. But he didn't listen. He thought Jake Wolf must have done something to her. So he went after him. My guess is, the wife was telling the truth. She shot him in self-defense. That's how my son ended up dead. But I didn't do any of that."

Myron waited. Her lips were trembling, but Edna fought through it. She would not collapse. She would not show weakness, not even now when it was all unraveling, when her actions not only failed to produce the desired results but had ended the life of her own son.

"All I wanted to do was save my grandchild's life," she said. "How else could I have done it?"

Myron still didn't reply.

"Well?"

"I don't know."

"Please." Edna Skylar clutched his arm as if it were a life preserver. "What is she going to do about the baby?"

"I don't know that either."

"You'll never be able to prove any of this."

"That's up to the police. I just wanted to keep my promise."

"What promise?"

Myron looked down the corridor and called out, "It's okay now."

When Aimee Biel stepped into view, Edna Skylar gasped and put her hand to her mouth. Erik was there too, on one side of Aimee. Claire stood on the other. They both had their arms around their daughter.

Myron walked away then, smiling. His step felt light. Outside the sun would still be shining. He knew that. The radio would play his favorite songs. He had the whole conversation on tape—yes, he'd lied to her about that—and he'd give it to Muse and Banner. They might make a case. They might not.

You do what you can.

Erik nodded at Myron as he passed. Claire reached out to him. There were tears of gratitude in her eyes. Myron touched her hand but he kept moving. Their eyes met. He saw her as a teen again, in high school, in the study hall. But none of that mattered anymore.

He had made a promise to Claire. He had promised to bring back her baby.

And now, at long last, he had.

Acknowledgments

Over the past six years, the one question I always get on the road is, "How tall are you?" The answer: Six-four. But the second most common question is, "When are you going to bring Myron and the gang back?" The answer: Now. I've always said that I wouldn't force his return, that I'd wait for the right idea. Well, the right idea came, but your encouragement and enthusiasm inspired and touched me. So first acknowledgment—to those who missed Myron, Win, Esperanza, Big Cyndi, El-Al and the rest of this motley crew. Hope you had fun. And for those of you who don't know what I'm talking about, there are seven other novels featuring Myron Bolitar. Go to HarlanCoben.com for more information.

This is my fourth book working with Mitch Hoffman as my editor and Lisa Johnson as my everything else. They both rock. Brian Tart, Susan Petersen Kennedy, Erika Kahn, Hector DeJean, Robert Kempe, and everyone at Dutton rock too. Lots of rocking. Thanks also to Jon Wood, Susan Lamb, Malcolm

Edwards, Aaron Priest, and Lisa Erbach Vance.

David Gold, M.D., had helped me with medical research on a lot of books. This time he even gets his name mentioned as a character. You're a good friend, David.

Christopher J. Christie, the U.S. Attorney for the state of New Jersey, provides great and wonderfully twisted legal insights. I've known Chris since we played Little League together when we were ten. For some reason, he does not put that on his resume.

I'm grateful to the Clarke family—Ray, Maureen, Andrew, Devin, Jeff, and Garrett—for inspiring the idea. The boys have always been open with me about what it's like to be a kid, a teenager, and now young men. I thank them for it.

Lastly, thanks to Linda Fairstein, Dyan Machan, and, of course, Anne Armstrong-Coben, M.D. Too much brains and beauty—that's the problem with all three of you.

Kat Donovan spun off her father's old stool, readying to leave O'Malley's pub, when Stacy said, "You're not going to like what I did."

The tone made Kat stop mid-stride. "What?"

O'Malley's used to be an old-school cop bar. Kat's grandfather had hung out here. So had her father and their fellow NYPD colleagues. Now it had been turned into a yuppie, preppy, master-of-the-universe, poser ass-hat bar, loaded up with guys who sported crisp white shirts under black suits, two-day stubble, manscaped to the max to look un-manscaped. They smirked a lot, these soft men, their hair moussed to the point of over-coif, and ordered Ketel One instead of Grey Goose because they watched some TV ad telling them that was what real men drink.

Stacy's eyes started darting around the bar. Avoidance. Kat didn't like that.

"What did you do?" Kat asked.

"Whoa," Stacy said.

"What?"

"A Punch-Worthy at five o'clock."

Kat swiveled to the right to take a peek.

"See him?" Stacy asked.

"Oh yeah."

Décor-wise, O'Malley's hadn't really changed much over the years. Sure, the old console TVs had been replaced by a host of flat screens showing too wide a variety of games—who cared about how the Edmonton Oilers did?—but outside of that, O'Malley's had kept the cop feel and that was what appealed to these posers, the faux authenticity, moving in and pushing out what made this place hum, turning it into some Disney Epcot version of what it had once been.

Kat was the only cop left in here. The others now went home after their shifts, or to AA meetings. Kat still came and tried to sit quietly on her father's old stool with the ghosts, especially tonight, with her father's murder haunting her anew. She just wanted to be here, to feel her father's presence, to—corny as it sounded—gather strength from it.

But the douchebags wouldn't let her be, would they?

This particular Punch-Worthy—shorthand for any guy deserving a fist to the face—had committed a classic punch-worthy sin. In this case, he was wearing sunglasses. At eleven o'clock at night. In a bar with poor lighting. Other punch-worthy indictments included wearing a chain on your wallet, doo-rags, unbuttoned silk shirts, an overabundance of tattoos (special category for those sporting tribal symbols), dog tags when you didn't serve in the military, and really big white wristwatches.

4

Sunglasses smirked and lifted his glass toward Kat and Stacy.

"He likes us," Stacy said.

"Stop stalling. What won't I like?"

When Stacy turned back toward her, Kat could see over her shoulder the disappointment on Punch-Worthy's glistening-with-overpriced-lotion face. Kat had seen that look a zillion times before. Men liked Stacy. That was probably something of an understatement. Stacy was frighteningly, knee-knockingly, teeth-and-bone-and-metal-meltingly hot. Men became both weak-legged and stupid around Stacy. Mostly stupid. Really, really stupid.

This was why it was probably a mistake to hang out with someone who looked like Stacy—guys often concluded that they had no shot when a woman looked like that. She seemed unapproachable.

Kat, in comparison, did not.

Sunglasses honed in on Kat and began to make his move. He didn't so much walk toward her as glide on his own slime.

Stacy suppressed a giggle. "This is going to be good."

Hoping to discourage him, Kat gave the guy flat eyes and a disdainful frown. Sunglasses was not deterred. He bebopped over, moving to some soundtrack that was only playing in his own head.

"Hey, babe," Sunglasses said. "Is your name Wi-Fi?"

Kat waited.

"Because I'm feeling a connection."

Stacy burst out laughing.

Kat just stared at him. He continued.

"I love you small chicks, you know? You're kinda adorable. A spinner, am I right? You know what would look good on me? You."

5

"Do these lines ever work?" Kat asked him.

"I'm not done yet." Sunglasses coughed into his fist, took out his iPhone, and held it up to Kat. "Hey, babe, congrats—you've just moved to the top of my 'to do' list."

Stacy loved it.

Kat said, "What's your name?"

He arched an eyebrow. "Whatever you want it to be, babe."

"How about Ass Waffle?" Kat opened her blazer, showing the weapon on her belt. "I'm going to reach for my gun now, Ass Waffle."

"Damn, woman, are you my new boss?" He pointed to his crotch. "Because you just gave me a raise."

"Go away."

"My love for you is like diarrhea," Sunglasses said. "I just can't hold it in."

Kat just looked at him, horrified.

"Too far?" he said.

"Oh man, that's just gross."

"Yeah, but I bet you never heard it before."

He'd win that bet. "Leave. Now."

"Really?"

Stacy was nearly on the floor with laughter.

Sunglasses started to turn away. "Wait. Is this a test? Is Ass Waffle, like, a compliment or something?"

"Go."

He shrugged, turned, spotted Stacy, figured why not. He looked her long body up and down and said, "The word of the day is legs. Let's go back to your place and spread the word."

Stacy was still loving it. "Take me, Ass Waffle. Right here. Right now."

6

"Really?"

"No."

Ass Waffle looked back at Kat. Kat put her hand on the butt of her gun. He held up his hands and slinked away.

Kat said, "Stacy?"

"Hmm?"

"Why do these guys keep thinking they have a chance with me?"

"Because you look cute and perky."

"I'm not perky."

"No, but you look perky."

"Seriously, do I look like that much of a loser?"

"You look damaged," Stacy said. "I hate to say it. But the damage . . . it comes off you like some kind of pheromone that douchebags can't resist."

They both took a sip of their drinks.

"So what won't I like?" Kat asked.

Stacy looked back toward Ass Waffle. "I feel bad for him now. Maybe I should throw him a quickie."

"Don't start."

"What?" Stacy crossed her show-off long legs and smiled at Ass Waffle. He made a face that reminded Kat of a dog left in a car too long. "Do you think this skirt is too short?"

"Skirt?" Kat said. "I thought it was a belt."

Stacy liked that. She loved the attention. She loved picking up men because she thought that a one-night stand with her was somehow life changing. It was also part of her job. Stacy owned a private investigation firm with two other gorgeous women. Their specialty? Catching (really, entrapping) cheating spouses.

"Stacy?"

"Hmm?"

"What won't I like?"

"This."

Still teasing Ass Waffle, Stacy handed Kat a piece of paper. Kat looked at the paper and frowned:

KD8115

HottestSexEvah

"What is this?"

"KD8115 is your username."

Her initials and badge number.

"HottestSexEvah is your password. Oh, and it's case sensitive."

"And these are for?"

"A website. JustMyType.com."

"Huh?"

"It's an online dating service."

Kat made a face. "Please tell me you're joking."

"It's upscale."

"That's what they say about strip clubs."

"I bought you a subscription," Stacy said. "It's good for a year."

"You're kidding, right?"

"I don't kid. I do some work for this company. They're good. And let's not fool ourselves. You need someone. You want someone. And you aren't going to find him in here."

Kat sighed, rose, and nodded to the bartender, a guy named Pete who looked like a character actor who always played the Irish bartender, which is what, in fact, he was. Pete nodded back, indicating that he'd put the drinks on Kat's tab.

"Who knows?" Stacy said. "You could end up meeting Mr. Right."

Kat started for the door. "But more likely, Mr. Ass Waffle."

Kat typed in JustMyType.com, hit the return button, and filled in her new username and the rather embarrassing password. She frowned when she saw the moniker at the top of the profile that Stacy had chosen for her:

"Cute and Perky!"

"She left off damaged," Kat muttered under her breath.

It was past midnight, but Kat wasn't much of a sleeper. She lived in an area far too upscale for her—West 67th Street off Central Park West, in the Atelier building. A hundred years ago, the Atelier and its neighboring buildings, including the famed Hotel des Artistes, had housed writers, painters, intellectuals—artists. The spacious old-world apartments faced the street, the smaller artist studios in the back. Eventually the old art studios were converted into one-bedroom apartments. Kat's father, a cop who watched his friends get rich doing nothing but buying real estate, had tried to find his way in. A guy whose life Dad had saved sold him the place on the cheap.

Kat had first used it as undergrad at Columbia University. She had paid for her Ivy League education with a NYPD financial aid scholarship. According to the life plan, she was then supposed to go to law school and join a big white-shoe firm in New York City, finally breaking away from the cursed family legacy of police work.

Alas, it hadn't worked out that way.

A glass of red wine sat next to her keyboard. Kat drank too much. She knew that was a cliché—a cop

9

who drank too much—but sometimes the clichés are there for a reason. She functioned fine. She didn't drink on the job. It didn't really affect her life in any noticeable way, but if Kat made calls or even decisions late at night, they tended to be, er, sloppy ones. She had learned over the years to turn off her mobile phone and stay away from email after ten P.M.

Yet here she was, late at night, checking out random dudes on a dating website.

Stacy had uploaded four photographs to Kat's page. Kat's profile picture, a headshot, had been cropped from a bridesmaid group photo taken at a wedding last year. Kat tried to view herself objectively, but that was impossible. She hated the picture. The woman in the photograph looked unsure of herself, her smile weak, almost as though she was waiting to be slapped or something. Every photograph—now that she went through the painful ritual of viewing them—had been cropped from group pictures and in every one Kat looked as though she were half wincing.

Okay, enough of her own profile.

On the job, the only men she met were cops. She didn't want a cop. Cops were good men and horrible husbands. She knew that only too well. When Grandma got terminally ill, her grandfather, unable to handle it, ran off until, well, it was too late. Pops never forgave himself for that. That was Kat's theory, anyway. He was lonely and while he had been a hero to many, Pops chickened out when it counted most and he couldn't live with that. His service revolver was sitting right there, right on the same top shelf in the kitchen where he'd always kept it, and so one night, Kat's grandfather reached up and took his piece down from that shelf and sat by himself at the kitchen table and . . .

Ka-boom.

Dad, too, would go on benders and disappear for days at a time. Mom would be extra cheery when this happened—which made it all the more scary and creepy—either pretending Dad was on an undercover mission or ignoring his disappearance altogether, literally out of sight, out of mind, and then, maybe a week later, Dad would waltz in with a fresh shave and smile and a dozen roses for Mom and everyone would act like this was normal.

JustMyType.com. She, the cute and perky Kat Donovan, was on an internet dating site. Man oh man, talk about the best-laid plans. She lifted the wine glass, made a toasting gesture toward the computer screen, and took too big a gulp.

The world sadly was no longer conducive to meeting a life partner. Sex, sure. That was easy. That was, in fact, the expectation, the elephant in the date room, if you will, and while she loved the pleasures of the flesh as much as the next gal, the truth was, when you went to bed with someone too quickly, rightly or wrongly, the chances of a long-term relationship took a major hit. She didn't put a moral judgment on this. It was just the way it was.

Her computer dinged. A message bubble popped up:

We have matches for you! Click here to see someone who might be perfect for you!

Kat finished the glass of wine. She debated pouring another, but really, enough. She took stock of herself and realized an obvious yet unspoken truth: She wanted someone in her life. Have the courage to admit that to yourself, okay? Much as she strove to be independent,

Kat wanted a man, a partner, someone in her bed at night. She didn't pine or force it or even make much of an effort. But she wasn't really built to be alone.

She began to click through the profiles. You got to be in it to win it, right?

Pathetic.

Some men could be eliminated with a quick glance at their profile photograph. It was key, when you thought about it. The profile portrait each man had painstakingly chosen was, in pretty much every way, the first (very controlled) impression. It thus spoke volumes.

So: If you made the conscious choice to wear a fedora, that was an automatic no. If you chose not to wear a shirt, no matter how well built, automatic no. If you had a Bluetooth in your ear—gosh, aren't you important?—automatic no. If you had a soul patch or sported a vest or winked or made hand gestures or chose a tangerine-hued shirt (personal bias) or balanced your sunglasses on top of your head, automatic no, no, no. If your profile name was ManStallion, SexySmile, RichPrettyBoy, LadySatisfier—you get the gist.

Kate clicked open a few where the guy looked . . . approachable, she guessed. There was a sad, depressing sameness to all the write-ups. Every person on the website enjoyed walks on a beach and dining out and exercising and exotic travel and wine tasting and theater and museums and being active and taking chances and grand adventures—yet they were equally content with staying home and watching a movie, coffee and conversation, cooking, reading a book, the simple pleasures. Every guy claimed that the "most important" quality they looked for in a woman was a "sense of humor"—right, sure—to the point where Kat wondered whether "sense of humor" was a euphemism for "big boobs." Of course, every man also listed preferred body type as "athletic, slender and curvy."

That seemed more accurate, if not downright wishful.

The profiles never reflected reality. Rather than being what you are, they were a wonderful if not futile exercise in what you *think* you are or what you want a potential partner to think you are—or most likely, the profiles (and man, shrinks would have a field day) simply reflect what you want to be.

The personal statements were all over the place, but if she had to use one word to sum them up, it would probably be treacle. The first read, "Every morning, life is a blank canvas waiting to be painted"—click. Some aimed for honest by telling you repeatedly that they were honest. Some faked sincerity. Some were highfalutin or showboating or insecure or needy. Just like real life, when Kat thought about it. Most were simply trying too hard. The stench of desperation came off the screen in bad-cologne, squiggly waves. The constant soulmate talk was, at best, off-putting. In real life, Kat thought, none of us can find someone we want to go out with more than once, yet somehow we believe that on JustMyType.com we will instantly find a person we want to wake up next to for the rest of our lives.

Delusional—or does hope spring eternal?

That was the flip side. It was easy to be cynical and poke fun, but when she stepped back, Kat realized something that pierced her straight through the heart: Every profile was a life. Simple, yep, but behind every cliché-ridden, please-like-me profile was a fellow human being with dreams and aspirations and desires. These people hadn't signed up, paid their fee, or filled

13

out this information idly. Think about it: Every one of these lonely people came to this website—signed in and clicked on profiles—hoping that it would be different this time, hoping against hope that finally they would meet the one person who, in the end, would be the most important person in their lives.

Wow. Just let that realization roll over you for a moment.

Kat had been lost in this thought, clicking through the profiles at a constantly increasing velocity, the faces of these men—men who had come here in the hopes of finding "the one"—blurring into a fleshy mess from the speed, when she spotted his picture.

For a second, maybe two, her brain didn't quite believe what her eyes had seen. It took another second for the finger to stop clicking the mouse button, another for the profile pictures tumbling by to slow down and come to a halt. Kat sat and took a deep breath.

It couldn't be.

She had been surfing at such a rapid pace, thinking about the men behind the photographs, their lives, their wants, their hopes. Her mind—and this was both Kat's strength and weakness as a cop—had been wandering, not necessarily concentrating on what was directly in front of her, yet was able to get a sense of the big picture. In law enforcement, it meant that she was able to see the possibilities, the escape routes, the alternate scenarios, the figure lurking behind the obstacles and obfuscations and hindrances and subterfuge.

But that also meant that sometimes Kat missed the obvious.

She slowly started to click the back arrow.

It couldn't be him.